An Ark in the Flood of Time

Chronicling the Further Adventures of Satanaya the Circassian

Christopher Ryan

HAKAWATI PRESS
HAWICK

Published by Hakawati Press, Hawick, Scotland

First published 2022
Copyright © Christopher Ryan 2022

Designed and produced by Ged Lennox – gedlennox@me.com
Set in 10/13 Minion Pro

Cover art: Christopher Ryan and Patrick Rafferty
(www.raffertyandrafferty.com)

Maps: Aliya Ryan – aliya@cantab.net

Printed the United Kingdom by Severn, Gloucester

ISBN 978-0-9569552-2-7

For further information: contact author at:
www.damascusdrum.co.uk
damascus_drum@yahoo.com

To Amaya

ACKNOWLEDGEMENTS

'Terroir' in the vinicultural sense could refer simply to the chemical composition and organic structure of the vine's soil, and its concomitant relationship with geographical location vis-à-vis climate, latitude, altitude etc.. Yet for lovers of the true wine, the true lovers of this beautiful creation that is no other than the expression of the vast unseen essence of things, terroir may also be the natural correlative of what poets, writers, and mystics sometimes refer to as 'spirit of place', that indefinable climate in the soul of a place, evidence of a specific anchoring in time and space of what the original peoples since the days of Adam refer to as 'The Great Spirit'; that outpouring of the cup of love that is the Unknown making Itself known to its No Other.

In this respect, therefore, in the matter of acknowledgements - where convention encourages the writer to mention with gratitude those friends and helpers, such as Ged Lennox, Pat Rafferty, Zimmy (editing) Aliya (maps) who supported this attempt to chronicle the adventures of the Circassian known as Satanaya – here we salute in fond remembrance the places themselves, embodiments of the muse, bringing the light of inspiration and nourishment of soul to this writer as he followed in her footsteps – those cities and towns, rivers, seas and lands which connect between, namely: Constantinople, Damascus, the Lebanon, Galilee, Nablus, Jerusalem, Famagusta, Mersin, Silifke, Karaman, the great plain of Konya, Smyrna, the Bosphorus, Gallipoli, Aleppo, Sofia, Salonica, Famagusta, and not forgetting those august and awe-inspiring institutions of learning, whether school, university, kitchen, ashram, tekke, business, and the sweet company of guides and mentors, of readers and friends, of lovers and marriage, of parents, children and grandchildren which prepared the pilgrim for this undertaking, especially those Masters of the Kitchen, Bülent Rauf, Bomer von Marx and my mother Patricia at whose apron strings I first learnt to appreciate *le bon goût*.

"Hopes are hundredfold in this present time. Step forward, O young one, and like a true lover leave off empty argument. Though your eyelids fall, you are asleep and voyaging in safety. For this the Prophet said: I am the Ark in the Flood of Time. That person who through their inner vision, holds this place as God's representative becomes an Ark in this Ocean of Oneness."
– Rumi

'Distance does not exist in what we aim.
Sweet company remains not through distance only,
but also through aeons of time.'
– Bülent Rauf

'Time is an ocean but it ends at the shore'
– Bob Dylan

ONE

Prolegomenon

Istanbul, 1976

T HAD BEEN predicted long ago that Constantinople would not be conquered again, but would fall from within.'

Prince Mehmet paused and gave me a look. It was a look intended to pique my curiosity, accompanied by a close-lipped smile and an almost imperceptible rocking of the head.

That morning we had gathered to cast the ashes of our Lady Satanaya upon the waters of the Bosphorus, according to her last wishes. After lunching well in a waterside restaurant, and resting in our hotel during the afternoon, we had met that evening to dine at the Yeni Rejans. A place we knew as the 'Russian Restaurant', it was a throwback to the days when Istiklal Caddesi ('Independence Avenue') was known as La Grande Rue de

1

Pera and was the heart of European Constantinople. The restaurant had been established some time after World War 1. In the wake of the 1917 Russian Revolution, bands of dispossessed Russian bourgeoisie, the so-called White Russians, fled the Bolsheviks, south into the lands of their former wartime enemy. Here they survived as best they could, selling their furs, their jewellery and themselves on the streets of the great city lost by their Orthodox Greek brethren to the Ottoman Turks in 1453.

The restaurant was now run by a bevy of white-haired ladies of Russian origin, daughters of refugees who had founded a place where their fellow exiles could eat piroshki and Chicken Kiev, and drink iced lemon vodka which, legend had it, was prepared in a bath out the back. We too ate piroshki and borscht, beef stroganoff and roast woodcock, crème caramel for dessert, and drank iced lemon vodka to excess; and the evening passed in a wonderful, numbing blur as Mehmet entertained us with stories of his remarkable past. Or, as the alcohol took hold and we became bolder and more reckless in our converse, he never failed to pounce on our foibles, mocking our seriousness, teasing us jovially but mercilessly. The one exception to his aim was the retired British Colonel, an older man for whom Mehmet always showed a companionable respect. They were in cahoots.

Our talk was really a continuation of the conversation earlier in the afternoon when Mehmet had handed me a portmanteau containing a second archive of Satanaya's personal writings and correspondence.

Now we were discussing the Battle of the Dardanelles in the First World War, and the part played in the defence of the Gallipoli Peninsula by the mysterious Captain Mustafa. Though they had not formally met, Satanaya and Mustafa's paths had crossed in those earlier days before all the wars.*

'Yet, whoever would credit the word of an Istanbul postmaster who announced that a man called Mustafa would be the saviour of the country.' The Prince paused again, smiling mischievously. He knew he had caught me.

'Go on...' I said.

'Remember our talk this afternoon, about the 'Büyükler', the 'Great Ones' who guide the destiny of this world. You must remember, Jacob, this

---

* As chronicled in the author's previous book, 'Satanaya and the Houses of Mercy'.

was perhaps Turkey's darkest hour of the war. The guns of the British battleships were pounding the hillsides of Gallipoli Peninsula. The bombardment was so fierce, so powerful, that the boom of the explosions could be heard after nightfall and in the early morning more than a hundred miles away in Istanbul. It sounded like dull and distant thunder. Foreign troops were landing by the thousands on Turkish soil, no one felt safe. The population in the capital feared the worst. A young civil servant, who was also a dervish, Mehmet Ali Özkadeş, had just heard he was being posted to Ankara and came to say goodbye to his teacher, Ahmet Süreyya Bey. This Süreyya Bey was an official in the Office of Post and Telegraph in Istanbul, but he was also a Qadiri sheykh*. Young Özkadeş poured out his heart to his sheykh his worries over the fate of his country. Süreyya Bey, then in his late sixties, told his young protégé, "Don't worry, my son. Go to Ankara. Do your duties. When you return I won't be here. But there is a person who has been chosen to save the country. And his name is Mustafa."

Prince Mehmet must have noticed my blank look, verging on incredulity.

'Come on, Jacob, surely by now you can see, while we imagine we are in control of things, greater destinies are being played out in the world.'

This was typical of him. He would say things that implied a deeper meaning, while leaving us to work things out for ourselves.

That night as I lay awake in my room in the Pera Palace Hotel, listening to the musical pipes of the ancient plumbing, I tried to take in the events of the day. It was curious to remember Satanaya, how we had felt at her departure. Our mourning had been an affair of joy, rather than sadness. Our reminiscences and speculations about her life had all been of a lively, friendly nature, wrapped in much fondness. And but for a moment of silent poignancy as the ashes flew among the shearwaters like some flamboyant greeting of fellow Ariels, swirling in the air above the sea as the urn with its burnt offering was shaken out into the blue ocean stream of the Bosphorus, it had been a wake of pleasure and pleasant recollection; a farewell, an *au revoir*, with no greater sense of finality than seeing a friend off on a journey, upon trails unseen where we too would inevitably tread in due course.

---

* A teacher in the line of the great Sufi master from Baghdad, Abdul Qadir Gilani (1078-1166)

✶ ✶ ✶

It wasn't until much later, on returning to Scotland, that I began the unravelling. There was far more in the portmanteau than at first met the eye. Lady Satanaya's letters were written in a very small hand. Likewise her diaries, which were plain notebooks, with entries dated and giving locations. Correspondence from the Turkish officer was simply signed 'M', but the handwriting was consistent throughout. Most of these letters would begin and end quite formally in French, though often breaking into Turkish, in the old script, when the writer's thoughts ran fast in describing events. Most were still in their envelopes, and some bore postmarks identifying the place of dispatch. Others had evidently been hand delivered. Most intriguing among the varied documents were those relating to Satanaya's early mentor, Lady Gülbahar: there were whole bundles of letters from admirers and friends, as well as what seemed a collection of stories, handwritten in Arabic and all rolled up together in a piece of goatskin, with a label which read, 'Daud's stories'.

But none of this seemed to explain how it all began – this business with the officer called Mustafa that is – until I opened a small parcel labelled 'Pelin'. Satanaya's letters to and from her old room-mate and adoptive sister in Beirut told of her travels in Anatolia, and how her and Mustafa's paths were continually crossing, so it seemed they were often travelling on the same journey. In the parcel also was a small bundle in a strange script which I conjectured to be Amharic, the language of Pelin's native Ethiopia. But we are getting ahead of ourselves.

✶ ✶ ✶

When a story may have many beginnings it is not completely true to say, 'once upon a time', unless we go back to Adam. And even then one is tempted to ask, 'which Adam?' For as tradition tells us, and the scientists are now very keen to explain, the worlds and universes, not to say quantum dimensions of existence bubbling away quietly under our thumbs, are well nigh, if not in actuality, infinite.

As far as Mustafa is concerned, his beginning, as the son of a minor official in the local Ottoman administration in Salonica*, is notable simply for the fact that he was born, as was Satanaya, in the same fateful year of

---

*   Now the city of Thessalonika in Northern Greece.

1881. These are all known knowns.

He was a sensitive child, – what they used to call 'highly strung', although this term was used more often in reference to girls and horses. Above all he was intelligent. From the start Mustafa seemed to know where he wasn't headed – to the religious school to wear baggy şalvar trousers and chant Koran all day, as his mother had hoped. He was set on going to the military preparatory school, wearing Western style military uniform and later a career in the modern world. In the end he got his way. By the time he graduated he had lost his father. When his mother remarried, he left home – there was no room for two top dogs in one Turkish household. Free to roam the cafes by Salonica's waterfront, he discovered a life beyond the classroom, where he was free to drink beer, to fall in love, to meet and mix with Jews and Christians, and people who had travelled in Europe beyond the confines of the Empire. In fin-de-siècle Ottoman Turkey, the city on the edge of the Balkans rivalled Constantinople as a melting pot of new political ideas.

From Salonica he went to military high school in Manastir, where he was to meet the infamous Enver, who was in the year above him. Thereafter, until Enver's own premature demise, he became a kind of nemesis to Mustafa, and his successes a goad to the younger boy's own frustrated ambitions: Enver always appeared where Mustafa would wish to be, while Mustafa seemed always one year, one step, behind the action. In 1899 Mustafa entered the prestigious *Mekteb-i Harbiye*, the Military Academy, in Constantinople. He graduated as Staff Captain in early 1905, which is where, as far as we are concerned in the story of Lady Satanaya, we may rejoin the threads of this tale.

Jacob Merdiven de la Scala

TWO

A Night Out in Damascus

Constantinople-Syria-Palestine, 1905

HERE ARE *muezzins* who can hold a note as pure as a nightingale, and there are those who, like revellers departing the tavern in the early hours, just pour salt in one's ear. And then there are those whose vocal virtue lies in bearing the beloved's image to within the border of the listener's heart. The *muezzin* who faithfully called to pray that afternoon might well have been a lover crying out to some unreachable beauty, such was he lost in adoration in his song.

For once Mustafa listened with pleasure as the *ezan* rang out. If only everyone could hear the beauty in that, he mused to himself, there would be no need of mosques and temples, and those filthy priests.

The waiter arrived with the raki, glasses and a jug of chilled water.

'This is what I like about Kuzguncuk,' he said to his friend Ali Fethi, 'it

6

has a certain style – quiet, unassuming, but definitely class. Why can't all of Turkey be like this? Instead they arrest us for wanting our country to progress.'

The waiter poured each a double measure of raki, and water in another glass. He went away and returned with a dish of *leblebi* – roasted chick peas – some crumbly white cheese and a basket of fresh bread.

'You want the impossible, Mustafa. Can't you just be happy that we weren't cashiered, and given a real exile? As it is we only have to cool our heels in Syria a while, behave ourselves and let things settle down. Constantinople wasn't built in a day, and this crazy Sultanate won't be dismantled so easily either.'

It was the two young officers' last evening in the old capital. They were spending it quietly on the Asian shore in a small *meyhane* run by an Armenian, in a little lane leading up from the Bosphorus. It was January and a cold wind was blowing down the Straits from beyond the Black Sea; otherwise they might have sat outside in their thick overcoats and black lambskin kalpaks and drunk beneath the ancient plane trees.

'I suppose you're right, Ali. But maybe we can also do things in the East. The change has to happen in the provinces too, not just here, in the City, '*eis tin polin*' – he rolled the Greek around his tongue – 'in Stamboul, which is mostly in Europe, after all. Look, the countries to the west are getting stronger, while Turkey only gets poorer. Even the Greeks have a country now – they let the British fool them into believing they invented democracy. And once they had their little country, and we had our Constitution, albeit short lived, didn't they start coming back? Because they knew this country was rich and theirs was just mountains and islands. You know, Ali, the very year I was born we lost Thessaly. And almost Salonica, the town where I was born. And if we had lost Salonica? Am I not a Turk!'

Mustafa slammed his raki glass down on the table, to emphasise his point. The other customers looked up and fell silent. Ali tried to speak but Mustafa railed on:

'And what do we get? A Sultan who is too afraid to show his face, while letting go of our Balkan provinces one by one to the Russians; and as for the Caucasus, ha! Russians again.* And North Africa – you know, those

---

* Kars, in far north-eastern Turkey, fell to Tsarist forces in the Russo-Turkish War of 1877-78, and was only recaptured late in World War 1.

Beys down there in Tripoli and Benghazi are either making a mint or they're being shafted three ways backwards by the local mullahs, because not a penny in taxes is getting back to the Porte. No wonder our army is in such a state, we've barely the funding to pay for ammunition, let alone to modernise. If it weren't for the German training, we'd be lost already. And another point... '

'Yes, I know, the railways, the tobacco tax...' Ali had finally got a word in. 'Enough Mustafa, enough. You don't have to paint the white dog white for me. I can see it clearly and you're beginning to repeat yourself. Let's go over to Pera and enjoy our last evening in Europe. Come on, we'll drink whisky and find some girls.'

'You're right, I'm talking into the wind. Yes, let's get soaked in Europe, for tomorrow we may be dry in Damascus!'

* * *

The Austrian steamboat sailed south from Constantinople across the Marmara Sea, through the lower straits of the Dardanelles. Hugging the coast of Anatolia, it called briefly at Smyrna* before heading on to Rhodes and Cyprus, reaching Beirut after a week. Here it was a different climate altogether, and Beirut, its administration overseen by the European powers, seemed to Mustafa and Ali no less cosmopolitan than the imperial capital: pavement cafés, and since the coming of the railway by the Germans, a beer hall. But these pleasures would have to wait. Mustafa and Ali Fethi were soon entrained for the 90 mile journey from the Mediterranean port with its boulevards and lively street life, over the hills and mountains of Lebanon to the ancient city of Damascus on the edge of the desert.

Damascus had been around for ten thousand years, and as far as Mustafa was concerned it was still living somewhere back in those dusty millennia. Religious, conservative – backward, even by Ottoman standards. And as for the plumbing... He felt he would suffocate here among the dirty, tumbling ruins, the women dressed head to foot in black, and the men of the desert in robes which made him think he'd returned to the time of the Prophet. At least in Constantinople the oriental aspect of the Empire was mostly Turkish, and that well leavened by centuries of European influence.

---

* Known as Izmir since 1930.

Mustafa and Ali reported to the commanding officer to receive their postings. Ali's family connections secured him an enviable position as part of the mounted guard of the Governor of Beirut. Mustafa drew the short straw and was destined to remain in the barracks in Damascus. Here he was joined by his friend Müfit, another drinking companion from Staff College in Constantinople.

As a staff captain, Mustafa would be involved in training exercises with the local troops. He was relieved to discover that the main task of their mission would be to sort out disputes between various tribal groups in the Hauran, the rough country south of Damascus, and the heights known as Golan which look down on Galilee. Here Druzes*, Circassian émigrés, and local Arabs all knocked against each other in their struggle to maintain body, soul and tribal claims.

The Turkish troops were there not only to keep order, but also were supposed to collect taxes on behalf of the Sultan. Ha! a joke. But it was a bad joke. The Circassians were not subservient by nature and culture, and the local Arabs, subsistence farmers and herders, as well as involved in their own intertribal disputes, were no innocent bystanders.

* * *

Mustafa was puzzled. An expeditionary force was being sent south to deal with some disturbances in the Hauran but he had not received orders to join it.

He met Müfit coming from the commander's office.

'What's up, Müfit'

His friend wore a grim expression.

'My unit's gone south, and I've been told to stay put here.'

'Same for me.'

Mustafa approached a group of officers who had just come from a meeting with the commander.

---

* The Druze are a secretive monotheistic sect, who revere the Prophet Jethro, known also as Shu'aib. Originally established in the Middle Ages in Egypt and the Levant, they were considered heretical by orthodox Muslims, and subsequently persecuted by Sunni Muslim rulers. They fought for centuries to maintain their independence from Ottoman rule eventually reaching an accommodation, as a bulwark against European intrusion in the Shouf region near Beirut. Later many Druze moved down into the Hauran as a result of political in-fighting in the 18th century.

'So, what's the deal? Where are you headed then?' he asked casually.

'Oh, the usual, down south around Kuneitra,' one of the younger officers volunteered. 'It'll be standard procedure. Chase the Druzes. Rumble a few Circassian villages. Maybe I'll be able to get a decent pair of boots out of it this time.'

'Yes,' said an older lieutenant, 'The Cherkez make very good boots!' and the group all laughed and walked on. But one of them lagged behind and when his companions had turned a corner out of sight, he returned to speak with Mustafa and Müfit.

'Look, chaps, I couldn't say this in front of the others, but I would be very careful, especially you, Mustafa. You're pretty well known down here already.'

'Oh? What do you mean?' Mustafa was sure this wasn't a compliment.

'Some of the older officers reckon you've got a broom up your arse and that you play strictly by the book. They say you got the top marks in Staff College. Well, maybe so, but it doesn't count for much down here. Look, things just aren't that simple. We haven't been paid in months – you saw Colonel Lütfi's uniform, he goes about in jodphurs and shoes. His boots wore out long ago. The only way we keep it all together and are able to send a little back home is if we play the tribes at their own game – you know, a raid here, a little rustling there. We're just combining taxcollecter with paymaster, that's all. Anyway, I thought I'd better warn you, some of the chaps won't take lightly to interference. You leave us to get along with our job. We'll do the same for you. You know how it is.'

'Yes, I know exactly how it is.' Mustafa's steely blue eyes took on a defiant edge, but Müfit delivered him a sharp kick to the side of his foot and he kept his peace.

The units from Mustafa's regiment left at dawn. Despite orders to the contrary, and after discussing it with Müfit, Mustafa saddled up and rode out after them a few hours later. He headed south from Damascus through the dry lands that led into the Hauran and the heights of Golan.

The seemingly endless countryside took him back to his boyhood. After his father died, his mother had taken him and his sister to live on her brother's farm outside Salonica. The days there seemed endless, hot and dry in summer and wet in winter. He remembered the times in spring when he and his sister would be sent to keep birds off the growing vegetables, when the land was sodden and marshy with the early rains. He remembered the cranes arriving in their thousands, resting after crossing the Bosphorus on their flight from Africa. They would appear through the early morning mist, roosting in the trees like pale monks, and later as the day warmed, wading in the flooded fields, picking out the frogs and tiny fish. Above, great birds of prey, also in transit to the north, circled like bandits around a caravan waiting for stragglers. Come March, and on their return in autumn, the same birds would appear here in Syria and Palestine, for he was riding the same migration route. He wondered how long before he too could return north.

Now winter wheat was showing green in the smallholdings scattered in the lower meadows where flooding streams of snowmelt had spread areas of fertile silt. Throughout the rough landscape olive trees clung on among the rocky slopes. Shadowing him to the west was the snow-covered massif of Mt Hermon – *Jebel al-Shaykh* – almost 9,000 feet, from whose southern flanks rise springs and streams which congregate to form the source of the River Jordan.

During the long ride Mustafa felt depressed. How on hearth had the situation come to this? Excellent graduation results from the prestigious Harbiye Military Academy and a promising career as a staff officer brought crashing down by his involvement in clandestine political activity. Carelessness, really. He had organised meetings with fellow students to air grievances about how the state was being mismanaged. But there had been an informer. They were arrested and interrogated, spending a few months in prison before being given these disagreeable postings. Although his loyalty was not seriously impugned, and higher ranking officers had pleaded his and his friends' case as youthful enthusiasm, for the time being Mustafa's ambitions appeared truncated. He had so wanted to get a posting to Salonica where he knew real action for change was brewing in the army. It was so depressing. Here in Syria, where corruption was the norm, he seemed helpless to influence things, and yet he resolved to try, and he knew he would have to watch his back here in the outlands.

He reached their camp after dark, and without his own tent and servant he bunked down with the enlisted men.

The expedition was as he suspected – nothing short of an excuse for a bit of looting. But Mustafa managed to keep his cool and even was able to rescue a major who had so riled the Druzes of one village that he had been taken prisoner and was in danger of being murdered. The Druzes had diverted a stream which fed the fields of a Circassian village lower down. The Circassians had complained before, but had had no redress. The Turks had first taken bribes from the Circassians, and the major had been trying to extort further currency from the Druzes, who naturally objected. When Mustafa rode into the village, he was surrounded by a shouting mob. He fired his pistol once into the air and replaced it in his holster. The hubbub ceased. Mustafa seized the moment. He dismounted and approached the crowd.

'Let that man go! He's a major in the army of your Sultan, the Caliph of God!' he spoke loudly and clearly. He didn't need an interpreter. They well knew the words *binbaşı, Padişah, Halifetallah*. His authority was inarguable.

'Who's in charge here?' he demanded, standing tall and with complete confidence. The gathered mob fell silent. A narrow-eyed grey-beard sidled forward, his head tilted slightly to the side, like a badly behaved dog brought to heel by its master.

'So, what's the problem?' said Mustafa

'Oh, no problem, *efendi*. But we don't have any gold to pay your major for the Cherkez. And we need the water for our animals.'

'You don't need to pay the major or the Cherkez, but you must reopen the stream. You'll just have to take your animals down below, well below their village. Is that clear?'

'Yes *efendi*, thank you *efendi*.'

'And give the major back his pistol and his horse!'

'Yes, *efendi*.'

The old Druze slunk back into the crowd, while the now-freed Turkish officer pushed his way out.

'Come on, sir. Let's get you out of here while the going's good.'

✳ ✳ ✳

Back in Damascus Mustafa met Müfit who had also joined an 'expedition', and had had a similar experience of looting and corruption.

'And they're offering me a share in the booty. Gold, mark you!'

'Are you going to accept it? Are you going to become one of them?'

Those eyes again. They said it all. Müfit smiled with relief. 'No, of course not.'

'Good, so you are a man of the future too.' said Mustafa, 'Bravo. We'll get them to change their ways yet. But not today, I fear.'

* * *

Mustafa wrote up his report and handed it in to the CO, who just gave a weak, defeated smile, and put the papers in a drawer.

'You don't understand, do you, Captain? You are still an ignorant officer with no experience. The Sultan doesn't want to hear that kind of story. Better to give a positive appraisal of how the Sultan's writ is maintained throughout his dominions. Here, like this.' He shoved a sheet of paper towards Mustafa. It detailed a successful offensive against rebellious tribes in the Hauran. 'This is what I want the Sultan to hear.'

Mustafa bridled. 'Yes, maybe I'm young. Maybe I'm ignorant. But I don't believe the Sultan should be kept in the dark about what is going on in his name.'

The Colonel glowered, and then looked down at his desk. He wasn't used to being spoken to in this way by subordinate officers, and yet it was a sign of the current state of affairs that the young man could take him to task in this way without fear of reprimand or worse. He knew Mustafa was right. Yet what could he do about it? He had taken over a situation not of his making. If he could only see out his term here in Syria, there would be a pension eventually, although it would be a pittance given the time he had spent sweating it out in the provinces. He didn't want to upset his chances of promotion either, however remote they were. 'This Mustafa seems to carry some weight,' he pondered. 'Perhaps I had better keep on the right side of him, just in case he is reporting directly to the Sultan.'

'Yes,' he said after a pause, lifting up his single sheet, 'maybe this is a little too optimistic.' He placed it in the drawer with Mustafa's report.

* * *

That evening Mustafa left his quarters and went into the old part of Damascus. He needed a break from the depressing atmosphere of the barracks.

He wandered down past the Citadel and entered the Old City through the great market place of the Souk Hamidiyeh, passing the Great Mosque of the Umayyads, and on across into Midhat Pasha Street. Eventually he emerged near Bāb Sharki, the Eastern Gate, in the Christian quarter of Damascus. Wandering a little further beyond the walls he heard distant strains of music. Not the expected *rebab* and *dümbelek* or *kanun*, playing in Oriental modes, but a lively mandolin, with handclapping and a fiddle too. He followed the sound until he found himself in front of a small café full of people eating at tables, drinking wine and dancing; men and unveiled women together, enjoying themselves. Mustafa felt a surge of excitement, and would have entered there and then, had he not been wearing the smart uniform of an Ottoman staff captain. 'What the heck,' he thought and hurried back to his quarters, changed into mufti, and returned to the cafe. There he joined Italian railway workers and their wives drinking wine and for a few brief hours sang and danced away his ennui. Late in the evening he called for food and was told that all that the kitchen had left was some lentil soup – *mercimek çorbası* – to which he was welcome.

He ordered a steaming bowl and tucked in. Something about the soup touched memories deep within, something familiar, like real home cooking, and he was transported momentarily to his childhood kitchen, his mother cooking, his little sister lying nearby in the cradle. Something very close in this memory had arrived in the tasting of this thick broth. He was so overcome by the emotion it provoked that he called for the cook to compliment and tip him.

'Not a 'him', *bey efendi*. Her.' said the patron, whose name was Domenico, a man of flagrantly Sicilian temper, a bald, good-looking man with a bandit's moustache and a comfortable belly. Domenico returned to the kitchen and emerged shortly afterwards with an apologetic look.

'I am sorry, but she's just left, she's away now back to Beirut. She's not our usual cook, just a friend filling in while our man Alfredo was unwell.'

'What a shame. Who knows, perhaps we would have danced!' Mustafa was in a light-hearted mood. 'Never mind, bring me another bottle of wine and I might take to the floor again.'

THREE

Secrets in Salonica, Lies in the Levant

Damascus – Salonica – Beirut, 1906/1907

 USTAFA PACED SLOWLY up and down the room. Every so often he would stop, put his hand on his forehead, and stare out of the window onto the barracks square. Soldiers and NCOs sat about in the shade in small groups, smoking, or playing dominoes, but most were dozing, their hats pulled down over their eyes. Nothing was happening. Nothing much ever seemed to happen. The autumn sun was still very hot and for once the tribes were not revolting. He turned back to his commanding officer,

'Colonel Lütfi sir, can't you see what's going on here? The Empire is slowly atrophying. It's as if the oxygen supply was being cut off from the body: the heart still pumps, but it's barely producing enough energy to stand still. That makes us vulnerable to every kind of meddling and attack. Look at how the British have taken over in Cyprus and Egypt. North Africa has rarely been compliant, but now with all the Italian interference… the French are here in Lebanon, the Russians in Macedonia, Bulgaria, and the Caucasus… Call this an Empire? We're like some ailing Pasha: his beautiful konak is in ruins, his land let out for peppercorn rents, but he's pawned his wife's jewellery so he can still ride around town in a carriage. It can't continue like this for much longer. You'll see, they'll find some excuse and the Greeks will be into Anatolia as quick as you can say Eleftherios Venizelos'.*

In spite of its difficult beginning, Mustafa's relationship with his CO had improved somewhat, and the Colonel quietly accepted much of Mustafa's criticism. He too wanted change, but he had a family to think of, and was not prepared to take risks like Mustafa.

'I agree with you, Captain Mustafa. But in my position it is impossible to do anything. However, I do know someone who may be able to help you get things moving down here.'

* * *

Mustafa and the Colonel arranged to cross paths with Müfit in front of the newly-erected Ottoman Railway station, and from there they walked the short distance to the Souk al-Hamidiyeh. They entered beneath the high awning that shaded the wide street of shops selling every kind of merchandise. Colonel Lütfi stopped outside one shop and nodded to the two men.

'This is the place. Give my regards to the *Hajji* and tell him you're friends of mine.' And with that the Colonel carried on through the souk towards the Omayyad Mosque.

The two officers went inside, where a man, who looked no different from any other Arab shopkeeper, greeted them in Turkish. The Hajji, whose name was Cantekin, was a former student of the Istanbul Military Medical School. He too had been imprisoned and exiled, for political activities judged to have revolutionary aims. Cantekin sat the two officers down on little wooden stools, and he ordered tea while Mustafa explained their mission.

'Many of us here would dearly like to see changes in the system but we

---

* 1864-1936, hero of the 1897 Cretan uprising and 7 times Prime Minister of Greece between 1910 and 1933.

have no organisation.'

'Then we must meet again.' said Cantekin, 'But take care – I'll arrange something.'

* * *

Later that week, a door opened in a dark and narrow street in the Old City of Damascus. A hand stretched out and held up a small oil lamp to view the faces of the four cloaked figures standing outside. Cantekin quickly ushered the visitors through to the reception room to join others sitting Arab-style on cushions and oriental rugs spread around the walls. Bottles of arak, glasses and a jug of water were set out on a brass tray in the middle of the floor.

Over the course of the evening the group talked, complained and proposed all manner of remedy for the state of the Ottoman Empire. The discussion covered the army, the government and the Sultan, becoming more and more heated as the night went on and the alcohol took effect.

Suddenly a young subaltern, overcome by emotion, stood up and raised his glass, shouting passionately, 'I am ready right now to die for this revolution!'

Mustafa knew this kind of talk. He banged his fist on the floor.

'No. No no no. You're missing the point.' His voice was calm but stern. He looked around the room, making eye contact with each member directly. Now he had everyone's attention, he continued:

'We'd be no use to anyone, let alone this land we say we love so much, if we are dead. I have no intention of dying for the 'vatan' (fatherland) if at all possible. But I definitely want to live for it.

'There's no point in us going off half-cocked: we must have a strategy. First we need to analyse the situation completely, then get organised. Clarify our aims and lay down a proper plan. And we need more of our officers involved. It should be nothing less than a proper military campaign.'

Then turning to the would-be martyr, he smiled: 'Keep your romance for the ladies, kardeşim, although I don't see the point in dying for them either. On the contrary, I prefer to be very much alive for them.'

The gathering burst into laughter, but they had heard Mustafa. From then on the conversation sharpened and they began to make concrete plans.

* * *

Within a short time the group had connected with other disaffected officers in Syria and Palestine. Mustafa's job as staff officer gave him freedom of movement, and as he rode the new tracks of the Hejaz Railway to all the major garrison towns, he made discreet contact with similarly-minded young officers. They formed a society called '*Vatan*' with cells in Damascus, Jaffa and Jerusalem. Ali led a cell in Beirut.

It was all very worthy, but for Mustafa things were happening too slowly. He needed to be where the action was, where the Empire itself was threatened at its western borders; and so, under the pretext of taking sick leave, he made a brief clandestine trip to Salonica. Here he renewed and extended his contacts among dissenting officers, before returning to Damascus.

* * *

September 1907 – Damascus barracks

'What news from Salonica?'

Mustafa looked up from his letter at Müfit.

'That new group, calls itself the Ottoman Freedom Society: it seems they've linked up with that firebrand Talaat, and a couple of other Salonica locals, old-time revolutionaries. They've amalgamated with our Vatan group' he scoffed; '"taken over" would be closer to the truth. Listen to this: "*Mustafa, you won't believe it. We had to put on these red cloaks, and veil our faces with black cloths. Then we were spirited away to a house somewhere where they chanted all this high and mighty stuff about the ideals of the society. You'd think we were in a Greek church at Easter. Then we had to swear on the Koran, and then on a pistol. Really, Mustafa, it would have been comical if weren't so serious. But you've got to hand it to them, they've got a big network, and their support is growing by the day.*"'

'So, there it is.' Mustafa put down the letter. 'And here we are left kicking our heels in this dustbowl. We're missing our chance. They're bound to screw it up. That fellow Talaat, the Postmaster, he's not interested in Turkey. He's a thug, he just wants to be the leader of the gang. And Enver, or Major Enver we should say, you remember him of course. Good soldier, very bright, if impetuous. But his politics are too conservative. The mullahs will be leading him round on a string before he knows it.'

'Do I detect a note of jealousy, Mustafa *canım*?' Müfit was smiling.

'Of course I'm jealous. You would be too if you knew you could do a much better job. I am jealous for my country's sake, not for myself.' Mustafa was now getting quite worked up. He was no longer addressing Müfit, but staring into some inner space with a faraway look in his blue-grey eyes.

'Old chap, you're getting maudlin. I tell you what, we need a night in Beirut to dust the cobwebs off – come on, we can get the afternoon train if we're quick about it.'

Müfit was just reaching for the door handle when a knock came from the opposite side. A young soldier stood there, saluting with one hand, an envelope in the other.

'For Major Mustafa, sir.'

Mustafa ripped open the brown envelope. As he read the contents his expression changed rapidly to one of complete satisfaction.

'Yes!' He held up the letter triumphantly to Müfit. 'Salonica – oh beautiful Salonica. My posting's come through at last. And promotion, to boot! You're right, tonight we shall drink champagne. And then arak. And then... ladies! Are you ready for those beauties of Beirut!'

'And not forgetting the slender boys!' said Müfit.

Mustafa gave him a rueful grin. 'Mmmm... yes, the boys... Well, it is Beirut, I guess anything's possible. Come on, *haydi gidelim!*'

FOUR

The Ripening of a Revolution

Constantinople, July 1908

HEN FRUIT IS RIPE, one day of sunshine may be sufficient to excite the sugars to bursting. So with revolutions, it takes but a spark to ignite a conflagration.

Within the high-walled enclosures of Yildiz Palace, with its hidden corners and secret by-ways, there at the centre of its own dark web of information and misinformation, spun by sycophantic courtiers out of the twisted visions of his multitude of spies and agents, deep within that meshed warp and weft of truths and lies, clinging like strands of mucus in the tubercular lungs of the teetering Empire's administration, the Old Man, petulant tyrant and indulgent father to his people, Sultan of Mood Swings, ever fearful to the point of psychopathic paranoia, Abdul Hamid II woke slowly into a fateful day.

The thin little man with the dark beard and the hooked nose, in the too large overcoat, gazed at the image in the mirror, and as though to another he spoke his thoughts to his own soul:

'What was this meeting in the Baltic all about?'* Why were the King of England and the Russian Tsar all of a sudden talking to each other in Reval?† Damn and blast that American journalist. It all started when he saw how we dealt with traitors in Bulgaria. And then he reports it to the European newspapers in all its ghastliness! Have they forgotten our sacrifice at Plevna? Do they not remember San Stefano in 1878, when the British fleet stood off Constantinople, the Russian army beneath their guns…? And anyway, it's not the dead they care about, but the interest outstanding on our loans. And why have we had to take these loans? Have they not taken so much and more from us in return? Egypt, Crete, Greece, Romania, half of Serbia, Cyprus and now most of Bulgaria! They want to destroy us and carve up the corpse…'

The Sultan was not having a good morning. This wasn't something new. It had been like this ever since that day in 1876 when he, the then-Sultan's younger brother, locked away for safe keeping in a palace with his concubines, had been dragged out of his comfortable berth and girded with the Sword of the House of Osman. Now over thirty years later the forces ranged against him were no longer just from without, but within his own army.

'We sent our commission to Macedonia to try and uncover the rot. And what happens? They shoot at our messengers. We send the army, and they seduce our troops into joining them. We try to reason with them, we are prepared to forgive, we offer them promotions. It no longer makes sense… was it for this that we survived the assassination attempts? Is this gratitude? Is this loyalty?'

The 'this' was an ultimatum. The 'Young Turks' had finally come out into the open. Prolonged fermentation after years of patient cultivating by young army officers had produced a heady revolutionary brew. The garrisons in Macedonia, the whole of the Second and Third Army Corps had come out under the banner of Major Enver and the Committee of Union and Progress (C.U.P) – the Young Turks – to demand a return to

---

* April 1908, the 'Baltic Agreement' between Germany, Russia, Denmark and Sweden, to guarantee the status of Baltic coasts and seaways.

† A meeting in Reval (now Tallin) to discuss reform in Macedonia.

the Constitution. And there was a twenty-four hour deadline, or else…
This was the original Constitution, promulgated by Grand Vizier Midhat
Pasha*, to which Abdul Hamid had consented back in 1876, in order to
appease the European Powers. It had been hastily dispensed with by the
Sultan two years later.

Abdul Hamid II called for his trusted Astrologer. The Astrologer consulted the stars, the Sultan's Council, the spies, the wives of the spies, and
the maids of the wives of the spies. Most importantly, he was made privy to
the telegrams arriving every moment from Macedonia forecasting the
gathering storm within the army. The Astrologer confirmed that it would
be in everyone's best interest to accede to the demands of the ultimatum
poste-haste. Which, to everyone's surprise, the Old Man did.

* * *

Salonica – July 1908

Major Enver alighted the train in Salonica station with due solemnity. The
cheering crowd on the platform were not disappointed and he received
their plaudits with aplomb. His moustachios seemed to have extra spring
in them today, and he had dressed in his best uniform for the occasion. It
made good theatre.

Mustafa and Enver were the same age, and socially were on a par, being
of humble, lower-middle class origins. Their families both came from the
European lands of the Empire. Both had made their mark gaining excellent
results at the Military Academy. Both were good looking officers, with the
vanity that goes with success. But in other ways they were opposites. Enver
the clean cut, don't smoke, don't drink kid with a marked leaning towards the
religious right, towards fanaticism even. Mustafa had definite socialist lean-
ings, and while he may have been obsessed with his country and its untapped
potential, the breadth of his thoughts took him far beyond the present,
correct and traditional forms of Ottoman religious culture. And Mustafa
enjoyed his drink, his cigarettes and the wilder delights of the flesh.

But if Mustafa was ahead in his thinking, it was Enver who later that day

---

*   Midhat Pasha (1822-1883) Grand Vizier and a leading figure in the 'Tanzimat'
     (modernisation) movement which brought about the first Ottoman constitution
     in 1876. Eventually he fell from grace and was exiled to Arabia, imprisoned and
     murdered.

stood before the masses of Salonica on the balcony of the Olympos Palace Hotel as the *kahraman* – the Hero – of freedom. While Mustafa skulked in the background, the crowds were hailing Enver as their Napoleon.

* * *

Two officers gazed out across the seafront towards the suburb of Perea on the far side of the bay, and beyond into the dark waters of the North Aegean. A hot southerly breeze was whipping up a white froth. Wavelets slapped the sides of small boats and dashed against the harbour wall.

From his shady cafe seat near the White Tower, Mustafa looked at the people in the street. It was a crazy sight, one that had probably never been seen before in Salonica, and maybe never would again. Everyone was out celebrating: Turks, Greeks, Armenians, Bulgars, Jews, Christians, Muslims, soldiers and sailors, ladies unveiled, all embracing and laughing with joy.

'Missed the boat, it seems, eh, Ali.' he said to his companion.

'You were there, Mustafa. It's happened and you were there. Isn't that enough?'

'But you saw him up on the balcony like some Roman Emperor, wooing the crowds, lapping up the cheers. And now, what's he doing? Parading round the streets in an open car. Does he know how to run a country, I wonder. We'll see.'

'Come on, let's at least enjoy today – a revolution without bloodshed, more or less, that doesn't happen often – and you were more than a small part in this.'

'Yes, but what now. The CUP don't seem to have an agenda, and there's so much to do. I wonder if they've even thought through how we are going to apply this new democratic system in the empire at large. Of course, it's easy here in Salonica or in Monastir, or even in Constantinople for that matter: we've had so much influence and interference from the Western Powers, we could slip into becoming European almost without noticing. But just let the bars of Pera and the unveiled women spread down the hills and over the Bosphorus – before we know it we'll have a counter-revolution. And as for the Arabs and Kurds in the East...' He rolled his eyes. 'But you're right, let's enjoy today while it lasts. Get in some more beers, and the *tavla* board.'

'Who knows, Mustafa, maybe it's better this way. Let Enver and Talaat fight it out.'

'Yeah? And leave me to pick up the pieces. And then what?' He shook his head. 'Well, at least I've got the army, I'll be busy enough without having to get involved in politics. I shall watch with interest, and try and hold my tongue.'

'Hah, Mustafa! I'd like to see that.'

Ali threw a five. Mustafa a six. The game began.

* * *

It was a balmy August night a few weeks after re-declaration of the Constitution. The town of Salonica stretched lazily up the hill from the water and seemed to sigh in the warm breeze at the day's end with a sense of relief verging on gaiety. Even the fishing boats rocking gently at their moorings seemed content.

But Mustafa wasn't content. He was holding forth to a group of fellow officers, in Salonica's newest cafe, the White Tower.

'What do we need party politics for? At this stage, we need consensus and carefully worked out programmes. Otherwise, will we have the right wing deciding for all of us, and keeping the power close to their chests? It would be just like the old days.'

'Or, if the liberals hold sway, you'll see the minorities demanding not just self-determination, but independence. Then before you know it we'll lose the provinces. And then what Empire?'

Mustafa poured himself another raki, and nibbled on a few *leblebi*, the little brown roasted chick peas which he found helped slow down the absorption of alcohol without him having to reduce his consumption.

Constantinople, September 1908

It wasn't long before Mustafa's continued harangues reached the ears of the CUP's leaders. The Committee, now removed to Constantinople, considered him a thorn in their side. To get him out of the way, they decided to send him on a mission to North Africa, to replace the provincial governor who had just died.

'To be frank, looking at the way things are developing in Constantinople, I'm glad to be out of it,' he said to Ali on receiving the news. 'I believe we soldiers should keep out of politics. Except when absolutely necessary of course.'

It was an early morning in Constantinople. The two friends stood on the passenger quayside at Salıpazarı gazing across the Bosphorus to Üskudar on the Asian shore. This pier, below the Ottoman arsenal of Tophane, has served the city for arrivals and departures by sea for seven centuries. A pleasant *meltem* breeze was blowing down from the hills above, causing the leaves on the giant plane trees shading the water's edge to shiver gently.

Mustafa's luggage had already been taken aboard the Italian steamer that was to carry him to Tripoli. The officers threw their cigarette butts into the water and a big gull dived down to investigate. A *simit* seller called his wares from a cart nearby. Ali went over and purchased a couple of the soft bread rings coated in sesame seeds, and handed one to Mustafa.

Whether it was the confidence which came from being born into privilege, or just his natural easy going approach to life, Ali didn't seem at all worried about their future prospects. He remained quite sure that their talents would get due recognition all in good time.

'Look here, Mustafa,' said Ali, brushing sesame seeds from his moustache and tunic, 'you're only twenty-eight, and already we've come so much further than we could have hoped since college. For heaven's sake, *canim*, it's only been five years! Let that lot make the mistakes that we might have made. There's so much more to learn, to do. Our time will come, mark my words.'

The ship's horn blasted three times, and a seaman by the gangplank began to ease the mooring cables. The two men embraced. Mustafa climbed aboard and without looking back he disappeared below to his cabin.

The vessel was underway in minutes, and when Mustafa came up on deck shortly afterwards, they were steaming past the thick green hillside of Saray Burnu. Peeping out above the treetops were the buildings of Topkapi Palace, the old lair of the sultans, with the little pointed chimneys of the harem, the kiosks and mosque, and as they gained the Sea of Marmara, the six spires of the Mosque of Sultan Ahmet and the great dome and minarets of the Aya Sofia arose in their stern, glowing in the morning light. Constantinople was radiant, lying there embedded in a sea of sapphire and pearl. Musing on this he murmured a couplet to himself:

O beauteous whore, whom everyone would own.
What filth you hide within your petticoats of stone.

FIVE

Counter-revolution

Constantinople, April 1909

PRIL, THE MONTH of the Judas Tree. The shores of the Bosphorus glowed magenta with the buds which flower directly from the branches before the heart-shaped leaves appear. And even more quickly than these fading blooms did the inevitable counter-revolution wither on the branch. Mustafa stood staring out of the window in the Harbiye Military College, his back to the room where the General sat at his desk.

'Well, he's done it again. Captain 'Death or Glory', that's what I'd call him. Great sense of drama, but I wonder how much common sense he really has.'

Mustafa was grumbling again. And as usual it was Enver who was the object of his derision. Mustafa had returned to Salonica from Libya in

January with his reputation enhanced after settling a revolt and establishing the new order of the Young Turks. Then the counter-revolution in Constantinople brought him to the city with the 'Army of Liberation'. On the morning of the 13th of April a rebellion from reactionary elements had arisen in the Topcu Barracks in Taksim Square and elsewhere in the city. It mainly involved the lower ranks and the conservative old guard, elements in the army which had remained stubbornly loyal to the Palace. It was rumoured that it had been funded by the Old Man himself, Sultan Abdul Hamid II.

Quashing the counter-revolution had been quick and decisive. A lightning offensive from Macedonia soon had Istanbul surrounded. Investing the city by land and sea, the army then slipped in under cover of darkness and apart from some minor street skirmishes and brief sieges at the Topcu Barracks in Taksim and the nearby Mecidiye Barracks, soon it was all over bar the shouting. And that was silenced once the ringleaders of the mutiny were hanged on Galata Bridge. Enver had acquitted himself in typical gung-ho style when he charged into the fray at the head of his men at the Topcu barracks.

General Mahmut Shevket Pasha smiled indulgently at the young staff officer – a rare smile from this otherwise serious, even ferocious, old Chechen. 'You've got to admit he's keen.' General Shevket was referring to Enver. 'I mean, look how he high-tailed it down here from Berlin, and got straight into the action'

'But that's exactly what I mean. He's all bull and bluster, but what is he actually doing about running the country?'

General Shevket sighed.

'Mustafa, my dear, this is just the beginning. You remember Osman's Dream? Haven't you seen what happens to a big tree when it outgrows itself? One of those huge çinars (plane trees) that grow in the village squares, or here along the Bosphorus. Eventually it becomes a victim of its own size. If it isn't looked after, trimmed down occasionally and its big old branches supported, eventually it will collapse under its own weight. Or maybe a storm will uproot it from the earth. It may continue to live a while sprouting new leaves for a season or two. But mark my words, in the end it will die, victim to frost and heat, and eaten up by all the tiny organisms which inhabit its crusty skin, then fall apart and crumble into the earth. In time this great mass that once filled the sky in its grandeur, is returned to

the soil whence it emerged from a tiny seed. Then other seeds will grow
and another tree will take its place. The Empire is like that tree. It has
collapsed under its own ancient mass, and still breathes a while, as its
final strength is sapped by all those who have lived off its wealth for so
long, and now take what they can and flee.'

'Yes, my Pasha,' said Mustafa, 'but look at the people. Their minds are
still running round and round on the same old tracks, afraid to open up to
new ideas. That is why this is not a real revolution. Imagine if they could
truly let go of the past; then what a new world would be possible?'

'Mustafa, of course you are right. But you are like the one lone ox
pulling forward against a whole train that wants to go back into the farm-
yard. In time, if you are given the strength and the help, it all will go
forward, I'm sure of it. But for now, let's consolidate what we've got.'

'That's easy for you to say, sir. You've already achieved more than a
lifetime's worth for any man. And you're still a big influence in the army,
even bigger now that you've brought Constantinople back in line. Perhaps
you're right. I wonder does one really become more patient as one gets
older? Perhaps one just gets worn down.'

'Come, come, Mustafa Bey, now you're beginning to sound like one of
the students from the staff college. Enver's glory will fade quick enough if
there is no substance to back it up. Time will tell.' The General rose from
his desk and stood beside Mustafa by the window. He spoke in a low voice:

'In the meantime, take care my young friend, these are dangerous
times for all of us. There's no telling what action people will take against
those whom they consider a threat to their ambitions.'

Mustafa took his leave of the General and made his way by tram back
down the Grande Rue de Pera. Avoiding the enticements of the Yüksek
Kaldırım – he had other business that night, and in any case he didn't
doubt the ladies would be fully occupied with entertaining the visiting
troops – he took the little one-stop *Tünel* underground railway down to
the waterfront at Karaköy from where he crossed the Golden Horn. Even
in the dark of the cloudy night, the fires of the chestnut sellers and the
braziers of the men frying fish in shallow pans gave off enough light to
adumbrate in slow-moving shadows the bodies of the traitors swinging
from the gibbets along the Galata Bridge. A few expectant rats crawled
around beneath the suspended corpses. He thought on General Shevket's
parting words, and moved his heavy Mauser C96 pistol from its holster

into his greatcoat pocket. It had not occurred to him before that anyone would want to assassinate him.

Was someone following? He had crossed and walked up the lane which ran along the right hand side of the Egyptian Market. The coffee seller on the corner was closed now, but the strong smell of the day's roasting and grinding permeated the air and covered the smells from the fish sellers and butchers nearby. At the top he turned left and immediately right and continued up the narrow lanes of Mahmutpasha, skirting the the lower side of the Grand Bazaar in the direction of the Suleymaniye Mosque. He was forced to walk slowly as the streets were poorly lit and the cobbles were in a bad state of repair. So many of the small streets in Istanbul had been neglected during the reign of Abdul Hamid and some were little better than dirt tracks, dusty in summer and slippery mud slides when it rained.

His suspicions were confirmed by footsteps about thirty or forty yards behind him. He waited until there was a kink in the lane and while out of view he backed into a doorway and slipped out his pistol. He held his breath and waited. As the man approached the clouds parted, and for the briefest of moments a glimmer of moonlight revealed the face of his pursuer. It was enough for Mustafa. In that moment he recognised the face of an uncle of Enver. The man continued walking. He could not have avoided seeing Mustafa lurking to his left, and would realise he had lost his advantage and was now the prey. Mustafa let him get a little ahead before stepping out and following close enough for the man to hear his footsteps. Close enough so his would-be assassin would be certain that Mustafa's pistol, if he chose to use it, would be effective. He followed him right up to the retaining walls below the Great Mosque of Süleyman, where at the top, just by the tomb of the Royal Architect Sinan, Mustafa let the man go ahead, and on into the night. For his part, Mustafa turned left, past the Dar'ul Ziyafe and around near the main entrance of the mosque, where opposite there were a number of food stalls. Here he paused, finding himself a late supper of *kuru fasuliye* (white beans in a tomato and pepper sauce) and pilaf.

Sitting in the moon shadow of Sinan's masterpiece, he reflected on General Shevket's mention of Osman's Dream, and his words about the declining old tree. This prophetic dream was a foundation myth of the Ottoman Empire. It concerned the young prince, Osman, the son of a leader of a small Turkish tribe which inhabited the region around Eskişehir, south-east of Constantinople in the 13th Century. Osman was the founder of what became the Ottoman dynasty, from whom the Empire, known in Turkish as 'Osmanlı' took its name.

Osman's Dream

Osman is passing the night in the house of a local holy man, Edebali, whose daughter he is courting. In the dream, Osman is sitting with Edebali, from whose breast he sees a full moon rise which then sets in his own breast. Now an enormous tree springs up, beautiful and verdant, growing ever bigger until its canopy covers the whole of the world. Its branches are supported by the mountains of the Caucausus, the Atlas, the Taurus and the Balkans, and from its roots flow the great rivers Tigris, Euphrates, Nile and Danube. Great ships ply their trade on the waters, the fields are spread with ripening corn, forest covers the hillsides, fabulous cities are evident throughout, and the crescent moon shines down upon domes and minarets. The muezzin's call to prayer intermingles with the song of nightingales and countless birds of marvellous beauty flying beneath the domed canopy of the great tree. A strong wind blows, transforming all the leaves of the tree into scimitars which point towards the cities, in particular towards Constantinople, which sits between two seas and two continents like a great diadem set in the bezel of a world-encompassing empire. And just as this jewelled ring is being placed upon his finger, Osman wakes up.

He tells Edebali who interprets the dream as a very positive sign for the young man's future and gladly gives him his daughter's hand. The rest is history.

✷ ✷ ✷

Within days of Mustafa and General Shevket's conversation, this circle of history took another momentous turn. The spiritual leader of the Muslim community in the Empire, the Sheikh-ul-Islam, was prevailed upon by the now re-instated Committee members in Parliament to issue a *fatwa* deposing Sultan Abdul Hamid II in favour of his brother, the mystically-inclined Mehmet Reshad, who had been kept under virtual 'palace-arrest' for the previous thirty years. An unworldly man, Sultan Mehmet V, as he became known, accepted his fate with the resignation of a dervish disinterested in the affairs of the world, a puppet for the ruling Junta now comprising a Triumvirate of Enver, Talaat and Major Djemal, who was an influential officer in the Macedonian army and prominent member of the CUP.

SIX

The Shore Road to Beylerbeyi

Haydarpaşa Station, Constantinople, March, 1911

NE MORNING in late March, Satanaya, still not yet thirty years old, newly arrived by train from deep in the Anatolian hinterland, stood on the grey stone steps outside the station, looked about her and shivered.
Unlike most of the great railway stations of the world's capitals, which present their majestic facades upon the grand plazas of consumer splendour and busy traffic of commercial thoroughfares, the passenger arriving at Haydarpaşa might imagine that she has attained some mystical station at the edge of the world.

On a good day, after long journeying through Middle Eastern deserts, high mountain barriers and the endless monotony of the Asian steppe, the traveller, on alighting her train, progresses through mahogany doors into the lofty arrivals and ticket hall. Here she pauses a moment upon the marble paving, happily perplexed beneath gently curved ceilings plastered in squares of pale cerulean, supported by pink walls pierced with arches and bordered in ornamental pargeting. Gazing ahead through a wall of glass brightly, she attains her first glimpse of the masterpiece for which the building is but a simple frame, and so moves outside onto descending steps and there beholds a sight of rare beauty: the blue ocean stream of the Bosphorus Strait, on whose opposite shore rise the fabled palaces, domes and minarets of the Queen of Cities, Constantinople, which under a rising sun gleam and glister in majesterial glory as if they were the monumental aigrette and crown, the orb and mace of Sultan and Emperor in whose honour these architectural jewels were unveiled.

But this was not that good day.

An icy blast drove curtains of rain down from the Black Sea whipping dark horse waves which leapt and crashed against the quayside below. A sea mist shrouded the far shore in a cloak of gloom.

'Never forget Beauty. Remember Beauty always, seek It out, yearn for It, and It will remember you, just as It seeks and yearns for you. That is what love is for, nothing else; and life is for learning to love.'

As Satanaya gazed into the gloom she remembered the words of Yeşil Efendi on their last night together – he had spoken them quietly, almost as an afterthought, a postscript to their long journey of the soul together. And yet now the words resounded in her as if he was present and speaking directly into her heart.

But where in all this gloom was Beauty? She concentrated, as if the beam of her sharpened mind could pierce the fog. And for a moment clarity came. Though sight still beheld the grey drizzle upon the roiling waters, the scene no longer oppressed, but appeared full of potential, and she resolved to enter her new adventure with the lightest of hearts.

Back in the station she disembarked her horse Tarçin from the livestock wagon, gently leading him up and down the platform until he was steady on his feet again. Then with directions from the Station Master, she proceeded north along the shore road, by now a muddy track, to the village of Beylerbeyi, by way of Üsküdar.

From Haydarpaşa she rode through Harem, and on to Salacak, with its long wooden pier to the ferry landing stage, the 'iskele'. Out beyond the waves she spied a tower upon a little island, battered by the rushing downward tide.* Further on she met the little Mosque of Shemsi Pasha†, a sad neglected ruin, its roof a garden of sprouting weeds and shoots of bushes, the whole complex in danger of slipping into the sea. Here the track came so close to the water's edge that the waves crashed upon it, soaking the shore-fishermen with their long bamboo rods, and sending them scurrying for cover. But the *hamsi* were running and the anglers soon returned, casting deep and reeling in their multi-hooked lines, now leafed in quivering tongues of silver anchovy. Cats, ragged in the rain, snatched up any sprats that danced loose off the lines even before the fishermen could unhook them, cheating the screaming gulls which wheeled above.

Had it been that other day, that fairer, brighter day, Satanaya without doubt would have noticed and been astounded by the bustling town of Üskudar, with its two huge Imperial mosques flanking the wide *meydan*; and by the water's edge the picturesque square-roofed fountain with its intricately carved marble facades with basins and spigots where the passing faithful quench their thirst and perform their ablutions.‡

As it was, she traversed Üskudar through a heavy curtain of rain, and saw little else but ramshackle wooden houses clustered along the mud-

---

* The Maiden's Tower, or 'Kiz Kulesi', has struggled with two millenia of Bosphorus tides and gales, and from its well-known location as a lighthouse it has guided to safety many a storm-tossed vessel. No such safety was granted the original inhabitant, a king's daughter, incarcerated there by her father who wished to preserve the girl from a soothsayer's prophecy that she would die by snakebite upon her eighteenth birthday. But death would not be cheated. An itinerant grocer passed by in his boat, from whom the maiden purchased a basket of fruit. She reached in among the peaches and cherries and a viper hidden in the basket bit her, obligingly fulfilling the requirements of her kismet (destiny).

† This mosque was the work of the 16th century Imperial Architect Sinan, who built it for the Grand Vizier Shemsi Pasha, by all accounts a flamboyant character who loved the perks and pomps of high office. It is said that he was the first official in the Ottoman court to accept a bribe, by the hand of the notorious Vizier, Rustem Pasha, the wealthy husband of Princess Mihrimar, the only daughter of Suleyman the Magnificent; and in that act of corruption was sowed the seeds of the future downfall of the empire. Shemsi Pasha had the mosque built as a penance and hoped-for expiation of this sin of corruption.

‡ later in the 20th century this fountain was moved back from the quayside and raised up as the surrounding area was raised.

filled lanes. Sodden pedestrians sheltered beneath the projecting bays of
upper floors – the '*cumba*' – from where on more clement days the occu-
pants would sit unseen behind latticed shutters and gaze below on
passers-by.

Passing the village of Kuzguncuk, the weather cleared, the clouds
backed off and the wind dropped. Sun and blue skies transformed the still-
choppy surface of the Bosphorus into gold-flecked lapiz lazuli. Looking up
at the hillsides, Satanaya now saw that the *erguvan* – the Judas trees – were
just coming into bloom. The bloody magenta buds and blossoms which
hint at the derivation of their name, glistened from the branches. Tradition
says the blooms were once white, but turned red in shame at the act of the
ill-starred disciple.

As followers of her earlier travels in Palestine and Syria will know,
Satanaya had recently been living in Konya*. There her host, a Persian lady
called Shireen, had provided her with an introduction to the wife of a
Turkish army colonel in Constantinople who required a lady's companion
and governess for her child.

This family lived in a villa in the next village, Beylerbeyi, within an
estate which stretched from the shore right to the top of the slopes behind.
The main building, the *konak*, was a large square three-storied wood-clad
structure with cantilevered *cumbas* on each side. Nearby was a coachhouse
and stables, and various other buildings. She paused, momentarily confused as to where she should present herself.†

She decided to investigate the main building. Facing the Bosphorus,
glazed double doors gave onto a small terrace beneath the cumba, with
steps leading down to the path which encircled the house. Clockwise to the
next side, three double French doors opened onto a paved terrace which
descended to a formal garden with rosebeds, shrubberies and lawns, and
an ornamental pool. Continuing around to the rear, fronting the hill, was
access to a gravelled area, and the coachhouse opposite. Completing her

---

*   see Satanaya and the Houses of Mercy, Hakawati Press, Hawick, 2018.

†   The typical Ottoman house of the period would have at least two entrances. There
    would be a main entrance to what was known as the Selamlık, where the man of the
    house received visitors, who would necessarily only be male, and there would be the
    private apartments known as the Haremlık, where the women of the house held
    sway, the bedrooms and the kitchen. An area called the 'Mabeyn' – meaning a place
    in between two – connected these two domains.

circumambulation on the final side she found a
with a wide panelled door. She decided to enter her
to an iron ring on a rail provided for this purpose.

She had chosen correctly, for her arrival was anticip
tachioed man dressed in traditional dark baggy breeches
over a white shirt, his close-cropped pate crowned with   ed fez,
allowed her entrance. Then a young couple dressed in modern European
clothes appeared in the doorway. They looked the visitor up and down,
then the lady burst into a little giggle.

'Welcome, welcome. I imagine you must be Satanaya. Please tell me it
is so?' The delight on the young lady's face was evident.

Satanaya for her part was a little non-plussed. She wasn't at all sure
what to make of this reception. But she smiled cautiously and said,

'Yes. Yes, and…?'

'I'm Amina, and this is my husband Colonel Mohammed.'

The tall young man bowed slightly, still smiling.

'Yes, welcome my dear, please come inside and let's get you dried off.'
he said.

'Thank you, *Bey Efendi, Hanım Efendi*.'

It was only as she stepped inside and saw her reflection in the tall
ormulu-framed hallway mirror that Satanaya realised the cause of her
hosts' amusement. Anyone opening a door to that sight would surely have
raised their eyebrows. What a mess. Her full length cloak, soaked and
muddied, and the once wide-brimmed felt hat melted and mingled with
her soggy locks, the kohl she had so lovingly applied before leaving the
train that morning streaked across her face, one might be forgiven for
imagining a ghoul had wandered in from a nearby graveyard.

'Oh dear' was all Satanaya could say.

'*Ma pauvre!*' said Amina Khanoum. 'I was so rude to laugh at you, but
our friends in Konya said you dressed like a European, and here you
appear, for all the world like Cosette sweeping the puddles in 'Les Miséra-
bles'. You poor little drowned thing!'

Satanaya managed a weak laugh.

'Perhaps I should change my clothes.'

Her room was two flights up. Here she found a bathroom plumbed in
the modern European fashion with a huge cast iron bath complete with an
overhead shower, and even a pedestal w.c.. Before long she returned to her

hosts clean, warm and dry.

Satanaya was invited into the family room on the first floor, to wit, the *haremlik*, furnished traditionally with ornately painted wooden ceiling and panelled walls with plaster alcoves frescoed with pastoral and sea views, recessed windows and sumptuously cushioned low divans. A brass brazier sat in the centre of the room, between two large Hereke carpets.

'Satanaya, dear,' said Amina Khanoum, 'You may imagine you are here with us due to the connection with your friend Shireen, and her father in Konya. But my mother also knew Lady Gülbahar through her husband the Ambassador, and they corresponded regularly, especially after the Ambassador died. It even turned out that she and mother were distantly related.'

Satanaya's surprise was evident. Amina Khanoum began to pour the tea, Turkish style in little glasses.

'Oh, it all goes back to the Caucasus,' she continued, 'Apparently we all have a bit of Cherkez in us, you know – all those Circassian slave girls who were our grandmothers and great-grandmothers, the pretty ones who caught the eyes of the Khedives. Sugar?'

'Thank you, just a little.'

Amina Khanoum then proceeded to give a brief run down of her family's history. It turned out that she was descended from the great Muhammed Ali of Egypt. His family had come from Konya to Thrace at the beginning of the 18th century, before Muhammed Ali became the Sultan's great nemesis in the 19th century and made of Egypt a semi-independent state within the Empire. He and his descendants, the Khedives, the hereditary Viceroys of Egypt, became so wealthy and powerful, they were considered rivals to the Sultan himself.

'I was named after his first wife – but you know, he had so many, aside from the four official ones. I think we counted at least twelve more, didn't we darling?' She turned to her husband seeking confirmation and he smiled indulgently. 'And of course they all had children, and so on. Our grandpa was the Khedive Ismail – you know, the one who had Verdi do that opera and...'

At this point a female servant appeared in the tow of a young child of about two years, and all attention turned to the little chap in his sailor suit who was insisting he be brought to his mother.

'*Annem, annem!*' he cried, 'Mama, biscuit, PLEASE. Ahmed needs a biscuit. Please!'

'Ah my sweet, *gel, buraya gel, canım*! Come here my darling.' said Amina, delighted.

The little boy detatched himself and trotted across the carpet, his nurse Subhana following closely, steering him round the brazier while cautioning in an urgent whisper, '*Dikkat* Ahmed! Be careful of the *mangal*, it's hot.' And to her mistress, ' I'm sorry Madam, but he just insisted.'

But Amina wasn't listening, she was hugging her child and introducing him to the guest.

'This is Satanaya *Khanoum*, who has come all the way from Arabia to help look after you. Ahmed – Satanaya. Satanaya – Ahmed.'

Ahmed stood in silence for a few moments, looking at Satanaya very intently, as if trying to fit this new arrival into his world view.

'Hello' said Satanaya, smiling.

'Hello' he said eventually, maintaining a cautious look.

'There, now you can have one biscuit, and then off you go with Subhana,' said Amina, and turning to Satanaya, 'You see – children – they are perfect lovers. All they see in their mothers is sweet nourishment.'

Little Ahmed, a biscuit in one hand, the other gripping the hand of the maid, departed.

At this point the Colonel, who up till then had been standing quietly by the brazier with his tea, spoke:

'You see, my wife is pregnant again, and Subhana, sweet as she is, cannot always be there to help. Her own mother is ill and her responsibilies are divided. And with a new baby, it would be even more difficult. Of course, there are any number of young women whom we could employ, among our servant's relations, but we thought it might be good for the young chap to experience slightly more educated company. You could be his '*mürebbiye*'.'' He used the Ottoman word with a meaning roughly equivalent to governess. But it also included the sense of nanny. 'You would have all the help you need. And of course, you would be a valued companion for my wife.'

'Oh please do say yes.' said Amina Khanoum. This bubbly young lady displayed all the gracious bloom of pregnancy and the effervescence of youth. 'The Colonel Efendi is so busy these days, and I so much would like someone to accompany me around town, visiting, shopping, picnicking. We shall see all of Constantinople, by boat and by carriage. Of course I shan't be doing that for much longer, but' she looked down and placed her hand upon her belly, a satisfying bump which Satanaya now noticed. 'I'm over the difficult bit and we're not expecting to deliver 'til summer.'

Suddenly Satanaya felt a deep longing for something she had missed in recent years. The sense of femininity that Amina Khanoum exuded, the love of fun and the frivolity of life. And the thought of children – perhaps it wasn't so frightening after all. Of course it was easy for Amina, she belonged to one of the richest dynasties in the world, and while only a minor relative, the privileges and possibilities were great.

'I would love to, but may I ask one thing?'

Amina looked concerned. 'Please, if it's in our power, whatever you wish.'

'May I go in the kitchen from time to time?'

Amina Khanoum laughed and clapped her hands.

'Oh yes, oh yes. Lady Gülbahar said you were the best. Oh you must make yourself at home there. I've already spoken to the cooks, and they are quite in awe. But I must warn you, they are all excellent cooks too, and can cook in the Palace way.'

'That is what I want, I am also here to learn.'

'Excellent. That's settled then.' said the Colonel. 'What say we take a walk around the garden now the sun's come out? You know, we Turks have always loved gardens, just as much as the Persians and the Indians. The old Persian word for a walled garden is *parideza* – paradise. The first Mughal emperor, Babur, as well as conquering India, in between his campaigns he had a garden built in Kabul. We all need a little paradise between our campaigns in this world, don't you think?'

✳ ✳ ✳

The fertile acres of the Beylerbeyi property were a mix of woodland and arable ground, with some pasture for a couple of dairy cows. As they walked among the chestnuts and walnuts coming into leaf, budding almond and cherry, and the flowering Judas trees, the Colonel explained the workings of the estate.

'Although we have a modern approach here using the latest scientific farming methods, we run the estate as one big family, with far less of a division between the master and mistress and our servants than you would find on a European estate.'

Satanaya thought of some of the English novels she had read while in

Beirut, where social stratas were rigidly defined with little if any movement between. Her time in Konya had shown her that while there was formality in the individual relations between people, there was a certain fluidity in the society, a recognition of the human person that preceded their apparent worldly status.

'In traditonal Ottoman society' continued the Colonel Efendi, 'anyone with ambition who showed real talent could rise, if one had the right backing.'

'If that person were a man' added Satanaya.

'Or, if she were to marry the right man' said the Colonel.

'Or he were to marry the right woman' quipped Amina Khanoum.

At the same time, it was evident to Satanaya that all, from the mistress Amina Khanoum down to the children of the cowherd, held their master the Colonel Efendi in the highest esteem.

'Yes, but here I imagine you are like the Sultan.' ventured Satanaya.

'Yes, here my word is law!' he laughed, 'But you will see, there is mutual respect, and affection we hope, from all sides. In some ways the set-up here does mimic the Sultan's palace. But with a difference – here you are free to go or stay. There are no wages, as such, but there are gifts, and no one goes wanting – it was not so long ago that many of these servants would have been slaves.'

The Colonel then explained how the gradual quasi-colonisation of Egypt by the British which followed on the building of the Suez Canal had brought about the banning of slavery in the Khedivate in 1896, although in Constantinople and elsewhere in the Empire some of the more traditional households still kept slaves. But the Colonel who had enjoyed both a European and Ottoman education would have none of it, and any slave he and his wife had inherited had been officially freed. In fact the change was more of status than of condition. Whether slave or servant, under the Ottoman system they were often better off in many ways than a servant in a European house, receiving education, often with the master's children, and enjoying many of the same privileges. As there was not the same cultural or social discrimination between ranks, marriages between freed slaves and their masters were not uncommon.

They were in the vegetable garden now, one of the Colonel's great enthusiasms.

'Look, the spinach is already flourishing, and the seedlings of the peppers and aubergines we started in the glass-house have already taken well.' he said. 'The garden provides the kitchen with most of our vegetables, and wood for the stove comes from husbanding the woodland.'

The Colonel's thrust for modernisation had recently manifested in the installation of a coal-fired boiler and central heating system to supplement the *mangals* during the cold winter months from January into March.

'But mostly we run it to heat the glass-houses so we can have flowers and fresh vegetables all year round.'

Living by the Bosphorus, and with the poor state of the roads, automobiles were a rarity still. The Colonel did own a private motor launch, but he preferred to use either an official Palace caique or one of the modern ferries when crossing to the European shore. From there he would take a horse-drawn cab to perform his duties within the offices of the state bureaucracy.

'And then, of course, we have chickens, and pigeons, and game birds.'

They were just beyond the glass-houses, in a fenced off area about the size of a tennis court, surrounded by closely-planted cypress trees. Low wooden huts housed dozens of chickens and guinea fowl which were currently busy scratching about in the muddy earth .

'We have so many eggs now they are laying again after the winter that we sell them in the market in Çengelköy. But my latest hobby is pigeons.'

The Colonel pointed over towards the coach house. Satanaya could just make out the bird houses beneath the eaves at one end of the building.

'They're shaded in summer by that large çinar. Now, when the leaves are gone, the winter sun warms the nests.'

'And do you eat them?' asked Satanaya, fondly remembering the taste of roast pigeons stuffed with *freekah* as she rode with Timur and Murat down through Palestine.

'Of course, we breed them for cooking. But also simply for the beauty of the birds and their flying. You know we have a long tradition of flying pigeons. You see on some of the large mosques, pigeon houses and dovecotes configured into the walls, imitating in miniature the very building of which they are a part.'

They inspected the coach house and stables, where Tarçin was receiving loving attention from young Fatih, the stable boy. He had brushed the horse of all the mud and dust from the journey until his coat was shining deep cinnamon brown. Here the tour came to an end.

Something in Colonel Efendi's manner made Satanaya feel immediately at home in her new surroundings. He was a charming guide, thoughtful and considerate. His enthusiasm to try out new ideas on his estate reminded her a little of Lady Gülbahar's late husband, the French Count. She felt safe here.

SEVEN

A Summer in Constantinople

Constantinople 1911

OLLOWING THE INITIAL excitement of arrival, and able at last to relax after so much journeying, something in Satanaya broke. She hadn't realised quite how much she had been living on her nerves during the past couple of years. What with all the travelling, the irregular diet and the intense and somewhat ascetic life she had led under the tutelage of Yeşil Efendi, she had lost the comfortable curves nurtured in the kitchens of the Beyt'ur-Rahma. She was exhausted down to the bones.

The day after her arrival she began to feel a little light-headed. This was followed by vomiting and the next day she came down with a fever and was immediately sent to bed. Amina tended to her initially with hot toddies and endless glasses of 'ıhlamur', the delicately scented infusion of linden blossom which helps the system fend off congestion and the dreaded 'grip'. But it was no simple 'flu.

The fever deepened and with it came the aches; she felt as if her whole being were dissolving. Every bone and joint seemed on fire and when she wasn't burning, she was shivering; perspiring so much that her bedding became soaked. She had no recollection of sleeping, instead drifting back and forth between liminal states. And it wasn't just physical. She was also experiencing a kind of mental hell. Her mind became overwhelmed with strange images, and she felt herself being pulled down by forces deep in her unconscious, as if something wanted to bury her in the earth of her own being. Each time she surfaced, her physical pain increased, and she began to believe, and at times to wish, that she would die. This cycle continued day and night until all her strength was gone and she felt alone in the darkness. She finally accepted the end. She no longer had the energy to fight the ineluctable tide drawing her further from the shore of her life.

Then, in the midst of this drowning frenzy, at a point where she had truly surrendered to whatever was assailing her, came a moment of calm. And with it a kind of inner sense of assurance, telling her that everything was going to be fine, all had been prepared, all she needed to do was to step away from her pain, her anguish, her life. It was a choice. She knew she was on the brink, and the next step could be a blissful entry into a world beyond suffering. The invitation was irresistible.

And then – something else. She recognised it immediately. It was not a voice exactly, but rather a tone of being, a kind of odour, upon which hinged a memory, of smoke and earth and the dry heat of summer in Meram. It was Yeşil Efendi, her erstwhile companion and mentor calling her to attention, with a reminder that there was work still to be done. She cried out from her delirium, a cry she thought must have shaken the wooden boards of the konak, a cry of desperate love for all that she ever knew herself to be, a cry for life. She woke to herself and realised the cry must have been purely internal.

She fell back asleep, but this time the phantasmagoria that had been haunting her for days had vanished. In their place came deep sleep and a dream of truth in which Satanaya found herself by the shore at Salacak, opposite the island with the Maiden's Tower. She was emerging dripping from the Bosphorus, being pulled to safety by a very old man who came to her walking upon the water. As she looked back at the island she thought, 'the snake bit me, but I didn't die.' She reached the beach, the sun was shining, the sea was calm, and a gentle breeze was blowing. She felt empty, purged, but cleaner than she had ever been. She looked at the old man, who smiled at her and said. 'You can return now. Yes, there is still work to be done. But first you must get back your strength.' And with that he turned and walked off up to a little mosque at the top the hill, a few hundred yards away, which he reached in two or three strides at most.

When she woke, the fever had broken. Her bedding and night gown were soaked through. Her body, though weakened, felt strangely light; it was comfortable and it was hers again. Through the window she saw dawn was breaking. The far shore of the Bosphorus was bathed in gold though the sun had not yet risen above the hills behind Beylerbeyi. No sounds came from the rest of the house. She stripped off her wet things, wrapped herself in a warm, dry blanket and went to the window. High in the heavens, lit by the unseen risen sun, flocked a great mass: circling in great spirals were thousands and thousands of wide-winged birds. It was the spring migration of storks. Having crossed from Africa by way of Palestine they were collecting over the Asian shore of the Bosphorus before flying north over the great Balkan mountain range which the Bulgarians call the 'Stara Planina', the Old Mountain, to their nesting grounds in Poland and beyond.

She remembered the storks she had seen circling above the Sea of Galilee, and thought of her putative husband, Timur and his lover Murat; and their desperate hidden love. Where were they now? Could they be in Constantinople? She thought of her mother and father back in Palestine, and felt a yearning for them and an impending sense of sadness for the little girl who had grown up and left home. Then she remembered the dream and reminded herself that like the circling storks, life was a series of migrations, of long journeys, before one could return home. For now she was alive, and happy to be so. She knew deep in her heart she was a warrior. There was lots of work to be done, but first she had to get back her strength.

Satanaya's return to life was greeted with joy by the household. Amina and Subhana worked hard to rehabilitate the Circassian lass, with meals of steamed chicken and vegetables, broths and 'yayla çorbası' – the Istanbul version of this soup, made with rice.

'You will stay in bed until we say you can get up,' was the daily chorus of these two guardian angels.

Thus Satanaya was under orders. She had shed a lot during her illness – to be sure, something of her old life had fallen away. But now, in spite of a queer light-headedness, she felt more than ever herself, clearer and more certain. She was happy just to lie there for as long as… well, as long as it takes to get completely bored. It was the third week of April before Amina allowed her to dress and come downstairs, and another week before it was deemed safe for her to venture into the outside world.

Daily life within the Beylerbeyi konak was in many ways similar to the Beyt, but with a fixed order to the day. Following a trip to Germany as a member of a fact-finding mission with a view to modernising the Sultan's army, the Colonel Efendi had instituted European timekeeping. He wished to establish a degree of uniformity in a land where the day was divided according to the times of sunrise and sunset, and the five times daily prayers of the faithful. His system only extended to the konak itself where a large hall clock fixed the meal times. Beyond the walls, time was anyone's guess, estimated by the height of the sun or the last call to prayer floating up from the mosque in Beylerbeyi village.

Lunch was at midday, after which everyone went off for a rest. Afternoon tea at 4 pm would be taken on the lawn if the weather was suitable; supper at 6.30. Evenings might be spent in conversation and card games, especially if there were house guests. There was a continual stream of female house guests as Amina had innumerable sisters and cousins. In addition there were regular formal receptions with government officials and visiting diplomats, as well as more informal parties beginning with cocktails on the terrace at 7 pm.

When Satanaya was fully recovered, what a world she began to discover. Amina had become so bored by the seemingly endless double confinement of winter and her pregnancy, that her only thought was to take off with her new companion in the konak's landau and go visiting. Each day saw the pair heading out to cousins and friends in the neighbourhood, bringing little neatly wrapped parcels of pastries from the kitchen.

And as Amina's condition progressed, and the days became hotter, they eschewed the bumpy roadways for the cool breezes of the Bosphorus. The boatman, the *kayıkcı*, would be summoned, and the ladies would descend with servants to the little inlet on the estate at the water's edge where a beautifully painted *kayık* would await them, a sleek open boat with a slender curving prow at both ends. A crew of brawny young shaven-headed oarsmen, in their regulation kit of baggy white trousers and open blouses displaying dark tanned chests, the *bekiars*, or bachelors, would row the party along the shore at a cracking pace, upstream to the Sweet Waters of Asia.

This grassy meadow bounded by two streams was a favourite picnic spot for parties of Turks and Europeans alike, who came by water, by *araba* or horseback to stroll in the fresh air of the countryside far from the crowded city. Upon colourful Anatolian carpets spread out on the grass they would wile away the afternoon, delighting in the fountain of Mihr-i-Şah, a square construction of delicately carved marble. Beneath its wide overhanging eaves holiday makers could take the 'sweet waters', while gazing upstream to the massive revetments of Rumeli and Anadolu Hisar.*

This was all in the days before the motor road was built, and the villages became linked in the urban sprawl that has become the mega-city of Istanbul. What Satanaya saw, as they glided serenely along were pretty waterside settlements of painted wooden houses, here and there a mosque, an Armenian or Greek church and a few coffee houses with fishermen sitting nearby mending nets. Between the villages along the shore stood elegant wooden villas – '*yalıs*' – set in sumptuous gardens housing the wealthy *beys* and *pashas* of Constantinople during the hot summers. Here Satanaya and Amina visited with their servants to enjoy conversation and refreshments in the cool shade of the mulberry trees and vine-covered pergolas; they would nibble savoury '*mezes*' and sip sherbets while watching the boats and ferries passing up and down stream.

As spring blossomed into early summer, the barrows of the fruit sellers in Çengelköy were piled high with purple mulberries which were sold in little punnets lined with mulberry leaves, and Satanaya and Amina would return home from their outings with fingertips stained, not with golden henna, as the Arab poets describe, but deep purple, and their guilty lips darker than was respectable. And as the bleeding branches of the Judas trees gave way to the pale blooms of almond and pomegranate, so too did the initial friendship of the two young ladies flourish and grow from convention to intimacy.

---

*   Two castles built by Sultan Mehmet II on opposite shores of the Bosphorus as part of the gradual encirclement of the Byzantine capital prior to its conquest by the Ottomans in 1453.

The outings were by tradition ladies-only affairs. But in the evening, especially once the warmer weather set in, the konak in Beylerbeyi became the backdrop for fascinating soirées, much more in line with what she had experienced in Lebanon, with male and female guests, mixing unselfconsciously in the modern European manner that the Colonel and his wife liked to promote. A string quartet would be hired to play in the garden. The French were keen to hear the more avant-garde works of their young Ravel, and if any Hungarians showed up, it might be Bartok. But Mozart was the Colonel's preference, and he generally had the last word.

These gatherings would often include foreign diplomats and their wives, when French would be spoken, and the tone would be earnest as the subject of the 'Young Turks' and the emerging constitutionalist state was discussed. But there also came visitors from Egypt, relations and friends from the Khedivate, many of whom decamped from the summer heat of Cairo to take up residence in their Bosphorus villas. Then the evenings were much more relaxed and the conversation was in Arabic.

And sometimes the Colonel's officer friends came over, when after a little initial polite conversation, the ladies would retire upstairs. Raki would flow and the men would sing the Türkü folk songs, like the stirring *türkü* of 'The Plevna March'*, recalling Osman Pasha and the heroes of the ill-fated siege; and Rembetiko songs popular in the cafes of Pera and Salonica – their favourite was the hauntingly beautiful 'My Nightingale in a Golden Cage'†.

These sessions went on late into the night. Wine and raki flowed, and if more *mezes* were required, Satanaya was invariably on hand. She developed a way of entering without disturbing the men at their conversation, so that they found her presence natural and she was able to linger. With the alcohol, inhibitions fell away, tongues loosened and opinions not aired publicly might be expressed freely among friends. Often an off-the-cuff remark from the Colonel, might entice an inexperienced diplomat to disclose more than he ought with regard to the intentions of his particular government. With the titbit of news in the bag, the Colonel would swiftly but subtly turn to another subject. By showing indifference he allayed any suspicions that he might also be fishing for information. It was a game they

---

* https://www.youtube.com/watch?v=EBQJvSGuEFc&t=70s

† https://youtu.be/pThuxkPZB8U

all played, guest and host alike, but the Colonel was the master; he would cast his fly long, wait patiently, and invariably land his fish.

Satanaya was a good listener and during these social evenings she learnt much about life in the capital: who were the main players in the political arena, their good points as well as their faults and foibles, and of the dark events that were brewing. It was knowledge that would stand her in good stead in the period of turbulent change that was to come. For the year 1911 heralded the onset of a series of wars which would embroil the Empire for more than a decade with barely a break. It began with the Italian invasion of the Ottoman province of Tripolitania – modern-day Libya – in September of that year. Later the Empire's borders would once again be reduced as a result of the machinations of certain Great Powers playing on the rising nationalist sentiments in the Balkan provinces. And all this was but a preamble to the greater conflicts which would ultimately see the Empire's disintegration in the global conflagration of a World War.

The Colonel Efendi, with his close court connections, was able to exercise a subtle influence in both the Palace and the Army during this period. He was known to be a modernist, in that he was not afraid to embrace the new, particularly when it came to things European, but politically he remained something of a celibate. Since Sultan Abdul Hamid II had been deposed, the Colonel, as an ADC to one of the old Generals, had been acting as a roving emissary between the influential families of the Ottoman elite and the new regime.

For Satanaya it was like watching a play unfold in which larger than life characters acted out an intriguing, but so far unfathomable plot. While for now she could only observe the drama from the periphery, something was telling her she needed to be at the heart of these events.

EIGHT

Sohbet, Sufism and Tariqat

Constantinople, 1911-1912

ND THEN THERE WERE evenings of '*sohbet*'. This was not the traditional *sohbet*, where close followers of a Sufi sect would gather in their '*tekke*' around a leader or a respected sheykh, for discourse and to put questions on matters spiritual or personal. While this aspect was not entirely absent, *sohbet* at the konak was more often in the nature of happy gatherings of folk simply for the pleasure of company and conversation.

Amina had close family links with a number of leading sheykhs of the Sufi *tariqas*, the mystical sects that were an integral part of the Ottoman culture and whose influence in affairs of state was significant. People from the humblest market porter to illustrious generals and viziers could be found with one *tariqa* or another. The Sultan himself, in his coronation ceremony, was traditionally girded with the sword of Osman, the founder of the dynasty, by the head of the Mevlevi Order of dervishes, a direct descendant of Jelaluddin Rumi. And it was not unheard of that a subordinate in the office of some high official, might be found in a gathering of the brethren for *zikr* or *sohbet* presiding as sheykh over his daytime boss.

Amina and her husband appeared to have no exclusive link to any particular band of dervishes. Their circle was wide and the *sohbet* was not of the common order. For a start, some of the '*efendis*' – as those elusive, not to say elevated, mystical personages were known – were of the '*melâmi*' way, i.e. the 'way of blame' – a kind of supra-*tarika*, but not a *tarika* in any formal sense with fixed rituals, initiations and membership etc., but each being responsible only to him or herself and to their maker.

Strange things could occur at these *sohbet*. It happened one evening that among the guests was a magician, a man said to be in league with a djinn. The magician could do tricks that did not depend on sleight of hand, for he was knowledgeable of the words and sounds that make things manifest, like the magicians of the Pharaoh who turned their rods into snakes before Moses. One time this fellow took a pack of cards and threw them up in the air. Each card landed on its edge atop one of the hanging crystals of the huge chandelier in the high hallway of the *selamlik*. The cards remained aloft in perfect balance until he clapped, when the pack returned obediently to his hand, correctly ordered in their suits. Another time he placed his evidently empty hands over those of a guest and lo! a dozen mint 500 *kuruş* gold coins, bearing the *tuğra*, the seal of Sultan Mehmet V, appeared out of thin air in the guest's hands. Long afterwards Satanaya heard that this magician had died by spontaneous self-combustion, while sitting in a cinema in Tunis. It was not a surprise because, as they said, 'he was one of those who went with djinn, whose element is fire', and those who live by fire die by fire.

* * *

It was a warm evening in May. The terrace was awash in lilac and blue beneath a cataract of wisteria blooms swaying in the light breeze. Satanaya and Amina Khanoum enjoying the sweet fragrance and the light glinting off the water through the trees. Satanaya was speaking of their mutual friend, Shireen, and this Konya lady's concern over the changes happening in the Empire.

'Well, yes, it is of concern,' said Amina, 'but tonight there will be *sohbet*, and then I will introduce you to someone who knows better than I these things...'

This 'someone' was one of those mysterious '*efendis*', a small, unassuming man, whom one might pass in the street without sparing a glance; a nobody, an unimportant person, which was how he liked to be seen, and how he would have described himself if asked. Yet, when Amina introduced him, Satanaya could not help notice the bright, penetrating eyes. He had a kind face, she thought – a face of humility perhaps, as if guarding some rare knowledge that she would like to know too, if only she could.

'*Salam aleykum.*' Satanaya gave the formal greeting of peace to the elderly bearded gentleman, in frock coat and fez sitting quietly in a corner by the window, his hands clasped over an ebony walking stick. She felt rather nervous before this man who could easily have been her grandfather.

'*Wa aleykum salam, wa rahmatullah wa barakatuhu.*' the man gave a traditional response, invoking the divine mercy and blessing. 'Come, *kızım*, sit down next to me, and tell me about yourself.' The Efendi smiled and patted the cushioned divan, putting Satanaya at her ease. 'I want to hear all about your adventures from the beginning.'

'Gosh. Well, I suppose it began in the convent, where I was a cook...' she said, embarking on her life story. Then realising that was not what the gentleman was asking, she hesitated, closing her eyes. A picture came into her mind of her first love, the young goatherd Yusuf, so many years before. She began again:

'It started with love. I suppose that's all there is to it really. And wanting to know who I am, what I am for. Here... My life... My journey that is. And wanting, longing to know love. I guess that's really how I came to be here now. I want to know love. It seems the only important thing to me, at times so beautiful and yet sometimes I feel as if I'm in the middle of a battlefield.'

Strangely she felt no inhibitions about opening her heart to this stranger. There was something about him that reminded her of Yeşil Efendi, the wild man of Anatolia whose severe kindnesses had so patiently unpicked her own selfish soul and opened up in her a heart she'd had no idea existed. But he was different too. This man was so gentle, though she didn't doubt his strength. He made her feel safe, as safe as a child upon her grandfather's knee.

'But you are so very brave. It must have been hard, all that travelling alone, as a woman. ' said the Efendi

'I got that from Lady Gülbahar,' she said. 'She taught me to think beyond my gender. I have always wanted the same things men have – this freedom, to choose, to go where I want. To do what I want. To love whom I want, and how I want. But society makes it so difficult.'

'Oh, we can't always have this kind of freedom.' said the old man. 'We men also have our constraints. But in matters of love, and knowledge, we are equal. In fact we are the same, in so far as we are nothing. Simply witnesses to events, passing time. But there can be a great freedom in being nothing, being a witness.'

'Yes, I can see that's true. From the inside, that is. But at the same time, I feel I must be doing something. And not just the usual. You know, not marriage, not the housekeeping, children…'

The Efendi smiled.

'Do you know what I do?' he asked Satanaya.

'I expect you have some important position in the government or something like that.'

'Well, I do work for the government in a way. But I'm certainly not important. I'm what might be called a 'technical expert'. But really, I just study the possibilities in things. I try to be witness to what is already present, waiting to be seen. Then I say what I see, if someone asks.'

'So, you're a scientist then? You deal with the realities of things, you try and distinguish between true and false. You experiment and make inferences from your observations.'

'Yes, I suppose you are right. Do you have any questions for a scientist?'

'Actually,' Satanaya hesitated again. She wasn't sure how to put her question. 'You know how the world seems to be changing so very fast these days. Not just outwardly, but the system itself, the ideology and the structure of how the world operates. This whole business of the Sultan ruling with absolute power as the Caliph, the "Representative of God on Earth". And now suddenly a revolution and we have a government of elected representatives, a constitutional democracy… well, how does that sit with what went before? I mean, if it was true in the past, the Caliph representing God, how is it not now? My friend Shireen in Konya was most upset. And she's someone who understands – or seems to – many of the inner mysteries of religion. And she follows a dervish path. Does all this no longer have a meaning?'

The Efendi sat with the question a while.

'Yes, and no.' he said. 'As with so many things when we discuss religion or philosophy, the truth is not so easily fixed in our relative language. Sometimes we say yes, and equally, sometimes we say no. It does depend on the point of view. If we paint a board white on one side, and black on the other, and then we look at it from one side, we say it is a white board. And another person looks from the opposite side and calls it black. Yet another looks from a point above and says, "maybe it's both." And yet another can't even see the board – so he says "what board?". And someone else who has heard all these persons' opinions, he gets confused and says "I don't know, maybe, maybe not." From where we stand among these contraries, each is correct from their own point of view. But at the same time, everyone doesn't have a vision that can encompass all the possibilities. So, it is possible to say, "this is true" as long as we allow for the opposite.'

'Yes, but how does this relate to the Caliphate, dispensing in the name of God – and now the will of the people enacted through the elected representatives? Whose will is the real will? Who is actually directing things? Who determines the relative truth?'

'My dear child,' said the Efendi, 'you are forgetting the basic premise, which I'm sure you learnt with Yeşil Efendi: that there is only one – one will, one being, one absolute wishing, willing to know and be known, showing itself to itself in every form, as in a mirror. Being relative in the relative, while remaining absolute in the absolute?

'Nothing comes out of nothing. Power, might, will, knowledge, voice and hearing – all these qualities exist as names which originate in this one source. And here, in this world, among the people, these qualities are received, as if into different cups. And some of these cups are small and some are large, and the larger the cup, the greater the dispensation of these qualities is possible. That is why some people are destined to have power over others. It's a matter of how much your cup can take. and the small cups submit to the large cups, and hand over their will, and their power and their voice to the big cups. But in fact, we are all actually drinking from the same cup. The one cup of the source of all things.'

With a jolt Satanaya remembered Yeşil Efendi's words, repeated ad infinitum: *How many beings are there in existence? One! Aside from which there is nothing else.*

The Efendi stood up.

'Come, let's go into the garden while there's still a little light. We can talk as we walk.'

Satanaya was still thinking of Yeşil Efendi. She took his arm and together they went out by the French doors and walked down towards the shore. It was warm in the konak and the cool air off the water refreshed them.

'So, your question – for a start, the idea behind the Caliphate – divine viceregency – didn't begin with Islam. Nor with Christianity for that matter. Nor with the Pharaohs of Egypt who were considered gods. We think that what we call Sufism or the tariqas – the mystical sects – originates with Islam. Not so. There have always been people for whom journeying between absolute and relative has been as natural as crossing the Bosphorus from Europe to Asia.'

The Efendi gestured down to where a ferry from Beşiktaş on the European shore was slowing before turning to berth at the Beylerbeyi landing stage. As it passed, a myriad of lights from the passenger lounge reflected and refracted in the churning water, cascading fiery sparks like shooting stars and roman candles.

'The scientists?' said Satanaya, using the words *'ilim adamı'* – man of knowledge.

'Or perhaps *'arif adamı'* – men of wisdom – would be more accurate. You see, there have always been people, men and women, whose vision went beyond the surface of things. And they have educated others in this science, what we call esoteric lore.'

They had reached the small beach where boatmen were sitting leaning against the boatshed smoking narghilehs, relaxing after a day at the oars of their *kayıks*. The sunset call to prayer began to sound from the minaret nearby. The boatmen got up and walked towards the village. Satanaya and the Efendi stood and listened in silence by the water's edge until the muezzin had finished his sweet song.

'You mean like the dervishes? The Mevlevis?' Satanaya picked up the thread again.

'Yes, and Qadiri, Rifa'i, Shadhili, and others, long before Islam. This inner wisdom comes in many other ways, like when Khidr appears to Moses.* There is a saying 'the one who knows his or her self will know the

___

* Quran 18:60-82

reality' – this thing called Sufism is only one name for a system of knowing according to reality. And this reality, this 'one being', this 'absolute that contains the relative', is in constant expression. It is unstoppable, evolving endlessly, arranging forms and meanings specifically relevant to the needs of each place where it appears: to each one of us, and in general to the demands of the era. We are not other than this 'one'. So, humanity's desire to know itself creates our future by demanding we outgrow our limits from one moment to the next. This is realising our potential.'

'And the *tarikas*? All these 'ways' to truth?' Satanaya persisted with her question.

'The quality of the great mystics' lives often inspired followers to come together to imitate and emulate. In time these groups became formalised in what were initially simple brotherhoods. Like the monkish orders of the Christians. What we call *tariq* or 'way', as in 'way of life', from which we get *tariqa*, that is, a religious sect or dervish order. They practised methods of meditation and invocation handed down from ancient sources – but ultimately from one single breath of wisdom – that intimate, return-to-hearth invitation, extended from this single origin directly into the hearts of these practitioners.

A ship's horn sounded in the darkness and a few moments later the ferry reappeared, moving away from the shore before heading up stream and turning into the current to cross again to Beşiktaş.

'And, as the spirit moved on, these *tarikas* developed and flourished. The simple virtues and subtle wisdoms of their originators were often obscured by convention and ritual. And though the jewels of wisdom remained, they became accessible only by the resolute, the independently-minded ones, the ones whose hearts had been purified, the true possessors of humility.'

'And how does this relate to the Caliph and religion?' said Satanaya.

'They represent outwardly what is the situation for every individual, where each person is a sovereign within their personal estate. Or not. If a person is subject to their states, then they do not fully serve their reality, but only their states. It is the same for the leaders in the world. They represent for their people, at least symbolically, the single, specific order of that world. Once there were prophet-kings who truly represented this order. Kings who were true servants, who served their people through serving the essential will.'

'And now? Where is this order? Who are the caliphs now?'

'Perhaps one should ask, where are they not?'

They had paused in the middle of the lawn on their way back up to the konak. The moon had risen, laying a path of golden steps upon the water, joining the near and the far shore. The Efendi's last words floated out like steps of light, and in Satanaya's mind, thoughts arose from the depths to join them, and an idea clarified.

'From what you say, then,' she ventured, 'each person, if he or she comes to know themselves – if they become, like you say, people of wisdom, people who can cross between the two sides of absolute and its relative, the ferry man between the one and the many, then surely each of us – in potential at least – is the representative, the caliph – of her own world. That makes us all responsible. No wonder the religious leaders are worried. It makes for a big change of mind-set.'

'Exactly,' said the Efendi, 'But who among us want this change. There is a lot of vested interest in things remaining just as they are. We don't like to give up what we are used to, for something that means we must take responsibility for ourselves. Then who could we blame but ourselves when things don't go the way we like?'

'It's no different from growing up, really.' said Satanaya

'True,' the Efendi said, 'but many will find it difficult, both in the mosques, and in the *tarikas*. Others are saying that these institutions have run their course, and a new way is necessary for the future – a way that is not fixed to specific religious beliefs or cultural ways but has universal application for humanity. It's inevitable, when you think about it, with the new education that is coming from Europe, in science and social philosophy, people's minds are broadening. Knowledge is being sought, both within and beyond religion. A lot changed with the printing press. Time was when a seeker would travel hundreds, even thousands of miles to sit at the feet of a particular Master, or someone who had a manuscript of the Master's book. Now one can go to the bookseller and just order a copy. That changes things a lot. People are finding out for themselves, thinking for themselves.'

'But these things can't be learnt from books, surely?'

'Certainly not, but neither can they be learnt from a master if the pupil has no aptitude. You know this of course – you're a cook. If the taste is there, if the desire is there, you don't need a recipe. But it may help to know what the ingredients are. Some of these books carry such words, and talk of such weighty matters with subtle explanations, but nothing can be gained if the students' minds are not open to read between the lines, and to dive to the kernel of the meanings within. Then – book or master – if the student's heart is established in taste, will it matter? These books, however, have a spirit. And need to be treated as one would a master, with cleanliness, respect and humility.'

Satanaya was reminded of her first taste of bouillabaisse at the Anonymous Fish Restaurant by the harbour in Beirut. And she remembered the words from Takla's Cookbook: *The dish itself will teach the cook, for no other reason than its own love to be known, tasted and consumed.*

'Then, it's about having the aptitude, the predisposition – the desire to know?'

They reached the terrace of the konak and sat down beneath the amethyst arch of shedding wisteria.

'Yes.' said the Efendi. 'And what has changed now is humanity's disposition, the capacity to receive these inner meanings and tastes; the availability of books are a reflection of this, proof if you will, that this aptitude has widened, evolved. Many people are no longer willing to accept blindly the words of the preachers in the pulpits. Why, there are people – intelligent people mind you, not necessarily religious, but people of real weight, men and women who are not controlled by their states – they are saying that religion in its present form is like a dead tree. It is still standing but the life has gone. Yet its seeds, its realities, have been spread everywhere, in the hearts of people not yet born, seeds which one day will flower in real universal understanding. But in the meantime the old tree still stands, and people imagine it is still living. Perhaps one day someone will come and push it and it will crumble to dust, or maybe they'll shore up the trunk with stones and put supports under its branches, so the form will still stand. There will be much pain because of the attachment to the form, rather than stepping into the unknown. If only we could, then it would be easy.'

'And in the meantime?' Satanaya's half-formed question hung in the air.

The Efendi fell silent a while, and looked down at his hands, turning them over upon the dark wood of his walking stick.

'Outwardly we may witness the negative effects of an inability to accept the changes. They will manifest in violence and war and an unwillingness to admit that here we make mistakes. It will show as a denial of the essential good, of the intended happiness of humanity and all creation. There will be war in the soul of Man, a war which may show itself here on the outside. But it won't last forever'

'But how? How will it end?' said Satanaya.

'Love. And knowledge of course. Recognising the origin and the object of love. Just as you said earlier. We must really want it, and to want, we must know love, and that is something I think you do know a little about, Satanaya.' The old man's eyes twinkled.

'But surely these *tarikas,* these orders, have been a good thing?'

'Of course. The essential dispensations of light which descend upon this world originate in a clean place – '*tayyib*', you know this word, the original purity, like the sweet smells of paradise, the pure breath of the spirit – it arrives in waves from the ocean of existence, and when a wave is spent, a new wave arises. In the meantime, the sea withdraws. This hiatus appears chaotic, empty perhaps, as this shore of time prepares to receive the new wave that is coming. The old ideas will not save one from the flood, only spirit takes one forward, whether in life or in death.

'You remember Noah, how he built the ark to carry his family and the pairs of animals, so that when the flood came, there would be a resource for the world to begin again, to continue. Perhaps there was also a spiritual resource that needed to be preserved, the covenant that Noah carried in his heart, that knowledge of union, the absolute unity of existence, of essence and its relative form, the real ark of salvation in the flood of time.'

'But what can I do?' Satanaya looked pleadingly at the old Efendi.

'You can do anything you want.' He gave her a slightly teasing smile. 'You don't want me to tell you what to do, do you? What do *you* want to do?'

'To be honest, I really don't know.'

'Look, my dear girl.' Again he called her '*kızım*', as if addressing a child or a daughter, as was fitting for an elderly gentleman to a young lady. 'Perhaps you know the Arabic word '*muktedir*' – "the one who has the power to do whatever it wants"? It is the name of the eternal choosing, the name by which we are able to move at all, permitting and enabling all the choices we make. But of course, here we must be careful, we need to ally our choices and actions with guidance and wisdom; to know what is appropriate, the right measure. That is wisdom. Again it depends on knowledge – science – the intellectual faculties, both of the mind and of the heart – reason and intuition. And if these appear to conflict – well, then intuition is the way forward. Reason will soon catch up. You might say, "reasoned intuition" is the way to go.'

'And where is this guide?' asked Satanaya.

'The guide for you is in everything – which is where your wisdom-intuition comes in. You look, you listen and in everything you will learn.'

Again she was drawn back to Meram, to the couplet she had read in the tomb of Rumi's cook, Shams Ateshbaz Wali:

'Whoever attains the true state of meditation
That person is educated by everything'

From out of the darkness came the sound of a nightingale, trilling and whistling, piping and warbling, its vibrant notes descending from the woods behind the konak. Satanaya found it beautiful beyond words, full of mystery yet as comforting to her heart as a well-loved melody.

As the Efendi rose to leave, Satanaya took his hand and bowing, attempted to kiss it, saying 'Thank you Efendi.' The Efendi responded pulling her hand to his own lips saying, 'But no, it is I who must thank *you*, kızım.' And Satanaya again said 'Thank you,' and there they stood for a brief moment each pulling the other's hand in a tender tug-of-war of mutual deference, until they both burst out laughing.

Then, his old coat swirling around him disturbing the fallen blossoms on the terrace, he disappeared within the konak. Satanaya was left wondering, 'Is that what is meant by a wind of change?'

NINE

Birth

Beylerbeyi, Constantinople, Summer 1911

PRING WARMED into early summer. Satanaya began each day looking after little Ahmed, or lending a hand in the kitchen. Once the weather settled she would take coffee with Amina Khanoum in the shade of the terrace. They talked and wrote letters; if they weren't visiting, Amina had the green baize games table brought down from the *haremlik* and they played cards beneath the shady canopy of a big ash tree. Satanaya watched a pair of great tits bring food to their chicks in a nest built under the eaves, in the angle where the *cumba* extended from the building. The little birds chattered and chuddered whenever crows came around, as they regularly did. And when the chicks had flown, starlings took over the nest, enlarged the apartment, and by early June they too had hatched a noisy brood.

The fruit seasons advanced in waves, falling over each other as each crop surged to ripeness. Black mulberries which had filled the market stalls from late April to late May gave way as cherries flowed down from the hills of the Black Sea, dark red or pink-yellow, growing in size and sweetness until they were superseded by peaches; the delicate white peaches of Thrace, and then the huge peaches of Bursa, gold and violet-red as bruises, firm fleshed and yielding to the tongue, their musk-scented juice expressed in torrents, overflowing mouths.

The Judas flowers had dropped in the heat, their negligent boughs now clothed in heart-shaped leaves. Jasmine arrived one morning, its perfume sudden and unexpected as first-sight love, confusing all the senses. It came out of hiding from one corner of the konak, while its honeysuckle suitor appeared from the opposite side, tangled in the small red blossoms of a climbing rose. Each wafted scent a lover's sigh and the terrace their trysting place.

The first melons appeared in late May. But Amina said they would not purchase until later in the season when the golden *kavun* from far off Çumra, a village near Konya, reputed to grow the finest melons in Turkey, would be at their peak of sweetness. Watermelons from the market gardens of the Meander Valley were brought up by steamer from Smyrna, and kept cool in the ice house dug deep up in the hillside.

* * *

The baby, a boy, arrived on a Monday in the middle of the month. Amina had dreamed his name in lights strung between the minarets of the Mosque of Süleyman the Magnificent. They named him Mohammed Ali, which pleased everyone, remembering as it did the dynasty's founder, Mohammed Ali Pasha*, as well as satisfying the religious sensibilities of the family. A number of Amina's cousins had moved into the konak for her final period of confinement, and Satanaya was happy to retreat to the busy kitchen which was now expected to turn out every kind of sweet and savoury delicacy by day and night.

---

* Mohammed Ali Pasha, an Ottoman commander who declared himself Governor of Egypt and eventually became Khedive (Viceroy). He ruled Egypt and Sudan from 1805 until his death in 1849 at the age of 80.

When the accouchement began, they called the midwife. Beulah was an old Jewish lady who had come to Constantinople as part of the gradual migration of Egyptian nobility following the deposing of Khedive Ismail in 1879.* She brought with her the venerable and sturdy walnut birthing chair that for decades had done royal hard labour supporting the safe arrival of many a child destined to take the Khedival throne, or to be a princess, or at the very least a senior ambassador, governor or military figure in the dynasty of Mohammed Ali Pasha.

The hours and days consequent to birth are a very precious time in which the soul of the newborn hovers upon an isthmus, between its origin within the ocean of absolute existence and the exterior world of form upon whose shore it has recently emerged.

The baby Mohammed Ali lay there in all his helplessness. And yet, in that state of absolute receptivity, arms, legs, eyes and mouth alert to the stimuli of his new environment, there was also a transmitting. This emanation was so strong that all who beheld the little baby in his impotence were themselves disarmed by the evident closeness of this creature's being to his origin, their hearts flooded by the pure outpouring of love and compassion in this little human place, springing directly from the source.

And in that movement of compassion in the child, came an ability, provoking a necessity, for all those who beheld him, to respond: to help, to care, to keep from harm, to nourish, to guide and to educate, to become themselves gods in reflection by enacting, enlivening and bringing to maturity and elevation in knowledge and in life this new emergence of the real, this most excellent manifestation of God, as child.

The only imperfection, if such a thing can be mentioned in the blessed occasion of birth, comes not from its origin in the Divine purity, but from our own inability to receive this gift; and from the place of decay we call our world, the world as we have made it.

---

* Khedive Ismail (ruled 1867-1879) initiated grand schemes to modernise Egypt, but when post-Civil War America's cotton industry revived and the price of cotton fell, the country was plunged into debt. In order to maintain the security of the Suez Canal, the Khedive, who had by then sold his shares in the canal company to the British Prime Minister Disraeli, was removed in favour of his son, Tewfik Pasha, and British and French financial and political control became established. Gradually under the British Consul, General Evelyn Baring ('over-Baring' as he became known) Egypt effectively became a part of the British Empire.

Satanaya felt all this and more when she came to visit. It was there in his eyes. She looked and something was looking back. Not a little thing, not a helpless little creature, but something vast. So vast. She looked into his eyes, and remembered the story of the Prophet Mohammed who wanted to look into Ayşe's eyes, 'to look into the eyes that looked into the eyes of Uways al-Qarani'*. Satanaya looked, and for a moment she vanished from herself into the baby's vision. But it was untenable. Sheer beauty leaves no handrails to hold or footprints to follow. She hovered an instant: captured, falling, and caught in the hint of a smile that passed over the tiny lips of the infant. The eyes were steadfast.

She smiled in response to this gaze coming unveiled from the origin, and wondered, 'Where has this being come from? What is it seeing?' As Satanaya leant over the cradle she also noticed the fragrant clean smell of the baby, a scent like a loving embrace, the milk of paradise, and remembered a moment in Meram, and Yeşil Efendi reading Ibn 'Arabi's words on the essential goodness of things, *'They emerge from the origin by original cleanliness and beauty and subtlety...'*

'They all enter life like that' said Beulah, observing from her seat in the corner as Satanaya looked up from kissing the baby, swaddled in his ornate gilt rocking cradle. 'But then for most, in time, the veils begin to fall. They become distracted by this world and they forget completely where they came from. But this little one – for him the veils will be thin. If he's looked after, and educated properly, he won't stray far from his source.'

'How can you tell?' said Satanaya.

'Look at the joy, it's so strong in him. It will keep him afloat. And look how well he took to the breast. He has a great thirst for life.'

It was true. Poor Amina had been complaining of soreness, and so Beulah had steeped fresh basil leaves in warm olive oil, which she rubbed on the mother's nipples after feeding, along with warm water and compresses before and after.

Following the birth various customs were observed. The sex of the child was proudly announced, the Colonel Efendi dispensed gifts to the staff and alms were distributed to the poor of the neighbourhood. Beulah cut the umbilical chord. Amina had a premonition that her child's destiny

---

* Uways al-Qarani, a Yemeni camel herder, an ascetic and saint who lived at the time of Mohammed, though they never met.

lay far from the shores of this land, so, according to the well-known tradition the cord had to be cast into water. In this case it went straight into the
Bosporus. The placenta, considered part of the child, its 'friend', had to be
disposed of with care and respect. It was wrapped in a piece of new cloth
and buried in a special place in the garden.

Beulah washed the baby and dusted him in salt, rubbing a tiny dab of
honey on his cheeks to ensure sweet character and good taste throughout
his life. The child was then swaddled and handed to the Colonel while
mother was washed, given fresh clothes and brought into a specially prepared bedroom, where little Mehmet (as Turks call Mohammed) was
returned to her. A small blue bead, the 'mavi boncuk' was sewn into the
swaddling, as a protection against the 'evil eye', and a Koran placed nearby.
Mother and child were closeted together, closely but quietly attended by
the midwife and a few intimate female friends, to help and encourage her
in her new state. The Colonel Efendi visited again on the third day and
after saying various prayers in Arabic, he pronounced the baby's name
three times into his ear. On the sixth day, all being well with mother and
child, a modest celebration took place.

Having survived the hazardous period of forty days after the birth,
known as loğusa, the period of puerperium when the woman's body
returns to its pre-pregnancy state, when quiet and little activity is recommended, the kırk hamamı, the Forty Day Bath, was held. A proper
celebration now, with friends, neighbours and relations, and serenaded by
a band of Roma musicians, Satanaya accompanied Amina Khanoum and
little Mohammed Ali, Subhana and Ahmed in the open landau as they
made their way ceremonially to the hamam. In the warm, womb-like environment of the Turkish bath, mother and baby were meticulously steamed,
cleaned, and all the guests fed throughout the day with endless plates of
sweets and savouries; litres of ayran were drunk out of brass beakers, songs
were sung, extravagant compliments paid, and hints and promises were
made of future brides.

After the celebrations, life returned to normal in the konak.

TEN

Latin Machinations

Beylerbeyi, Constantinople, summer 1911

T WAS A HOT EVENING later in the summer. Colonel Efendi was pacing up and down in the *selamlik*, smoking furiously and staring up at the wooden ceiling from time to time, as if some relief from his frustration might be found in the geometric patterns of the painted boards.

'We saw it coming, of course, but how could we avoid it? We tried to persuade the Italians to accept an arrangement like we have in Egypt – British management, Ottoman ownership – but they seem to want a fight.'

Colonel Efendi was referring to the Italian invasion of the Ottoman North African provinces of Cyrenaica and Tripolitania – that is, Libya. Satanaya and Amina sat in silence, the child feeding noisily at his mother's breast. The Colonel was speaking to no one in particular. He was letting off steam after a frantic and apparently fruitless few days of preventative diplomacy traipsing back and forth between the War Office, the Palace and various European legations, while at the same time being lobbied by government members in the Committee.

'The Palace feels something must be done to assert the Caliphate, otherwise it will look impotent. But even General Şevket Paşa believes the place is indefensible, and he should know.'

The venerable warhorse Mahmud Şevket Paşa had retired from the army but remained as Minister of War. The Palace's concerns were real. The Sultan of Turkey had a spiritual remit that extended far beyond his earthly realms, for as Caliph, he represented God Almighty to the many millions of Muslims outwith the Empire's borders, in particular the Faithful in the Indian subcontinent.

'This invasion is completely illegal on the part of the Italians of course. But Izzet Paşa* says we are equally to blame for letting the country get into such a parlous state that we can't even protect the lands we purport to govern; and I'm afraid I must agree.'

The Colonel paused in his soliloquy when Subhana entered the *harem-lik* to take the baby away for the night. He suddenly became aware of his son.

'But how is my little fellow?' he cooed, leaning down over his wife and picking up the child, holding him before him. 'My, he's growing. Is he feeding well, then?'

'More than well.' said Amina, 'He loves his milk, and at the rate he drinks, I'll soon be dry and we'll have to employ a wet nurse to top him up.'

Subhana took the baby and left the room. The Colonel resumed his peripatetic oration:

'Even if we had our troops in Africa, what use would they be against the guns of the Italian ships. We've heard that the Committee are independently raising a secret force of Turkish officers to rally the local tribes. Apparently Major Enver is at this moment hot-footing it from his post in Berlin. He's organising a group to enter Tripoli undercover through Egypt. Of course, officially we have had to wash our hands of these kind of adventurers. But what an opportunist he is! Ever since he caught the eye of little

---

* Marshall Ahmet Izzet Paşa, Chief of the Ottoman General Staff 1908-1911

Princess Najiye and they became engaged, he's started behaving like some kind of Mahdi*. No wonder they're calling him 'little Napoleon'. I wouldn't be surprised if he uses his connection as *damad*, as a future son-in-law of the Sultan, to authorise a *jihad* among the tribes.'

'But he is terribly good looking, don't you think?' remarked Amina.

This comment puzzled the Colonel and brought to a stop his interminable pacing. He looked at his wife and frowned. She smiled back at him.

'Only teasing, my darling. They say he now waxes his moustache so it stands up just like little Willy Kaiser's, so that counts him out as far as I'm concerned. But what about your Captain Mustafa? The one who so impressed you on your trip to France?† I remember you saying he had all the older staff officers frantic because he had such a good grasp of strategy. And that he was able to criticise– correctly you said – some of the manoeuvres. I wonder what's he up to now?…'

'And I remember also how taken you were by that Frenchman, Monsieur Bleriot and his aeroplane. You were convinced his machines would revolutionise military tactics. You couldn't stop talking about it. And then you invited him to Constantinople to demonstrate his 'plane and when he got here he crashed it into a house.'

The Colonel laughed. 'Yes, and we spent weeks visiting him in hospital while the poor fellow recovered. But still, I believe those flying machines are going to bring changes, just as the motor car has.'

Something stirred in Satanaya throughout this exchange. She put down her needlework.

'And this Captain Mustafa…?' she enquired.

'Oh yes, Captain Mustafa - or I should say Major – he's only an adjutant-major now, but I see that fellow rising. I have no doubt about him. He has all the good qualities of Enver, but without the egotism. He appears to have Turkey at heart rather than personal ambition. Something of a political rebel, and really a wild card in the Young Turk pack. He and Enver… well, let's just say theirs is not a comfortable relationship.'

---

*   Mahdi: the rightly guided one, who will come to cleanse the Muslim religion, and who will join with Jesus to destroy the anti-christ at the end of days. Historically, there have been half a dozen claimants to date.

†   Multilateral military exercises held in Picardy in 1910, which had been attended by military attachés and observers from most of the Great Powers of Europe including Turkey.

* * *

Even as Colonel Efendi held forth in the cosy living room of his Bosphorus mansion, former Captain, now Adjutant-Major Mustafa was somewhere between Constantinople and Cairo, travelling incognito to Libya.

After a number of mishaps during which he had survived being shot at by a wandering desert warrior, and subsequently succoured by an Egyptian border guard who was sympathetic to the Ottoman cause, Mustafa crossed into Libya, finally meeting up with Ottoman forces in December 1911. He received his promotion to full Major in late November and was given command of forces outside the port of Derne in Cyrenaica in Western Libya. Enver, however, had beaten Mustafa to the beachhead, and as senior officer was in overall command.

What followed was ultimately a disastrous campaign for the Ottomans. Lieutenant-Colonel Enver Bey had taken upon himself the mantle of a kind of crusading hero to the tribespeople. They gathered around the banner of his *jihad* and selflessly entered the fray under the Turkish commanders. Enver had also enlisted the support and backing of the Grand Senussi, a respected Sufi mystic and tribal leader who was the *de facto* ruler in Cyrenaica.

While the Italians controlled the narrow strip of coastal settlements, the desert tribes under Turkish commanders were able to prevent further incursion into the vast hinterland. But it was always going to be an unequal fight. It needed much more than religiously-inspired tribesmen and a charismatic leader to dislodge the modern well-armed forces of the Italians, equipped now with their Bleriot monoplanes.* Still, Enver pushed on month after month in the misguided belief that in the end they would be victorious. But to little effect. The outcome could at best be considered a stalemate; in fact it was a disastrous waste of lives. All the while Enver was sending positive reports to Constantinople of their 'progress in the field'.

The Italian forces remained in occupation of the coastal towns and cities throughout most of 1912. In order to put pressure on the Ottoman government, they began a series of naval raids in the eastern Mediterranean, bombing Beirut and the forts at the Dardanelles, as well as occupying

---

*   On October 22/23 1911, Captain Carlo Piazza of the Italian Royal Army Air Services conducted the first aerial reconnaissance flight between Tripoli & Aziza during the Italo-Turkish War.

Rhodes and some of the Dodecanese islands. It was only when things began to stir in the Balkan states, with Greece, Montenegro, Bulgaria and Serbia putting on an uncharacteristic united front against the Ottomans, that the Italian threat became too serious to ignore. Then Turks and Italians sat down together in the town of Ouchy in Switzerland, and Italy formally annexed the whole of Libya. Major Mustafa and his fellow officers accepted the inevitable and made their way back to Constantinople.

Lieutenant-Colonel Enver, the golden boy of the Young Turk Revolution, standard bearer of the Libyan *jihad* and soon to be *Damad* Enver Paşa, son-in-law of the Sultan, Shadow of God on Earth, at first refused to leave Africa. He was ready to set up an alternative government in the Saharan sands with himself as leader. But as the Balkan situation worsened, he saw that better opportunities for the advancement of his Napoleonic ambitions lay closer to home, and off he went, simply abandoning his loyal tribal fighters to their own devices. Any begrudging illusions that Major Mustafa might have entertained in the past about his fellow officer's long term credibility were irrevocably broken.

ELEVEN

Trouble in the Balkans

Constantinople, October 1912.

VENTS MOMENTOUS within the immediate context of their time often become submerged beneath the wider inundations of history, in consequence of which these initial floods are subsequently viewed as mere surge of tides in distant backwaters. Such were the wars in the Balkans when measured against the greater conflict that followed. Yet, for the millions of Turks, Greeks, Albanians, Macedonians, Serbs, Montenegrins, Bulgarians, Roma and Nomad herders who inhabited Rumelia, (as the Ottomans styled their European lands west from the Bosphorus, all the way to the Adriatic Sea, and that once stretched north to Budapest and twice, briefly, to the walls of Vienna) the consequences of the First and Second Balkan Wars, in terms of death, massacre, starvation and the wholesale upheaval of these communities was at least as tragic and long lasting in effect as the so-called 'Great War' in western Europe.

And yet it is the question of the Middle East that remains: the cause and continued effects of the collapse of the Ottoman Empire, and the end of the Islamic Caliphate, the removal of which heralded a new order in the world, an order which emerges in spasms like some beautiful child struggling for breath in intensive care while the physicians argue over symptoms, diagnoses and cures, and within which blind witnessing we slouch towards this ever-shifting mirage of Bethlehem.

There had been rumblings among the Albanians on the western edge of the Empire ever since the 1878 Treaty of Berlin, which had allocated much of the area they occupied to their Balkan neighbours. Now, with Serbia, Montenegro and Romania emerging as independent nations and Bulgaria and Macedonia gaining increasing autonomy within the Ottoman Empire, the Albanians feared that their lands would be absorbed and their Muslim identity, disappear completely. An insurgency throughout the summer of 1912 culminated in Albanian revolutionaries capturing Skopje in Macedonia. This in turn brought the Ottoman government to the negotiating table, and by September agreements were being drawn up which would establish Albanian autonomy in four regions where there were ethnic Albanian majorities.

However, Serbia, Montenegro, Greece and Bulgaria had a more pressing and altogether different agenda.

* * *

Satanaya was now experiencing for herself that which had precipitated her own family's exodus from the Caucasus more than thirty years earlier. The harsh and indiscriminate effect of the war was brought home to her with the sudden appearance on the streets of Constantinople of an increasing number of destitute families arriving daily from the west. Ramshackle carts piled with meagre possessions, upon which children and chickens were tethered, pulled by skinny ladies with dirty faces and unkempt hair clad in unwashed rags of clothes. Lean-to's and tents sprang up on unoccupied ground around the old Byzantine walls of the city, and on the edges of the Bosphorus villages. The refugees didn't linger long as the authorities were constantly moving them on, into the hinterland of Anatolia where poor land was being allocated to them. Scattered upon the roads and fields around the city lay the starved and abandoned the corpses of those destitute ones, too worn out to continue.

＊ ＊ ＊

In Beylerbeyi Amina Khanoum looked over the dinner table and carefully inspected each place setting. It was her birthday and Satanaya had helped the cooks prepare a special celebratory dinner for two. But where was the Colonel Efendi? He had not returned, as promised, on the early evening ferry. The trouble with having a husband in the administration, was that every evening was unpredictable. Months would go by with him arriving home at lunchtime, spending the remainder of the day fussing about in the garden, and later enjoying supper on the terrace, relaxed and happy. But this past year had seen a complete upheaval of his routine. First the Italians, then the Albanians, and just as things appeared to be settling down – Amina Khanoum tried to remember what her husband had said a few days earlier – something about a message from the German ambassador relating to unusual troop movements on their Balkan borders. Since then he had arrived home later and later. Tonight he had promised to be home early.

Amina left the table, informing the kitchen that things might have to be postponed. She went upstairs and ate a light supper with Satanaya.

'This is the lot of a wife in the administration. No matter that I'm a princess, State comes first, always.' Amina wasn't so much unhappy – she couldn't blame her dear Colonel, it was just how it was – as frustrated by not knowing the cause of the delay.

'Doesn't it bother you?' asked Satanaya, whose life had rarely been ruled by such outwardly imposed sanctions.

'Personally, no. But I do feel a little sad after all the efforts of the kitchen…' she sighed. 'it could have been such a lovely evening.'

'Well, at least the food won't be wasted. Pheasant eats as well cold as hot. And I'm sure when he does come, he'll enjoy it with some champagne.'

'Champagne! That's just what we need. Come on Satanaya, let's celebrate a little together, while there's still light, and the roses are so sweet on the terrace.'

Two hours later the bottle of 1893 vintage Louis Roederer 'Cuvee de Prestige', floated empty in the silver ice bucket. Satanaya and Amina themselves were floating in the sea of stars that glowed in the night sky above when the sound of boots on the path announced the return of a very haggard Colonel Efendi.

He pulled up a chair, flopped down unceremoniously between the two ladies and waved a hand at the bottle while simultaneously giving a nod to the attendant butler who had followed him in. The butler returned minutes later with a fresh bottle, already chilled, and was about to open it when the Colonel stood up and grabbed it from him.

'In times of war...' he began, and stepping inside the konak he reappeared brandishing a sabre. With a deft swipe he decapitated the noble flask and poured its frothing contents into a glass, raised it up to the dark sky and pronounced his toast:

'For God and the Sultan, may we be given victory.'

He drained the glass and sat down. Turning to his wife, he said, 'I apologise for bringing such bad tidings but it was hell in the War Office today. The Montenegrins declared war on Turkey, and the Bulgarians have mobilised their armies – they're probably crossing the border into Thrace at this very moment. The Greeks are moving north into Thessaly and Epirus. Heaven knows what the Serbians are doing, but their armies are mobilised too. They want to squeeze us out of the Balkans.'

He paused, filling and draining his glass once more before continuing.

'I have to report to my regiment tomorrow. After that, who knows when I'll be back. I'll probably have to rig up a cot in the War Office, but at least I shan't be out of the city for now.'

The two ladies sat in stunned silence. Then Amina Khanoum rose and stood behind her husband,

'You know, darling, I am with you, wherever your duty calls. Satanaya and I have already eaten, so why don't you have some cold pheasant and forget about all this until tomorrow.'

And in an uncharacteristically intimate display of affection, she wrapped her arms around his neck and kissed his cheek, over and over, while tears poured from her own eyes.

* * *

Shortly after the Montenegrin declaration, two other partners in the Balkan League, Serbia and Bulgaria, sent in their demand for ethnic autonomy in the Empire. This ultimatum was considered an unacceptable threat to Turkish sovereignty and on 17th October the Ottoman Empire declared war. Subsequently full scale hostilities broke out on all fronts of Ottoman Balkan lands.

A week later, Colonel Efendi returned briefly to Beylerbeyi.

'The Greeks are continuing their offensive and the Bulgarians are pouring down from the north. It looks like they intend to invest Salonica. I have orders to escort two of the princes to bring old Abdul Hamid back from exile by ship. If the Sultan were to fall into enemy hands, it would be unforgivable.'

'But Salonica, that's impossible!' cried Amina Khanoum. The Colonel's favourite aunt had married into a Salonica family, and they still had relatives in the city. 'Is there anything you can do?'

'They are already here, or on their way. Let's pray they are safe.'

* * *

That evening the armed steam yacht *Lorelei* of the Imperial German Navy sailed from its permanent berth north of the city, off the village of Tarabya. The vessel served as '*stationnaire*' or 'guard ship', a concession only Germany had been granted, in order to protect the country's interests in the region. Mostly *Lorelei* was used as the Ambassador's private yacht or for official jollies into the Black Sea or Aegean. It had hosted Kaiser Wilhelm II during his 1898 visit to Constantinople, conveying him to Palestine. Its mission to collect ex-Sultan Abdul Hamid II from Salonica, where he lived under house arrest in the villa of the prominent Jewish merchant family Allatini, was considered a necessarily acceptable breach of Germany's neutrality in the ongoing conflict.

* * *

The Colonel Efendi, who had grown up in the shadow of this old man, was shocked to see how his former lord had shrunk even more since his departure from the capital less than four years earlier.

Abdul Hamid had been informed of his imminent change of residence and was having none of it. Even the sight of the two princes, each the husband of one of his daughters, filled him with suspicion.

'You know well what they will do to me when they get me back in their hands.' he said. He looked down at the fine Ushak carpet upon which his slippered feet rested and exhaled slowly. In that moment it seemed he sank his whole being into the repeating blue star pattern of the rich pile, as if some kind of internal drowning might save him from facing the inevitable. Then he clutched an embroidered cushion to his chest and looking up into the eyes of the escort, made as if to pull the fabric apart. His next words came as an almost inaudible hiss: 'Like this, *they* will tear me to pieces.'

The princes were in a quandary. 'But the Greeks will be here in a matter of days, and the Bulgarians are also close. We can't leave you here.'

'And the others? What about all my people? Are you going to leave my people to the Greeks and the Bulgarians? That is what *they* want.' A ghost of a younger sultan with an empire at his feet seemed to enter for a moment, a shade quickly carried off by the breeze across the bay.

Their assurances carried no weight as far as the old man was concerned, and no amount of pleading would persuade him to leave. The escort party were obliged to beat a temporary retreat.

Kapitan Joachim von Arnim paced the teak boards of the wardroom aboard *Lorelei* as he pondered the report that Colonel Efendi conveyed from the princes. He fixed his eyes on the Colonel as he might his own First Mate.

'So what do you suggest?'

'His Majesty... his ex-Majesty that is, has always held your country in highest esteem. Perhaps if you wore your dress uniform it might appeal to his sense of pomp and pride?'

'Mmm. Why not. It's worth a try. And what about a band?'

'I think a band might just be gilding the lily, don't you? Besides, it would draw too much attention, and we haven't much time.'

'You're right. And if that doesn't work, then it will have to be a forced evacuation under cover of darkness. Perhaps a few random gunshots could be arranged near the mansion, a simulated attack to rattle the old fellow into leaving. I understand our orders are we must embark tonight.'

'Quite so.' replied the Colonel.

In the event, when the returning shore party appeared before the ex-Sultan, the German naval officers arrayed in crisp white Number Ones with all the gold braid, medals and sashes that Kapitan von Arnim and his officers could muster flashing in the sharp autumn light, dress swords and scabbards jangling from their hips, something of the Abdul Hamid of old stirred the little man from his gloom. He slowly rose to his feet and with a smile of resignation addressed the German captain and his entourage:

'The loyalty and companionship of our dear friend Kaiser Wilhelm is not forgotten. Today this gives us such confidence that under your protection this poor servant of Allah willingly submits to your command wherever it shall lead us.'

Discreet glances of relief passed between the Colonel and the Captain. The ex-sultan, his two young sons-in-law, his two wives and their ten ladies-in-waiting were accompanied to the German vessel and embarked without further delay.

The voyage home was uneventful, save that even as the ship passed out of the bay and into the Gulf of Thermaikos, sporadic rifle fire was heard coming from the outskirts of the town, and the distant boom of cannon echoed from the west. Salonica surrendered to the Greeks on 9th November.

TWELVE

Coup d'État

Constantinople, 1913

WENTY MILES WEST of Constantinople, the hills edging the Çatalca plateau look down upon a fertile plain of small holdings bordered with hedges, ditches and areas of rough scrub and marshland. The Black Sea is visible to the north, and to the south, the Sea of Marmara. In springtime, through the early morning mists, ghostly sentinels of roosting storks emerge shrouded in black and white upon the tops of pines. It is the migration. By day they peck for frogs and worms in the green pastures, while buzzards and eagles, also heading north, perch nearby, harassed by hooded crows and jackdaws. Small birds – wagtails and finches – fuss about among the grazing stock, while swallows soar and dive over flooded fields, snatching insects on the wing. Godwits and avocets pace the edges of small lakes, while shel-

77

duck and teal take off and land, disturbing the resident coots and grebes. In autumn the migrants return in even greater numbers. Storks and eagles, having passed en masse over the high peaks of Bulgaria's Stara Planina, and eager to escape the coming snows to winter in Africa, head on east to rendezvous upon the great thermals rising above the Bosphorus.

The Bulgarians who advanced that autumn upon the Çatalca Lines, the series of forts which stretched from Kıyıköy on the Black Sea to Tekirdağ* on the Marmara Sea were no mere passerines. They had it in mind to reach the Straits at Europe's edge and remain there. It was only eight days since the fall of Salonica; they had Edirne under siege, and now the Great City of Constantinople seemed to be within their grasp. But below the hills of Çatalca they came to a halt. The two armies faced each other, a third of a million men and nearly eight hundred cannon. The Bulgarians had a slight numerical superiority but the Turkish positions commanded the heights and with their troops well dug in the defenders clearly had the advantage. Nevertheless the Bulgarians pressed their attack relentlessly for two weeks.

But those greater birds of prey watching from their eyries in London, Paris, Berlin and St Petersburg had no intention of allowing the Turkish capital to fall into the hands of the Bulgarians. An armistice was mooted. The parties gathered in London, and the truce began on 3rd December, with the Bulgarians demanding Edirne.

It had been a chaotic year for the newly reborn Turkish parliament. By early 1912, with many of their leading members off fighting in the Libyan adventure, the influence of the Committee of Union and Progress was greatly weakened. Only by rigging elections in January and February had they attained a semblance of control, and by mid-summer conservatives had regained power. But with the outbreak of war, the Sultan dissolved Parliament and a new government formed, headed by the venerable four-times Grand Vizier, Kamil Pasha†. The War Ministry was given to another old soldier, Nazım Pasha. Rather than adopting the accepted defensive stance which had been Ottoman military doctrine since the recent reorganisation of the army under German instructors, Nazım Pasha took the offensive with disastrous results.

---

* Tekirdağ – formerly Rodosto

† known as 'Ingiliz' Kamil, because of his strong sympathies with Great Britain.

* * *

One evening in late January 1913, the Colonel Efendi returned home. His face was ashen, and even in the well-padded greatcoat with epaulettes and braid of rank glistening from the spray off the Bosphorus, his shoulders looked slumped. In the *haremlik*, well warmed by the brazier fire glowing beneath its ornate brass cover, he did indeed slump into his favourite armchair, and took the large whisky which the butler had already placed on a silver coaster at his right hand. He swilled the drink gently, letting the ice slake the sting of the alcohol, then took a good swig. The taste of the whisky released a little of his gloom. He sighed deeply and contemplated the liquid, pale against the lamplight in the room.

'Oh *canım*, what a day, what a day. You wouldn't believe it. They've gone mad, I tell you.' He was gazing up at the painted panels of the ceiling, although his wife was sitting opposite, a book on her lap. Satanaya entered at that moment, but hesitated on the threshold when she saw the Colonel.

'Come in my dear, come in, you can hear this too. You might as well know what a pretty mess we've come to.' he said.

'I didn't think it could have got much worse. Has Edirne fallen?' Amina said. She put her book down and came and sat on the carpet by her husband's chair and began stroking his arm.

'It might just as well have, and Constantinople to boot. It was this afternoon. I was delivering communiqués from the British Ambassador to the Parliament. The Powers were recommending that we give in to the Bulgarians' demands and surrender Edirne, and in return they would guarantee Constantinople's safety. When I arrived there was a huge crowd outside the Sublime Porte; scores of Committee members and their thugs. I could see Enver and Talaat and others forcing their way in to the Parliament building. Then I heard gunshots. I tried to get into the building but I was prevented by some of Talaat's bullies. I even had my own pistol out; it was awful. Eventually I managed to get in and I discovered that someone had shot old Nazım Pasha, the Minister of War. Afterwards they forced the Grand Vizier Kamil Pasha, one of our few causes for hope in all this mess, to sign his resignation.'

'So, what now? Who is the Government?' asked Satanaya.

'Exactly.' said Colonel Efendi. 'We have just witnessed a *coup d'état*, which means, my dear, that power is taken by force. With the CUP seizing control like this, the future becomes uncertain and unpredictable.

'And the Sultan?'

'The Sultan is in God's hands. Unfortunately, for the moment, it looks very much as if those hands are being manipulated by Talaat and Enver to their own ends. Clouds are gathering, it would seem, and we have no choice but to wait out the inevitable storm.'

When the armistice expired on 3 February 1913, the fighting recommenced. A month passed, during which the Committee in the form of the hard-line triumvirate of Enver, Talaat and Djemal consolidated their control over the Turkish Parliament. They installed a reluctant General Mahmud Şevket Paşa as Grand Vizier, the titular Prime Minister. And so began the darkest days of Turkey.

Winter deepened its grip, snow came and the war dragged on with defeats for the Turkish armies through Thrace, Macedonia and into Albania. The Bulgarians were still encamped in front of the Çatalca Lines, experiencing the hardships of trench warfare; the rats came and joined them after their Serbian allies left to fight other offensives further west. And the vultures, the apocalyptic-winged Griffons that nest in the craggy heights of Losinj Island in the northern reaches of the Adriatic, they too stayed and grew fat on the corpses of the battle-wasted fields.

* * *

Major Mustafa was not at all pleased. When he arrived back in Constantinople from the Libyan campaign, the war had been in progress for more than a fortnight. He had been ill and now on his recovery he discovered that his hometown of Salonica, along with most of his country's European territory, was occupied by Greeks.

He was posted to the Dardanelles which had been cut off by the Bulgarians' lightning advance down to the Marmara Sea at Tekirdağ and was put in charge of operations at Bulayır*, a small town on the narrow neck of land at the top of the Gallipoli Peninsula. As the siege of Edirne worsened, Enver conceived a plan to land troops from the Tenth Army at Şarköy, west of Bulayır, from where they would push the Bulgarians back, and join up with the Turkish forces before moving north to relieve the besieged city.

The plan was ill-conceived and hastily enacted, and it failed with much loss of life. A row developed between the two commanders. Mustafa, the

---

* Bolayır – burial place of nationalist poet and activist Namik Kemal (1840-1888)

contender, sparred with the self-appointed champion Enver, and only by the personal intervention of General Mahmud Şevket Pasha was some kind of reconciliation effected.

Edirne fell to the Bulgarians on 24th March 1913 and the loss of this former capital sent shockwaves throughout the Ottoman Empire. The stalemate at the Çatalca Lines continued into spring with little loss or gain of territory on either side. Eventually at the end of May another armistice was signed, giving over to the Balkan League all the European Ottoman lands west of a line between the Black Sea at Kıyıköy* and Enez on the Marmara Sea coast.†

* * *

It was a Wednesday morning in June when Satanaya and Amina Khanoum set off early to deliver a parcel of fresh clothes and pastries from the konak kitchen to the Colonel Efendi. Amina Khanoum had been concerned about her husband's appearance. He had been holed up in his office for days, putting in place administrative details at the Turkish end for the recently achieved armistice.

The two ladies left the War Ministry later that morning and were walking across the square in front of the Bayezid Mosque. They were intending to pick up their waiting carriage which would take them onto Divan Yolu, the main thoroughfare towards the Aya Sofia Mosque and then down to the ferry station. A motor vehicle exited the gateway of the Ministry and drove slowly past them; a noticeable event as there were so few automobiles yet in the city. Then came the sound of pistol shots. Satanaya saw the car had come to a halt just in front of them. Everything seemed to be happening so slowly. That is how she noticed the bullet holes and cracked glass of the car windows; they seemed out of place. A man in a military uniform jumped from the rear compartment of the car, a pistol in his hand as he ran down the street chasing someone. Then more shots, and a man fell. Moustachioed men in jackets, shirts and ties

---

* Kıyıköy – formerly Midye

† Following the peace agreement, former Grand Vizier İngiliz Kamil Pasha returned from exile in Egypt. The venerable statesman, thinking the time was ripe to raise opposition in Parliament to the CUP, had not reckoned with Talaat, who immediately had him put under house arrest. The British Ambassador intervened and Kamil Pasha was allowed to leave for Cyprus, the land of his birth.

were running everywhere, waving revolvers. A woman selling fruit from
a barrow began to scream. A flock of turkeys on the far side of the square
tried to fly, their hysterical gobbling providing an eccentric chorus to the
call to prayer which floated down from the minaret of the Bayezid
Mosque. Satanaya just stood there, as if watching a play; or perhaps an
opera. The timpani of gunshots; the aria of the fruit seller. The chorus of
frightened birds. The finale of the call to prayer.

Then soldiers appeared and the scene became confused. Amina
Khanoum had collapsed to her knees and begun to say the *Fatiha*.[*] Satanaya
pulled her back on her feet and taking her hand dragged her away. No one
stopped them. She saw blood on the road; a pistol lay abandoned. Instinctively she felt in her purse for her own small pistol that she always carried
nowadays.[†] The feel of the cold steel woke her up, and they walked on
without stopping or looking back. Their carriage was nowhere to be seen.
They carried on walking all the way down to the ferry station by the Galata
Bridge. She released her grip on the firearm only when she had to find
change for the ferry fare.

---

[*] 'The Chapter of the Opening' – the short prayer which opens the Koran.

[†] Since arriving in Constantinople, Satanaya had exchanged the heavy French
   military pistol, which had accompanied her through Anatolia, in favour of a smaller
   pocket pistol, a Belgium-made FN 1910, of 590 gms.

THIRTEEN

The Tragic Assassination
of a Grand Vizier

Constantinople, 1913

HE IRONY OF IT ALL. A long, illustrious career ending in assassination by revolver in the back of a car. Born in 1858, Mahmud Şevket Paşa was the bright hope of a noble family of Baghdad. Raised in Basra on the confluence of the Tigris and Euphrates, and schooled in Constantinople from the age of thirteen, he chose the life of soldiering, entering the Harbiye military college where he rose quickly to a position on the general staff. There he caught the eye of the German military advisor, General von der Goltz, who sent him to study armaments at the famous pistol manufacturer Mauser in Germany as part of the programme to re-organise and re-equip the Turkish Army.

Appointed as governor of the province of Kosovo, and now with the rank
of general, he led the army which crushed the counter-revolution against
the Young Turks in April 1909, hastening the deposing of Sultan Abdul
Hamid II. A modernist, he introduced the first automobile to Constantinople and as Minister of War helped bring about an aviation programme
in the Ottoman military.

This particular Wednesday morning in June when the General is to
meet his fate, comes four hectic months after the assassination of Nazım
Paşa, and the ousting of the Grand Vizier Kamil Paşa, in the coup d'état.
General Şevket Paşa had accepted the vacant position of Prime Minister
only with much persuading. In the end he felt some responsibility to try
and steer from the back seat this unruly bunch of thugs who had taken
over the wheel of the state. After all, it had been his 'heroic' move with the
army in 1909 that had brought about the return of the constitution and
parliamentary rule. He had supported the CUP then but subsequently
baulked at what he saw to be military rule in the guise of parliamentary
democracy. Soldiering for soldiers, Parliament for politicians, that was his
way, and the way of that young Major Mustafa whom he hoped one day
would exert a stronger influence in the affairs of state. But not today.
Mustafa preferred to keep his head down in the army, while he, at fifty-five,
a General at the peak of his powers, was parading about as Grand Vizier,
and definitely not keeping his head down.

'Come on, Eshref Bey, it's time we got going,' the General calls across
the big mahogany desk into the far corner of his office in the War Ministry
to where his ADC sits at a similar, but much smaller bureau.

'Sir?' Captain Eshref stands at attention.

'We're going to the Parliament again. It is my job, after all. Well, one of
them.' He smiles resignedly and turns to address the servant standing
silently on his left. 'Go and make sure the car is waiting, Kazım Ağa, we'll
be down in a moment.'

Kazım slips out while the Grand Vizier places the large red fez on his
head, straightens his richly-braided dolman jacket and buckles up the belt
which he had eased while sitting at his desk. Captain Eshref Bey speaks
softly into a black phone – a most recent innovation in Turkey since they
had been banned during the rule of Abdul Hamid for security reasons –
replaces the earpiece and puts on his own cloth kalpak. A knock at the
door a moment later precedes the appearance of Lieutenant Ibrahim, his

ADC representing the Navy. With his aides in train, the General marches smartly from the room, receiving salutes all the way down the staircase of the War Ministry and out into the wide Courtyard where his recently-acquired 1912 Laffly automobile is waiting.

Although Sultan Abdul Hamid had once bought a car, it had never been driven outside the bounds of Yildiz Palace. Mahmud Şevket Paşa was proud of this modern addition to the workings of state. He looked to the day when the whole military machine would be motorised. The Laffly has an open-sided box at the front where the driver sits with the mechanic – in this case Mahmud Şevket Paşa's manservant, Kazım Ağa – and behind is a closed compartment with thick glass windows and facing bench seats making room for four passengers. It is the latest in French automobile design.

The entrance to the extensive Court in front of the Seraskeriat – the War Ministry – comprises a mock barbican of three horseshoe-arches, with sentry boxes either side of the central carriage entrance, and shouldered left and right by squat crenelated towers, each turret sporting its own clock. The clocks chime the hour of eleven as the Laffly passes out into the *meydan* in front of the Bayezid Mosque. According to the local newspaper reports to follow, witnesses will say the General was sitting facing forwards on the right hand side, his aide Captain Eshref Bey on his left, with Naval Lieutenant Ibrahim Bey sitting opposite.

Bayezid Square, originally 'The Forum of the Bull' built by Constantine I, has always been a place of public gathering and markets. As the officers drive from the Seraskeriat, they pass to their left a group of geese sitting in the dust, tended by a lone young boy in striped shirt and ragged trousers. A crowd of sightseers line the railings along the outer wall, peering into the Court where some soldiers are being drilled; further along a shepherd corrals his flock of fat-tailed sheep and a row of barbers in aprons and polka-dotted shirts are busy giving shaves to patrons seated on little stools. A pair of buffaloes pulling a cart laden with a huge barrel trundle slowly towards the Ministry gateway while around the periphery moustachioed men in dark coats and fezzes idly stroll.

Crossing the square the chauffeur steers the Laffly towards the Bayezid Tramway Terminus, intending to enter Divan Yolu en route to the Sublime Porte. At this point the vehicle is forced to give way to allow a funeral cortège to pass. Mahmud Şevket Paşa was a pragmatist. Nevertheless, perhaps from a habit ingrained since childhood, this proximity to death compels him to repeat on his breath the formula, *La hawla wa la quwata illa billahi'l ali al-azim* – 'There is no power nor strength save in God, the High, the Mighty' – hoping to ward off any immediate attraction which the next world might be exerting on his soul. Perhaps also in this moment of bearing witness to a superior order, as the Grand Vizier of a superpower on the brink of collapse, he is consciously or subconsciously offering his submission to the necessities of the Empire's destiny. Will he too to be part of the death of the great tree of Osman's dream, another old branch cracking beneath the weight of time, unable to extend beyond its allotted reach? And he, being merely the nominal incumbent, when removed from the seat of power, must he sink or swim according to his own poor abilities?

The cortège moves on. The Laffly remains at a standstill. The sound of gunfire. The glass in the left-hand window smashes. A thumping on the running boards of the car. The doors open. Feet appear on the threshold. Arms stretch inside. A pistol in each hand. All the tired general sees are faces. Small faces with narrowed frightened eyes and thin mouths. He will carry these faces with him into the next world. The first bullet enters his right temple and exits through his left. Vision fades into a thick red mist, but hearing remains, carrying the sound of the fusillade; and sensations remain, the thumping upon his body reluctantly receiving the cloth-buffeted lead, and on his left side he feels his aide Ibrahim Bey fall against him. The pain begins, a sharp burning feeling which distances in his consciousness as the red mist brightens and turns to light. He tries to hold on. Later the surgeons will extract five bullets from the General.

The chauffeur and Kazım Ağa dive from the car at the first sound of shots. The General falls forward onto Eshref Bey, who has somehow escaped being hit. The assailants disperse. Pushing back the bloodied body of his commander, Captain Eshref draws his gun, but it misfires. He reaches into the general's jacket for his pistol, but that too fails him. Taking the fallen Ibrahim Bey's weapon, he jumps from the vehicle and gives chase, managing to wound one of the assassins as they climb into their own car and make their escape.

Soldiers reach the scene in minutes and the Laffly is brought back to the Ministry. Lieutenant Ibrahim Bey is dead, having been killed instantly from a bullet in the head. The now unconscious Grand Vizier is carried into a building where resident medical staff attempt to treat his wounds. In spite of the expert ministrations of the Chief Medical Officer Besim Paşa, assisted by Lambeki Paşa and Dr. Süleyman Numan Bey, Mahmud Şevket Paşa is dead within half an hour of the shooting.

* * *

The newspapers the following day were filled with lurid and varying accounts of the event which Satanaya and Amina Khanoum themselves had witnessed. By then they had already heard from Colonel Efendi that the General had been murdered. The Colonel had left his office on hearing the commotion in Bayezid Meydan, concerned that his wife and Satanaya might have been caught up in the melée, and worrying even further when he could not find them. Ascertaining that no women had been arrested in the usual indiscriminate round-up that would have ensued from such an attack, he had set off for Beylerbeyi.

'Eliminated. That is the term they use, I believe. He objected to his employers' methods, it seems.' commented the Colonel. 'You'll see. They've already arrested suspects, mostly people running gambling dens, and a couple of notables who have opposed them openly. They'll hang, of course, and that will be the end of that. Mahmud Şevket Paşa was an inconvenient convenience. He never wanted a political post, but he might have been eliminated sooner had he not accepted it. They will say he was done in by the Liberals, but I wouldn't put it past Talaat to have had him removed. They always saw him as a threat in waiting. Now Enver will take the War Ministry.'

They were gathered in the *haremlık*. The Colonel was drinking whisky, while his wife dandled young Mohammed Ali on her lap. The child was asking for food as his mother tried to persuade him to say please. He was nearly two now and growing rapidly. Finally he said the magic word. Language was coming easily to the intelligent child. She gave him a date from which she had first removed the stone, and he sucked it with delight as she spoke.

'I've heard on the Khedival grapevine that our uncle Prince Sa'id Halim has been given the nod for the Grand Vizierate.'

Amina Khanoum was referring to her great uncle, His Highness Prince Muhammad Sa'id Halim Pasha, one of the thirty-two children of Mohammed Ali Pasha of Egypt. He had been educated in Switzerland, become a general in the Ottoman army and as a member of the CUP had recently been appointed Foreign Minister. He was an obvious choice: ostensibly neutral, necessarily pliable, he had been happy enough enjoying the privileged life under the old order, and his courtly background had prepared him well for treading a path of studied diplomacy in the tumultuous atmosphere of the new constitutional Turkey.

'He's being handed a poisoned chalice, whichever way you look at it.' said the Colonel Efendi.

'How long will he last, I wonder?' said Amina.*

Ever since the rise of the CUP, assassinations had become the order of the day. Typically it was the Committee's political opponents and journalists who were the victims, though anyone who voiced protest, even from within their own ranks, might be found early one morning in an alley way, with a bullet in the head.

* * *

It was a sad peace that came with the armistice of 30 May. For Turkey, the loss of Edirne, barely 150 miles from the capital, was a national catastrophe. Founded by the Roman Emperor Hadrian it became known as Adrianople and had been a Bulgarian city since the 9th century until captured in 1361 by the third Ottoman Sultan, Murad I. The city became the first European capital of the Ottoman Empire before Constantinople was conquered in 1453. Edirne served as the forward post for the many Ottoman expeditions into Europe against the Austro-Hungarian Empire, campaigns which saw them twice pulled up before the walls of Vienna, while for over five hundred years the Turks maintained greater and lesser degrees of control throughout the Balkans.

And yet, even as the peace was being agreed, further trouble was brewing beneath the surface. The members of the Balkan Pact, once united in greed, having achieved many of their goals, became divided over the spoils of war, notably the division of Macedonia. Disagreements brought Serbia and Greece into confrontation with Bulgaria. By late June, the Bulgarian army, without even the consent of their own government, attacked both the Greeks and the Serbs, but were repulsed. Romania now joined in and the Bulgarians subsequently lost much of the territory they

---

* Prince Mohammed Sa'id Halim Paşa, held the post of Prime Minister until 1917. He was assassinated by Armenian agents in Rome on St Nicholas' Day, 1921.

had fought so hard to win.

This was Turkey's chance, and the government didn't waste time. Talaat persuaded the Sultan to order the Ottoman Army into battle. Turkish forces broke out from the Çatalca Lines on 18th July and within three days had retaken Edirne. With Bulgaria now having to defend itself on all sides, it relinquished eastern Thrace to Turkey, signing a peace agreement on 29th September 1913, a bare three months after the conflict had erupted. Enver Pasha had ensured once again that he was in poll position for the final push to take the city, and now bathed in the glory of being a second Conqueror of Edirne after Sultan Murad I.

The government in Constantinople was now stacked with cronies and henchmen of the regime's three leaders, Talaat, Enver and Djemal Pasha. Mustafa had little chance of having his own policies considered within such a scenario. He was offered, and accepted, the position of military attaché in the embassy in Sofia. Fethi, his former commander from the Bulayır campaign, and a Committee member, had retired from the army and had been appointed Turkish Ambassador to Bulgaria. Whether it was promotion or relegation, Mustafa was going to take advantage of a post among the Europeans and bide his time.

FOURTEEN

A Bulgarian Intermezzo

Constantinople – Sofia, 1913

OMETHING THAT particularly impressed Satanaya during her time among the Ottomans, Khedivial Egyptians, and the high born people with whom they mingled, was the extraordinary certainty with which these grandees assumed their position in the world, and the complete self-assurance with which they conducted themselves. Even during the most dreadful periods of political crisis and war, none of them, not the Colonel Efendi, nor Amina Khanoum, nor the many officials and ministers with whom she had come into contact in the konak, showed the slightest deviation in maintaining a positive attitude, impeccable manners and strong presence of mind in whatever apparent adversity was shaking the state at the time. It was uncanny. Their sense of self-possession, of command, even when they lost power, seemed innate. She was impressed too by those unusual people, the efendis and the sheykhs who would arrive in the konak like a fragrance or a fine mood, who would fill the space with their otherworldly conviviality for a brief, bright, alluring moment; and after their departure there would remain a timeless contentment, as the sunset glow of a summer's evening at the edge of clear night. It was as if their interior character reflected a more original and comprehensive force than the mere pretence of authority exercised by the so-called powers that be; and hence exerted a more encompassing influence upon events in this outer universe.

Satanaya had seen at first hand how this influence was brought to bear, if in just a small way, in the manner with which the two small boys were being brought up. At one level they were indulged; clearly loved, but never spoilt. Their nascent intelligences were not patronised, but clear boundaries between licit and illicit behaviour were set and observed. If expressions of rebelliousness arose, it was not punished by bastinado, nor even a slap, but that cruellest of punishments: the questioning frown and the withdrawal of attention. It was not a withdrawal of love, but a shuttering of the mirror in which that love appeared. Any selfish, egotistic stance or recalcitrant mood in the child would melt quickly before the fire of their greater need, for their mother's – or indeed any of the servants' performing their duty *in loco parentis* – love. And mother knew how to turn it off and on like a tap. A roll of the eyes was often enough, and if that did not get the required response, silence accompanied by a certain uninterested attitude would begin to eat away at the child's egoism, until like sandcastles eroding before the inexorable tide, it would dissolve in tears of regret and sorrow, love's longing in the form of surrender.

The boys were encouraged to express themselves in the best manner, to respond when spoken to, to be patient and not interrupt. Even at an early age, young Ahmad had begun to carry himself with a certain serious-ness that might have been mistaken for aloofness were it not for his wicked sense of humour, evident in the flash of his eyes which always seemed to see more than was immediately obvious in a situation. To all appearances a quiet child, his intellect whirred away inside him; continually weighing up, calculating, discriminating, and arriving at considered conclusions. Little Mohammed Ali, on the other hand, always knew the value of a well-timed smile, and disguised with charm the penetrating intelligence that lay behind it. Satanaya had from the start found something unsettling about this child. She would catch him looking at her, and the look was of someone observing distantly as if from another time, as a very old person might look down from the height and wisdom of age at the foibles of the world. And at the instant that she caught the look, out would come that irresistible smile and she would have to pick him up and give him a hug.

Late summer eased into autumn. The heat had gone out of the sun and since the retaking of Edirne and the subsequent signing of the peace treaty with the Bulgarians in Constantinople, the political temperature had also somewhat cooled. The Colonel Efendi was taking extended leave, accompanying Amina's family on the yearly trip to winter in Egypt. For the sea voyage to Alexandria, his mother-in-law, a Royal princess of the House of Mohammed Ali Pasha the Great, and who now lived in a palace on the Bosphorus at Emirgan, had chartered an entire passenger steamer from a European shipping company. She'd had the captain's apartments refitted to her own requirements, and claimed the ballroom as her personal stateroom, the rest of the family having to do with mere First Class suites and cabins.

Satanaya, meanwhile, had other plans. Although things had quietened down in the city, it was the kind of surface stillness that belies a seething in its turbid depths. Curfews and martial law had blanketed any possibility of objection to the Triumvirate. The hangings and disappearances of suspected dissenters bred fear among the regime's opponents and a surliness amongst the population, reminiscent of the worst periods during the reign of Abdul Hamid. The gaiety of the konak too had disappeared, under the dust cloths which now covered the furniture in the *selamlık;* just as Constantinople's spirit sank under the gloomy clouds of a persistent *lodos* wind.

At a gathering one evening in the konak before the Balkan wars, Satanaya had made the acquaintance of a Parisian lady living in Sofia, the new Bulgarian capital. Madame Sultana Hortense was a society dame who opened her house to the kind of soirées familiar to Satanaya from her time in the Beyt'ur-Rahma. She had extended to Satanaya an open invitation to come and spend time with her, and to enjoy the modern society of this new 'European' capital.

'There will be balls, parties, opera! Who knows? You might even find a husband.' Madame Hortense had enthused.

Satanaya had no wish for a husband, but the thought of balls and opera was certainly attractive. To visit Europe, ever since Lady Gülbahar had planted the idea back in Beirut and begun teaching her French, had been a constant dream, although the recent war had driven such notions to the back of her mind. Now, in what would turn out to be such a brief window of peace, she remembered the invitation and sent a telegram proposing a visit.

Madame Hortense's reply arrived in the first week of November. It said simply, '*Chère Satanaya nous sommes impatients de vous accueillir*'.

Much as Satanaya might have wished, in her custom, to travel on horseback, this was a different kind of journey. And anyway, with her newly-opened account at the Ottoman Bank, she was beginning to enjoy the benefits of the substantial inheritance bequeathed her by Lady Gülbahar. She could well afford to travel in style. She packed two trunks with her favourite ball gowns and warmest furs, and with tickets purchased through Wagons-Lits*, she took an overnight steamer from the quay at Karaköy to the Bulgarian port of Varna on the Black Sea. There she boarded the Orient Express to Sofia, the direct route from Constantinople rendered impossible due to war damage on the tracks.

∗ ∗ ∗

Snow was falling in the gas-lit streets of Sofia. Satanaya felt a chill of excitement as she pulled her fur coat close around her and settled herself into the phaeton at the central station. They set off down the wide Maria Luisa Boulevard and over the Lion Bridge, before turning right into Tsar Simeon Street. Barely ten minutes later the cab stopped in front of an impressive three-storied stone house where the driver jumped out and rang the door bell. A liveried doorman appeared, followed closely by the tall figure of a woman.

Madame Sultana Hortense descended the steps pulling on a cloak over a black taffeta dress. Her great tresses of thick wavy blonde hair were dressed loose in the Grecian style with a large bun at the back of her head, all crowned with a stunning tiara aigrette of flashing diamonds and white

---

* Compagnie Internationale des Wagons-Lits was the historical operator of the Orient Express train service. Founded in 1872, it was the premier provider and operator of European railway sleeping and dining cars during the late 19th and the 20th centuries.

peacock feathers. Her face glowed with life: her full cheeks rouged a soft pink, her eyes strikingly enlarged by the careful use of a smouldering grey kohl, and dark eyeliner extending her already dark eyebrows. Full lips on a wide mouth seemed further plumped with ruby gloss, and her neck sparkled within a broad diamond choker set with a single teardrop emerald. She presented an imposing figure in all the joyful extravagance of La Belle Époque.

'Darling Satanaya, oh but you have arrived just in time. Quickly, we must get you ready, the Swedes are holding a party in the ballroom of the Grand Hotel and it promises to be quite an evening. The Russians are coming, and the Germans, and the Turks of course, so some diplomatic sparks may fly… Come on Igor, hurry along and get the lady's trunks up to her room. Cab driver, be a good chap and give him a hand – there's *rakija* waiting for you in the kitchen… Now, Satanaya, do come inside out of the cold.'

While the two men struggled with Satanaya's luggage, Madame Hortense led Satanaya up the main staircase into a large drawing room on the first floor. It was furnished over-abundantly with deep divan-type sofas and chaises draped with lace covers; Turkish rugs covered the floors, and small tables held Art Nouveau lamps. The walls, meanwhile, were papered in a deep maroon floral pattern, and liberally hung with original paintings by some of the young artists of the new Modernist movement working in Paris. Satanaya was initially startled by the strangeness of the various styles which confronted her: the early cubism of Picasso and Braque, the pointillism of Seurat; but in time she would come to appreciate the strength of life that sprang from these images. In time, too, she would learn to enjoy the easy lifestyle of the expatriate community in this little enclave of modernity in the former Ottoman dependency.

'Now, perhaps a glass of šljivovica to fortify you against the weather, then there will be time for you to bathe and change for the evening.'

The plum brandy went quite to her head, and as she contemplated which of her gowns would best suit her entrance into Sofia society, a warm glow of happy anticipation spread through her.

* * *

Sofia, set in a plateau at the junction of three mountain passes connecting it to Western Europe and the Adriatic Sea, and the orient, suffers cold and snowy winters, hot humid summers, and turbulent intervening seasons. The city dedicated to the Holy Wisdom became the capital of the nominally independent Principality of Bulgaria following the Seige of Plevna in 1877-78, when Turkey lost much of its European lands to Russian advances. A city situated at a geographical, meteorological, ethnic and religious crossroads, the fortunes of Sofia have vacillated between war and peace in the Balkans for two millennia.

The recent tumultuous events in the Balkans brought about a changing parade of neighbours: Greece, Macedonia, Serbia, Romania, variously friend and foe. And after more than four hundred years of relative stability under Ottoman rule, Bulgaria now had Turkey outside its borders.

The years since independence had also ushered in dramatic changes to Sofia. Gone were the narrow muddy lanes winding between timber-framed houses with overhanging upper stories, the *harem* windows shuttered from public gaze with trellis-work *kafes* from where the veiled wives of the Muslim overlords looked down. Gone were most of the mosques and hamams, and the Ottoman civil buildings where the ruling class had maintained their authority. Instead a new city in the modern European style had sprung up. Broad avenues and streets laid out in straight parallel rows were lined with municipal buildings in the neo-classical style and stone villas and townhouses such as Madame Hortense occupied. During this short period the population had grown tenfold to over 100,000 inhabitants. The Principality promoted itself to a Kingdom in 1908, when the incumbent – 'Foxy' Ferdinand I, a Saxe-Coburg-Gotha prince and cousined to most of the Royal Houses of Europe – proclaimed himself Tsar.

* * *

While Satanaya was getting ready for her first outing in Sofia, in another part of the city the young Turkish military attaché stood before the cheval mirror in his room in the Splendide Palace Hotel and adjusted his white tie. He looked at his friend Shakir Bey, another smartly-dressed and bright-eyed young buck preparing for a night on the town.

'So, apart from the wives of the Ambassadors and Ministers, who are we likely to bump into tonight? Will there be any eligible young ladies for these eminently eligible young gentlemen?'

'Eligible for what exactly, Mustafa?' Shakir laughed. 'There are not likely to be any ladies of the night, if that's what you're after. Later perhaps. No, but these Bulgars do like to show off their daughters who make pleasant enough company, and are certainly happy to get to grips with one on the dance floor. How are you with the waltz or the tango?'

Mustafa grimaced. He'd had little opportunity for such extra-curricular distractions in recent years, but the carefree atmosphere in post-war Sofia had inspired him to take up dancing lessons again. Still, he wasn't at all sure he would be able to cut a rug in modern European society.

'So so… but I can always watch you.' said Mustafa.

'No chance. I know you like to dance. I've seen you in the cafés after you've had a few. This won't be any different, except we'll be drinking champagne not raki.'

＊ ＊ ＊

When Madame Hortense and Satanaya entered the ballroom, Shakir Bey and Mustafa were already on their second glass of Hungarian 'Törley' Champagne. Although it was nearly seven years since their paths had crossed so briefly in Lebanon at the Beyt'ur-Rahma, recognition came instantly. Both Mustafa and Satanaya were stopped in their tracks.

'Do you know each other?' Madame Hortense asked Satanaya.

'Yes…no… we have never actually met… he came to Lady Gülbahar's once, and also in Damascus…' her voice trailed off. Satanaya experienced a curious sensation where time and space seemed to fold up and connect her to the immediate presence of those earlier events.

It was the same for Mustafa, as if something begun one evening in the hills above Beirut continued now in Sofia without even an interval.

'Someone you know?' said Shakir Bey, under his breath. 'You lucky bugger, she's a stunner. Come on, introduce us.'

'Actually we've never been formally introduced.'

Mustafa wanted to back away, but it was too late. Madame Hortense had taken Satanaya's arm and launched a pre-emptive strike across the large open space of the ballroom. Shakir Bey in his eagerness responded, leading the hapless military attaché into the field. Coming to attention before the two ladies he took the elder's gloved hand and with a discreet bow pressed it lightly to his lips.

'Good evening, Madame Hortense, how lovely you look tonight.' Shakir Bey was ladling on the charm.

'Ah, Monsieur Shakir, Bey Efendi, how naughty you are to flatter the daisy in the presence of the rose. May I introduce my guest, the Baroness Satanaya. She came just this evening from Constantinople.'

Naturally all eyes fell upon the radiant Satanaya, whose face, already flushed with cold and *šljivovica*, blushed even more and managed a generous smile. She had never been introduced as Baroness before. She was still suffering that state of arrival where everything appears so new, and so exciting. It would have taken little to sweep her from her feet altogether. From the intensely serious yet handsome face of the tall young man standing back a little from the cheerful Shakir Bey, two eyes of blue steel surveyed her with a strangely soothing curiosity. Mustafa's gaze had the effect of anchoring her back in herself. Then his eyes softened as he returned her smile, and kissing her hand he answered, 'A rose… ah, then I must beware, for they say that the rarest essence of the rose lives in its thorns.'

'Oh, and I thought I was meeting the brave Captain who led the army against the counter-revolution. The one who fought bravely against the Italians and the Greeks. I'm so sorry, I must have mistaken you for another Captain Mustafa.' Satanaya smiled kindly.

Now it was Mustafa's turn to blush.

'Yes, it must have been another. I am just a simple soldier who does his duty faithfully,' he replied

'And is it a soldier's duty to raise a lady's hopes by bringing fine words of flowers and scent? Alas, words without action bring poor satisfaction.' Satanaya was beginning to enjoy herself.

'Then at the risk of my pride being pricked, would you do me the honour of the next dance?'

Satanaya's smile broadened and her eyes sparkled. 'The honour is mine.'

Madame Hortense and Shakir Bey stepped aside as she took Mustafa's arm and they made their way towards the orchestra where a waltz was just beginning.

The evening went by in a flash. Satanaya felt extraordinarily happy. The weight of the past year in Constantinople lifted as if it had never been and she drank deeply of the gay European spirit investing this lively new city. Just how much of this spirit was due to the handsome man whose strong arms encircled her in the dance, and how much was simply relief at having escaped out of the shadowy night of the Turkish capital now in the stranglehold of a gangster regime, who could tell. The man, certainly, was a bonus. Although his movements were at first stiff, Mustafa soon loosened up in the close presence of this beautiful young woman who danced with easy and spontaneous movements. For Satanaya the waltz was a joyful escape after the formal steps of Circassian dances, and she felt herself turning like a dervish in the captain's hands, while enjoying a gentle pleasure and innocent abandonment.

Satanaya's entrance to Sofia society was a success. Next she danced with Shakir Bey, who flirted amusingly throughout. Madame Hortense then led her on a whirl of introductions, and after an energetic polka with the head of the Swedish diplomatic mission, she ended the evening once again on the arm of the enigmatic Captain Mustafa. If any diplomatic sparks flew that night, it was between the young men vying for Satanaya's attention. But on account of her long day, the ladies excused themselves early and returned to the house in Tsar Simeon Street.

Mustafa and Shakir extended their evening in a *café chantant*, drinking raki and being entertained by a couple of lubricious Hungarian singers who joined them after their performance. Mustafa was not in the mood.

He was thinking of the Circassian girl that he had held in the dance. Something about her deep blue eyes had struck him, not simply their beauty, but... what? Some kind of intelligent light. It was not something he had ever noticed, at least consciously, in a woman before. It was an irritation in the usual scheme of things. He would have been content simply to have fallen a little in love, to see where it led. But this was not so simple. Mustafa returned alone to his hotel, wondering how he could see Satanaya again, leaving Shakir in a quandary as to which of the two Hungarian chanteuses he was to disappoint that night.

Meanwhile, Satanaya lay snug beneath goose down quilts in her new home. She too was thinking of her evening and the Turkish officer. She was glad to have met him that way, on neutral ground, and as equals. She no longer felt the perturbation she had experienced in those earlier encounters. He was the same lonely hunter she had glimpsed distantly in Damascus, but her heart had now been strengthened. No pretty pigeon to his hawk. Dangerous, perhaps he was, but she no longer feared him. She fell quickly asleep.

FIFTEEN

Sofia and the Drums of War

Sofia, 1913-1914

HRISTMAS CAME and went, and Satanaya played the seasonal roulette of parties and receptions. To begin with she was chaperoned by her host; Madame Hortense appeared to be on everybody's guest list. But soon Satanaya became sought after in her own right, as the ladies of Sofia society knew that the presence of this exotic Circassian baroness would attract all the eligible young men. And as it seemed the Turkish attaché had placed his chips on Satanaya's number, and she likewise found herself spinning ineluctably towards the corresponding pocket, the Sofia mothers saw the odds of their own daughters' making a winning play among suitable European stock only improved.

This kind of gaiety, the feasting and dancing, taffeta and tails, ropes of pearls and diamond tie-pins, while not in itself conducive to deeper relationships may nonetheless assist in penetrating the gloss of mere acquaintance. In the dark days of February, with little relief from the unrelenting snow and grey skies, Satanaya decided to host a party of her own around the warm hearth of Madame Hortense's reception rooms. While the expected crowd were invited, it was with Mustafa in mind that she took charge of the kitchen and embarked upon a feast of hot and cold mezes, grilled kebabs and exotic desserts.

She consulted Takla's Cookbook for inspiration on the Turkish kitchen. Now, it is well known that there is no single form of cooking that can be designated purely Turkish. Perhaps it is like the Turkish meal itself, a subtle combination of tastes, various and complimentary, without any single monumental dish to swamp the many possibilities inherent in such an eclectic cuisine. Byzantine, Egyptian, Phoenician, even Arab influences all find a place. Yogurts of the Balkans, the hearth-cooked food of the Turkic steppe nomads, the flat breads and meats grilled on skewers; even pasta, attributed to Marco Polo returning from his eastern adventures in Xanadu, arrived in Constantinople prior to entertaining the palates of the Venetian nobles. For this cuisine is peripatetic and one may journey without fixed itinerary, confident that the discerning cook will not set forth dishes one against the other, thereby ensuring each diner a safe and happy passage.

To begin, there were cold *mezes* – hors d'oeuvres – comprising seasonal vegetables cooked in olive oil: tiny leeks cooked with a little macédoine of carrot and potato and flavoured with dill; fritters of thinly sliced aubergines and courgettes; peppers stuffed with rice and fresh parsley, dill, mint and thyme; ironmongers' salad and *taze fasulye* – fresh green beans. Then the hot mezes: a variety of *börek* – savoury pastries variously filled with homemade white cheese, spinach, spice-cured beef cut wafer-thin, and hard *kaşar* cheese. The meats followed: tender lamb chops, trimmed and flattened, basted with a little olive oil and oregano and grilled over charcoal; grilled köfte – of minced beef and lamb, parsley, grated onion and breadcrumbs – each shaped into tiny furrowed patties by being pressed between the first three slender fingers of Satanaya's hands; kidneys and chicken pieces also found their place above the charcoal. For desserts, two milk puddings: baked rice pudding – *sütlaç*, and her favourite ground almond and semolina pudding – *keşkül*, flavoured with vanilla and a hint of rose; as well as *ayva tatlısı* – baked quince dessert topped with thick clotted buffalo cream.

Madame Hortense came into the kitchen in the late afternoon to see how things were shaping up, and was amazed at the ordered chaos and energy in the room. Satanaya had commandeered most of the staff who were hard at it under her competent direction, peeling and scraping, chopping and mixing, frying and steaming. Madame Hortense looked at the proposed menu and laughed.

'But why have you included this peasant dish of lentil soup, when there are so many subtle and delicious dishes here?'

'Ah,' Satanaya's blue eyes sparkled, 'it's a long story – about memory and taste. If my intuition is correct, something may be revealed tonight. If not, I promise I'll tell you tomorrow.' She smiled mischievously and Madame Hortense just laughed again.

The guests that evening were mostly Turks, expatriates and Bulgarian-born residents. Shakir Bey, who was one of a small number of Turkish members of the Bulgarian parliament, was invited, and also Mustafa's friend and head of the Turkish diplomatic mission, Fethi Bey.

As people arrived a small '*saz takımı*' struck up some traditional songs from Salonica, in honour of Mustafa and Fethi. Drinks were served, raki and local wines, and the conversation was lively. Keenly discussed was the current state of affairs in China where the General Yuan Shih-k'ai had ushered in the end of the Qing Dynasty forcing the abdication of the child-emperor Pu Yi. After leading a brief period of democracy as President, General Yuan had had his opponents removed and himself set up as absolute ruler.

'It all sounds so familiar.' mused Shakir Bey. 'I shouldn't wonder if our own dear Napoleon, Enver Bey, entertains similar pretentions, now that he's married the princess.'

'Then he would have to rid himself of Talaat and Djemal… and the Sultan too, for that matter. It would take a bigger man than Enver Pasha. I doubt if such a one could be found, and still manage to keep the people on his side.' said one of the musicians, a dark, handsome man called Hakan, a political refugee who had found Sofia a safer bet than Constantinople during the recent purges.

Mustafa was about to enter the discourse when Fethi Bey tapped him gently on the arm, and said quietly: 'Perhaps now is not the best time to promote your ideas, *canım*. The ears of the Committee may reach even to Sofia. Let Enver do what Enver does. Our time will come.'

After an hour or so of drinking, Madame Hortense sounded a little gong and invited the guests to move into an adjoining room where on a large table the buffet was laid out. It was familiar fare to the assembled party and guaranteed to stir fond memories of home. They first admired with their eyes, complimenting the elegant array of dishes surrounding floral displays. They began to eat, trying a little of this and a little of that, no greedy piling of plates, content to savour rather than stuff. For a while the conversation gave way to pleasant hums of delight and satisfied sighs.

A large soup tureen in the centre of the spread seemed neglected. Mustafa leant across and sniffed. A frown of perplexity spread over his face.

'No, not possible!' he said to himself. He took a bowl and gave himself a couple of ladles full, squeezing lemon liberally over all. He tasted. The frown gave way to a smile, yet the perplexity remained.

'Damascus! Domenico's...' he said out loud. 'It's the same. How could it be?'

Mustafa looked around for the Circassian girl, but she was nowhere to be seen. With bowl in hand he made his way downstairs to the kitchen where he found Satanaya supervising the arrangement of the shish kebabs and köfte onto two large platters as the meat came sizzling off the grill.

'Away with them, quickly, while they're hot.' she commanded the two waiters. Mustafa stepped back to let them pass. Satanaya sat down and wiped her brow with a cloth and took a large swig from a glass of water. She looked up and noticed the visitor.

'So, it was *you*!' began Mustafa. 'Tell me I'm not imagining it. In Damascus. Gosh, it must be more than ten years ago.'

'So, you remember.'

'You were there? I asked to see the chef, but they said you'd left.'

'Look, I was tired. It had been a long day. I just wanted to get to bed.'

'So, who are you exactly? One day you are working in an Italian cook-shop in Damascus, then you are a waitress in a Beirut villa. I heard you lived with an Egyptian princess in Constantinople and next you appear as a baroness waltzing among the elite of Sofia. And now here you are back in the kitchen cooking lentil soup like only my mother ever made for me.

SOFIA AND THE DRUMS OF WAR   103

What next, the first female Grand Vizier?'

Satanaya grinned. 'Here, have a glass of our best cooking brandy.' She got a bottle down from a shelf, filled two glasses and pushed one across the table. 'We have dear old Sultan Abdul Hamid to thank,' she said, and gave a brief synopsis of her family's flight from the Caucasus to Palestine.

Satanaya and Mustafa barely made it back upstairs to the party that evening. They sat across from each other at the kitchen table recounting their life stories. Mustafa told of his early years in Salonica,.

'It was a great place to grow up. It was just as cosmopolitan as Constantinople, and much more modern in its thinking. Everyone seemed to get on, whatever their religion or race. There were a lot of Jews, and Greeks of course. My mother had insisted I go to a religious school, which I did briefly. But it was so conservative, all we seemed to do was recite Koran. And we had to wear those baggy pants – *shalwar* – that kind of thing. You would have laughed.

'Anyway, my father hated all this, but he didn't like to go against Mother who is so traditional. In the end he persuaded her that the local state school with a modern secular curriculum would be more suitable.'

When Mustafa was seven, his father, a customs officer with a failing timber business, died of drink and depression. His mother, a young woman of twenty-seven was left to raise him and his sister on a meagre pension. They went to live in the country a while, but later returned to Salonica where he was enrolled in the military secondary school.

'After school we used to hang around the cafés on the waterfront. That was where the revolution really began. We were too young of course. We would get chased out of the drinking places. But we knew what was going on and wanted to be involved. It was a struggle between the old and the new, and of course, we wanted the new, it was so exciting.'

'It still is, don't you think?' said Satanaya.

'Yes, but it's got bogged down in politics. Look at the way the Committee have been handling things back home. That was never the way we wanted it. If you had been in Salonica the day the Sultan gave in and re-instated the Constitution! People were dancing in the streets, everyone was hugging, everyone was everyone's brother. What happened? The same greed and self-interest, the same petty power struggles carried on. And now everyone is an enemy of the State. And who is the State? Well, we don't have to mention names, do we?'

'Yes, I heard them talking upstairs. Do you really think Enver Pasha wants to be Sultan?'

'He'd like to be. He probably thinks he is already, having married a princess. But he'll get us all into trouble with his Pan-Islamic fantasies. He's courting the Germans, but that'll end in tears. Anyone who allies himself with the crazy Wilhelm is bound to end up in trouble.'

'So what are you going to do about it?'

'I'm not afraid to speak my mind, but I'm a soldier. I don't believe in mixing soldiering with politics. It's one or the other. So, for now, I'll just try and do this job as best I can, and hope the politicians don't interfere too much.'

'But how does your being in the army improve the country? Surely it needs political guidance?'

'Of course. Look, the country – Turkey that is – is in a poor state. But we need to be able to defend our borders, otherwise there'll be no Turkey. And first, the army needs completely overhauling; modernising; we have got rid of most of the old guard, but old habits die hard. The Committee is asking the Germans to come and reorganise and train us. But you'll see, the Germans aren't doing this out of kindness. Why do you think they are paying for the railways? They smell Persian oil. At the end of the day, they are after an empire. They envy the British and the French with their colonies in Africa and Asia. But I believe those times are over. And a strong modern army is our only hope of retaining our lands and consolidating our heritage. Look how the Russians and Austrians have already eaten away at our Balkan territories, and Britain all but owns Cyprus and Egypt. I know we only have ourselves to blame – but the time comes when it has to stop.'

'Wow! You really do believe this, don't you? You really are a revolutionary.' Satanaya wasn't being facetious. She was secretly impressed by the force of Mustafa's little oration.

'You do see this, don't you?' Mustafa looked at Satanaya as if for confirmation. But Satanaya wasn't simply an audience. Her listening became for him a mirror where his ideas could be mapped out and considered, then judged. Primarily by himself, and accepted, or not, as the case may be.

'Go on.' she said.

'Look how your family was driven from the Caucasus. It was the same here in the Balkans. My own homeland, my heartland – Salonica – gone. And all those thousands of dead, and more fleeing and homeless. Even my mother and sister, refugees like your parents, forced to flee, walking hundreds of miles, leaving everything. It doesn't make sense, but it happens. It's essential that we first stabilise things, and that means a strong army to stand up against these crazy people who would destroy us. Then the real revolution can happen, the revolution in the minds of the people. And the people become a nation.'

'Does the Committee understand this? Does Enver?'

'Yes, but sometimes I think Enver's more interested in his own self-image than the safety of the country. More interested in his beautiful engraved rifles and his tailored uniforms….'

Footsteps on the stairs and the figure of Madame Hortense loomed in the kitchen doorway.

'Ah, so that's where you've been hiding.' said the hostess, 'We thought Major Mustafa had kidnapped you and ridden off into the Stara Planina, but it seems it's Satanaya who has captured the Turk.'

'Ah, if only I had my horse,' Satanaya sighed. 'That's the one thing I do miss here in Bulgaria.'

'Circassians and their horses. Of course.' said Mustafa, 'That can easily be arranged. A military attaché has of necessity certain privileges. Perhaps you would accompany me on a ride out to Mount Vitosha when the fine weather comes.'

'If you provide the horses, I'll bring the picnic' said Satanaya.

'Yes, Vitosha in the springtime.' said Madame Hortense, 'You have a treat in store, Satanaya. Now, come on you two, join us for coffee and sweets. Everybody is raving about the quince dessert – Mustafa, you simply must try it.'

SIXTEEN

Delirium on Mount Vitosha

Sofia, 1914

ITH THE LENGTHENING days at the end of March, the air warmed and the first storks of the year appeared in the skies above Sofia. They circled, gathering in groups and performing their helicoidal dance on the rising thermals over Mount Vitosha and all along the Stara Planina, the great Balkan range which stretches east across northern Bulgaria to the Black Sea.

Mustafa and Satanaya set out early on horseback from the stables of the Turkish Legation with a substantial picnic of *börek*, a humus of *fava* beans, fat Gemlik olives, stuffed cabbage leaves and a couple of bottles of Hungarian champagne. Before them the morning sunshine reflected in a bright haze off the eastern flank of the mountain.

The outskirts of Sofia still showed the scattered remnants of wooden houses of the old Turkish town. These poorer quarters, simple timber-framed hovels with walls made of adobe and flattened tin cans, their canvas roofs weighed down with rocks, had been erected by refugees from the Balkan Wars. Though poor in contrast to the newly-built central city, nonetheless there reigned an atmosphere of light-heartedness as the inhabitants went about their business in the open air markets, at the wood-fired bakeries and street cafes. Smoke from breakfast fires drifted over the settlements. The roads here were mostly unpaved, and aside from the very occasional omnibus or lorry, little in the way of motorised transport frequented these outlying parts.

The suburbs gave way to small farms, laid out with terraced orchards where the land stepped up the first slopes of the Vitosha massif. The plan was to head up to the village of Vladaya by following the river Vladayska, up to the famous Golden Bridges, a river of stones, where they would have their picnic. The track was lined with spindly birch, conifers and thick shrubbery. The spilt coin of last year's leaves covered the ground, glowing wet and dark in the morning light. As they climbed higher, ebullient streams of snowmelt crashed down through rocky crevasses, the turbulent water raising a fine mist over the land. They led their horses on foot over narrow wooden bridges, or waded them through the smaller rivulets. By mid-morning they reached a spot high enough to see the whole of Sofia spread out below them. The spring sun was warm and they dismounted. The land was alive with the drip-plop tinkle of water and the twitter and chatter of songbirds, flitting from bush to branch, dipping and drinking from rocks in the stream.

Mustafa's duties as military attaché involved establishing and main-taining a network of sympathetic agents around the country. Often busy with trips out of the city, today was the first opportunity he'd had to spend time with Satanaya since their conversation in Madame Hortense's kitchen. He had recently been promoted Lieutenant-Colonel and this invitation to Vitosha was by way of celebration.

'I'm so glad you agreed to come today,' said Mustafa, 'This takes me back to my childhood. After my father died, we moved from Salonica to my uncle's farm in the country. I loved it there – the hard work, the fresh air, working with animals and the land. I missed school, but being close to nature I learnt to appreciate what most of my fellow Turks do all their lives, scraping a living from the earth.'

'You were lucky then. Some would say blessed.' said Satanaya.

'How do you mean?'

'Well, you were educated by nature itself.'

'I'm not sure I follow.'

'You were made aware of the earth from an early age, you learnt to respect your origin. Some people say that's the half of religion, to appreciate life from the ground up.'

'And what's the other half? The mullah and the *papaz*?' Mustafa looked mockingly at Satanaya.

'No, I don't mean that, not at all...' Satanaya wondered why he was covering up his sensitive side, with his jokes, and his severity. 'I don't know... perhaps that's just it, the not knowing, and then the wanting to know. The discovering, the yearning we have, to rise up from the earth, like a plant or a tree, to fly like the birds, to be magnificent like this mountain.' She turned and gazed up at the brooding mass of Vitosha. She was quiet for a while, lost in this vision. She continued:

'When I see all this magnificence, all this beauty outside, it stirs something within me... something in me wants to connect with this beauty but I can only gaze at it in wonder... and the more I gaze, the more the beauty in the scene seems to fade and I'm left with rocks and trees, and all the while this something inside me is still yearning. It frustrates me. It irritates me. And it makes me want to discover what that something is. To discover myself from the outside in.'

Mustafa was silent. He looked around at the wide horizon, and then back at the Circassian girl. 'Yes,' he thought to himself, 'there is something to be discovered, something of value in this world, and something of value inside me.' But he kept these thoughts to himself.

'My country is my religion.' he said. 'This is what I am discovering, that is what I value above all else. It's with me all the time. That's my connection, to the earth beneath me. And not just the land, but the people in it. It's the people who carry the soul of the country, who make it not simply an expanse of trees and rocks and earth. They give it meaning. Can you understand that, Satanaya? It's my passion. I don't know how to explain it, but like your beauty and magnificence, I believe it is something concrete, to be held onto, cared for, valued. And perhaps we have to fight for this too. I don't mean war for war's sake, but to protect it and struggle to bring it to its real potential. And not to give in to those who would take that potential for their own ends, whether inside or outside. We need to discover who we are as a nation and bring that to light. Maybe you think that's blasphemous, but that is my religion, my faith.'

'Then it is a religion of love.' said Satanaya

'Yes, I suppose you could call it that. It certainly has the power to keep me awake at night.' Mustafa laughed.

They rode on and by mid-morning they reached Vladaya, a large village surrounded by small holdings. It was a purely Bulgarian village, with a small Roma camp on the outskirts. The rich smell of coffee brewing wafted up from a little shack on the street outside of which a few old men sat smoking pipes. The two riders were observed with some curiosity, and not a little suspicion. They sorely would have liked to stop for a coffee but memories of the Turkish occupation and the recent conflict were still very much alive in the rural population. Mustafa's Turkish-accented Bulgarian would immediately have been recognised and Satanaya could only have communicated in Russian, which might not have been welcome either, so they didn't linger.

From Vladaya the riverside path took a turn to the left, and they rode on until midday when they arrived at the famous Golden Bridges of the Vladayska River. These 'bridges' were in fact a 'stone river' – a mile-long cascade of massive rounded boulders which poured down the mountain-side in a swathe more than a hundred yards wide. The 'golden' stones, some taller than Satanaya and Mustafa, and weighing hundreds of tons, were named for the bright yellow-coloured lichens which covered their smooth surface. Scattered around were smaller stones, thousands of evenly shaped cobbles just like the ones that paved the streets of Sofia. They stopped for lunch. The horses drank from the river. The air was still and the sun warm.

'I wonder if we can reach the top of the mountain?' said Satanaya.

'We could try, it doesn't look too far. We're already more than a thousand metres up, just another thousand to go. ' Mustafa had a military map of the area. 'Of course we'll have to avoid the stone runs, it's dangerous for the horses. And there may be too much snow right at the top. We'd better not waste time if we don't want to be caught in the dark.'

They set off, the horses making good way, as the land plateaued out from time to time in wide flat steps bare of any substantial vegetation.

They had been going for about an hour when the first clouds appeared, floating in the deep blue high over the summit of Vitosha. They hadn't worried at first, as they didn't look like rainclouds. Then the temperature dropped and with it descended a fine mist, rolling in billows from higher up the mountain. Mustafa now led the way from the front, but in minutes they were wrapped in a dense fog, so thick that Satanaya could no longer make out the shape of horse and rider in front.

'Mustafa, where are you?'

'Here, I've stopped. Can you see me? Follow my voice.'

'Keep talking. I'm dismounting. I'll walk towards you.'

Mustafa began to sing, a song of the cafes in Salonica:*

> 'We were caught in a storm
> driven to endless depths
>
> Our union, my love
> must wait until life unfurls
>
> Our union, my love
> comes to us in the next world
>
> And as the coffee in the pot began to boil and rise
> so my coy love's words flowed o'er her lips and eyes
>
> Fresh coffee boils and swirls upon the stove
> dagger in my belt and rifle in my arms, my love
>
> Rotting in this prison, tossing side to side
> I look through every window for my brown-eyed girl'

It took some time before Satanaya got her bearings from Mustafa's singing. The sound did strange things in the mist, and more than once she was fooled by the echo. She was no more than a foot away when she spied the dark saddle and khaki-clad leg of the rider. She grabbed hold of his boot.

'There you are at last.' she said

Mustafa leant down and looked closely at her face.

---

* Bir fırtına tuttu bizi deryaya kardı –
  https://www.youtube.com/watch?v=O1IAn0nYiIU

'Ah, it seems I have acquired a *rikab-dar*.'*

'Oh, and look who thinks he's the Sultan! Or did you just catch the eye of his horse? You should be so lucky!'

'My God, this mist is thick. I thought you must have been wandering about on purpose to tease me! What took you so long?'

'Well, the singing for one. It sounded like a shepherd calling his sheep.'

A strong breeze blew across the mountain side, and for a moment the mist cleared. Then the sky darkened and the first snow began to fall. Within minutes they were wrapped inside a blizzard. Mustafa dismounted.

'We must find somewhere to sit this out,' he said. 'There are some big trees up ahead, I saw them when the mist cleared. Here, give me your hand, I don't want to lose you again.'

Something in the way he said this warmed Satanaya. She'd weathered worse storms on the plains of Konya, but his words were comforting nonetheless. They reached the trees, which sheltered them from the worst of the snow. But the storm didn't show any signs of letting up.

Mustafa unrolled the map again.

'We must be about here,' he said, pointing with his gloved finger to an elevation line at fourteen hundred metres. 'If we cross this woods, and skirt round the side of the mountain, we should end up at this monastery, marked here.' He pointed on the map to a small cross in a circle.

'Why can't we go back the way we came?' queried Satanaya.

'We could, but crossing the stone river in this snow would be dangerous – not just for us, but for the horses. You saw those cobbles – in the snow they'd be invisible and we don't want to risk laming these fellows. Then we'd really be stuck. The monastery – if it still exists, this is a pre-war map – is on a road that would bring us back to Vladaya.'

They led their mounts slowly through the gloomy woods, the snow gaining depth as they went. Mustafa was well trained in orienteering, and with his compass, and a good sense of keeping on a level altitude, after about an hour he reckoned that they were more or less above the supposed monastery. They began a slow, careful descent. By now the snow was too deep for Satanaya to walk in her thick skirts, so she remounted and with the horses tied in line, Mustafa led the way. Twenty minutes later they

---

* literally: one who holds the stirrup, a high-ranking member of the Sultan's personal household.

came to a tumbledown stone wall.

The monastery did indeed exist, though in a state of dilapidation. It comprised just a couple of buildings, no different from the farm buildings of the area, and a chapel. They unsaddled the horses in an empty stable, gave them a good rubbing down with a couple of old grain sacks and went to explore the rest of the property. The chapel had a big padlock on the door, but Mustafa had no trouble disengaging the levers of the simple lock with a long nail. Inside it was dark. He struck a match, and found some candle stumps in a niche by the door. He lit them, and held them aloft.

They found themselves surrounded by the most magnificent gallery of wall paintings. In bright colours were depicted the trials, tribulations and temptations of a holy man, glowingly handsome angels fighting shrivelled black devils, and vivid portrayals of well known biblical scenes: there was Solomon, sword in one hand while holding aloft a naked babe in the other, solving the dispute between the two claimant mothers; here Abraham's raised dagger was being stayed by the angel above poor little Isaac, the substitute ram quivering in the background; another showed Jesus touching the eyes of the blind man and delivering the healing spirit. In the centre of one wall, a large portrait: the red-robed Saint Nikola, kindly-faced and forgiving. Beneath a pair of carved gilded dragons, the iconostasis showed a regular line-up of the usual suspects: gold-haloed disciples six-a-side of the team coach, but with one telling empty frame.

'Beautiful, aren't they?' The owner of this soft voice had slipped in unnoticed. 'I'm sorry I wasn't able to greet you. The snow you see. It makes everything so quiet. I was coming in myself to light a candle, but I saw someone had beaten me to it.'

The voice carried on in Turkish. 'I saw your horses, too – Turkish saddles, not those awful wooden Bulgarian ones – I should know, I bought and sold enough of them during the war.'

The speaker turned out to be a Roma horse-trader, who had worked both sides of the border in the troubles, and now was employed with his wife as caretaker for the monastery which had been deserted since the last abbot died.

'You are welcome to stay here the night. I don't expect you want to go back out in this weather. My wife is cooking some dinner; perhaps you would honour us with your company?'

The horse-trader's name was Pipindorio. His family was originally

Iberian and had fled Lisbon in the 16th century after the massacres had made things difficult for anyone with such loose affiliations as the Roma. They came to Salonica, along with the Jews and the remnants of the Moors. His wife, Merripen, he claimed (for she only spoke Bulgarian) came from Persia.

Pipindorio led them back across the yard and up some stone steps to a large room above the stables. Merripen was sitting in front of a grate, stirring onions in a pot over a small fire. She blushed when they entered. Supper was a simple country stew of vegetables and potatoes, bread, and supplemented with the remains of the picnic. A bottle of Hungarian champagne seemed to work magic on the old couple, and when Pipindorio brought down an old violin and began to play in the style of the Roma, Merripen got up and danced.

It was a slow dance, in which she distilled all the wild movements and controlled abandon of her youth, when she had danced around the open fire on the plains of Hungary, her emerald green eyes and flashing teeth capturing all the restless hearts of the boys. Now she simply turned and swayed with the calm repose of river water reaching a bend, smiling eyes resting on the chosen Pipindorio. The mood came upon Pipindorio and with it a bottle of sljivo, from which he filled four glasses. With an heroic call, he downed his drink in one and signalled the others to do likewise. He refilled the glasses and took up his fiddle again, this time playing some more uptempo melodies, in a style all his own, a kind of marriage of Andalusian flamenco rhythms with local Balkan melodies. More sljivo was drunk and soon Mustafa was on his feet singing.

Mustafa sang a few of the folk songs he remembered from his Salonica days, tunes which Pipindorio picked up instantly, and together they danced a brisk *kalamatianos* around the room. Satanaya joined in, improvising on traditional Circassian steps. Even Merripen caught the mood and before long the old beams of the monastery kitchen were resounding to stamping feet and the rippling crescendos of Pipindorio's bow. The music and dance continued until a second bottle of slivo had been drained.

Then, at the height of their joyful delirium, in one of those moments when all fall silent in unison, as when angels pass overhead, they realised how late it was and how tired they were. Merripen without ceremony shooed the young couple into a small adjoining room with a bundle of blankets and quilts, while she and her husband curled up for the night on the rough divan that lined one wall of the kitchen.

✳ ✳ ✳

A moment of delicious tension stretched time for the two riders, lost and found on Mount Vitosha, as they faced each other beneath the roof beams in the candlelight. Both were drunk, it has to be said. And although sentiments of intimacy naturally arose, Satanaya was still able to find a mindful place from where she could observe the situation beyond the attraction, the weighty gravitational pull of her own physical wants. If there was to be a relationship with this man, it was going to have to be on different terms. Mustafa for his part, was strangely shy again. In his own mind Satanaya represented a possibility of a type of relationship that he was only beginning to comprehend – that of equality, of partnership. The fact that this was in his mind more than in his body was also something new. Although he too felt drawn towards a physical union, yet he knew he could not be the one to make the first move. And Satanaya knew this too. They looked at each other with such fondness, such warmth, as waves of emotion met between them and mingled. Yet each held back.

Afterwards they often wondered why. It was a perfect situation, made for love. Maybe that was it. There was no doubting that some kind of union was occurring in their eyes, their breath even, lightly mingling in the small room. Could that possibly be enough? In the event, Satanaya took the initiative, expressing how happily tired she was, and embraced Mustafa closely and long. Then she kissed him gently once below his ear, and declared that she must sleep. This sustained contact between clothed bodies was sufficient to dissolve the tension Mustafa felt in himself, so that he too meekly succumbed to the suggestion, and the two rolled themselves up side by side in their separate cocoons of quilts and blankets, each wondering, in their own way, as they melted into their chrysalid sleep whether the imaginal cells of their desires might transform them in the night to wake as butterflies.

They woke to a world by light transformed, the brightness of a deep blue heaven above a pure white earth. At least it was white for the first hour of their return journey along the riverside track. Then as quickly as the snow had come, like a dreamt vision it faded, as a warm wind moved up from the south and snow in great clumps began to fall from the trees. Soon the view took on the appearance of a mangy magpied landscape. The two riders looked at each other with a strange longing. Each knew something had passed between them. Something that would remain. A connection. A relationship. Whether it was love, and love in time, time alone would tell. For now the snow, like the memory, was melting, and the so-solid earth that yesterday had lost them to themselves, returned them to itself today.

SEVENTEEN

A Night at the Opera

Sofia – Constantinople, April-May 1914

ATANAYA RETURNED from her excursion on Mount Vitosha in a strangely buoyant mood. In spite of the natural longing that the affair had awoken in her, she was rather pleased that she had not fallen under the spell of the handsome Lieutenant-Colonel. Well, not completely. Just a little fallen. She had enjoyed herself in the shallow waters and though the open seas were attractive, she knew the currents were unpredictable and she was hesitant to let herself be drawn in deeper.

The conversation as they rode back into Sofia was a didactic affair. This time Satanaya felt less like a mirror and more like a blackboard upon which the teacher inscribed his lesson. Nevertheless she listened with interest as Mustafa expounded his ideas on modernising Turkey. He had come across Bulgarian Turks who had successfully entered commerce, running modern businesses and trading generally – occupations which in the Ottoman Empire were for the most part the preserve of foreigners. His friend Shakir was a Member of Parliament and also engaged in manufacturing and export. And Mustafa was impressed by the way many Turkish ladies in Bulgaria had stopped wearing the veil.

'The key to progress,' said Mustafa confidently to the air around him, as if addressing a crowded auditorium, 'lies in education. Modern education, like in Europe, based in science and the arts. An education for all, men and women, from the peasants to the bourgeoisie. It's the only way we can rescue the Empire from this sinkhole of despond we have fallen into. We must become a viable player in the modern world, and this won't happen as long as we remain bound to the past, to the superstitions of the mullahs and the greed and corruption of the officials. We have to free ourselves of the baggage of past centuries.'

The biggest obstacles in educating the masses, he told Satanaya, were the language and the script. The language of all official communication and documentation was Ottoman, a hybrid of Turkish, Persian and Arabic vocabulary and constructions set within a Turkish syntax. Turkish has at least eight vowel sounds and was written in the Arabic alphabet, which script allows for only three vowel indicators, and even these were commonly omitted in printed texts.

'It's no wonder most of the population has remained illiterate. If you try to talk to the country people in the court language of Constantinople, they just laugh. We must have a new script, based on the Latin alphabet. And simplify the language, bring back the everyday words which the country folk still use. We need to drop all these elaborate Persian phrases and Arabic religious language if our people are going to be able to communicate with each other and be taken seriously in the modern world.'

Mustafa talked in this vein most of the way back to the stables, reiterating his view that before anything else, Turkey must secure its borders with a strong military force, well trained with modern weapons.

'And manufacturing. We must learn to manufacture goods for ourselves instead of having to import everything. Look at the influence Germany is gaining over us with its railway projects. And all our armaments come from abroad. If we don't learn to make things for ourselves and stand on our own feet, we'll always be the Sick Man of Europe.'

Although Satanaya just nodded as Mustafa poured out his ideas, she was secretly excited by the strength of vision that animated his words. She wondered at the changes that would be needed in order to bring his revolutionary ideas to pass. Again she had sensed something out of the ordinary in this man. And while previously she had sensed it as a danger to herself, now she saw something else, a glimpse of the unstoppable, like the tide itself, a movement of destiny that enveloped his being and drew her into its flow. Could she be a part of that process? Or would a relationship hinder or divert this? To be witness to the unfolding of this dream... the thought both thrilled and scared her.

They parted at the tram stop.

'I really enjoyed our time together, Satanaya,' said Mustafa, as he took her hand in a farewell gesture. 'It meant a lot to me.'

'I'm sure you say that to all the girls you lure up to your mountain hideaway.' She laughed gaily. 'And then you cast us away as soon as a fresh face appears. I know all about you army officers.'

Mustafa blushed. 'Not at all, truly.' he began. But remembering the all-too-brief liaisons of the past he blushed even deeper. 'No, I felt we... something... you know... Look, we must meet again, and soon I hope.'

'So you can tell me more of your plans for when you conquer the world?'

'The world? No, that would be Enver you're thinking of. Turkey is enough for me.'

'And would he lure me up the mountain?'

'No, not you, you're a mere baroness. He prefers princesses.'

The clanging bell of the approaching tram cut short their words of farewell.

'And I prefer Lieutenant-Colonels.' said Satanaya, smiling as she stepped onto the tram. They exchanged a brief but lingering look sewn with shy threads of longing. Mustafa savoured the sweetness of Satanaya's parting words as he walked back to his hotel.

Shortly afterwards, Mustafa and Shakir Bey rented a house together, not far from where Fethi Bey, the head of the Turkish Diplomatic Mission, lived. To celebrate, they held a small housewarming party, and Mustafa called on Satanaya for help with the catering side of things. The guest of honour was the Bulgarian Minister of Justice, and the fare included the finest Russian caviar and Louis Roederer Cristal champagne which Satanaya procured through her Khedivial contacts in Constantinople, and plenty of quadruple-distilled arak from the Touma distillery in Lebanon.

The evening was a great success, and word of the excellent hospitality quickly went round the corridors of power in the Bulgarian Parliament. Soon afterwards a little bird intimated to Shakir Bey that General Kovatchev, the Minister of War, would entertain positively an invitation from the dashing young Turkish Military Attaché. For such an occasion an even greater effort was required, especially as Madame Kovatcheva was also attending. Satanaya presented a choice of hors d'oeuvres – mezes – prepared in the Palace style: baby bamya – ladies fingers – no bigger than the end of one's finger, and tiny yaprak dolması made from the first translucent vine leaves of the season, delicate mücver – fritters of grated courgette and white cheese, and Sarayiçi artichokes purchased out of the back gate of the Topkapi Palace. The entrée was a dish of tender braised lamb wrapped in aubergine, and almond keşkül for dessert. The evening proved a diplomatic triumph for Mustafa, on the strength of which he gained entry to the upper echelons of Bulgarian society.

* * *

In Constantinople, spring turned into early summer. In May, Amina Khanoum and the Colonel Efendi arrived home from Egypt, and sent word inviting Satanaya to rejoin them in the konak without delay. This sudden recall confirmed a prescience in Satanaya that her time in Bulgaria was coming to an end. But she couldn't leave without a proper farewell to her friend Mustafa who was up country at the time, meeting some factory owners in Plevna. The trip was a cover for his main task in making contact with his agents. While gathering useful knowledge of a military nature, he was also indulging his passion for battle strategy, sizing up the terrain and inspecting the ruined redoubts of the great seige of 1877-78. It was a shame, for that coming Saturday Verdi's opera Aida, which Amina Khanoum's grandfather, the Khedive Ismail, had commissioned, was to be performed at the theatre in Slavskaya Street. She telegraphed Mustafa from the Legation, informing him of her decision to return to Constantinople the following week, and hoping he could make it back to Sofia in time for a farewell evening at the opera.

* * *

With his slim build Mustafa always cut a fine figure however he dressed, and that evening in his top hat and swallowtail coat, white silk waistcoat and tie, with a fine diamond pin lent him by Shakir, he sparkled more than ever. The opera too seemed to have lit a fire in him. Although the humble staging by the recently formed company of Sofia might not have impressed the habitués of the Wiener Hofoper or La Scala, the singing was competent enough; and what the production lacked in costume and decor was adequately compensated by the ostentation of the female members of the audience, who offered an abundance of organdie, tulle and chiffon in gowns of lemon yellow, cornflower blue, ivory and blushing pink, their strings of pearls clasped with diamonds and sapphire, rubies and emeralds. It was joked that the burglars of Sofia had taken the night off, as their potential swag had all gone to the opera. Most of the Cabinet were attending along with many Members of Parliament, high level military personel and most of the Corps Diplomatiques, as well as the Exarch of the Bulgarian Orthodox Church and anyone at all with pretentions to Sofia society.

As the audience mingled during an interval in the performance, General Kovatchev beckoned Mustafa and his friends to join his party. Introductions were made: another old soldier, former Chief of Staff, General Petrov, was there with his family, as well as Kovatchev's younger daughter, Dimitrina, recently returned from studying music in Geneva, and who was just coming out in society. This convivial meeting was a continuation of the *entente cordiale* begun previously when they had all attended a fancy dress ball. On that occasion, Mustafa had been the talk of the ball, when he had appeared in the flowing robes and headdress of a Turkish Janissary, especially procured for the evening from the military museum in Constantinople.

Kovatchev was himself a revolutionary in his youth, and had like Mustafa become a Lieutenant-Colonel at the age of thirty-two. Recently he had led the opposing Bulgarian forces against Mustafa during the battle of Bulayır in the Balkan Campaign. They had a lot in common. And Madame Kovatcheva was a well-known hostess in her own right. Now here they were all together performing intricate diplomatic *pas de deux* surrounded by family members.

'It's all so cosy.' Satanaya was thinking to herself, remembering the difficult war years she had spent in Constantinople, 'Can it really be so simple, so easy? To fight, then sit down and chat as if those terrible events had never happened?'

Mustafa was playing to the crowd that evening, being charming to the ladies, making sage and intelligent conversation with his male counterparts. Satanaya looked at the young Dimitrina, hardly more than half her age, the same age when she herself had set out from Seydnaya with a broken heart. And she noticed how the girl was gazing up with wide eyes at Mustafa, hanging on his every word, unaware of just how dangerous it would be if… No, Satanaya said to herself, she mustn't let herself think like that. She was leaving in a few days, anyway, leaving all this behind, perhaps for good. Nevertheless, in her heart she felt banished to a no man's land of confusion in her emotions.

In the event their parting, which took place later that night after the opera, was an awkward affair. What might have been an intimate, tender moment was inhibited by the good-hearted bonhomie of the gathered force of marshals, matrons and maidens of the Bulgarian elite. A polite kiss upon a gloved hand, a frustrated exchange of glances as Mustafa helped her into her carriage, a brief wave, and that was that.

✳ ✳ ✳

With Satanaya gone, Mustafa, whose heart had for months past been so gently prised open with the culinary delights and conversational pleasures of this beautiful Circassian lady, slowly but surely tumbled into love with the lovely Dimitrina. And Dimitrina, the innocent girl from a wealthy and successful Bulgarian family, also fell head over her tiny heels in love with Mustafa.

Mustafa entered this new career phase with ease. Companioned by his friend Fethi, who had himself become enamoured of General Petrov's daughter, their lights were shining brightly in the crepuscular interlude which presaged the darkness about to descend upon Europe and the Middle East. Back in Turkey, the Triumvirate had established a degree of stability, albeit at the price of democracy. But at least the army and navy were being revitalised under Enver and Djemal respectively. For the time being Mustafa felt he could relax and benefit from this excursion in Europe.

Mustafa became a regular visitor at the Kovatchevs, discussing strategy and politics with the General, and at the balls that Balkan spring he danced almost exclusively with Dimitrina. It was assumed to be a political liaison, the Turk paying court to the Bulgar by paying compliments to his daughter. But the conversation on the dance floor was of music and love, albeit with a good dose of Mustafa's ideologies for a new Turkey; and as both were the outcome of his inner passion, even his talk of women's rights were to the open heart of Dimitrina a kind of wooing. And Dimitrina responded with all the puppy-eyed devotion of a young girl's first falling in love.

That thoughts of marriage should eventually come to speech between them was inevitable. Love's malaise is infectious. Paralleling the blossoming romance between Mustafa and Dimitrina, Fethi Bey's liaison with the daughter of General Petrov continued apace. Both paramours had marriage in their sights. But after the balls were over, and the most subtle of diplomatic overtures sounded, the drawbridge to the castle of their desires was raised and the portcullis of parental disapproval lowered. It seemed that although the wounds of recent conflicts might have healed, the cultural dread of the heathen Turk that had existed for centuries in Christian lands proved an irremediable affliction.

While General Kovatchev and his wife discreetly dropped Mustafa from their social list, the father of Fethi's beloved declared he would sooner submit to the stake of Vlad the Impaler than have his daughter impaled by the love lance of a Turk, or words to that effect.

✳ ✳ ✳

Satanaya's return from Sofia was greeted with much joy and fuss from Amina Khanoum, whose well-informed social network had already apprised her of her companion's burgeoning relationship with the dashing young officer from Salonica. It was with some sadness that Satanaya had to update her friend with her suspicions regarding the young Bulgarian maiden.

Eventually a letter came from Mustafa confirming her fears. For some reason it was written in awkward French. Perhaps he had forgotten that Satanaya's Turkish was now quite advanced. Whatever, it was definitely awkward. In it he urged her to forget him, saying he knew he wasn't worthy, that they would always have Mount Vitosha, its misty snows, the plum brandy and the music.

Yet, while Mustafa's heart may have turned upon a different mountain track of hopeless yearning for the young Dimitrina Kovatcheva, a heart is still a heart. Its nature is to feel and love, even in the wilderness of separation, and Satanaya's heart felt hurt. Memories of misty snows and plum brandy are poor compensation when not accompanied in the flesh by a good man who sings and dances rebetiko. Perhaps he wasn't such a good man after all. Well, she had always known he was dangerous, right from the first time she saw him across a crowded cafe in Damascus those years before. So there was no surprise really. And although hurt, and perhaps also angry with Mustafa, she couldn't feel jealousy for Dimitrina, young, beautiful and European. His letter continued in florid poesy (a cover for his own personal guilt – so obvious, thought Satanaya) on themes of the impossibility of distant love and the futility of unrequited longing in such uncertain times.

She confided her feelings in a letter to Madame Hortense who replied, reassuringly, that the young Turk would soon discover a lot more of the impossibility of Bulgarian love and longing when General and Madame Kovatchev got to hear of their daughter's affair.

And so it had turned out. While in military matters Mustafa may have been a brilliant strategist, Satanaya concluded with a certain sweet bitterness that when it came to romance he was a novice. The General easily out-manoeuvered the Lieutenant-Colonel, even if simply by parental force majeure. Mustafa could have taken a lesson from the Circassians and galloped off into the sunset with the sweet Bulgarian maid. That might have proved his love, though at the risk of a third Balkan conflict. In the end she remembered the look on Mustafa's face as they rode back that morning from Vitosha, when he spoke in almost fanatical terms of his concern for his country. She knew then who was his real love, the one he would never exchange for any pretty face. And so while her heart forgave him for all that never was, she did not forget.

EIGHTEEN

When the Blast of War Blows

Bosnia, Bulgaria, Turkey, June 1914 –April 1915

 IKE THE GREAT *Nouras* of Hama, the waterwheel of time turns and returns refreshing with each repeated irrigation the slowly changing fields of human destiny. If we sow wheat, then wheat is harvested. If blood, then blood. In the relentless onslaught of Ottoman armies into Europe, on 28th June 1389, Sultan Murat sows Serbian blood on Kosovo's Field of Blackbirds, where he too succumbs to the curved blade of the assassin-knight Miloš Obilić.

Five hundred years pass and twenty-five more, and in 1914, on this date long drenched in mourning *in memoriam*, but since the Balkan Wars now a day of celebration, a rogue seed, done languishing in drawn out germination, pushes up in re-won Serbian soil. Its vigorous shoots surface in Sarajevo, where Catholics, Orthodox and Muslims, Serb, Croat and

Roma, have coexisted in explosive mix since 1909 when Austria-Hungary annexed Bosnia and Herzegovina.

What delinquent thought of the Austrian Emperor Franz Joseph prompts him to order his son Franz Ferdinand, a man of significant moustache and nervous eyes, to oversee military manoeuvres in Bosnia this June? And what arrogant whim decides the Archduke to visit Sarajevo on this day of such ill-omen?

The assassins and their Serbian nationalist controllers are evidently amateurs. The Archduke's car passes the Mostar Café where Mehmedbašić waits with his bomb. But the would-be assassin loses his nerve. The second assassin, Vaso, packing a pistol in addition to a bomb, also fails to make the grade. A third man, Nedelijko, positioned further down by the Miljacka River, manages to throw his bomb. However it falls into the folded-open canvas hood of Franz Ferdinand's car. Franz just flips it out behind him, where it explodes beneath the following vehicle, injuring more than a dozen bystanders. Nedelijko, having failed to kill the Archduke, is also unsuccessful in his suicide attempt. He takes his cyanide pill, and jumps into the river. Sadly for Nedelijko, the fates are against him. Bad cyanide, past its sell-by-date, he vomits up. And the river, down to a trickle in midsummer, denies him the luxury of drowning. The crowd grabs him and beats him up before he is arrested. Suicide bombing is still in its infancy.

One would think the Austrians and their entourage would get the message. But things now go from bad to worse, as Franz decides to press on with the programme. A suggestion that troops taking part in the manoeuvres might now be drafted in to guard the route is vetoed because the soldiers would not be dressed appropriately for the occasion. The show must go on, but standards must not be seen to slip.

Destiny is no amateur. Destiny is patient. Destiny has all the time in the world. It has covered the bases in Sarajevo today with a full chamber of assassins. Gavrilo (Gabriel) Princip, a thin-faced Bosnian of nineteen years is the son of a poor but rigorously strict farmer. At school he has been radicalised as a Serbian nationalist. To him, all things Austrian are anathema. The Archduke is delivered up to him on a plate, as the royal vehicle comes to a halt five feet from where the boy stands. Gavrilo's moment of destiny. He fires his pistol twice. In a matter of minutes both the Archduke Franz Ferdinand and his wife Sophie are dead. It is their wedding anniversary. Gavrilo is part of history. Now comes the reaping.

* * *

The telegram bringing news of the assassination in Sarajevo, barely 250 miles as the Serbian eagles fly over the Stara Planina to Sofia, dropped upon Mustafa's desk in the Turkish Legation unwelcome as a sprig of wormwood, that dark star bitter herb, precursor of death. It didn't take long for him to realise that this dirty and almost bungled murder in the Bosnian city would have repercussions far beyond the Balkans.

The Great Powers – Britain, France and Russia comprising the 'Entente', and Austria-Hungary, the 'Central Powers' – circled and parried in a preliminary *danse macabre*, choosing their partners for the inevitable conflagration. Turkey looked on. Most would have thought, leave well alone. But things are never that simple. Germany sided with the Austro-Hungarians, who saw themselves as the offended party. Austria-Hungary declared war on Serbia on 28th July. Germany declared war on Russia four days later, and on France two days afterwards. Germany wrong-footed their opponents by invading via Belgium, thus circumventing the line of forts on France's northern border. Germany expected that this strategy would win them France in six weeks. When they used this tactic twenty-five years later, with the advantage of fast modern tanks, they were successful. In 1914, however, the Belgian army, with the help of the British who declared war on 4th August, slowed the momentum of the Kaiser's troops sufficient for the French to mobilise and halt the advance at the Battle of the Marne in early September. Meanwhile, the Russians mobilised with uncharacteristic haste and attacked the Germany/Austria-Hungary alliance in the east, thus drawing troops of the Central Powers away from the Western Front to defend their eastern borders. And so the general situation of the war in Europe would remain thus, more or less, with a certain amount of to-ing and fro-ing as the Balkan countries entered the fray, and the Bolshevik Revolution occurred in 1917, until the Armistice in November 1918 brought most fighting to an end.

Turkey appeared to bide its time. Yet, even as the European powers began hostilities, Turkey had already initiated secret agreements to enter the war on the side of the 'Central Powers'. While the country remained neutral, the army was put on a war footing. Then in a covert operation ordered by Talaat Pasha, the Interior Minister and Enver Pasha, the Minister of War, the Ottoman navy bombarded Russian coastal towns in the Black Sea and sank a number of Russian vessels. Neither the Sultan himself, nor the Prime Minister nor the Ottoman High Command were privy to this decision. Britain, France and Russia declared war on Turkey which officially entered the war on 11th November 1914.*

Russia now began a push into eastern Turkey. At the same time Enver Pasha, as Commander in Chief, ordered an offensive to take the town of Sarıkamış on the Russian border.

Mustafa opposed the idea of war, for he doubted Germany could win. Like many in the Turkish military, he would have preferred an alliance with the Entente Powers. But the die was cast and his duty as a soldier was to serve his country as best he could. For now, however, in Sofia he felt hobbled like a camel, away from the action. Meanwhile Enver travelled to the army in Eastern Anatolia to try and sort out the chaos that had ensued in the wake of his ill-starred offensive.

Winter in the steppes of north-east Turkey is unrelenting: temperatures may fall below minus 30 degrees Centigrade. For months deep snow covers the plains; blizzards rage in the mountains which rise to over 3,000 metres, the whole within the purview of Mount Ararat, Noah's Landing, at 5,137 metres. In the final analysis, the battle for Sarıkamış represents perhaps the point of nemesis for Enver's ambitions. What possessed this man, in spite of the advice of his officers, to prosecute an offensive campaign, with insufficient preparation and support and complete disregard for the climatic conditions, resulting in the reduction of a force of 80,000 men to a tenth of that number, the greater part simply freezing to death where they collapsed on some ice-blasted mountain path? The same hubris that visited Napoleon when he took on the Russians? But Enver was no Napoleon.

The third member of the dictatorial triumvirate, the gangsters who were to run Turkey for the next four years, was Djemal Pasha, the Minister for the Navy. He was now appointed Governor of Syria from where he led a force against the British at the Suez Canal, with losses of 3,000 men. Turkish troops suffered a further 2,000 casualties in fighting near the Abadan oil refinery, in a futile attempt to gain control over British oil interests in the Persian Gulf.

---

* In later years people would accuse Mustafa of having brought down the Sultan, but really it was Enver who took the country to war, something which constitutionally only the Sultan had the authority to do.

With defeats on three widely separated fronts, Turkey's war had not begun well.

* * *

In late January 1915 Mustafa at last gained release from his Bulgarian post and returned to Constantinople to take up an appointment as commander of a Division. At the War Office he met Enver Pasha and was shocked at what he saw. No longer the bright star rising in the Ottoman firmament, he cut a pale, subdued figure.

'So, how was it?' said Mustafa. He was trying to find suitable words to greet his leader, something positive, but all that came out were words of pity. 'You look all in.'

'Oh no, not really… You know, war… We fight, don't we?' Enver seemed distracted, distant. He too wasn't comfortable with this meeting.

'And now, how is it out there?' Mustafa persisted, referring to the war in the east.

'Oh, fine, fine. It's all going to plan.' Enver's detachment was evident, as if addressing some irrelevant bystander, rather than one of his commanders. That the battle for Sarıkamış had been an unmitigated disaster was no secret, in spite of the ban on reporting which Enver had ordered.

Mustafa felt strangely ashamed, embarrassed even, by this exchange. Ashamed for his country having been led into such a pass. And embarrassed that this person, his commander, once heralded as hero, could appear in such denial. Enver didn't seem to know anything about Mustafa's appointment and referred him to his general staff, who seemed to share their commander's vacuity.

* * *

In the event, it was the fear of an invasion much closer to home that resolved the issue for Mustafa. He was sent to Tekirdağ, a modest seaport town of ancient heritage west of Constantinople where he took the command of the newly-formed 19th division. With barely time to organise a single regiment he was ordered to the Gallipoli Peninsula following the commencement of the Allied naval bombardment of the Dardanelles Straits.

This narrow waterway stretches between the Gallipoli Peninsula on the European side, and Turkey in Asia. It is the gateway from the Aegean

Sea to Constantinople on the Marmara Sea, and thence through the Bosphorus to the Black Sea and Russia.

The details of Mustafa's role in the Gallipoli campaign has become the stuff of myth and mystery. Month on month of savage trench warfare, of young men charging at dawn with unloaded rifles – 'nothing up the spout!' – only fixed bayonets to ensure that they must reach the enemy trench or die in the attempt, to take a few feet of ground, only to be cut down by the deadly sickle of machine gun fire. It would be easy in the tidal wash of history to absolve ourselves of the responsibility of war. Yet we relive the battle of Gallipoli, as we do all the battles before Troy and since, as if some lesson we never quite learn… and so, once more unto the breach…

But for Mustafa it was simple. His homeland was being invaded, and his job was to defend it. Never mind that some old men in London had sat around for months discussing the possibility of the great Royal Navy charging through the Dardanelles with their mighty dreadnoughts to stand off Constantinople and bring the Ottoman state to its knees, just as it had forced the Russians to back down in 1878. Never mind that a wise old Sufi mystic had foretold that Constantinople would never be taken by force, but only from within. For each actor is privy only to his own lines, yet still must play his part, willy nilly, following the director's prompts, until the final act and curtain.

Unlike Enver whose impetuosity might have captured a hill, only to lose the mountain range, Mustafa had learned a lot over the years from sitting on the sidelines. He had developed the ability to see the big picture, the significance in the apparently insignificant; he was a natural strategist, with a chess player's ability to hold many 'what-ifs' while discerning the best move for the long term advantage. He knew to wait for the right moment, and sieze it.

From the beginning Mustafa held more cards than the Allied Admirals and Generals hidden in the safety of their great fleet behind the offshore islands. Mustafa's intelligence was native, he knew the lie of the land and he held the high ground; what his troops lacked in equipment was more than compensated for by patriotic fervour. Everything turned upon their ability to defend the sea passage.

The British plan was to blast their way past the Turkish forts on either shore of the Dardanelles, thence to Constantinople and demand a Turkish surrender. An exploratory attack by sea in November appeared to show the defenses to be weak, which encouraged the Allies to further attempts. These failed due to the resilience of the Turkish batteries, combined with a lot of luck.

The subsequent naval offensive in March 1915 was a disaster. Three battleships were sunk and three disabled. The assault was called off. It is an irony that in the year-long struggle at Gallipoli where half a million men fell dead or wounded it was something as prosaic as mines which decided the issue. This army of remote and unmanned irregulars, these random floating drones, rolled upon the tidal baize like loaded dice, required no human agent to wreak their wrath.

By now the Turkish shore batteries' ammunition was reduced to a mere twenty-seven long range shells. The assault by sea was not repeated. The Allied strategy changed to a land offensive.

When the landings of the French, British and Anzac forces began, Lieutenant-Colonel Mustafa was with his troops, in a village halfway down the Gallipoli Peninsula.

NINETEEN

The Antakliyan

Constantinople, 1914

HE JOY OF SATANAYA'S welcome back into the Beylerbeyi household lost its shine in the weeks following the
assassination in Sarajevo. Mustafa's awkward letter, which
had arrived a few weeks after their parting at the opera in
Sofia, showed that when it came to love, he could too easily lose his way.
Since then she had heard nothing.

Satanaya sat on the landing stage and gazed out over the Bosphorus.
Back and forth the slender four-oared caiques skimmed the water; beautiful pinewood craft, painted red and green trimmed with gold leaf. The
young oarsmen, tanned, bare chests, muscles taut and glistening with
sweat, stroked the gentle swell with their long blades with such supple

grace it seemed her own skin yielded to their distant caress. She felt herself leaning towards the fine features of these dark-faced Albanians and Greeks as they laboured with a kind of joy that only the freedom of open water gives. She could love these men on their looks alone.

She wondered what really attracted her gaze. What was this urge to love, and to be loved; this simple, essential need to surrender to a mundane beauty when her heart was being driven further, to a vision beyond the crudely physical? Was it the light, the glimmering gold and amethyst sheen crowning the waves, the creamy flume of the boat's wake, the glowing torsos of these handsome boys, the white lightning flash of their teeth and eyes? This light was tossing her heart like a ball, back and forth between the horizon of distant domes and minarets and the firmament of her own breast, just as the warmth of the sun and the breeze played on her skin, and she felt helpless to resist. And yet nostalgia was no substitute for love itself, and yearning needed a concrete object of desire; an action, and a firm response to this beauty that was playing her like a maestro on a damp piano.

The dull days of summer brought an ennui to Satanaya and the Bey-lerbeyi konak. Even the distracting laughter of the two young boys jostling in the garden with the servants' children was insufficient to lift her spirits. Perhaps the time had come to move on, she thought.

With war approaching, nothing felt stable any more. Even upon the Bosphorus, where the frantic quotidian traffic of caiques and ferries and small fishing boats continued unabated, something had changed. Where before these local craft had skirted and dodged between a larger fleet of merchant vessels of both sail and steam, trading in and out of Constan-tinople from the east via Suez and west from the Americas, a strange calm had descended. One of the world's busiest maritime passages had suddenly become a by-water.

The outbreak of war was a slowly spreading plague. What began in Sarajevo infected Europe. Turkey would not be immune. The talk among the military and in parliament was confused and contradictory as to whether the country could remain neutral when both sides in the conflict had influential support in Constantinople. Rumours reached Beylerbeyi from Amina's cousins in Egypt indicating that the Khedive would call for a jihad to support the Sultan and Caliph, in spite of the fact that his country was de facto a part of the British Empire.

* * *

One evening a small gathering took place in the konak, attended by some
of those mysterious friends of Amina Khanoum. From the particular
deference that Subhana and others among the staff showed them, Satanaya
understood that these were sheykhs, or dervishes perhaps. The talk,
naturally, was of the impending conflict. She was struck particularly by a
brief snippet of conversation she overheard, between an elderly man, and
his young protégé, a civil servant about to leave the city for a posting in
Ankara.

The older man was reassuring the younger, with his hand upon his
shoulder, saying, 'Don't worry, my son, you go and do your duties. When
you come back, I won't be here. But there is a certain person who has been
chosen by God to save the country – his name is Mustafa.'

Satanaya had been on her way out of the *selamlık* with a tray of empty
cups. When she returned a few minutes later, both men had left. The
gathering continued but it was as if those two had never been there. She
wondered if she had heard right. But the older man's words kept ringing
in her head as clearly as if they had just been spoken. No, she wasn't
imagining things. Later, when the guests had all left, she told Amina
Khanoum what she had witnessed.

'Ah yes, that must have been Süreyya Efendi and his pupil.'

'And who is Süreyya Efendi?'

'Well, it's difficult to say really. He was an inventor when he was young
– some sort of new cannon for the army. And then he worked in the
Ministry of Posts and Telegraph. Now – well, let's just say he's one of the
very special ones.'

'How do you mean?'

'Some say he can raise the dead.'

Satanaya laughed. 'You're joking!' But Amina Khanoum's look told her
she was deadly serious.

'And this Mustafa who is going to save Turkey?'

'Well, one in ten Turkish boys are called Mustafa…' Amina Khanoum
seemed evasive. 'Why these questions all of a sudden, Satanaya *canım*?'

Satanaya blushed.

'Oh nothing, I was just wondering,' she said, and carried on clearing
away the glasses and coffee cups.

* * *

During one of the last soirées in Beylerbeyi, as summer exhausted itself and Turkey drifted inexorably towards war, the compass of Satanaya's journey pointed her on a new course.

'Oh look, there's a new hotel opening up in Pera; by a wealthy Egyptian, apparently. I wonder if we're related.' Amina Khanoum was reading from one of the French language newspapers published in Constantinople.

'How strange, and at such a time as this. What does he know that we don't?' said the Colonel Efendi. 'Perhaps we should invite him. I'll find out more.'

The Colonel was sitting with his feet up on a footstool, a pile of official papers on his lap. He spent a lot of time at home these days, as the Triumvirate had sidelined so many of the honest men in preference to their own corruptible stooges. With Turkey's involvement in the war appearing unavoidable, he expected to be called up any day for active service.

Two weeks later, among the guests at the konak appeared a middle-aged man, who was introduced as Zeki al Antakyalı. A successful Levantine merchant, Zeki al Antakyalı had made his fortune in the burgeoning Egyptian tourist trade which followed the British invasion in 1882. He was of mid-height, soft-skinned, tending a little to corpulence, but not disproportionately; his handsome face glowed healthily with few care lines, and deep brown eyes twinkled behind long lashes.

Satanaya spied him across the *selamlık*. Something familiar. Something unmistakable in that face, but also out of place. As if she were seeing a long lost item of one's own apparel being worn by someone else. She approached the small group where he was holding forth in impeccable French.

'Yes, we hope to open in the new year, although I still haven't found the right man to manage the kitchens.' Zeki al Antakyalı was explaining to the Colonel Efendi.

'Or woman, perhaps?' joked the Colonel.

'And why not?' Satanaya said, slightly piqued by the Colonel's tone.

'Yes, why not indeed!' said al Antakyalı, turning towards Satanaya with a broad smile. Their eyes met, and mutual recognition came slowly but certainly. Satanaya blushed and the gathering laughed, completely misinterpreting her response. And in that momentary distraction the Egyptian managed a conspiratorial wink, the import of which was not lost on Satanaya.

'May I introduce you,' said Amina Khanoum, 'Lady Satanaya, companion to my late friend Gülbahar Khanoum of Beirut – Sayyed Zeki al Antakyalı Bey Efendi from Cairo. He's opening a hotel in Pera. Isn't it exciting!'

'*Enchanté*, Madamoiselle. Just Zeki, please. I was sorry to hear of the loss of that great lady. Our paths crossed, you know, in the dim and distant past. And of course, the Beyt al Rahma was a byword for all manner of good taste in *l'Orient Prochaine*. I understand that you too are a person of accomplishment in the kitchen. I'm sure any protégé of the Lady Gülbahar will have many talents hidden up her sleeves.'

'Thank you, Zeki Bey, you are too kind, but it is surely not so. I'm just a cook.' Satanaya pleaded demurely. 'I seem to recollect something also, perhaps it was you… or perhaps not… But we had so many visitors, and I was so much in the kitchen. And as we say, time is an ocean of unknowing in which the salt of memory dissolves into forgetfulness, perchance to non-existence.' Now it was the guest's turn to blush. Satanaya grinned, she was happy to enter this little game of hidden confidences.

'But then, you must become the ocean, what could be better!' the Antakyalı laughed. 'I insist you come and visit us in our little hostelry, I would value your advice.' Then turning to his hosts, 'And now I would like to propose a toast, which I hope is not presumptuous: to my future, and my future clientele at 'The Hotel Grand Antakya'.'

'What kind of future can we toast in these times, I wonder?' mused the Colonel, 'Will you be serving schnapps or champagne this New Year's Eve?'

'Whatever the outcome, there should always be champagne. If we remain neutral, Constantinople will be at the heart of things. In any case, there is always the need for an oasis of civilisation in such times, good or bad. So I feel confident we can provide a worthwhile service.'

That night Satanaya couldn't sleep. For a start, she had been astonished to discover that the owner of this new hotel in Pera was none other than little Zeki. Little Zeki who had been the teaboy at the same brothel where Lady Gülbahar had spent her youth prior to being rescued by that valiant soul, Daud the Arwadi. Zeki, the pretty little boy whom, according to Lady Gülbahar, the ladies of the house would dress up like a doll in women's clothes, put make-up on and have him dance before the clients who were being served drinks prior to engaging a girl. Later it was discovered that he had a fine singing voice, and he frequented the salon of Lady Gülbahar in her last years. When Satanaya first met him he had grown into an attractive young man – he had that youthful androgynous face, slim build with narrow hips, and deep brown eyes behind long dark lashes that attract the attention of both sexes. It was inevitable that one of these admirers, a rich Egyptian pasha whose family were originally from Antioch, would fall head over heels in love with Zeki. This Antakyan became his patron and took him off to Cairo as his butler.

In time the Pasha was widowed. The Pasha had never been able to fully experience conjugality with his wife, and so when he too died, childless, his beloved Zeki inherited all his wealth and property. By now Zeki had become the toast of Cairo, performing as a singer, ostensibly as a woman, and gained notoriety in some of the less salubrious Alexandrian night clubs for his own version of the Dance of the Seven Veils. It was a performance guaranteed to shock newcomers to Egypt – when he relinquished the last piece of diaphanous gauze blowing in the light breeze of the overhead fans they were confronted momentarily by a male member of extensive proportions.

Before he died, the Pasha had bestowed on Zeki his own patronym, Antakyalı. But in Egypt Zeki had become too well known as drag queen and erstwhile catamite to the Pasha. Now with no protector, he decided to recreate himself abroad as a sober businessman who had made his money in the hotel trade. He knew the industry backwards. With war approaching, Zeki decided to try his luck in the wicked city of Constantinople.

As Satanaya's imagination over Zeki's sudden re-appearance finally exhausted itself, and she was drifting off to sleep, she remembered his words. 'And why not!'. The look he had given her then was no patronising gesture, but was, she was quite certain, a genuine invitation. She sat up in bed and repeated to herself, 'And why not!' She had enjoyed the past three years in Beylerbeyi, not solely because of the generous good nature of her hosts, but for the unique insight it had given her into the workings of an empire, albeit one in the process of dissolution. Or perhaps it was evolution, as Mustafa had described it. Change, certainly, and she too felt ready for a change. Her excursion into Bulgaria had re-awakened her taste for adventure, and notwithstanding her obvious devotion to Amina's two little boys with whom she had formed strong, almost motherly, bonds, she knew the time was approaching for her to move on.

At breakfast she shared her thoughts with Amina and the Colonel.

'But I would only be across the water. It's about time I put some of my experience into practical use. Zeki Bey certainly seemed genuine. Anyway, I promise I'll visit often. Of course, maybe he won't want me after all. Then you'll still be lumbered with me, I'm afraid.'

Satanaya said this, knowing full well that Zeki was not one to make an empty invitation. If he had said, 'Why not?', it meant he wanted her.

Amina sighed and looked kindly at Satanaya. She was not in the least surprised on hearing the news. 'I've been wondering how much longer you would be with us. I know you've enjoyed being here as we have enjoyed your company. You really have become part of the family. But you're young and I know that whatever it was that Lady Gülbahar was cultivating in you must continue to grow. Actually, I rather envy you – living in a big hotel, it's all rather exciting. And as you say, it's only a strip of water that will separate us, even if we are on different continents. But we'll miss you, just the same.'

'There's just one thing.' Satanaya hesitated. 'My Ottoman identity papers still state that I reside in Beirut. My French identity papers may not be helpful if Turkey joins Germany.'

'Don't worry.' the Colonel reassured her, 'I'll sort that out. After all, you were the ward of a Turkish ambassador's second wife as well as a French baroness. It won't be a problem – and Amina Khanoum's uncle is still the Prime Minister… at least for now.'

TWENTY

The Hotel Grand Antakya

Constantinople – 1914-15

S THIS HOW it feels – the prelude to war? The normality of it all? The birds are twittering in the fig trees, whose paling leaves still shelter the dessicated scrota of unpicked fruit, and the waning sun shines weakly before the advent of winter's death. Is this how it sounds? The waterseller keeps calling in the street – what imperceptible fog upon the ear mutes the knell of his clanging cups? And with what hesitancy is the shopkeeper possessed? The confusion of mislaid keys, the shutters rattling in the dawning light, he looks left and right, and wonders if when the parade comes will it arrive gaily coloured, chattering and with the ease of small worries, or will it march in drab, humdrum, muffle-mouthed to the thud of a dull tattoo? It is the sleep of minds that impresses. How else do sacrificial beasts come to slaughter?

In the weeks following Zeki's visit, reports began to filter through of the Turkish attack upon the Russian fleet. One evening the Colonel Efendi arrived home bringing news that the country was now at war. They sat up late that night drinking whisky, talking as one might at a wake of a dear friend. They drank as if in hope that the spirit might somehow illuminate a future beyond their perceived loss, aware that an indeterminate purgatory of grief lay ahead. Yet they drank and talked, yearning for a glimmer of that light which must eventually return.

✳ ✳ ✳

In Constantinople the mood on the streets descended gradually into fear.

'I can't bear it much longer.' the Colonel Efendi exploded one bitterly cold evening in late January 'The city's going crazy. Everyone knows the eastern campaigns have been a disaster, and now it looks as if the British are getting ready to invade through the Dardanelles.'

Only that day he had heard that the Germans doubted they could hold off the Russians if they attacked Constantinople from the north.

'Even the Government is planning to leave the City and move into Anatolia, probably to Eskişehir. They've got trains ready and waiting at Haydarpaşa. The gold has all been taken out of the banks. They want the Sultan and his family to go too, but he's refusing. Apparently his brother here in Beylerbeyi* said if he left he would never be able to return. That appears to have settled it.'

'If only the British would come and rid us of those thugs in the Committee.' said Amina Khanoum. 'I was speaking to Josephine Morgenthau today. Apparently that monster Talaat told the Ambassador† that he'll have Aya Sofia blown up, rather than let it fall into British hands. The Committee are not interested in old things, he said.'

'If the Americans would only join the British and French! But I guess they're playing a waiting game,' the Colonel sighed. 'At least Enver is convinced the British won't succeed. He's forming a new army with the German General Liman von Sanders in charge, to defend the Dardanelles.

---

* deposed Sultan Abdul Hamid II, confined to Beylerbeyi Palace.

† Henry Morgenthau Sr. United States Ambassador to the Ottoman Empire, 1913-1916.

I gather that young Colonel Mustafa will command a division, so there is some hope.'

Satanaya sipped her whisky. The words 'Mustafa' and 'hope' had the same bitter-sweet taste.

∗ ∗ ∗

One morning Satanaya woke when it was still dark, dressed, and went into the garden. Gazing at the pre-dawn streaks of light behind Çamlica Hill she remembered her arrival at the konak more than three years earlier, when she had woken from her fever and gazed up into the morning. No birds now filled these winter skies. The storks had long since flown to Africa as the guns of Europe had begun to fire.

A dull and distant rumble punctuated the silence. Thunder, she thought, but no clouds veiled the stars and lightning did not flash. On and on the booming sound continued, culminating in a louder prolonged thundery roll, then silence. Unbeknownst to her then, she was witnessing at over a hundred miles distance, audible through the clear cold air across the Sea of Marmara, the big guns firing from the Allied battleships as they began their operation to force the sea passage of the Dardanelles, and the explosions as Turkish mines hit home and took their toll. The war was suddenly close to home.

'You know, Satanaya,' said Amina Khanoum later that day, 'it does feel strange to be carrying on enjoying life as if nothing had happened, while all the men are off on this war business. I feel we ought to be contributing somehow. '

'But you have your two sons to look after, canım, what could you be expected to do?'

'Well, there's the *Hilal-i Ahmer* – The Red Crescent. They need women to train as nurses. They've been saying this ever since the Balkan Wars.'

'You couldn't become a nurse – you have a horror of blood!'

'Well, maybe I could roll bandages, or something. Knitting. That's it. I could knit gloves or sweaters. And I already support them with money as we all do.'

'I suppose you're right...' she thought for a moment. 'I could do the training, couldn't I?'

'Of course! And you could tell me everything you learn. Just in case, you know.'

And so Satanaya enrolled at the local branch of Red Crescent and was soon attending daily classes in the old hospital near Haydarpaşa. Initially she did report details of her lessons, such as how to clean wounds and assist at amputations. But Amina was more interested in hearing who was taking part, if any of her friends were there, and were the teachers really as strict as she'd heard? Satanaya fed her the gossip so her friend would feel she was also taking part, as they sat knitting socks together in the evenings.

* * *

Satanaya completed the initial training to become a nurse. She had passed the exam and soon there would be practical training with casualties returned from the Dardanelles. With time on her hands, she began to think again of Zeki and his hotel project. What a crazy idea. Why would anyone want to open a hotel in Pera at the start of a war?

One morning she crossed over by ferry from Üskudar to Beşiktaş and caught the newly-electrified tram, taking a cushioned seat in the ladies' compartment of the First Class car, along the Bosphorus as far as Karaköy. She felt so excited that she decided to walk the 118 steep steps of Yüksek Kaldırım, carefully stepping back at the cries of '*destur! destur!*' – 'make way!' of the bent-backed *hamals* as they carried their heavy loads up from the docks at Tophane. She passed the brothel street, the Genoese Tower, to the Mevlevi Tekke and on into La Grande Rue de Pera at Tünel Square. Cutting down a side street on her left she emerged onto Kabristan Street, the area where many of the big hotels were situated, including the Hotel Grand Antakya.

Pera, the enclave of late 19th century western Europe: one side of its hill looked over the Golden Horn to the old Moslem city of Stamboul, while the other gave on to steamers and sailing vessels berthed in rows below on the Bosphorus shore, and to the Asian hills across the water. The trams still clanged out warnings to pedestrians, the bells on the reception desks of the splendid hotels still summoned porters to attention, and cash registers continued to ring out the change in the cafes along the Grande Rue. While there was more than the usual activity around the entrances to the various European embassies where those with the means applied for *laisser-passez* to safer climes, for the most part it was business as usual in the couturiers and milliners, jewellers, perfumiers and confectioners.

The Hotel Grand Antakya does not exist any more. The premises were situated between the Pera Palace Hotel and the Grand Hotel de Londres, an area now the site of a car park and exhibition centre. The cemetery which gave Kabristan Street its name has been built upon, and the road is now Meşrutiyet Caddesi (Constitution Avenue).

The hotel building had originally housed a bank on the ground floor, with apartments upstairs and vaults below. It had been closed for a number of years when Zeki managed to pick it up cheap from its previous owners – venture capitalists who had gone bust following the recent conflict. He brought in an Italian architect and his own team of builders, and had the interior redone in the current Art Nouveau style, even having Lalique provide designs for panels and mirrors in the public areas.

The Hotel Grand Antakya never attained the status which the Orient Express brought to the Pera Palace, nor could it rely on a long-standing reputation such as antiquity bestowed upon the Grand Hotel de Londres. It has never been mentioned in literature as a rendezvous for spies, clandestine trysts and the dalliances of diplomats with *femmes de nuit*, although its bars and bedrooms witnessed its own fair share of intrigue – this was Constantinople, after all. It appeared as if *ex nihilo* as war began and faded without visible trace shortly afterwards. Yet for all its apparent anonymity, during its brief flowering, Zeki's establishment outdid its more famous rivals in the breadth of provision: Its kitchens, *chambres privées*, the flexible terms of the house bank on the roulette and baccarat tables, the willingness of its footmen and maids to procure with discretion the necessary creature comforts for its clientele. And of course, its inimitable cabaret, choreographed by Zeki himself and in which, on special request, he might also perform (but only as a sturdy, veiled chanteuse); and so Hotel Grand Antakya remained as a secret, yet fondly remembered affair in the intimate recollections of its patrons until they too gradually passed into non-existence in the ebb and flow of time.

Unlike its neighbouring hostelries, the building did not itself announce itself with a grand porch, a glazed canopy fanned like a peacock's tail, nor balconies supported by busty, lusty caryatids. Entrance was business-like, up three steps and through a pair of somewhat austere brass-framed plate-glass doors, attended by a doorman in livery of green and gold. Yet from the moment one stepped upon the deep maroon and gold pile of the lobby carpet, or sank down into the luxurious leather chesterfields in the bar, one felt instinctively that one was in good hands and all one's needs would be well attended.

But we jump ahead. Following Satanaya's re-acquaintance with Zeki Bey at the konak, they had begun a correspondence in which she advised him on the layout of the kitchens and possible menus for the hotel's restaurant. The advent of war had delayed considerably the refurbishment of the building from bank into hotel, as difficulties arose with regard to payments to foreign suppliers. Shortly before the proposed opening, which had been postponed until the end of winter, Satanaya had written and asked to meet Zeki; and it is on the appointed day that we find her, making the journey with the 118 steps. When she finally fetched up at the hotel, the proprietor was awaiting her anxiously in the foyer, and immediately ushered her into a private office.

'Thank you so much for coming, Satanaya. You have no idea how relieved I was to get your message. But I am still wondering, what exactly is this meeting about? Not blackmail, I hope!' Zeki giggled nervously.

'As if that would worry you, of all people. I'm sure you are privy to enough guilty secrets that your safety is more secure than if you had the wealth of the Nizam of Hyderabad.'

'Ah, yes, that might be so. And that is why I have deposited so many little notes, my 'securities' shall we say, with my solicitors. If anything untoward should happen to me... But there, times change, and there is little certainty in the world these days. We have to make the best of what we have.'

'And you haven't a cook?'

'Ah, cooks aplenty, but no chef.'

'Then perhaps I might be of assistance. I don't call myself a chef, it would be too difficult under the circumstances – no doubt you have an all-male crew here. But perhaps a more neutral title, such as 'catering manager', would take the sting out of your chaps having to submit to a female order.'

'Excellent. When would you like to start?'

'I'm here, aren't I? Why don't you introduce me to the brigade?'

And so it was that by the afternoon, with sleeves rolled up she set to work in the kitchen. She explained to the assembled brigade that, while she recognised that each of them had their particular talents, the important thing was to work as a team serving a single order. And the order for now was the menu that she was preparing.

'Many of the dishes we are going to serve will be variations of what you know already. But,' she stressed, 'if we were going to make the Antakya shine out among so many other bright lights, our table must be the best example, the standard, so to speak, of good taste.' Satanaya was consciously drawing on themes from Takla's cookbook. 'This means starting out fresh each day as if from a point of complete unknowing, so that our customers will always receive something new, something original. Even if they imagine they have eaten such and such a stuffed mackerel or Özbek Pilav before, it won't be this stuffed mackerel or pilav. And they will remember and tell their friends. The idea is not to be different, but simply to make people notice. There is no need to innovate, but perfection today can always be surpassed tomorrow.'

The best way to get the team on her side, she knew, was by example, and so she found herself the next morning surrounded by her team as she demonstrated a simple vegetable '*turlu*', a versatile dish that could be eaten hot or cold, or with meat added to make a substantial stew.

Satayana peeled and chopped the red onions in big chunks and put them in a large oven tray. She scrubbed the pale courgettes and sliced them in small barrels. Now she rinsed and squeezed the aubergines, which she had cut and salted earlier, and in they went. The long Charliston peppers she scrubbed well and added whole. To this mélange she poured virgin olive oil from the Komili estates near Ayvalık, sweet sun-dried paprika paste dissolved in water, a light dusting of ground cummin, cinnamon, pepper, nutmeg and fenugreek, a good dash of pomegranate molasses and just enough water to encourage the vegetables with a little steam. Then with both hands she mixed all this up before adding thick rounds of tomato, a little oregano, salt and sugar. She placed the tray into the hot part of the oven for about thirty minutes, until the vegetables were beginning to brown on top, then a further twenty minutes or so cooking at a lower heat, with occasional gentle turning, not disturbing the tomato slices, and adding a little more water if the dish looked to be drying out too much.

Satanaya stood back and wiped her brow. The hotel was built on a slope, so the kitchens, while being in the basement, had the rare luxury of an open side facing the Golden Horn, allowing gentle airs to enter. Still, it was a hot place to work, summer or winter, as the wood-fired ovens were rarely allowed to go out. But she was happy to be back in her own element.

And so it began. There were a few hiccups: lost tempers and displays of stubbornness from some of the more entrenched members of staff. One or two of the most intransigent were encouraged to move on. Yet those who remained soon fell under the spell of this charismatic young lady, with her cheeky sense of humour – she joked with them knowingly as she removed the outer membranes of a pair of 'koç yumurtası', or patted the plump 'kadın budu' into shape – and while she didn't conform to their accustomed view of what constituted propriety for a woman, the convivial atmosphere and the fulsome compliments returning with the empty plates from the dining room soon welded them into a team happy to submit to their coach's demands.

TWENTY ONE

The Watchers on the Hills

Gallipoli Peninsula – 25 April 1915

HE WATCHERS on the hill tops of Sarıbayır Range stared into the black abyss of night. The wind carried rain mingled with spray from the sea into their eyes and the looming well of darkness revealed nothing. They waited and watched as they had done now for weeks, scanning in vain the dreadful depth with their blind telescopes. Earlier that night there had been moonlight over the sea and ship shapes had appeared in the distance, moving towards the coast from the direction of Imbros*, the large island about fifteen miles to the west. When the moon set, just after 2 a.m., the ships vanished into the murk. Poor weather set in and a pall fell upon land and sea.

---

* now Gökçeada (Turkey)

146

For months now, the Allied battlefleet had been lurking out of sight in the sheltered harbour of Mudros on the Aegean island of Lemnos further south-west. From here it had made regular sorties to bombard the Turkish positions on the peninsula. Also gathered at Lemnos, having been transported from Egypt, were the Allied armies: the British and French, and the Anzacs – the Australian and New Zealand Army Corps.

The prize was Constantinople, the aim to force Germany's ally out of the war. Ever since the failure by the British and French navies to force their way through the Dardanelles, an invasion by land had been expected. The Turks poured reinforcements into the peninsula. United in a new 'Fifth Army' under the command of the German General, Otto Liman von Sanders, small detachments were spread along the coast on the steep heights above the beaches as an initial line of defence, in three main areas: Bolayır in the north of the peninsula, Seddülbahir /Cape Helles at the southern tip, and on the Asian shore at Besika Bay. The main body of the army was held inland, to counterattack once it was known where the enemy had landed. The need for secrecy and to avoid being targets for the regular bombardments from the sea meant that Turkish troop movements on the peninsula took place by night. The German general had got two right out of three, with the main British attack taking place at Cape Helles, while the French landed on the Asian side. A major diversionary assault by the Royal Navy in the north had blind-sided von Sanders. The southern coastal area where the Anzacs landed, between Gaba Tepe and Ari Burnu, remained wide open with weak defences.

The Anzacs came by night hidden beneath the same shroud that veiled the watchers in the hills. No preparatory softening up of Turkish defenses by naval bombardment heralded their silent approach. At five miles off-shore three battleships disembarked a first wave of fifteen hundred warriors into whalers manned by young midshipmen, which were then towed in train by small motor boats, and cast off near the shore. With rag-muffled rollocks the only sounds were the creak of spars, the splash of the oars and lap of waves barely audible within the wet wind blowing and the gentle roll of the Aegean surf.

Like the mines in the Straits, the fate of the expedition now turned, not simply on ingenuity or heroism or human will in the first instance, but on a mistake. No one yet has determined categorically how, or even whether, the Australian and New Zealand forces were landed in error more than a

mile north of the designated beach. Some reached shore upon a small
sandy bay, known ever since as Anzac Cove. From here they charged up
the steep slopes and surprised the flimsy troop of eighty Turkish soldiers
monitoring this section. Other boats came to land a little further north
around the point known as Ari Burnu where they were faced with almost
sheer cliffs and withering machine gun fire from Turkish positions. A
communications breakdown seems the most likely culprit, but even there
the pundits disagree on exactly who to blame. Perhaps even the grandest
of schemes can be undermined if the fates decree otherwise. Nevertheless,
in spite of the difficulties, the Anzacs made speedy inroads, their reckless
bravery and great numbers – by now four thousand had landed – baffling
the small contingents of astonished Turks who were driven back, leaving
the invaders in command of the near-shore heights by shortly after day-
break. Of the eighty Turks who had faced the original landing force, only
three survived the day.

✳ ✳ ✳

Five miles inland at Bigalı, a village where the peninsula narrows, Mustafa's
19th Division had just come off night manoeuvres. In the early hours,
Mustafa woke to the sound of distant rifle and machine gun fire coming
over the Sarıbayır range. Around sunrise he received an urgent request for
back-up from the commander of the 9th Division who had made initial
contact with the invaders. Mustafa set off in urgent haste with a company
of cavalry and some artillery. Mustafa rode on ahead. Nearing the scene of
the fighting he crested a hill and stopped to wait while his men caught up.
Through the scrub ahead the fleeing remnants of the 9th Division, wide-
eyed and confused, came running towards him, a rout of young soldiers
with not an officer within sight.

Mustafa could not believe it. He was livid. 'Halt! What's going on?
Why are you retreating?'

A corporal, barely stopping in his flight, cried out, 'It's the enemy, sir!
They're right behind us.'

'Where?'

The man pointed. Mustafa could see a line of soldiers advancing
towards a hill in the distance. The enemy were closer to his position than
his own men coming up behind.

'We mustn't let them pass.' Mustafa ordered them.

'But we're out of ammo, sir.'

'You've got bayonets, haven't you? Then fix them. Now lie down and wait.'

Then a remarkable thing happened. As the soldiers obeyed Mustafa's commands, the enemy troops advancing in the near distance halted and also lay down. Perhaps they thought they were being drawn into an ambush. But it didn't matter, for now there would be enough time for reinforcements to arrive. Still, Mustafa's company were only a small detachment, and it was evident that they were far outnumbered.

A runner arrived with reports that the Anzacs were capturing the heights to the north. His small company didn't stand a chance against the superior forces. Yet he had no choice. If the enemy were able to continue their advance, they would soon command the high ground which overlooked the narrow part of the Dardanelles above Eceabat/Maydos. This mustn't be allowed to happen, whatever the cost. If Eceabat were taken, it would open the passage for the enemy navy. The defenders' local knowledge of the terrain and the desperateness of the situation were to their advantage. At least they might hold up the Anzac advance until further reinforcements arrived.

He gathered his troops together, and when he spoke he didn't mince his words:

'There'll be no running away,' he ordered them, 'and no surrender. Not like those who gave up our Balkan lands. It would be better you were shot right here than let you give up a yard.'

Still the men hesitated, and he pressed them further:

'I'm not ordering you to attack, I'm ordering you to die. By the time we are dead, our places will have been taken by the troops coming up behind us.'

And so it was that Mustafa led them back into battle. By 10 a.m. they had taken the high ground at a hill called Conkbayırı. From here he organised a counter-offensive, fighting relentlessly through the day and into the evening while the rest of his division made it up from Bolayır. He had not spoken idly about their chances of survival. In the coming days while the defense was consolidated, wave upon wave of men fought and died, pushing the Anzacs back into a section barely a mile from where they had landed that morning.

Meanwhile, the French landed a brigade on the Asian shore as a diversion. The main British landings took place on the southern tip of the peninsula on beaches around Cape Helles, at the entrance to the Straits. Here a huge naval bombardment preceded the attack, forewarning the Turks to bring up reinforcements. When the invasion forces began to come ashore, it was a massacre and they were unable to make any significant progress inland. The Turkish troops had pulled back from the shoreline to secure positions on the ridges above. As the British boats reached the beaches the defenders opened up with incessant fusillades of rifle fire. The incoming troops were slaughtered as they became entangled in the thick Turkish barbed wire, which their poor quality wire cutters were unable to cope with. A hundred years later, half-buried in the undulations of time-collapsed trenches, spikes and spurs of rusted wire remain, still sufficiently potent to rip cloth and puncture the hide of the unwary intruder.

By next morning, reinforcements had brought Turkish strength up to around ten thousand men in Mustafa's sector at Arıburnu, with machine guns and batteries of artillery. But the Anzacs had now landed twice that number, and, following a strong naval bombardment, renewed their attacks. Inconclusive skirmishing continued throughout the day. On the morning of 27th April, Mustafa lead a major counterattack and succeeded in pushing back the enemy, but a night attack failed to consolidate these gains. With further reinforcements and significant artillery and machine guns now positioned among the scrub oak and pines of the steep slope, a major Turkish push began before dawn on 1st May. By now the Anzacs were firmly entrenched and the Turks, having suffered around six thousand casualties, were unable to break the invaders' lines. Like their Antipodean foes, the Turks began to dig in for the long haul.

TWENTY-TWO

Josephine and the Armenian Escape Routes

Constantinople – 1915

 INCE SO MANY of the young Turkish officers who frequented the bar of the Hotel Grand Antakya were now
engaged in the Gallipoli defensive, the mood in Constantinople had become somewhat depressed. One day when
trade was slow, Satanaya took time off to visit Amina at the konak. It
coincided with a visit by Josephine Morgenthau, wife and stalwart
support of Henry Morgenthau, Ambassador to the United States of
America.

'It will be a good chance to catch up on some of the diplomatic gossip,' said Amina, 'Since this war started, we rarely get news from the other side.'

Satanaya and Amina met the Ambassador's launch at the konak's landing stage.

'Josephine, my dear, so good of you to come.' Amina Khanoum greeted her friend. 'And so brave! All this way, with all those British submarines lurking beneath the waves, like sharks waiting to devour you.'

'Nonsense, Amina, don't be so dramatic. You might be able to put off your Egyptian friends with such tales, but we Americans are neutrals, as you know. And if the British want us on their side – which, mark my words, they surely do – they better not go sinking our little boat.'

'İnşallah, maşallah.' Amina said quietly, ushering her guest inside.

Once the three ladies had settled down in the *haremlik* and tea had been served, Amina inquired about the gossip of the court.

'What I have to say isn't gossip, though there is plenty of that.' said Josephine, 'I'm afraid the real news is all rather tragic.'

Satanaya and Amina glanced at each other.

'You see,' Josephine began again, 'it's about the Armenians. Henry, he's such a dear, he just won't let this go. And how can I blame him. He's been back to see that ghastly man, Talaat Pasha at the Interior Ministry. You remember last time, I told you the Minister had been in one of his moods, over the release of some crony of his whom the British are holding in Malta, and poor Henry was as usual pleading the cause of the Christians.'

Amina had heard the tales, but held her peace and let her friend speak. Satanaya too was aware of the terrible state of affairs that had ensued for the Armenians following the defeat at Sarıkamış that winter. While it was true that some Armenians in the Ottoman army had switched to the Russian side, the mass of the Christian population, caught between the two armies, were simply victims of circumstance, being in the wrong place at the wrong time. Though it was also a convenience for those in the Committee to cover their military defeats with stories of treason. The solution, as far as the local Ottoman authorities were concerned, was a blanket proscription of the Armenians within the Empire; in short, a brutal and inhuman persecution.

'You know Mr White, one of our Consuls in the east, has been sending back the most distressing reports, of massacres and torture of tens of thousands of Armenians in the region round Harput. He told us how he went out into the countryside himself. He saw the emptied villages and then the piles of corpses rotting in the wilderness where the poor souls had been marched, exhausted, starving, then shot and left to die. He has given refuge to a few he was able to hide within the consulate grounds – at risk of his own life, I must add. And some he could furnish with papers to get them out of the country. But it is so little. Mr White has tried to reason with the local Governor and the Chief of Police, but they want him to sign a paper saying the deported Armenians were criminals. And similar reports of murders and so-called deportations have come from Mr Jackson, our man in Aleppo, as well as from American missionaries.'

Satanaya sat silently through this, trying to take it all in. She knew from her parents' stories that similar atrocities had been meted out to the Circassians as they were removed from their lands by the Tsarist forces half a century earlier. She remembered what her father had said on the subject, when speaking to some of his young pupils who wished to revenge their ancestors: 'Only love can free the soul from the fears and iniquities of this world. Revenge may assuage the pains of the afflicted soul, but will harden the heart. Love, unconditional surrender to the onslaught of compassion upon the heart, only this will melt the soul and all its preconceptions. All the hurt in the world is no excuse not to love, for only by letting go into love are we able to escape this vale of tears.'

She thought of these dispossessed and orphaned, the innocent refugees treading their road of sorrow. Would they, she wondered, be adopted by some inner power of love and be brought to that salving union where no terror strikes? And she thought of her friend Shirin in Konya, who feared for what might come about when the Sultan was no longer in place, when the established order was broken. Something deep within revolted in horror as she pictured the events related by Josephine. A thought came to her, something that old gentleman, the Efendi, had said to her the night they walked and talked in the garden by the Bosphorus, about inability to accept change, and an unwillingness to accept mistakes… this becomes a conflict in the soul of Man which may manifest as actual war. All this she thought, but in this she felt so small. At least, in her heart, she knew she must preserve the notion of the essential good, and nurture it, feel it, protect it. As the winds of war prevailed in this time, it was not easy. Yet it was all she could do, all she had to cling to.

Amina spoke: 'But the government here, how can they allow this?'

'Of course, Talaat denies it on the one hand,' said Josephine. 'Perhaps he's afraid that admitting it might bring the United States into the war alongside the Entente. But he also seems perversely proud of what is happening; his arrogance is only matched by his boorishness. The Armenians come to poor Henry at the Embassy, but what can he do? We even have German missionaries asking us to put the case to our government because their own is saying nothing. Oh dear. It's so horrible.'

'The man's insane.' Amina was indignant.

'No, Talaat isn't insane. That's the point. He knows exactly what he's doing. He plays with us as if we were fish on a line.'

At this point Josephine stopped. The cheerful front she had presented on her arrival had vanished, and she began to sob quietly.

'Please forgive me. It's just… well, I get so angry and there's nothing I can do. Poor Mr White, I do worry so for him. He's a most unassuming man, you know, but such a brave soul.'

Amina went and sat next to Josephine and put her arms around her like a sister.

'*Istağfurallah*! On the contrary, it's us who should be begging your forgiveness.' Amina said. 'We are all shamed by these men. But what can we do. It is a fire that once lit must consume itself. All we can do is try and prevent it spreading.'

Satanaya passed around the eau de cologne. Josephine dabbed her hands and face, and wiped her tears away with a small lace handkerchief. She gave a little laugh, and regained her composure.

'They deny it all of course, the Committee men. But Henry says the Consuls' letters are being heavily censored, and their travel severely restricted. There's a lot the authorities want to keep hidden, and if it wasn't for the bravery of our Consuls and the missionaries we'd hear even less.'

'And I suppose Talaat Pasha will claim it's all a domestic affair anyway.' said Amina Khanoum. She knew enough of the man to understand his ways.

'Exactly. He just stonewalls Henry if he questions him too deeply. And he gets angry, though he tries to pretend otherwise. He sits at his desk puffed up like some big bullfrog, with those huge hands of his clasped together, and if Henry mentions any of the witnesses, Talaat just accuses them of being British or Russian spies.'

'And is it just Talaat who is responsible?' asked Satanaya.

'Henry is convinced that it begins and ends with him, but the local authorites are all colluding. And it seems, once out there in the hinterland, there is no one to report; that's where the worst of it, the really horrible things are happening. And even those Turks who are against it are too afraid to say anything. They are calling it a 'punitive deportation', but there are no controls at all. It's in effect a death sentence to a whole people.'

'Is this happening to Armenians in Constantinople too?' Amina asked.

'Yes. Unfortunately. All the civil leaders, the politicians and priests, and the intellectuals of course. Anyone with a voice is sent into Anatolia, where they can't be heard, where they can be 'disappeared' without trace.' said Josephine. 'And if that wasn't enough, that monster wanted my husband to provide him with the names of any dead Armenians who had life insurance policies with American companies, so that they could claim the money for the State. It implies that not only were the policy holders deceased, but the beneficiaries too. That man's cruelty knows no bounds.'

Satanaya thought of a number of Armenian friends she had made since she began working at the Hotel Grand Antakya. A baker whose family lived in Van, but years ago had come to the city, learnt his trade and who was now a regular supplier. A banker friend who had advised her on managing her funds. And not a few of the hotel staff were Armenians, though you wouldn't know them from any of the other nationalities, the Greeks, Jews, and Alevis, who performed all the many and varied tasks which supported the smooth running of the establishment.

No one had touched the tea, which now had gone cold in their cups. A fresh brew was brought, and baklava to sweeten the bitter taste of their conversation. Afterwards they went into the garden for fresh air and admired the Colonel Efendi's latest blooms in the greenhouse.

Late in the afternoon Josephine and Satanaya boarded a ferry at Beylerbeyi. They sat in the stern of the paddle steamer, close together against the cool breeze. As the landing stage fell away behind them, the pink-gold light of late afternoon sun painted a rosy glow upon the white-washed buildings of Üsküdar which gently stepped the slopes of the Asian shore. The view helped Josephine to cast off the dreadful images of earlier, and remember instead the bleached towns of the Amalfi Coast where she and Henry had cruised in happier days before the war.

Satanaya was still thinking of her friends, as more and more faces came to her, Armenian friends for whom she now was becoming worried. But she had an idea. She turned to Josephine and spoke quietly into her ear.

'If there are Armenians – not politicals, but people you know well, who can be trusted absolutely to keep silent, whatever the pressure, – who need to 'escape', I know who might be able to help.'

Josephine sat up. She had not expected to hear such things from this young friend of Amina's. She looked again at Satanaya, the beautiful, innocent, hard working, educated Circassian baroness, and discerned a glint of steel in those powder blue eyes. Josephine smiled. She recognised a little of herself, of her own quiet indomitableness, in the lady at her side.

'Thank you. Yes, I'll give it some thought.' she said, and resumed her gazing at the receding shore, wishing herself sailing again upon the blue Tyrhennian Sea.

∗ ∗ ∗

In times of war, it is always good to have an escape plan. Whatever one's loyalties, one is no use to anyone if one is dead. And if one's loyalty is to the love of humanity, and the continuation of that emergence, whether in one's own skin, but also of those of similar persuasion, it is prudent to keep one's plans updated to the ever-present possibility of disaster. Zeki had prepared his exit strategy in the form of a secret escape corridor.

Few were aware (for his name could not be linked to it) that while negotiating the purchase of the Antakya hotel property, Zeki had also bought the property next door, through a Lebanese shell company. The ground floor of this adjoining building presented a shop-front next door to the rear of the hotel, and was occupied by a trading company which stored all manner of merchandise, textiles, food stuffs. The upper floors housed private flats with a separate side-street entrance. These apartments were rented out, except for the top two floors. The penultimate floor, where the stairway ended, was kept un-let. From inside this apartment a secret staircase gave access to the penthouse floor, which in turn was connected by a hidden way, the secret corridor, to Zeki's apartments in the top floor of the Hotel Grand Antakya. There was also a further route down to the street via the roofs of the adjoining buildings. In this way, all manner of clandestine arrivals and covert departures, evasions of pursuers intent on malfeasance, and even the avoidance of jealous wives and husbands, could be effected. This arrangement also allowed Zeki some security against the uncertainties of war.

And so it was that a few days later in the fashionable Lebon Patisserie in the Grand Rue de Pera, two respectable European ladies were observed meeting for morning coffee, a pastry and a chat. No one would have suspected this cosy rendezvous was cover for Josephine and Satanaya to finalise the escape plan of an Armenian banker, about to be arrested by Talaat's agents on trumped up charges of money laundering.

That night, while the dining room was in full flow, a tall man dressed as a *hamal* delivering a case of fish arrived at the rear of the hotel. Having been relieved of his load of turbot he was directed to Satanaya's office where he exchanged his clothes for those of a hotel porter. Satanaya accompanied him in the service lift to a room upstairs where he changed again into the clothes of a Greek seaman. He was blindfolded and after many deliberately disorienting turns was led through the secret passage into the apartment next door. That night when the streets were busiest, he was taken down to the Galata Quay where he boarded a small caique belonging to a Greek fisherman. And thence by a circuitous journey of island hopping he made it eventually to Athens and a new life. It was the first of a number of escapes that the crew of the Antakya managed during this difficult period. Zeki was amply recompensed by his wealthier fugitives, which funds subsidised some of the more needy cases that so often appeared upon his doorstep.

TWENTY-THREE

The Submarine, the Cavalry and the Paddle Steamer

Part 1 – A Maritime Triangulation

The Sea of Marmara – May 1915

 IEUTENANT Commander Martin Nasmith R.N., master of His Majesty's Submarine 'E.11', raised the periscope and peered out over the smooth waters of the Sea of Marmara. It was late May, barely 4.30 a.m., the moon in its first quarter had left the night in darkness hours ago and now the sun had just edged above the horizon; the morning breeze had not yet risen and the water was still calm. He too felt calm. It was barely five days since he and his crew had managed to navigate the treacherous two-layered currents of

158

the Dardanelles Straits and slip through the minefields and shore batteries of the Turkish defences. The mission was 'search and destroy', to interrupt the seaborne transport of military supplies from the Ottoman capital to its army on the Gallipoli Peninsula. It had been a tense and frustrating few days; until yesterday. An early morning reconnaissance of the entrance roads to Constantinople harbour and the Bosphorus Strait had yielded the submarine its first success – a small gun boat lying at anchor. E.11's torpedo was on target, yet even as the unlucky boat was sinking before Nasmith's eyes an heroic Turkish seaman had got off a couple of lucky rounds from the deck gun, and his periscope was plunged into darkness. Frantic temporary repairs later that day had restored the submarine's vision, albeit with a slightly truncated scope. But this morning he felt confident, and casting caution aside, he now surfaced and scanned the sea from the open conning tower. A pod of dolphins breaking the water ahead of his ship only reinforced his sense of tranquillity.

Even as Lt. Cdr. Nasmith enjoyed this placid interlude, a thin wisp of smoke appeared distantly through his binoculars. But it was too far away, and after a brief chase whatever it was vanished from his horizon. Around ten o'clock more tell-tale smoke alerted him to a steamer approaching from the west. He gave the order to dive the submarine and a short while later surfaced alongside the steamer. Nasmith returned to the conning tower with his megaphone.

'Stop your engines and abandon ship.' he called out.

For a while nothing happened. Then the steamer changed course. Nasmith picked up his Lee Enfield and fired a couple of warning shots over the ship's bridge. Chaos ensued. As the steamer continued to make way in the water, the crew began to lower lifeboats, which immediately capsized. Men were jumping overboard in panic. Suddenly a strange figure appeared on deck dressed in a checkered knickerbocker suit, as if setting out for a day on the golf course. The man called down to the submarine:

'Good day, Captain. How can we help you?' He spoke in English, but the accent was American.

'And who the hell are you?' replied Nasmith.

'Raymond Swing of the Chicago Daily News. Pleased to meet you.' *

---

* Raymond Gram Swing (1887-1968) influential American journalist and broadcaster throughout WW1 and WW2.

'Well, whoever you are, kindly ask the Captain to stop engines. We are the Royal Navy and you are about to be sunk.'

The message was quickly relayed to the bridge, then E.11's marines boarded the ship. A quick inspection revealed a cargo of armaments and ammunition of German manufacture. While some marines laid explosive charges in the ship's hold below the waterline, others helped the unfortunate crew to right their lifeboats, while still others replenished the submarine's food supplies with fresh victuals from the ship's galley. The Turkish crew began the long row to shore taking with them the American, a neutral, a journalist on his way to cover the fighting in Gallipoli. The submarine pulled away to a safe distance, the explosives detonated, and the ship, *Nagara* out of Constantinople, began to sink. Shortly after, her boilers blew, producing a brief bouillon in the water and leaving a modicum of flotsam including some dead fish and a couple of bewildered ducks which the boarding party had missed, the only evidence of her passing.

No sooner had the sea regained its dark composure than Nasmith sighted another vessel. E11 dived and began to stalk its prey. Something, perhaps the smoke from the explosion on *Nagara* drifting over the water, must have alerted the Turkish captain. The vessel, which appeared heavily laden, veered suddenly off course and made full steam towards the little coastal town of Tekirdağ, sounding the ship's horn loudly as she went. E11 surfaced and gave chase. Bringing the ship alongside the sea jetty, the crew and passengers scrambled off and ran helter skelter down the length of the wooden pier. At half a mile out, E11 released its torpedo. The missile struck amidships, detonating its cargo of ammunition and in the process destroying the end of the jetty. A third ship was added to E11's tally. Nasmith had scored his hat trick.

* * *

While his cavalry troop of fifty Circassian irregulars finished breakfast and struck camp, Captain Timur rode his mount to a rise above the shore and contemplated the sea through his field glasses. Dolphins were crossing from the east, skipping the surface like smooth stones, blending deep in their element. He saw the smoke of a steamer coming from the direction of Constantinople, and carefully followed its progress across the horizon. His ADC, Lieutenant Murat appeared at his side with a sergeant bringing them coffee and some fried pastries. The air was quiet after the early dawn birdsong.

'For a moment you could forget there was a war on.' said Lieutenant Murat.

Captain Timur turned and looked at his friend but said nothing. Then a low rumble rolling in from the west signalled the beginning of the morning barrage from the British battleships over the Gallipoli Peninsula, clear as thunder across the water. There could be no forgetting.

In mid-morning Captain Timur halted the troop on the outskirts of Tekirdağ, on high ground above the sea. Again he scanned the horizon. Again the smoke of a ship. But this time the vessel was evidently in distress; a couple of lifeboats were hanging from their davits at odd angles, and people were falling in the sea. Then he spied the submarine. Now the ship had stopped and lifeboats were heading towards the shore. Next came the explosion and the submarine disappeared from view.

The rumbling from the west had ceased and again the air became still. The day was warming up. High above from the east came flocks of storks in great numbers, their flight in stages, stepping and circling upon the thermals. Eagles followed, dozens at a time, harried by the local crows, but moving inexorably north in their migration. Timur and Murat exchanged glances, reminded of happier, more urgent days of their youth, beneath the skies of Gallilee.

Timur looked back into the sea. The action was now close up, and he had no need of his field glasses. The Turkish cargo ship, well laden and low in the water, came careening in with its fog horns blaring, towards the extended jetty of Tekirdağ harbour. He watched the crew and passengers scrambling off and running as if for their lives. He saw villagers running away from the harbour. And he saw the cause of this effect, the black pipe fin of a submarine's periscope slicing the water, and then, when still a thousand yards out, the detaching of its steely phallus, the milky wake and then the climax as it penetrated the ship and impregnated its explosive cargo.

From their hillside vantage point Timur's sharp shooters fired a few rounds which plinked impotently upon the periscope as the submarine withdrew into deeper water.

* * *

In the Hotel Grand Antakya Satanaya felt she was simply treading water. Reports came in from the various battle fronts in a haphazard fashion, but were so heavily censored that it was hard to get a real sense of the situation, for better or worse. No one, least of all Satanaya, could be unaware, however, of the constant stream of wounded arriving in the hospitals by road and sea.

'Zeki Bey,' she said one day, 'I hate not knowing what's going on out there. Constantinople is beginning to feel like an enormous prison, where we are all waiting for the executioner.'

'I know, my dear. The whole world seems to have gone mad.'

'Well, I've decided that I want to go out to the Dardanelles and see for myself.'

'You mean, like a tourist?' Zeki laughed. 'The authorities would never allow it.'

'No, not as a tourist. But what if I was doing something worthwhile, like bringing a cargo of medical supplies? We're always hearing reports about the lack of dressings, and morphine. If we buy them on the black market, I can take them directly to the troops.'

'Satanaya, you're crazy. Apart from anything else, the danger involved?'

She smiled in relief. 'Oh, is that all? I thought you were going to say I was needed here.'

Zeki knew he was cornered. The only thing to do was to agree and support her plan, in the faint hope that something would occur to change her mind. And yet, when he saw her off in the old ferry, the *Ağrı Dağı*, a side-paddle steamer with the passenger saloons now filled to the ceiling with splints and crutches, blankets and stretchers, sterilising equipment, boxes of bandages, gauze and disinfectants, cases of morphine and an operating table arrayed with knives, saws, forceps and syringes, he felt nothing but pride. On deck thererewas even a couple of *arabas* complete with horses.

The weeks leading up to her departure had seen Satanaya moving frantically up and down the Bosphorus garnering donations from Amina Khanoum's friends and relatives in their splendid *yalıs*, wealthy people who were well aware that to be seen supporting the troops would keep them out of the eye of the Committee. Hotel Grand Antakya even imposed a hefty 'bar tax' of fifty percent on every drink, and a 'girl tax', on the escorts' earnings. Permission to accompany the cargo had been arranged, most reluctantly, by the Colonel Efendi, with an escort of young cadet officers of good standing. Amina Khanoum thought the whole project thrilling and pleaded to be allowed to accompany her friend, but here the Colonel had put his foot down. In any case the permit only allowed Satanaya to travel as far as Tekirdağ.

'Well, we'll see about that when the time comes.' was Satanaya's thought, as from the depths of her mind the image of Colonel Mustafa rose like a bubble to the surface.

One evening shortly after sunset, the old paddle steamer set off, hugging the coast and observing black-out.

Satanaya went and lay on her bunk in the stuffy cabin. Although exhausted from being up all the previous night with last minute preparations, she was unable to relax. She found herself assailed by doubts about her decision. Not being a fully trained nurse, she had little hands-on experience with wounded; and the horror stories she'd overheard at the bar from soldiers, which then had filled her with concern, now came back to haunt her. Added to that the responsibility of her valuable cargo and the recent news of British submarines in the Sea of Marmara… it had all seemed such an adventure as she planned it from the comfort of the hotel, but parted now from all the familiar, she felt afraid. Eventually she gave up trying to sleep, and wrapped up in her cloak, she went up on deck.

Breathing the fresh sea air was a relief, and helped her think clearly again. That she had come so far, there had to be a good reason. She simply had to trust that whatever happened now, was ultimately in her destiny. A memory appeared of a moment years before, of leaving the hammam where she had met the wonderful ladies of Karaman, the town where Rumi's mother was buried. Above the lintel was this calligraphy: '*If it is your allotted portion, it will come to you, whether or not it comes from Yemen or Baghdad.*' So, having no choice in that moment other than to be present where she was, she accepted her lot of being borne upon the ocean's breast into the ever-unknown future.

She stood for ages leaning on the taffrail as night fell, gazing over the sea which spread as a dark mirror to an unseen horizon. Lazy water, she called it, when the sea becomes calm, between tides, between storms, a laziness neither reprehensible nor blameworthy, but simply a time of rest; as all the perturbations of external influences subsided, leaving it in blessed peace.

And although she knew the scientists did not attribute the oceans' actions to the mass of water itself, but to its involuntary response to the moon's attractions, she knew also that this was only one point of view. Was not this water alive, breathing, absorbing from the air, and exhaling, while enfolding the whole of the vast earth in its embrace? Like the net of mace upon nutmeg, or a caul, clasping, a part inseparable but distinct. Was this water not the earth's closest lover, the spirit to its matter, and for now, in this moment of idleness, did these two not lie close as elemental lovers entwined and at rest in each other's arms?

With such thoughts Satanaya lay down beneath the stars in the bed of one of the *arabas*, and fell asleep to the rhythmic slap and dribble of the two paddle wheels choogling on down the European shore of the Marmara Sea.

TWENTY-FOUR

The Submarine, the Cavalry and the Paddle Steamer

Part two – Quod Erat Demonstrandum

The Sea of Marmara – May 1915

 T. CDR. NASMITH had tasted the sweet smell of victory, and he liked it. But the day was still young and the game was afoot. He kept E.11 close to the surface, and his eyes glued to the periscope. Before long another target presented itself; an old paddle steamer, evidently heading towards Tekirdağ; a requisitioned ferry, the sort that in happier days would be transporting the inhabitants of Constantinople between Europe and Asia, or on day trips up the Bosphorus and to the Princes' Islands. Nasmith was now able to make out horses coralled on the open deck at the stern, and rolls of barbed wire piled in the companion ways. 'An easy target, nice and slow. We'll just arrest her, get the passengers off and set charges,' he thought, as the submarine gradually closed the gap and surfaced in the vessel's wake.

'Stop and abandon ship!' Nasmith ordered through the megaphone.

The big paddle wheels slowed and the ferry drifted to a stop. Then the paddles began to rotate, each in a different direction as the boat turned around to face E.11. Then suddenly it picked up speed and charged towards the submarine, evidently intent on ramming it broadside. Nasmith was barely able to steer the sub clear in time to avoid a collision. Meanwhile his marines opened fire on the wheelhouse. The wheelman disappeared, the paddles stopped and the ferry was left to drift. Then the man returned to the helm and steered his ship back on course to ram E.11. Another volley of shots from the submarine brought the ferry to a halt. But only briefly. Once more the wheelman powered up the paddles but this time he steered the ferry directly for the shore, still some miles distant. The big paddle wheels churned the sea in a desperate attempt to escape as Nasmith closed in, this time with a torpedo loaded and ready. Then, like a little yappy dog standing bravely at the gate of its own yard, the ferry turned around to face its aggressor once more, before making a final dash for the safety of the shore, riding up the beach below some low sandy cliffs. Passengers and crew quickly disembarked over the side and headed off along the beach in the direction of Tekirdağ, while the poor ferry, its paddles still turning, futilely thrashed the shallows like a beached leviathan.

'Now we have her!' Nasmith shouted in his excitement. 'Prepare to board.' Then he inched the submarine right up against the vessel's stern.

* * *

Captain Timur and his detachment of Circassian cavalry continued their patrol along the north coast of the Sea of Marmara. Timur kept his field glasses to hand, and whenever their route took them by the shore, he scanned the waves. From the crest of a sandy cliff just short of Tekirdağ he spied an approaching ship. As its silhouette became more defined he recognised it as an old side-paddle *vapur*, one of the requisitioned Bosphorus ferries.

Suddenly, like a gamebird sensing the eyes of a hunter, the ferry stopped dead in the water. Then, in a slow dance, it wheeled around 180 degrees and headed back at full steam. Timur was intrigued. A white streak in the water just ahead of the ferry boat revealed the presence of its contender, a submarine, taking evasive action. Again the ferry slowed, stopped, and drifted, before turning and heading straight towards the shore below the cavalry troop. As the unlikely battle between the paddle steamer and the submarine unfolded before their eyes, the Circassian horsemen needed no prompting. Captain Timur, rifle in hand, led his men in a charge down the crumbling dunes through a break in the cliff. They galloped along the beach towards the stricken vessel, firing from the saddle as they went.

Fifty mounted Circassian cavalry in full charge along a Turkish strand was an irresistible sight to the boarding party from the submarine. Valour not withstanding, they knew they were outnumbered, and a discrete retreat was ordered. The cavalry continued to fire as the submariners scrambled back on board while their vessel reversed slowly away from the shore. When all his men were safely back inside, as Nasmith left the conning tower, a parting bullet zipped the crest of his cap.

'That's one lucky fox.' he muttered, and then wondered to himself, 'But who was the fox and who the hounds?' He went below, and took his ship out into deeper water.

* * *

Satanaya was in a quandary. She had been with the skipper, Orhan Kaptan, in the wheelhouse of the ferry when the submarine appeared and the first shots came; when the captain was hit, she had run to get a first aid kit. The ship had begun to drift, and when she returned to the wheelhouse, Orhan Kaptan, now lying groaning on the floor of the bridge, had croaked out some instructions.

'Turn her round, quick: squeeze that lever and push it back to reverse the starboard paddles, until we are facing the submarine, then push both levers all the way forward again and steer straight at her. Call down below for all the steam they can give her. We're not done yet, by any means. If we don't ram her, then we'll head for the shore – and if she gives chase we'll turn on her again. Don't worry, we'll make it.'

Orhan Kaptan was an old hand, he knew his ship well, and although an 'elderly lady', she was still quietly agile. He was confident the submarine could not manoeuvre as quickly. Maybe with the right moves they could gain time. It all depended on the girl. He had not been happy initially taking this passenger, but she had shown a real interest in his ship and her workings, and he had been enjoying her conversation as they steamed along that morning. Now perhaps she could show her worth.

Satanaya relayed the captain's orders to the stokers below, while pulling on the klaxon string. The ferry gained speed as the paddles frantically clawed through the water and it came within a few feet of clipping the submarine's tail as it ran off on their port side. She then turned towards the shore, fixed the wheel and began to tend the bullet wound in captain's shoulder. She tore off his shirt – he had bled a lot where the bullet had evidently passed through his right shoulder, breaking a bone before exiting but missing any significant artery. She hoped it had not pierced his lung. Removing bits of torn shirt from the wound, she staunched the bleeding with a big wad of cottonwool wrapped round his chest and was bandaging it when more rifle fire began to shatter the wooden walls of the wheel-house.

'Disengage the wheels, let them think we've stopped. And for heaven's sake take cover.'

'OK, but hold that dressing down as hard as you can. I'll be back in a moment.'

Satanaya did as she was told, briefly skipping out and hiding behind the funnel. As soon as the ferry had begun to drift, she slipped back in, turned it round and had another go at ramming the submarine. She knew the idea was to scare it off, gain time and hopefully a little distance. Once again the submarine dodged the old paddle steamer's bows and began to turn laboriously in a big arc. Meanwhile the ferry, with independently geared wheels, could turn on a penny and gain valuable ground.

They were getting very near the shore now, horn blaring, funnel steaming, paddles going full tilt.

'Just keep on going now, leave her in gear and hope we get well up and out of harm's way. Then get off quickly. Don't worry about me.' said Orhan Kaptan.

'Sure.' said Satanaya, while knowing she would not leave her patient.

A brief, gravelly scraping sound and then a shattering lurch as the ferry beached and sent Satanaya tumbling across the wheelhouse.

One of her escort cadets appeared, white as a sheet.

'Quick, we must get off!'

'I'm going to take care of the horses' replied Satanaya firmly, 'Find the others and get the captain ashore. Gently. Now.'

People were climbing over the sides and down mooring ropes and dropping, some into the water, some into the sand. Just as the dark hull of the submarine appeared alongside, and armed seamen were clambering aboard, cavalry arrived at the scene, racing along the shoreline, guns ablaze.

After a brief defensive firefight from the ferry's deck, the submariners withdrew to the safety of their own vessel.

* * *

It was a toss-up who was the more surprised. Satanaya in her relief at finding help at hand did not immediately recognise the battle-hardened face of the cavalry officer jumping directly from his saddle onto the side of the ferry. Yet those were the eyes of Timur, her putative Circassian bridegroom and quasi-kidnapper. It had been more than fifteen years since their parting on the quay in Beirut after journeying together through Palestine. As for Captain Timur, at first he was puzzled, then delighted. He would have embraced her there and then but a burst of fire from the deck of the retreating submarine put paid to a dignified reunion as he pushed her roughly down onto the deck.

'Gosh, you haven't changed your style much, have you?'

'Sorry. Stay down,' he said, then crept along the deck to the stern and managed a few return shots. He later swore he had hit the cap of the retreating submarine captain, though his men laughed at this boast.

'Satanaya, we must get off immediately. He'll torpedo the ship once he gets into deeper water. He's already done it once this morning, to a much bigger ship.'

'But the horses. What about the horses? And all my medicines?'

'Better you're alive, better we're both alive. Now come on.'

She didn't argue. Timur slid down the rope to his waiting mount and Satanaya followed, falling across his saddle, and together they galloped away from the stranded ferry in a somewhat surreal parody of the earlier mock-abduction in distant Gallilee. His troop, who had been firing from positions in the sand, followed, still letting off the occasional volley for effect upon the fast-submerging steel hull.

After a few hundred yards the cavalry dismounted on the dunes to observe the expected outcome. Sure enough, they had barely taken cover when the slick needle of a torpedo scribed a milky wake beneath the surface of the sea. They followed its steady course and it looked to be right on target, until it slid from the water to the left of the ferry and buried itself in the soft sandy cliff before detonating. The horses on the ferry reared and shrieked in their stalls, but otherwise no damage resulted.

Still, there was work to be done, and Satanaya and Timur had to postpone their personal reunion until the captain had been properly seen to.

Orhan Kaptan was not unknown in Tekirdağ. He had spent most of his life sailing the coast of the Sea of Marmara before retiring after the Balkan Wars and was well-liked by the seafaring community in those parts. Like so many of his age he had been pressed back into service when hostilities commenced. When Satanaya found him, he was already in the hands of Dr. Fikret Bey, the local *hakîm*. The prognosis was fair as long as infection didn't set in; he had been given a good dose of morphine and he would remain in the town's care for the time being.

As for the ferry, the crew refloated her in the rising tide, with the help of the Circassian cavalry and a couple of fishing *kayıks*. Under guidance from the crew, Satanaya took the helm, now designated honorary First Mate by Orhan Kaptan, and brought the old ship into the haven of Tekirdağ. While Satanaya enjoyed the hospitality of Dr Fikret and his Kosovan wife Sevil Khanoum, the escort of young cadets bunked down in camp with the Circassian cavalry.

* * *

Later that evening Timur called on Satanaya at the doctor's house. Her hosts left them sitting together on the terrace, beneath the vine's new leaves, in the early summer warmth.

'Look at you!' said Satanaya.

'And look at you.' said Timur.

'You and Murat, you stayed together. I'm so glad.' said Satanaya.

Timur smiled. 'He keeps me sane, you know, in this insanity. I always take things so seriously. I forget, with all this responsibility, my company, eighty men to look after and I can barely look after myself. If it wasn't for Murat… he brings me joy, with just a word, a look.'

'And maybe a kiss, on Mount Tabor?'

They laughed, then sank into silence awhile. Neither wanted to break the moment with history, to fill this shared space of friendship with an unshared past. But they did talk of the past, telling each other their stories until late into the night. And those unshared spaces too became by this friendship shared experience. When Timur rode off to his camp, their parting did not separate them; for some unions are established in a place where time and distance hold no sway, where the bond of true friendship holds no obligations.

TWENTY-FIVE

Soups for Troops

Sea of Marmara – Gallipoli Peninsula, May-June 1915

N THE AFTERMATH of their first military engagement, the four young staff cadets were somewhat embarrassed that they hadn't been more effective in the fight. Although they had managed to disembark the ferry captain without further harm and bring him to Dr Fikret, they felt they had rather funked their part in the actual attack.

'We did try,' one of them said, when they reconvened for a meeting with Satanaya and Timur. 'We lay in the dunes and I used up nearly all my ammunition firing at the submarine.'

'But at that range, our pistols were not much use,' said another cadet. 'If only we had been issued with rifles.' he added, wistfully.

'Well, you may get another chance to be heroes.' Satanaya reassured them, 'We can't abandon the ship now. And when Orhan Kaptan is well enough, we must see him and our cargo at least as far as Gallipoli, and perhaps into the battle zone at Maydos* itself.'

Although Maydos was vulnerable to bombardment from British battleships firing from behind their island shield of Lemnos, she explained that the ferry would be of great help to the Red Crescent in bringing wounded out of the battle zone. 'But… the Colonel Efendi gave us orders to accompany you here, and then bring you back…' the third young soldier piped up.

'Don't worry, I'll fix it all with the Colonel.' Satanaya replied.

That wasn't the point. What if she was no longer around to fix things? Here Captain Timur stepped in.

'Look,' he explained, 'I'm the senior officer here, so you are now under my command; and frankly I would rather face the Colonel Efendi under any circumstances than try to change the mind of this headstrong Circassian lady. Your duty is to protect her, and you shall; but for the time being you will make yourself useful with our troop. I shall telegraph the Colonel explaining the unusual circumstances necessitating your delayed return.'

'Besides,' added Satanaya, keen to instil in them a degree of her unconditional positive regard to life, 'I will need your help to load and drive the *arabas*, and to set up the hospital. And then, when everything is working well, we can go home. You'll see; it will stand you in good stead in your future careers.'

With that they dropped their arguments and submitted to their destiny with Satanaya and the Circassian irregulars.

Tekirdağ was the busy forward staging post for troops moving up to the front, and the transfer point for the wounded being brought out of the battle zone. A small tent-city had sprung up behind the town, where troops in reserve were being drilled, and the town's infirmary was now a military field hospital.

Orhan Kaptan was recovering rapidly thanks to the Dr Fikret's ministrations and Satanaya's restorative soups. While the crew and passengers waited in Tekirdağ, Captain Timur and Lieutenant Murat looked after the young cadets. The cavalry troop was being held in reserve, performing

---

*   now Eceabat.

simple patrol duties along the coast. Each day the cadets saddled the *arabas'* draft horses and rode out with the troop. Murat issued them with rifles and gave them target practice. The Circassians soldiers taught the boys skills they would never have learned in the gloomy classrooms of the Harbiye Military Academy. By the end of ten days, they could shoot from the saddle at a gallop and swing down on one stirrup to fire below the horses belly, though when they would ever get to exercise this skill they had no idea.

Ten days after the beaching, Orhan Kaptan was well enough to walk. Shortly afterwards under the captain's instructions, the little ferry *Ağrı Dağı* left the safety of the Tekirdağ breakwater after sunset and paddled quietly south-west along the coast towards the Dardanelles. The moon was in its last quarter, and when it set, and it was too dark to make way safely, they lay up in a small fisherman's *barınak,* a tiny cove invisible from the sea until you were almost inside it.

In the half-light before dawn they made a dash, keeping close inshore, and reached Maydos safely at sunrise. Satanaya was on deck as they steamed inside the protective arm of the harbour's old stone breakwater. A pall of smoke hung over the town blotting out the sun so that all the buildings appeared in an eerie mauve twilight. As the ferry was being made fast to the quay, a high pitched whistling sound rent the air. The soldiers on board looked to the sky. On shore people flattened themselves on the ground. But the explosion, when it came a second or two later, was behind the town to the west. Further siren shrieks and explosions followed, and then silence, and the descent of smoke and ash. Within the stillness Satanaya became aware of a distant chorus of gunfire, a backdrop of sound like the rolling of shingle or rain falling on leaves, that was to continue throughout her stay. Then people began to move again and everything returned to normal.

But it was a different normal. Everyone, crew and shore labourers, lent a hand unloading the cargo and harnessing the *arabas* and reloading the medical supplies. Almost immediately the ship had docked, an endless train of horse carts, hand carts and stretcher-bearers poured onto the quay carrying dozens of wounded men; pale-faced figures wrapped in blankets and bandages brown with old blood. Their eyes, if not closed, appeared blind to the outside world as in impotence they sought an inner relief from their pain.

Once the ferry had been unloaded, the wounded were taken straight on board where huge banners bearing the moon and star symbol of the Red Crescent now hung down the sides of the ship, designating it a medical evacuation transport. Satanaya and her little team had barely assembled themselves ashore when Orhan Kaptan sounded the klaxon from his seat in the newly repaired wheelhouse and began a slow turn out of the harbour for the return to Constantinople.

The new arrivals followed the band of stretcher-bearers back through the streets to the Maydos hospital on the outskirts of the town, one of the main transfer hospitals where casualties were brought. The Ottoman army had a well-established system for dealing with casualties from the battle-front, which here was barely five miles beyond over the rough scrubby hills and ravines. The wounded men were first brought back from the trench line to a casualty receiving station where immediate first aid would be administered by battalion medical staff. Less serious wounds would be treated at a field hospital, and the patient sent back to the lines. There was no mechanical transport on this part of the peninsula. Of the seriously wounded, those that were likely to survive were carried by hand or cart down to the transfer hospitals on the coast, and from there sent on by road or sea to hospitals in the interior of Turkey. Maydos hospital served as a major transfer point for casualties who would then be taken to Constantinople and thence by rail to Eskişehir for longer term rehabilitation. Those poor souls who had fallen in battle with fatal wounds were gently carried to quiet places in the shade of trees and left to nature's mercy. When the fighting was particularly fierce, medical companies would come into the trenches under fire and administer immediate emergency first aid within the 'golden hour': the first hour after serious wounding when a casualty's chances of survival are highest.

Nothing could have prepared Satanaya for what she encountered at Maydos. Earlier that month it had been targeted by British naval artillery and two dozen high explosive shells had wreaked havoc, killing hundreds of already wounded patients and destroying much of the hospital facilities. Now many of the patients were being treated in makeshift structures while repairs to the buildings were carried out. Large tents spread across the open land at the edge of the town and field kitchens were operating in the open air. But it was the smell that Satanaya noticed first, even before the evident chaos of the situation: raw sewage, decaying flesh and the burning of amputated limbs. She stifled the natural urge to retch as she blanked her mind as well as her senses, knowing there was no turning away. So this was the reality then, she thought. The bombing, the chaos and the filth, the apparent degradation of the human image – it was outside her experience and seemed unreal. In this pivotal moment she hovered above her own impending panic. Yet she knew she had to see it as it was; she had made the choice long ago.

Then someone called out her name.

'Satanaya, hi! So you did come after all.'

She recognised one of the nurses she had trained with in the hospital at Haydarpaşa, a girl called Melek.

Melek was smiling at her across the body of young soldier struggling with pain from a bloody leg wound she was dressing, while two male orderlies held the boy down.

'Have you got any morphine in those packages? And atropine?'

Satanaya knew there was nothing for it but to jump right in.

'Yes, of course. Coming right up.'

She climbed onto the *araba* and sorted through the packets until she found what was wanted. Within minutes of arrival she was helping Melek, going from patient to patient, some of whom were still lying on the stretchers they had been brought in on. Sometimes her job was simply to bring water to a young soldier, or to change a dressing. Sometimes it was to place a morphine tablet under the tongue of one crying in pain, or to close the vacant eyes of one who had found the ultimate relief. Before she knew it half a day had passed and she hadn't had a moment to think of her own needs.

She quartered with Melek and half a dozen other nurses in a part of the hospital building still standing; since the water supply had been damaged ablutions were a hit and miss affair. Casualties seemed to arrive without a break, at all hours, as many as five hundred in a day, sometimes more. Although Satanaya seemed to manage, even with her admittedly minimal training, she quickly realised direct patient care was not her particular strength. On the other hand, while the field kitchens were run efficiently enough, she felt there was room for improvement. If the meals could be made just that little bit more appetising, she thought, it might also improve the condition of the wounded men.

No one complained when she took over as *ahçıbaşı* – chef. It was a thankless task, cooking for such numbers in trying conditions, and too often the best intentions were wasted by overcooking and inappropriate seasoning. Cooking for the infirm is a particular science. Heavy wounding needs good protein to aid repair, and here Satanaya was able to use her skills by putting aside her natural distaste for the odiferous garlic by producing nourishing 'paça' broths of sheep's heads and feet and 'işkembe çorbası' from tripe, and her favourite, Uncle Mevlut's lentil soup. More often the choice of meat was horse, as so many wounded horses had to be put down, and the meat then quickly butchered; sheep were not so easily come by.

Something had taken possession of Satanaya. She stood at her field kitchen from morning until late in the evening, chopping and stirring, tasting and pouring out of the large military-size kazans, gallon upon gallon of rich soup which was gladly taken up by the endlessly passing train of casualties. It was a simple act of love, inexplicable, as she disappeared in the action. In spite of the apparent tragedy of her surroundings she found a quiet joy simply in preparing and serving the soup. Some might see it as a kind of self-hypnosis, to protect herself from the distressing situation, but that was only a secondary effect, when the cause was the necessity itself: the demand to serve the humanity of the young men, their poor bodies broken beneath the abuse of war. Satanaya poured out her soups of compassion upon their frail beings, and the benefit was reciprocal.

Most days Satanaya took a cart into Maydos town to fetch supplies. Much of the bread was brought up daily from the big bakery in Gallipoli, and other supplies from the depot in nearby Akbaş. Yoghurt and tobacco were also essential – the first to treat sunstroke*, the other for the nerves.

Maydos was a busy thoroughfare day and night, as more and more troops arrived, taking the place of the dead and wounded. One morning while collecting a load of *simits*, Satanaya heard in the distance the sound of flutes rising above a chorus of boot heels marching. Then around the corner of the street came a strange-looking band of men, bearing arms: the Regiment of the Mevlevi Dervishes. In their midst was their standard bearer holding aloft the *sancak*, the huge bright crimson emblem of the

---

* Take 2 tablespoons of yogurt and blend it with water. Add a little salt and ground cumin. Mix well and drink it thrice a day.

regiment, embroidered in silver silk picturing the '*sikka*', the dervish hat, its turban outlined in dark green thread, and the words '*Ya Hazreti Mevlana*' – 'O Blessed Mevlana' stitched in silver thread within, and high in one corner the crescent moon and star.

Four *ney* players led the troop, all wearing the tall tombstone dervish hats of felt, with rifles slung over their belted long-sleeved coats. The drummer, a small young fellow, solemnly beat out a marching rhythm. Another minstrel, a young Kurd, half-hidden in the crowd, a look of ancient sadness clothed his face, plucked a stringed instrument, a half-heard glimpse of lost love's pain and on he passed. High up in their midst rode the Colonel, mounted on a snowy white Arab horse. And following him, his troops. They sang as they marched, a *zikr*, gently chanted on their breath which rose as the hum of bees: *hu allah, hu allah, hu allah*. Satanaya flew in her mind to Konya years before when the white-skirted *semazen* led the dervishes as they spun in their planetary dance of the Sema within the mausoleum of Jelaluddin Rumi. She was transfixed and transported. Time and space folded up and the vast plains of the central Anatolian steppe, the conical red stone domes, the smell of cedar and soft footfall upon ancient carpets in the tombs of the saints, became present to her. And for a moment she saw again her mysterious guide, Yeşil Efendi, the man in the tattered green kalpak. Like a face peering from behind the curtain at the edge of a stage, he looked kindly at the soldiers, then vanished. There was a strange dignity in the manner of this passing troop, as if all were held within a protective cloak which, while it might not hold off the inevitability of their physical sacrifice, yet preserved their spirit from fear and the sadness of facing death. She returned to herself as the heels of the dervishes fell silent behind the street walls, and the notes of the flutes, full of dread and longing, faded as the regiment marched out to battle.

When the Medical General Inspectorate Director, Dr. Colonel Süley-man, brought her Colonel Efendi's telegram enquiring about her return, she knew her job was done. Dr. Colonel Süleyman thanked her for her efforts training the hospital cooks in the production of soups and pinned a campaign medal to her apron.

During her brief time at the front, Satanaya had not come across Mustafa. The story of how he had personally halted the invading troops at Arıburnu with a mere battalion of men was much talked about; as well as the praise of his men, it had earned him a breast of medals. Word reached the newly-promoted Colonel Mustafa in his headquarters, that the soups of Maydos hospital were having a good effect on the recovery and morale of his troops, and when one day an orderly brought him a steaming kazan of lentil soup, he recognised its provenance. He sent a message inviting this mysterious cook to visit his camp, but it was too late. Satanaya had left the hospital that morning, and the message was never delivered.

Here in Maydos Satanaya had found that even in the midst of hell there existed a paradise. On the face of it, it was simply a shambles, a butchery. The men were brought, like a driven herd, to die in this abattoir of hills and ravines. Their carcasses came back, seared and broken; and the nurses and doctors were expected to kiss it all better. Where they could, they did with the care of angels, comforting the frightened of dying, giving solace to the hurt. That such compassion existed alongside the denaturing devilry of war opened Satanaya's eyes to something beyond the obvious. Those who went before the guns were not simply cattle, for their sacrifice became an act of love. They were known as *shahid* – witness – for the martyrs of the battlefields are said to go straight to paradise. And among the mayhem, the cries of pain of the wounded, Satanaya knew with every last breath of the dying that she too became a witness, to the souls' transition from this valley of death to a greater freedom. In this shared witnessing, she felt an accompanying breath of compassion, a light upon their hearts within the gathered darkness of the place. Yes, there was love. Whether it was love of country or comrade, a wife or lover, a belief imagined or real, whatever, it moved their souls to surrender to beauty as a child will rush to its mother, in the midst of this decay.

But it was enough. In the end, her own yearning for beauty could take no more in this dreadful estate. As she began her journey to the harbour she passed two dervishes, cloaks stained with blood and filth, their felt hats bent but still atop their bearded faces. They bore between them a stretcher on which lay a small figure, his face bandaged blind as if embalmed for burial, yet by his side a hand protruding from the covering blanket clutched the neck of a broken lute. For the first time since coming to Maydos, she burst into tears. She wept for herself, for all those days she had, along with her soup, poured cheer into the hearts of her patients. And she wept for the boy with the broken lute, and all the boys returning blind to beauty's light of day that was their mortal birthright.

TWENTY-SIX

Secrets of the Hotel Grand Antakya

Constantinople – 1915

ERA. A CITY within The City. Since early Ottoman times Christian nations, initially Genoa and then France, Venice and many others were granted 'capitulations' – written documents which gave foreign traders the right to reside and operate within the Ottoman Empire. They lived under their own laws, collected their own taxes, and were exempt from military conscription and prosecution under Ottoman law. They settled in Galata, the area across the Golden Horn from the old city of Stamboul. Here they lived in a walled neighbourhood on the steep hillside which stretches up to present day Tepebaşı. In the 19th century, the walls were demolished and the 'European quarter' expanded north along the hill. The whole district became known as Pera, which the Turks call Beyoğlu. Pera also became the site of the European legations and was witness to a changing population of foreign travellers and transients as well as generations of Christian residents of Greek, Italian, Armenian and Jewish origin.

Pera was where the Turks went to 'visit' Europe and enjoy its manner upon their own soil. The main thoroughfare, 'Grand Rue de Pera', was where all the best shops were situated. Here were to be found the latest Paris fashions, and the finest imported goods from around the world. Here, and also in adjacent lanes, in the early 20th century could be met with the full panoply of Western consumerism: cinemas, restaurants, cafes and hotels. Here too the churches of Christendom had the freedom to flourish, whatever their flavour – Armenian, Orthodox, Catholic, Protestant. The *lingua franca* was just that – French – though a dozen languages would be heard in the street and understood: Turkish, Greek, Italian were most common, with Arabic, Armenian and Persian, and the Ladino of the descendants of the Spanish Jews who migrated after the fall of Granada.

Nothing was so very different in 1915.

In spite of the onset of war, or perhaps as a response to these extreme times, the Hotel Grand Antakya, situated in the heart of Pera, was a success. It was particularly popular with the young officers of the new Turkish army, as their superior officers (and their German counterparts) tended to patronise the grander establishments. But the Antakya also attracted a mixed clientele of foreign businessmen and second-tier diplomats, particular those of a Balkan persuasion; and once word got round that the catering manager was Circassian, a number of the more well-heeled survivors of the 19th century migrations who had business in the area would turn up, hoping to find some Cherkez dishes on the menu. Satanaya was always happy to oblige them with poached *mataza,* a kind of ravioli, little pastries in half-moon shapes, filled sometimes with meat and greens, or with Circassian white cheese, paprika and onion, and which they would eat solemnly, while attentive waiters refilled little glasses with vodka.

The menu was quite eclectic, comprising classic dishes from both the French and the Ottoman East Mediterranean canon. Despite the deprivations that war brought to Constantinople and the country as a whole, Satanaya, once she had returned from the front, made good use of her connections in Beylerbeyi. She frequented the market gardens in the Bosphorus villages, and in the little valleys that ran off behind, where she knew she could rely on the women to provide her with the best courgettes and tomatoes, onions and potatoes, at prices well below those of the black market in Pera. She kept her horse, Tarçin, stabled at the konak, and once a week she would cross the water and ride out to visit this or that little farm and come back with sacks of greens and root vegetables. So much food was being requisitioned by the army that if she hadn't had the Josephian vision early on to lay in a couple of years supplies of staples such as rice and bulgur, chick peas, lentils and beans, olives and oil – it is unlikely they would have managed to keep the kitchens going. These stores she kept safe from thieves and vermin by turning the great bank vault into a dry store to which she and Zeki were the sole key-holders. In the hardest times, she would exchange grains against fresh produce: eggs, salads, fruit and green vegetables.

Similarly large stores of vodka, brandy and raki were laid down in the vault, although curiously these liquid refreshments never seemed to be in such short supply as solid food. Wine for general consumption she ordered in from Bulgaria, through Madame Hortense. Following the Sarajevo incident, on the Colonel Efendi's advice, she had shipped to Constantinople her own share of the fine aged wines and brandies from the *caves* of Beyt al-Rahma. These few thousand bottles included the Beyt's own renowned Château Miséricorde; as well as Champagne, Bordeaux and Burgundy from the finest domaines which she stored in the konak's cellars and brought them to the hotel as needed. Thanks to the Alliance, German wines were also not hard to come by; and the late French Ambassador's relatives in Homburg ensured the hotel had a good selection of rare *spätlesen* and *auslesen* wines of the Mosel and Rhine from the personal cellars of the Ritter von Marx.

It had been mutually agreed between Satanaya and Zeki that should she decide to stay, she would have an opportunity to become a shareholder in the hotel venture. As Satanaya did not want to be completely tied down by property, it was settled that she would take her dividend as a percentage of the bar and restaurant's gross earnings for as long as she remained with the hotel.

Zeki took in hand the entertainments. He rounded up the best of the Roma musicians from among the fiddlers and accordionists who played for pennies around the taverns and waterfront eateries in Galata, but others he brought in from the east; Copts from Egypt and a few Jewish girls he had known in Beirut – dancers, acrobats, jugglers and magicians – talented artistes singing for their suppers, and perhaps a warm berth out of the chill winds off the Black Sea.

Zeki also had other avenues for attracting income. While operating a brothel as such would have been too unsavoury even for a Beiruti, he did employ a number of beautiful and cheerful young ladies, and some athletic young men, to act as escorts for single guests should they desire company. What went on behind closed doors, (and sometimes not so closed), was between guest and escort. Zeki's cut came simply from increasing the room charge. 'The upkeep is so expensive!' was his mantra. This wasn't entirely untrue, as he really did make an effort to provide the best, and there were of course bribes to pay. Sadly, for both Zeki and his girls, the supply of young men dwindled as the war took its course, and the attrition of the battlefields meant even physically disabled candidates didn't necessarily escape the draft.

The regular income came from the room charges and the bar, both of which did excellent business, especially when officers were on leave. As time went by, Zeki developed a sideline procuring documents, forged or genuine, for the illegals, refugees and people needing permits or exit visas, particularly Ottoman Greeks and Armenians. In some cases Zeki took payment in kind, providing cash and jewellery in exchange for property and goods being left behind. This enabled him to maintain cheap housing for the constant stream of refugees who came to his door and also to subsidise the poorest to escape. He was a true businessman, the kind who recognised that the universe operated according to unconditioned generosity, providing a vast table of wealth from which one was free to take and use, and then reinvest one's returns to the table. The table, as he saw it, was life itself. To amass and hold onto one's gains would be to succumb to greed, and so limit the generosity and constrict the possibilities of life.

Proximity to the port allowed Zeki to get to know the captains of the few deep sea vessels that continued to navigate the Marmara Sea and Bosphorus littoral. Some of these mariners were integral to his people-smuggling network, sailing out clandestinely on moonless nights, waiting out the day in hidden coves, hugging the coast and running the blockade through the Dardanelles, or up into the Black Sea to Varna and beyond.

These extra-curricular activities of the hotel, however, could not have been undertaken successfully in these dark times had it not been for the 'co-operation' of a certain middle-ranking police officer and Committee member. Colonel Karagöz, the Black-Eyed Colonel, owed his position to his distant but highly placed relative, the Interior Minister Talaat Pasha. Karagöz was definitely a cop going places; a seemingly jovial character with a substantial 'balcony' – his large belly evidencing his penchant for pilafs, pide and patlican – who proved able, for a reasonable retainer, to turn a blind eye and 'regularise' things with the authorities should the need arise. Karagöz had his own table in the hotel dining room, his favourite seat in the bar, and a weekly arrangement with a stunning and startlingly large lady, a Dinka from Khartoum called Madiha.

Madiha had been discovered by Zeki in Egypt where in the less salubrious dives of the Alexandrian dockside she was famous for being the possessor of a certain unusual appendage, usually vestigial in her sex; yet like some freakishly large vegetable one might find in competition at a village fete, this member had grown to a size comparable with, if not quite outstripping, its reciprocal organ in the opposite sex. How she had escaped the barbarous customs visited upon the females of her tribe was down to her father; he had recognised the financial potential of such a generous prolongation and had seen it as the means to escape the life of a poor herdsman in the upper Nile. He brought her to Egypt, but contracted typhus and died before he had time to profit from his plan.

In time Madiha grew from street child singing and dancing for piastres, to a dancer of some renown. Her great strength and majestic size had made her the equal of any man who tried to submit her to his own designs – she was known to have laid out many a drunk, including an overenthusiastic Swedish seaman, with a single punch. Within the limits of the docklands milieu her capital rose as an independent artiste, highly prized and well-paid by the Alexandrian club owners. Encouraged by Zeki, with whom for a time she enjoyed an affectionate and mutually satisfying relationship, Madiha embarked upon a grand tour of the Eastern Mediterranean hotspots. Unfortunately, while performing in Beirut, her progress folded following the outbreak of hostilities and the British takeover of Egypt-Sudan. She joined Zeki in Constantinople and soon was an indispensable member of the team at Grand Antakya, keeping things smooth with the authorities, specifically Colonel Karagöz. With Madiha, it seemed he became a different person. He felt able to

relax into his true self by taking over the submissive role in their relationship, and becoming the slave of the magnificent dominatrix.

Colonel Karagöz's official job was to keep track of the comings and
goings in the Hotel Grand Antakya and to relay back information to Talaat
Pasha. Zeki knew this of course, and it became a bit of a game, feeding him
via Madiha with choice tidbits of irrelevant gossip, as well as planting
important items of misinformation in order to protect his friends.

While Zeki was the charming and ever present Master of Ceremonies
during the entertainments at the Grand Antakyan, most of the day-to-day
responsibilities fell to the chief desk clerk, Fatih Bey, who doubled as night
manager, concierge and accountant. From early evening until after breakfast it was Fatih Bey whom one found at the front desk.

Fatih Bey was the one true Antakyan in the place, having been born in
Antioch in the plain of the Orontes River. He was an Alevi, that unique
descendant sect of original Islam that some would align with Shi'ism,
because of their particular reverence for Ali, but which in Turkey closely
follows precepts set down by the prominent Turkish Sufi Haji Bektash, a
contemporary of Rumi.

Alevis belong to a sect considered socially more developed than traditional Sunni Muslims. It advocates education for women, does not require
them to be veiled, and is considered by its adherents to be an inner or
esoteric path in Islam. Their ceremony, the Jem, incorporates dancing, the
singing of spiritual verses and may include the drinking of alcohol. In these
activities, like some Sufis, the Alevis show perhaps a more tolerant face of
the religion of Mohammed. And this tolerance was evident in Fatih Bey's
manner: he was the epitome of grace and politeness, helpful and without
judgement, whatever problem, crisis or embarrassment with which the
guests or staff presented him. He was a discreet soul possessing an inner
state which combined between the resourcefulness of a helpful djinn and
the comfort of a protecting angel. Satanaya fell in love with him at first
sight. It was not a lover's love, but she sensed in him a special presence of
trust and security. Like an elder brother, Fatih Bey always made her feel at
ease, accepted and safe.

'Oh, if only all religions could teach their followers to behave like Fatih
Bey,' Satanaya thought, when observing how he handled the escape of
some young Armenian fugitives. When they arrived breathless, seeking
his help, he first calmed them with kind words, and quickly dressed them

in bellboy outfits. Shortly afterwards when the jandarma arrived he feigned complete surprise saying that he had no idea what they were after, but they were free to search the place and these bellboys would show them around. Such occurrences were not common, but when called upon, Fatih Bey never failed to rise to the occasion.

In addition to these noble qualities, Fatih Bey had great business acumen, having once been account manager in the bank that used to inhabit the building. He showed himself dextrous at manipulating Zeki Bey's incomes and outgoings to the hotel's best advantage, suggesting adjustments and economies where and when necessary. While he ran a tight ship, in keeping with Zeki's own financial policy, Fatih Bey didn't hesitate to provide monetary aid to staff in need, and in addition made sure the local beggary kept off the hotel steps by providing them with a small stipend each week. Similarly Satanaya fed half a dozen refugee families with choice restaurant leftovers, out of the back door by the kitchens.

Fatih Bey kept a parrot in a large cage in the seating area of the foyer, an African Grey called Xenophon who could swear in eight languages, though not in Turkish or Arabic. Xenophon would recite Persian poet Sa'di's famous line, *bani aadam 'azaa-i yek peykarand* (the sons of Adam are limbs of a single form) when the better class courtesans and call girls came in off their night shifts for early breakfast before heading off to sleep. Fatih Bey would still be wide awake, impeccably attired in his well-pressed suit, with his dark smiling face, his large, bald shining pate. At Xenophon's sonorous call, he would rise and welcome the ladies as if they were countesses returning late from a ball. And when the chill winds blew down from beyond the Black Sea he would encourage them to warm themselves by the great enamelled coal stove which belted out heat through the hotel foyer. In wartime coal became another rare commodity. But again, Zeki's foresight had early on ensured their bunkers were brim full of hard coal, utilising one of the lockable basement vault rooms.

Fatih Bey read all the foreign newspapers avidly. He was fascinated by modern science and in particular the latest developments in psychotherapy, psychoanalysis and theories of the mind as propounded by the Vienna school. On long winter evenings after the dinner service was done and the bar had closed, he would sit with Satanaya and they would relax together, she with a glass of slivo, he with a small Syrian coffee, and read aloud the most interesting stories of the day. If there was something referring to the theories of Freud or Adler, or even the maverick Jung, conversation would inevitably ensue.

Satanaya preferred to be the one asking the questions, getting Fatih to explain what he understood of a particular theory, and then testing it against her own understanding of the mind's dimensions, as it had unfolded from her various mentors, noticing where a particular conjecture did not conform to the revelations of her own heart, and where one did.

Some nights the mood demanded otherwise and they might play a little *tavla*, a game at which they were evenly matched, and then the play would become ribald and competitive, demanding game after game until eventually Satanaya would begin to yawn. Then she would apologise and slip away to bed, while Fatih Bey remained on watch through to the dawn.

TWENTY-SEVEN

The Heroes of Anafartalar

Gallipoli Peninsula – August 1915

"If princes and kings were able to maintain it, all things would of themselves be transformed by them. If this transformation became to me an object of desire, I would express the desire by the nameless simplicity."
Lao Tse, on the exercise of government.

"Psychological powers triumphed over physical, the spiritual over the material"
Colonel Hans Kannengiesser, Commander, Ottoman 9th Division, Gallipoli.

ND SO IT CONTINUED through the long hot summer. Back and forth the battles raged, thousands upon thousands of human bodies cast before the shredding metal of modern munitions, for a few feet of dry blasted earth. To survive mentally and still function in this inferno, all kinds of human beliefs and conditioned responses need to be suspended. No rational person, let alone a person of heart, would entertain such behaviour, faced with the destruction of his own image.

It is perhaps, in the final analysis, that the emotion we so keenly parade as love – (not the eternal universal compassion upon all existence, but that complicated bundle of human desires that animates our best and worst aspirations) – is but a partial effect of our imagined autonomous existence. For such shadows of love divide and engender their opposites, and ultimately require annihilation of the illusory other which our selfishness creates.

War is pure annihilation. It is not simply a matter of hate, unless we accept that it is ourselves we are hating. It is a failure to comprehend the significance of a real totality, a failure to recognise that what we are looking at is the same as what is looking; that the seer, the seen and the seeing are one. Until then, war, the destruction of any human image that appears to contradict – rather than reflect or better, complement our own – will remain the prevailing *modus operandi* for emptying ourselves of our selves in the hope that after annihilation, something real might be revealed.

And so, as eternal qualities danced together, contending for dominance in the heavenly spheres, the mundane beastliness of their human manifestation, continued to roll out upon the plains and scrubby hillsides of Gallipoli and nearby Troy. And through it all Mustafa had only one thought, to perform his duty in protecting his homeland to the best of his ability. Due to his uncompromising (some would say intransigent) nature, this brought him into conflict with his superiors. He clashed with the German General, Liman von Sanders, over how the overall campaign was being conducted. He even complained directly to Enver, inviting him to take over the command. Enver visited, medals were pinned to Mustafa's chest, including from the Sultan, the Kaiser and the Bulgarian King Ferdinand, for his timely action on the first day of the invasion back in April, and his promotion to full Colonel came on 1st June. Still Mustafa continued to criticise the senior command. Following an unsuccessful attack by Mustafa's forces and some external criticism of his own subordinate officers for their lack of enterprise, Enver once more clipped our eagle's wings: Mustafa was removed from the position of Corps commander, at the same time being offered promotion to Brigadier if he would consider taking over the campaign in progress in Tripoli-Cyrenaica. But Mustafa's hour was yet to come. A second major landing on the Gallipoli Peninsula by the British in early August 1915 thrust Mustafa once more into the forefront of the action.

✷ ✷ ✷

From out of the sea, escaping their shells and bursting upon the shore, pearls. Pearls of humanity, strung in lines and threading the chasms, encircling the hills, rolling on up across the ridges, shining in the dark, trapping moonlight and starlight on their skin, the oh so delicate mother of pearl skins of their birth, glowing in the dawn. And opposite from out of earth-cracking rock came pouring as rain the sapphire drops of humanity upon steep slopes, catching the crescent light and returning it as starbursts as their mortal carapace is broadcast beneath day's luminous advent on peaks and hillsides. The jewels of the hearts, the treasure that is this Man, scattered across the land, resplendent a moment in glorious cognition of Its possibility. But the world could not bear their brightness. One by one and in company of thousands, their exquisite lights extinguished and their hearts returned into the chest of non-existence.

The battles of Chunuk Bayırı and Anafarta are a perfect example of the principle of unity overcoming division. And it is the submission to this principle, rather than the simple though commendable heroics of the individuals involved, that is the necessary action that brings victory in war, whether it is a struggle against outward forces or inner contests of the soul. This submission, this submitting to one's own death, comes only with any degree of usefulness, when made willingly. Or perhaps, leaning upon a greater will, towards a single idea of perfection strongly held by the heart, whether this is envisioned in country, comrades, or a moral sense of purpose.

The position that Mustafa and the Turkish commanders in the central region of the Gallipoli Peninsula found themselves in August 1915 was precarious, and could easily have led to defeat. The Turks knew another landing was imminent, but there was no definite information as to where

it would take place. The Allies had gathered a far superior force for their
August push. Twenty-five thousand troops had been landed and concealed
at Anzac Cove. Four miles to the north, twenty thousand more of Kitchener's
'New Army' sat virtually unopposed at Suvla Bay.

But General von Sanders believed the new invasion force would attack
further north, at the neck of the peninsula at Bulayır, where Mustafa had
fought the Bulgarians in the Balkan War of 1913.

'It doesn't make sense,' said Mustafa, on hearing this from his immediate
commander General Esat Pasha, who like many was inclining to the
German commander's view. 'They would only go so far north if they were
considering a land push to Constantinople. Not even Churchill would be
that stupid. It would be suicide. More likely they'll try and outflank us
north of where we are here in order to break through to Maydos. I would
expect they might try somewhere like Suvla Bay, where our defences are
weak and the immediate terrain is far less hilly.'

In the event, Mustafa was right. The landing at Suvla came on the
evening of 6th August, and in the following days some of the most desperate
fighting of the campaign took place. At this time Mustafa was one of a
number of divisional commanders in the central Arıburnu sector, an area
extending roughly six miles from Anzac Cove and the Sari Bayır Range in
the south, to the Anafarta Range overlooking Suvla Bay in the north. The
high points of Chunuk Bayırı in the southern area and the Anafarta Hills
in the north were crucial to the defence of the peninsula. As battle was
joined, after the failure of General Esat Pasha to press home a counterattack, General von Sanders offered Colonel Mustafa the command again.
Mustafa insisted on being given overall control over the forces north of
Arıburnu, and the General acquiesced, recognising that if anyone was
qualified for the task ahead, it was the forthright, obstreperous, but
ultimately fearless and willing young Turkish colonel.

The approach to Chunuk Bayır from Anzac Cove, on the west side, is
along steep narrow valleys between spurs leading to a gradually rising
ridge. From the east, the terrain is marginally less rugged, at least in the
environs of Bigalı, but the difficulty increases with altitude. Chunuk Bayır
is one of the highest points on the Gallipoli Peninsula, and from the top of
the ridge one can see north to flat land around Suvla Bay, south west to
Anzac Cove, east to Mustafa's headquarters a mile or so at Bigalı, and
further south east down to the coast at Maydos where the dark blue waters

of the Dardanelles sparkle enticingly. On a clear day from up on Chunuk Bayır one could make out the forms of sailors on vessels in the Straits.

At Chunuk and Anafarta, the strength and certainty of Mustafa's vision – to save his nation at all costs – infected all those around him. Time and time again he led his men from the front, facing the enemy not so much without fear, but as if wrapped in a cloak of invincibility such that the enemy's bullets and bombs could not enter his sacred sphere. His men, while not invulnerable, nonetheless imbibed this spirit.

Early in the morning of 8th August, after a long night-time slog up from Anzac, the Allied invaders had taken possession of the heights of the Sari Bayır range at its summit of Chunuk Bayır. Two days later, at dawn, Mustafa led a surprise attack with fixed bayonets into the heart of the Allied position and secured the summit.

With this success the invading forces were pushed back towards the shore. But both sides suffered massive casualties – over nine thousand on the Turkish side alone. Mustafa himself was hit in the chest by a piece of shrapnel, which smashed the watch in his breast pocket, but left him unscathed. This lucky escape confirmed again his belief that destiny was ruling events.

Meanwhile, the British landing at Suvla Bay went ahead with inexplicable slowness. Mustafa, with more and more troops now available, set about consolidating the Turkish position further on the high ground of the Anafarta Hills. The highest point in the range was Tekke Tepe, from where there is an almost unobstructed view down over the plain to the sea, and in what became a race for the summit, Mustafa's troops just managed to reach the top before the Allies, who were driven back down. The fighting was vicious over the next few weeks as the Allies tried to gain the high ground, but the Turkish divisions, content to hold their strategic position saw no need to advance, and dug in. Trench warfare again became the order of the day.

Once more Mustafa's instinctive approach to war had proved the man. But at a cost. He was exhausted from days without sleep, staving off sickness by force of will, and fed up with having to berate his own superiors whose petty fears and jealousies had prevented them from following his lead like the brave subordinates who had willingly, if blindly, given their lives by the tens of thousands. Mustafa grew tired of the bickering and infighting that went on at field headquarters between the German and

Turkish commanders. Eventually he succumbed to malaria and took to his bed.

At the end of September Enver visited the peninsula on an inspection tour of the front line, but failed to visit the sick hero; Mustafa, out of sheer frustration at this lack of recognition, promptly tendered his resignation. By now Liman von Sanders valued Mustafa so highly that he took pains to broker peace between the colonel and the War Minister, and Enver even wrote a conciliatory letter to Mustafa, pleading with him to return to duty. Mustafa was not to be so easily placated and pitched for a command in Mesopotamia. When this post was given to the German Marshall von der Goltz, Mustafa's objections to German officers interfering in Turkish military affairs came out into the open, until eventually there was a complete breakdown in his relations with General von Sanders.

In September the Allies landed a force in Salonica. In October Bulgaria entered the war in an alliance with Turkey and the Central Powers, thus providing a protective bulwark between Allied forces in Greece and the Gallipoli Peninsula.

By December the weather had turned bitter in the North Aegean and the whole Gallipoli campaign became a stalemate, at least from the invaders' point of view. Mustafa was convinced the Allies were going to withdraw, and pushed the Turkish command to go for an all out attack on the Ariburnu/Anzac beachhead, which was refused on the grounds that the Turkish Army no longer had men to spare for such a fight. Mustafa felt a great chance had been wasted. He packed his bags and returned to Constantinople.[*]

---

[*] Ten days later, on the night of 8th/9th January 1916, in one of the most remarkable occurences of WW1, the Allied armies evacuated the Gallipoli Peninsula without a single life lost.

TWENTY-EIGHT

No One Remembers The Eighth Raki

Constantinople, 1915-1916

ETURNING TO CONSTANTINOPLE, sunk as it was within it's own gloom, did little to lift Mustafa's spirits. Even the Bosphorus seemed depressed. The British submarines, that earlier had managed to negotiate the double defence of minefields and strong currents in the Dardanelles, had for a while terrified the population of the city by sinking Turkish shipping in the Marmara Sea. Lieutenant Commander Nasmith's submarine, E.11, had even ventured into the Bosphorus and torpedoed a transport ship at the Tophane arsenal. That August, while Mustafa had been leading his troops against the Allied offensive at Anafarta, the same submarine had sunk the venerable Ottoman battleship, *Hayreddin Barbarossa*, lying offshore near Bulayır, at a cost of 250 Turkish lives.* Supplying the Dardanelles had become a hazardous

---

* Originally built in Germany, this ship was commissioned in 1894 as *Kurfürst Friedrich Wilhelm* and served as the flagship of the Kaiser's navy; a veteran of the Boxer Rebellion in 1901, she was sold to Turkey in 1910.

business, with much of the materiel and men now going by road, or by the very circuitous rail route via Izmir/Smyrna and Bandırma.

Beylerbeyi Palace, built in the mid-19th century close by the Bosphorus' Asian shore as a summer palace, had never been fitted with central heating, and wartime fuel shortages forbade electricity or gas in the city. In the main reception hall the oil lamps gave out a ghostly light, which sparkled and multiplied off the Bohemian crystal chandeliers above, the bright coloured glazes of the enormous Chinese vases and the gilded capitals of the massive columns.

Upstairs, in a corridor off the '*Mavi Tören Salon*', the resplendent ceremonial hall with its deep blue columns painted in imitation lapis lazuli, and murals depicting naval scenes, was the private apartment of ex-Sultan Abdul Hamid II. This comprised a bedroom, a study, a *hammam* and a w.c.. all simply furnished – a plain double bed in the corner of the bedroom, a dressing table *cum* washstand with a brown marble top; and in the study, which doubled as a reception room, were eight chairs and a sofa, a desk with a large chair and a couple of wooden cabinets all ornately carved. The ceilings were of traditional Ottoman painted wood design, decorated with Koranic verses in calligraphy of gold on blue.

Within his shrunken estate in the rear of the palace, its windows facing away from the Bosphorus, sat the old Sultan, dethroned and depressed, living out his life under constant guard. On the floor below, Colonel Mustafa and his cousin Salih paced the length of the great hall. Although indoors, they still wore greatcoats and kalpaks against the damp December chill that blew down from the Black Sea.

Now Mustafa embarked on one of his perorations. Not that he was trying to impress his cousin in any way, but he wanted to order the thoughts that he had kept firmly on the back burner during the past seven months of frontline duty at Gallipoli.

'In battle, when a soldier properly submits to the task he has demanded of himself, he may go beyond his fear – beyond his fear of dying, and begin to live beyond his mortal skin.'

Salih looked at him quizzically. Mustafa continued:

'In this way he may find himself capable of deeds beyond his known abilities.'

Mustafa paused again, as if allowing the next thought to form before he expressed himself.

'He may find even that he is invested with a power that protects him from harm, a weapon more powerful than his guns and swords. This is because he comes prepared, he has already made the sacrifice of his self, his life, when he stepped out above the parapet despite his fears. This is important. He is not without fear, but he has let go of himself, surrendered that place where the fear resides, before a greater unknown. But it is an unknown that he has accepted, through faith, or belief, or certainty, or even love. But it comes with a sense of truth, that it is right, a reality that he is part of.'

He let his words hang there, settling, as if visible and readable in the air before him. Salih knew not to interrupt. Then he went on:

'Whether he lives or dies now is no longer the question, for he is already seeing the world beyond the veil of mortality. He has secured a victory that is not measured in the conquest of cities and nations for he has come into possession of something which cannot be taken from him – he has joined the moment, joined life itself. After that, it really doesn't matter whether his body lives or dies.'

Mustafa stopped his pacing and lit a cigarette. For Salih, this was above his head. But he loved his cousin and was too in awe of him even to begin to question. Instead, he now took the opportunity to divert him from his sombre mood.

'Oh Mustafa, are you really so bored?' said his cousin, 'Do you really miss the trenches? You miss the flies and the corpses, and the shells bursting overhead, and the dysentery and the mud and the lack of sleep, and the crazy arguments with the Germans over strategy? And of course you miss the abstinence and the foul water, and the male company. All those stinking sweaty men, down there in the tunnels and the trenches. Yes, I quite see what you're getting at, no wonder you seem depressed. But across the water there's a city – it's still *our* city, thank God! And somewhere there, even in all this madness, there are bars and restaurants and girls and raki. And some places still have gas lights on. And music. Music, Mustafa, like in Salonica. You remember Salonica, don't you? Come on, let's get out of here. There must be something going on over in Pera, even with the war on.'

* * *

An hour later they were sitting in the little underground funicular railway that climbed the hill from near Galata Bridge to Pera. They reached the Pera Palas Hotel, and were just about to enter when they bumped into a group of officers coming out whom Mustafa knew.

'You won't like it in there tonight, Colonel,' said a young lieutenant. 'The place is filled with the German top brass, and there's a band playing 'oompah', we're going to try the new place, the Antakyan.'

And so it was that Mustafa, Salih and half a dozen or so other Turkish officers found themselves at a table in Zeki's cabaret. And it was just as Salih had offered, and just what Mustafa needed. The music was pure Salonica, with *türkü* folk songs and *rembetika*, and with it, raki; a lot of raki. It began in a fairly civilised fashion, but there is an old saying, on nights such as these, that 'no one remembers the eighth raki'; and indeed, it was such a night. The soldiers took a table in the large dining room close to a small stage. It was a modest performance, a small orchestra, of *saz* and violin, *kanun*, *ney* and *darbuka*, and the soldiers joining in the familiar songs. They nibbled on *leblebi* and white cheese, and drank more raki.

Mustafa closed his eyes as the music took him back to the sounds and smells of the city of his youth: the seafront cafes around the White Tower, and the mass of sailing ships jostling and snapping their rigging as the dark waters of the Gulf of Salonica slapped the harbour wall. Nostalgia released in him a flood of long suppressed emotion. An *efe* in full bandit regalia of black boots and sash, herioc moustachios, crossed bandoliers, sword and bandana, with arms outstretched, appeared from behind the stage and the musicians began a *zeybek*. Mustafa arose to meet him spreading his arms out wide like wings, and together they moved with precise and deliberate steps around the floor, two great raptors turning about their prey. Then the other soldiers got up, tables were moved back and together they all danced the *zeybek* like some great convocation of eagles.

The *efe* eventually stepped away, and the stage was taken by some Romani musicians playing fast frenzied tunes on violin, clarinet and hand drums. The drinking continued. As a finale, a portly dame made her entrance, heavily made-up, her dress decolletée above a generous bust veiled beneath layers of fine lace, and an acre of pink chiffon falling behind her in a short train, her ensemble topped with a pink wig and a wide-brimmed straw hat festooned with pink cloth roses.

This grande dame performed some popular French cabaret songs in a husky voice that betrayed somewhat her natal gender, but she sang well.

Her renditions of slow waltzes had the well-lubricated audience weeping into their cups. The ever popular *'Je te veux'*, made famous by Paulette Darty and the young Eric Satie, had the soldiers transported.

> *'Enlacés pour toujours*
> *Brûlés des mêmes flammes*
> *Dans des rêves d'amours*
> *Nous échangerons nos deux âmes.'*

> Entwined forever
> Burnt within the same flame
> In dreams of love
> Our two souls become one

And her coy, seductive manner when singing songs of plaintive yearning in Arabic, had many of the mostly male audience sending little *billets* via the waiter to invite the chanteuse to their table for champagne. Zeki did not disappoint them, and came briefly among the audience, surprising some with kisses on the lips. And to the more forward (and drunk) of the suitors who pulled her onto their laps she gave a mild slap on the cheek with her gloved hand.

As word got round the bars of Pera that Colonel Mustafa, hero of Gallipoli, was here in the Hotel Antakya, officers, young and old, crowded round his table, hanging on his words, keen to hear news from the mouth of the lion himself.

'So, go on Colonel Mustafa Bey, tell us what it was like,' said an eager young lieutenant, not long out of Staff College and soon to head out to the Macedonian front.

Mustafa sat, bottle in one hand, his glass in the other; he was drinking the rakı neat now. He looked into the eyes of the young officer, trying to gauge the man. He took his time to answer.

'It's not how they tell you,' he said, eventually. 'Operations to take this hill or that trench, to hold a line, or fall back when the shells were landing. It was not like that at all. We were all just cells, blood cells in a body, the life blood of the land, called here and there as the need arose. It was not a matter of choice – we had made our choice and gone beyond it to submit to the necessity. We didn't count the dead because we were still alive. This body had become joined to another, a greater body. It was as if a great smothering fever was trying to overcome us, and we simply had to survive long enough and we would throw it off. The others count the dead.'

Mustafa paused and let his words sink in. The soldiers around were silent, listening intently, as pupils before their master. He took a long sip of his drink, lit another cigarette and continued.

'But our losses built our strength. How can I explain it? – Their spirit, the spirit that grew and strengthened in the moment of their sacrifice, grew and strengthened in the spirit of those of us who remained, and gradually the body threw off the attack. Not in some great battle where the victors take the vanquished away in chains and leave the slain on the field for the ravens. We simply recovered what we were, became again who we had always been. And the enemy melted away like a nightmare that dissolves in the light of day. War – it is like the Arabs say, war is *'fana'*, the passing away of things, things that in the end don't really matter. What is the *'baqa'*? What remains after this *'fana'*?'

He looked around at the faces puzzling at his last remark.

An old soldier who had been sitting listening at the edge of the group remarked

'What remains is the woman, no?'

Some of the more experienced soldiers gathered there laughed quietly, they understood. Those who had known war, who had peered over the brink of life knew that what remained in them was like a great hole, an emptiness, a huge need which only the love of a good woman could fill, however it came. In a wife or a daughter, or a song or a whore. Or, failing that, in drink.

Mustafa raised his glass. 'And the spirit. Always, the spirit remains.' Mustafa was quite drunk now, and became drunker still as he drained his glass. Yet he managed somehow to maintain a strong presence before his audience who continued to listen spellbound. Most of the other tables had finished their meals and left after the cabaret had ended. Gradually the soldiers too began to drift away, leaving Mustafa and Salih alone.

'Food. A soldier cannot fight without a full belly! Bring me a capon. And mustard!' he demanded. Mustafa was somewhere else altogether now. A waiter approached rather nervously and whispered to Salih that the kitchen had closed an hour ago and the cooks had gone.

'Oh do try and find something if you can, just to shut him up' Salih begged.

But as the waiter departed, Mustafa slumped forward on the table and began to snore.

Zeki appeared. He had changed back into his accustomed 'smoking' and had removed his wig and all the makeup except for a little smudge of kohl around the eyes.

'Don't worry, sir,' he said to Salih. 'We'll look after him. Heroes need a way to return to earth after soaring so high. We'll find him a bed, don't you fret.'

Salih left Mustafa where he was, sleeping like a baby among the ashtrays and empty glasses, his head nestling among crumpled napkins upon a table cloth stained with wine and cigarette ash.

Mustafa dreamed he was back in Damascus. An unseen figure had just placed before him a bowl of steaming lentil soup. *That* soup. But he wasn't in Damascus, and he wasn't dreaming either. There by his head, on a table now clear of the detritus of the night, was a soup tureen and ladle, a bowl and spoon, a quartered lemon, a glass and jug of water, and a fresh napkin. He lifted the lid of the tureen. He was not dreaming. It was *that* soup. The creamy sweet scent of lentils and butter invaded his nostrils. He began to wake up, but remained somewhat confused. He drank a glass of water then ladled some soup into the bowl, squeezed over some lemon, and ate. He then woke up properly and was properly confused. But something as delightful as lentil soup at three o'clock in the morning must presage even greater wonder. That empty place in himself of which he had spoken earlier was now growing in the pit of his stomach in a deep yet not altogether unpleasant longing, for any bitterness that imagination may place upon his sense of '*fana*', the passing away of things, was assuaged by the comfortable sense of remaining, the '*baqa*', which the soup brought to his inner being.

He wiped his lips and moustache with the clean napkin and got up to investigate, making his way towards the kitchen.

TWENTY-NINE

War is *Fana,* Woman is *Baqa*

Constantinople – 1915/1916

 HERE IS A YEARNING in love that is akin to union, which draws into expression the continually devolving qualities of the object of its desire, the moments of true creation – in the anticipation of her skin, the annihilation in his eyes, the drowning scents of her breath: this mingling of souls is the nearest bodies come to an actual physical union, and so it is the yearning that is to be desired more than the impossible joining of parts.

When Mustafa finally made a move to kiss her – he found her standing half-way in and half out of the doorway – an isthmus rather than an impasse – inclining, between the kitchen and the dining room – she did not resist; she did not turn away, but stood there with him. And while no voluntary movement proceeded from her, yet her whole body received him. The only evidence, subtle as it was, of her agreement was in the sheer soft swelling of her lips as he pressed upon her half-open mouth and, had he been aware beyond his own overpowering physical awakening, he would have noticed the same soft swelling receptivity of her entire body blooming, as when the slack sails of a long becalmed vessel billow with sweet zephyrs from a gentle west wind and stir her to be moved upon the water.

What is it about the kiss on the mouth that makes it more intimate an exchange than even the sexual act, so much so that among those who earn their living by sharing their body, most will not permit their clientele to kiss them on the lips? For the intercourse of bodies is of far less consequence in the long run than is the exchange and mingling of the breath, the joining of the soul itself in a moment of eternity.

For Mustafa this was too much after the long months of personal restraint, the single-minded and sustained focus of attention that is the diktat for successful prosecution of war, his sense of self strained to places beyond accustomed mentality. Desire for union now rose in him as a pent up spring that has sought for aeons within dark caves the light of day and bursts through rock and earth into the sun and air; as a dam resisting a flood beyond its capacity overflows, drenching the grass of its chosen meadow. And his meadow, the being of Satanaya, neither willing nor yet unwilling dissolved in unrequested but grateful ecstasy.

Half an hour later Satanaya came back to herself, and found Mustafa smiling behind closed eyes, breathing softly. They were wrapped in each other's arms, lying where they had fallen between the two rooms, still soaked in the honeyed nimbus of their union. Their coming together had been unexpected but not a surprise. The timing was perfect.

* * *

When Mustafa woke it was to the melody and words of '*Je te veux*' going round in his head: '*Dans des rêves d'amours, nous échangerons nos deux âmes...*' A low wintry sun shone through the half-moon window of the little apartment. The bed in which he lay was no narrow canvas army cot, but comfortable and generously-sized in a polished walnut frame, and the space to his left still exuded a faint warmth where the sleeper had recently lain. He breathed in lily of the valley upon the pillow next to his, and felt uncommonly good.

He looked around. Opposite was a dressing table laid out with the usual accoutrements of female toilette: silver-backed hair brushes, pots and vials of unguents and potions, a little simple jewellery hanging over the mirror. He noticed that he was dressed in a long cotton night gown. As he thought back to the events of the previous evening, there were some disconcerting gaps in his recollection. He hauled himself out of bed and went to the window.

The city had been transformed. Snow had fallen in the night and the streets below were unusually quiet. He recognised the view, on his right, over the cemetery of Petit Champs down to the Golden Horn, shining deep cobalt, and beyond to the hills of Stamboul, the domes of the imperial mosques resplendent in ermine cloaks, their minarets glowing spears of silver. To the left he could just make out the Marmara Sea and the entrance to the Bosphorus Strait.

Then that song again. Coming from an adjoining room. Not now the smoky sultry voice of a transvestite, but the bright notes of a singing girl: '*Enlacés pour toujours, brûlés des mêmes flammes...*' Then it all came back to him.

In the little kitchenette adjoining her bedroom, Satanaya placed a folded napkin on the breakfast tray. She had prepared a large *cezve* of coffee, some *açma*, various cheeses, conserves of quince and fig, olives green and black, and lastly a little frying pan with the *menemen* – the full Turkish breakfast. She too was remembering the events of the night. How with the help of Madiha, who had lifted with ease the barely conscious Mustafa and carried him to Satanaya's room, they had stripped him and put him into one of Madiha's extra large nightgowns, a kind of *dishdasha* that the Arabs wear. How she had seen him then, not so much as a lover might, but as a nurse, or a mother, with pity, and concern for his lean and wasted flesh. How vulnerable he had looked without his uniform, still a boy in her eyes. Well, almost.

Hearing the floorboards creak in the bedroom, she pushed open the door to find Mustafa standing, gazing out over the snowcovered rooftops.

'Well, you're looking a lot better than you were last night. You must have been exhausted. Do you know how long you've been sleeping? It's almost midday.' She placed the tray on the table by the window and sat down.

Mustafa found himself without an answer. He began to stutter. He looked down at the flowing white robe and then at Satanaya: 'How…?'

Satanaya laughed, 'Don't you remember? Come on, don't tell me you don't remember?'

'Yes, up to a point, at the kitchen door, but then…'

'Don't worry, after we met, well… Whatever happened, and I'm not sure exactly what actually happened, but no matter – afterwards you were pretty much out for the count.' Satanaya paused. They looked at each other. It was obvious to each then, the closeness. For whatever tensions, whatever veils of caution or inhibition they had maintained between themselves in the past, had disappeared.

'Now, for heaven's sake, have some coffee And eat some *menemen* before it gets cold.' She poured for both of them.

Mustafa smiled as he sniffed the steaming cup and took a sip.

'Mmmm, that's good. The cardamom, it reminds me of Damascus.' he said.

Now as they looked at each other, in daylight, each became a question in the sight of the other.

And yet not. It had been such a long time coming. The almost meetings in Damascus and again in the Beyt'ul Rahma, the almost fallings in love in Sofia and Vitosha, then the break up of what had never actually been. Or had it? Wasn't this in fact the natural, slow returning of an encircling comet, the dance of twin stars around each other, so close that the question of who is orbiting whom becomes ambiguous. Is this the closest we come in this world, however we love? We share each other's auras, whether with our bodies or our minds, just as the earth shares in the aura of the sun, whether it is day or night. It was the normality of it, their sitting together now, no drama, just acceptance of each other at a level that time has brought about without farness or nearness interfering. The normality. But never a banality. Absence and presence become the same thing, seen from different points of view.

'Satanaya, what is it about you? How is it you appear like this in the strangest of places? What's going on?' He looked at this woman, and couldn't understand how he could not place this wild thing in his romantic imagination. And yet with her the sense of the familiar was almost overpowering. As if he were looking at himself, and realising there was so much he did not know.

'I was thinking the same about you, Mustafa. You are a mystery, and yet I feel so close to you.'

Satanaya continued to look at him. She had never really taken in how shy he was. Perhaps it was just being out of uniform. Had she been expecting too much too soon? Perhaps she should not expect anything at all?

'So, that last night in Sofia,' she said, 'at the opera, we never really got to say goodbye. Gosh, it seems so long ago now.'

The sweetness, the gentility of small talk. The intimacy.

'Yes, that was a war ago. A whole lifetime. Things change. What was once is no longer.'

'You talk like an old man, Mustafa. You've seen war before. What's so different now?'

'This war… it was a mistake, surely. we shouldn't have gone along with the Germans. We should have stayed neutral. We could have. But, once started, better finish.'

'Even if we lose?'

'It's not the 'if', but the 'when' and 'how' that concerns me. In the meantime, we soldier on, as they say.'

'So where next?'

'I'm hoping for a command in Macedonia. But Enver still finds it necessary to keep me where I won't be a threat to his precedence, so more likely it'll be out east, trying to make the best of the mess he made there.'

'It's not all as bad as you think, Mustafa.' Satanaya broke off a piece of bread roll and smeared it with fig jam, 'Even Enver hasn't been able to hide the fact that what you did at Anafarta and Ariburnu has saved this city, and therefore the country. The people, the soldiers, they talk among themselves. They would follow you now wherever you led them. And there are few who support the Triumvirate, but wouldn't openly admit it. Especially after the situation of the past year. Food is getting short – most of the supplies go to the army. It's only because of our inside contacts that we can carry on here at the hotel as we do. The powers that be would like to give the impression that all is well, and so they allow us to provide these little luxuries, and our *divertissements*. They say it's good for morale, that's why you see so many officers, and business people here. But your name has been on everyone's lips these past months. In a good way. There is opportunity there. Why don't you take it?'

Mustafa turned in his chair as if looking for something.

'Here, is this what you're after?' Satanaya handed him a packet of cigarettes and a lighter, then got up and brought an ashtray.

'Thank you. If only it was so simple,' he said, after lighting up and taking a long drag. 'I don't want a revolution on my hands. Well, not at the moment, at any rate. You see, there is an order to this, and an order for me in this, too. If I've learnt anything, it's to bide my time. And if that means sitting back and watching the whole thing collapse because of their mismanagement, I can't be seen to have engineered it. On the contrary, I must work to prevent it, or at least be in a position to lessen the damage. You know, it's like being a doctor. When the patient is ill, but before the amputation one has to work to strengthen, to prepare the body.'

'You sound as if you've got it all worked out!'

'If only.' Mustafa made a snorting sound and gave a little laugh. 'What you see is what you get. But there are some things that have to change, and this will take time.'

'Such as?'

'Well, for one, this country is still being run as some kind of theocracy, but it's a complete sham. The sultan, God bless the poor old man, is a puppet. Has been since they installed him. How does that look, I ask you? He's meant to be the *halifa*, Caliph, Viceroy of God on earth – at least that's what the masses still believe. You should hear them when they go into battle, the young men and the older ones – it's all 'Allahu Akbar' and 'Long live our Padishah!' They're not doing it for me, but for some strange belief that this is what Allah and their Sultan wants.

'That lot,' Mustafa was now referring to the Triumvirate, and gestured with his head as if indicating people in another room, 'have been using the same sort of ploy to cover all their mistakes – "It's the will of God" they say. Nonsense. If God allows such madness, it's only to show them by the results the folly of it all.'

'And to point out a better way? A kind of universal compassion?'

'If you will. Perhaps. But I ask, are we still learning from our mistakes? You know, the Prophet Mohammed once said, "No more war." Did they listen? Did they believe? The hell they did! No, they took religion and shaped it according to their own desires, and now most religion has changed and become self-seeking. It's time it went.'

'Huh?'

'You know, Satanaya, if I could I would sink all the religions to the bottom of the sea.'

'How can you say that?' she said, 'Do you not love Mohammed? Are you not a 'true believer'?'

'How can I not love Mohammed? He was a lover of Truth. He fought for Truth. He risked his life for Truth. But religion nowadays, what's that got to do with matters of truth? The prophets planted a sapling, but the ones who came after cut the tree before it was grown, and built a house when they could have waited for the fruit – and now they starve, morally that is. If they had only taken on board the character of the man, and not simply copied how he cut his toenails, or what side of the bed he got out of, they might have become worthy of this *'islam'*, this 'surrender' they keep on about. And now they plant trees of their own imagination and expect them to bear the fruit of truth. It's not like that.'

Mustafa paused, lost in thought.

'Perhaps some were wise enough to take cuttings of these trees, graft them or keep them hidden and alive somewhere,' said Satanaya. She was thinking of her father and the Adige traditions, of the man in the green kalpak, Yesil Efendi, and the mysterious people who had appeared from time to time at the konak.

'Hmmm… Maybe… Yes, I remember an old Mevlevi sheikh in Salonica… he told me things that would have had him strung up for a heretic if he'd said them publicly… but there…' and was just about to launch into a further diatribe when Satanaya stopped his mouth with her hand.

'Enough. Eat. We'll talk more later. I'm just going to pop down and leave some instructions with the kitchen for the evening. Then let's go for a walk.'

He looked at the food on the table and suddenly realised how hungry he was. Apart from the lentil soup, he'd had nothing since lunch the day before.

The Istanbulus have a horror of snow. The steep hills upon which the city is built make the cobbled thoroughfares slippery and dangerous in bad weather for pedestrians and horse-drawn traffic alike, and more so for the modern motor vehicle. Snow is an excuse to remain indoors and keep warm, drinking tea around braziers and wood burning stoves. The damp air held the smoke of these fires close in to the ground. And so it was, that when the lovers left the hotel (by a private route to avoid the Reception desk) they found the streets to be almost empty, although the snow was beginning to melt.

They rode the Tünel down to Galata rather than risk the treacherous descent along Yüksek Kaldırım, and strolled out onto the bridge at the mouth of the Golden Horn where the usual crowd of hawkers and fishermen had made a thin showing that day. They found a quiet spot to lean against the balustrade and chat while gazing out to Asia across the water. To their right, above the green woods of Saray Burnu, in the Topkapi Palace, the half-melted snow bedraggled the little cupolas of the harem. Nearby, the Baghdad Kiosk perched pristine and empty above the tree tops in the cold evening light. Below them, at the entrance to the Golden Horn, ferries churned the water between the opposing shores of Karaköy and Eminönü, belching black smoke from their tall, raked funnels. Behind, high on the hill the lowering sun was split by one of the four minarets of the great cathedral mosque of Suleyman the Magnificent. Constantinople sighed, and the last drawn-out breath of the day passed as a balm upon the blue ocean stream of the Bosphorus. Flocks of shearwaters shimmered in mercurial flight over the darkening waters, and the far shore glowed in the last remnants of sunshine upon the hills above Üskudar and Salacak. Mustafa pointed to the green sward below the long pale buildings of the Selimiye Barracks:

'Those fields are where the British soldiers had their camp and paraded sixty years ago, before they marched off alongside our soldiers to fight the Russians in the Crimea. And now we are fighting them both. You know, we never wanted their lands, but they keep taking ours: Egypt, Iraq, Crimea, and the Russians have always wanted Constantinople. Did you know they call it 'Tsargrad'?'

'Yes,' Satanaya replied, 'and by those fields is the hospital where the wounded were brought to die of infections, until Florence Nightingale started a clean up.'

'War is *fana*' – عانف ?'

'And woman makes *baqa*'- عاقب '

He looked at her strangely. 'You were there? Last night?'

Satanaya looked away, across the water. 'Oh, it's just an Arabic saying, don't you know? *Al harbu tufni wa'l mar atu tubqi* – War desolates, woman restores. Come on, it's getting colder. Let's walk back before it gets dark.'

She took his arm and pulled herself close to him. She was surprised how she felt in his company, here in this big city, in the cold of winter, as if his presence was a protective wing shielding her from harm. Not that she needed protection, but it did feel good. Like being with her father, or simply sharing deep companionship. Perhaps this was a love too? But she shied away from that thought. Mustafa would have spoken of love. His heart was open and vulnerable. If he only knew what turmoil she felt; a wonderful turmoil, admittedly; a whirlpool in an ocean. She let herself be pulled into its current, no longer worrying how deep she would go, nor where nor when she would resurface. In love, past regrets and future fears remain hidden in the pleasure of the moment's timelessness.

Many things happen during a period of war – strange things, terrible things, and also beautiful things. Why should this surprise us? When great changes are required in humanity's destiny, and when our minds struggle with these changes, is it any wonder that such things occur?

When the natural run of water through familiar courses, the time-honoured channels of its dispensation, is blocked, then to reach its appointed destination the stream will rise up against these impediments, break its banks, burst the dams, and flood in wide search to create new pathways. So too, when the compassionate mercy that gives being to this ark of possibilities that is the human emergence finds the hearts of the people constricted and unable to receive the flow of its bounty, it too builds up pressure; testing the limits of the old creations to breaking point, bringing new worlds into being in their place. War, like a cardiac arrest, is an outcome, not out of a necessity for pain and death, but of the necessity for change. It demands a surgical procedure, ultimately for and because of the expansion of love.

Mustafa said goodbye to Satanaya in the dark of the street by the back door to the hotel kitchens. A pale moon in the dwindling twilight barely lit her face. Her eyes unblinking looked into his with a calm, unwavering receptivity. They kissed again, lightly, longingly. No winter's wind could chill the warmth they shared within the closeness of their hearts.

THIRTY

War in the East

Constantinople, 1916 – 1917

 ATANAYA STIRRED the pot. The steam rising out of the old Konya *kazan* moistened her brow, and her knuckles were hot from holding the wooden spoon as she turned the barely rolling velouté sauce. Later she would add some cream and a little mushroom juice and coat pieces of freshly poached chicken breast for the Suprême de Volaille on the evening's menu. It was a rare and special treat to be able to serve fresh chicken. The poultry had come from Beykoz, a village far up the Asian shore of the Bosphorus. Its source was an old acquaintance of the Lady Gülbahar's, an ageing Polish nobleman who had hung on in his dilapidated estate through all the turmoil of recent years, hoping to be forgotten by the authorities. But his horses had been sequestered by the army in the first weeks of the war, and he feared his chickens would be taken too, so from time to time he sent a dozen birds by trusted messenger across the water. Rather they go to the sweet Satanaya, who would send in return a supply of coffee, sugar and grains, and perhaps a case of Domaine de Misericorde or a bottle of fine brandy.

But she was not thinking of chickens now, although perhaps her mind was turned in a mother hen sort of way to the events of the previous day. For her feelings for Mustafa were not simply romantic; she worried for him. He had changed so much since Bulgaria. The exciting young diplomat of the dance floors of Sofia had retreated inside himself, and a harder, more resolute person had emerged in the soldier. But there was sadness too, born, she felt, of the horrors and waste of life he had experienced, and of the frustration of simply being a cog, albeit a significant cog with responsibilities, in the great machine of war.

Her maternal pity and concern were further provoked by the sweetest consideration he had shown towards her. And yet she recognised in this a neediness. There was love too in his approach – how could there not be? But the love he took and gave, with such grave passion, was only a portion of that inner engine driving him. It was fuel and lubricant to ease the movement of a greater will, this overpowering notion that his soul, like some prophet of old, was tied to the soul of his nation and its people.

And even though Satanaya had an ocean of love for Mustafa, and would gladly give freely, she knew that this would only compete for a place in his soul. Eventually one or the other – her self or his destiny – would become derailed in the confusion of human emotions, or necessarily abandoned in the flood of events.

Their union, such as it was that first night in the Hotel Grand Antakya, seemed hardly of their doing, though certainly it was of their willing. But Satanaya knew from now on the tension of lovers' longing was the safest bridge upon which their souls could meet – a union without mixing, in which both their destinies would be free to run their course, if only on parallel lines, for as long as they moved in the same direction. Intimacy, certainly, but within limits. Besides, Mustafa was a man – he could fulfil those particular desires anywhere, easily, with any woman or man; sex was simply a biological cycle and she knew he knew this. But love, that was both a medicine and an intoxicating drug – and depending on the dose, even a poison. It could bring to wholeness or break down the structure of any relationship, leaving it open to changes, desirable and undesirable. So, whatever one may conjecture – the real affair between them was happening in a place where closeness did not depend so much on physical proximity, but in the play and interplay of their words, the contortions and conjoining of their minds as they struggled to penetrate the depths in each other's souls.

* * *

Mustafa's hopes of a Macedonian command came to nothing; the Triumvirate were not going to risk having him so close to the capital. Heaven knows, there were precedents enough of successful generals marching on Rome. And besides, since Bulgaria had joined the alliance of the Central Powers in September 1915, the Turkish western front was secure. Since the group he had commanded in Gallipoli was now disbanded – it had been a special corps arranged for him by General Liman von Sanders – he was now effectively unemployed. In spite of this setback, with the newfound political credit he had earned on the battlefield Mustafa spent what time he had lobbying certain of his friends in the Committee, putting forward his ideas not just on how the war might better be prosecuted for Turkey's advantage, but also his vision for a modern nation based on the latest thinking in science and education.

Though the victor's laurels were denied him in the Triumvirate's stronghold of Constantinople, he was given a hero's welcome when he visited Edirne in late January to take up command of the 16th Corps, again under overall command of Liman von Sanders. Cries of '*Çok yaşa Mustafa!* – long live Mustafa!' rang through the streets of the ancient capital as his victory parade wound its way to the Friday prayers in the grand Selimiye Mosque.

At this point in the war, the Ottoman army was fighting on many fronts. Aside from defending the western borders in Macedonia, the Dardanelles and in the Balkans, troops were fending off Russian attacks throughout much of eastern Anatolia, and were being pressed by the British in Iraq and Palestine. The Empire had been on the defensive since its initial ill-fated naval attack on Odessa.

When Mustafa's new orders came through, it was to counter-attack following Russia's taking of Erzurum, almost a thousand miles to the

east, in February 1916. He travelled by train as far as Aleppo, followed by
a gruelling journey north-east by car and horseback, eventually reaching
Diyarbakır in late March. White blossoms burst hopefully upon the
dark-skinned almond trees beneath the city's black basalt walls, and sour
erik plums ripened along the banks of the Tigris. But Mustafa had little
time for poetry as he set about assembling his troops, and establishing
headquarters in nearby Silvan. On 1ˢᵗ April Mustafa was promoted to
Brigadier-General. He was thirty-five.

A long and miserable campaign followed for the army, and more so
for the civilians. Caught in the path of two rabid fighting machines, the
peasants of the land were driven this way and that, and either fled or died
of hunger and disease. Winter came, the land slept under snow, and major
offensives ceased for the duration. But a secure front had been established
under the new Brigadier-General's command. This held until the Russian
appetite for war against the Turks disintegrated as the Russian Revolution
took hold from March 1917, culminating in an armistice that December.

✱ ✱ ✱

Mustafa did not see Constantinople again until August 1917. Baghdad had
fallen to the British in March, sending shock waves through the Ottoman
Empire; unlike Enver's earlier disaster in the Caucasus, news of which had
been well covered up, the loss of Baghdad struck right at the heart of the
people's confidence in the government. There were calls for Enver to stand
down as Minister of War. But there was no one, except perhaps Mustafa,
who could have taken his place, an event which the Committee knew
would bring their own downfall. So, as a panacea to the popular uncer-
tainty, a grand counter-offensive was being planned: Enver had put
together a large force comprising three Turkish armies, the *Yıldırım Grubu*
– 'Lightning Group' – plus a German brigade, to retake Baghdad. Mustafa
was now appointed to command the newly formed 7th Army in Aleppo.

This brief interlude in the capital was filled with hectic daily meetings
at his headquarters in the Old City of Stamboul, and when evening came
Mustafa made his way across the Galata Bridge and up to Pera where he
had taken a room at the Pera Palas Hotel. After joining companions for a
session in the bar, he made his excuses as if to bed and slipped out to the
Hotel Grand Antakya. There, in spite of his long absence he was warmly
received by Satanaya.

'Hah! he comes at last. My Pasha has not forgotten me!'

Satanaya was mocking him in a friendly way, hiding feelings that otherwise might have reduced her to tears of relief and joy. His new rank had also meant promotion from *bey* – gentleman, to *pasha* – lord.

'So, what will you eat? The kitchen is at your command – we have caviar, courtesy of a cook I know in Enver Pasha's kitchens, and some fine horse meat steaks. Food fit for a General. '

'Can you do me a simple dish of beans and rice?'

From her balcony high above the city, a light breeze from the Bosphorus drifted across the hill, but did little to remove the oppressive heat of August. The waning moon had not yet risen. Below, the turbid waters of the Golden Horn reflected the lamps of the little fishing craft and created a strangely festive atmosphere; the silence of the night was broken only by the occasional clang of a late tram, and the metal scrape of wheels on tracks. In the Old City beyond, all was dark save for the outline of the domes and minarets of the imperial mosques, their hilltop silhouettes darkly visible against a star-jewelled sky.

They ate in silence. Mustafa seemed subdued. Satanaya asked him how it had been, the past year in the east; he opened his mouth to speak, but nothing came out. He just stared into his plate. Then he looked up into her eyes; and when finally he spoke, the words came as a confession drawn from a well of deeply hidden thoughts.

'You cannot imagine, what this war is doing to them.'

'Who? Your men?'

'Not them; they are soldiers, they've adjusted. It's the civilians. They don't understand. They are simple people. We tell them we are fighting to save the country, yet we destroy the country. Their fields are wasted, their villages are destroyed. They have nothing left to eat, no homes to go to. So they just walk. Everywhere, people are just walking. And when you see their eyes… nothing. It's as if their souls have fled, and their bodies just go on like a motor. They have lost humanity in a way that even shocks the soldiers.'

He lifted his head and looked directly at her.

'I saw a child, Satanaya, he couldn't have been more than four or five years old, stumbling along behind this couple – a man and a woman who had just walked past. I called after them and asked them why they wouldn't take the child with them. And you know, they looked at me as though I was

stupid. "He's not ours." they said. Unbelievable. And as for the atrocities…
between the Armenians and Kurds, on both sides, Christians and Muslims.
Crazy. You do wonder what part of "there is only one God" they don't
understand. Do they believe God is a nation? Are they so stupid – their
leaders, that is? Their priests and mullahs, who think only of their positions and not of the flocks they lead. And the flocks follow obediently
because that is the nature of a flock, they haven't been taught otherwise.'

When they had finished eating, Mustafa lit up a cigarette and drew
deeply of the mellow Yenidje tobacco, then watched the wreath of exhaled
smoke drift out and fade in the air beyond the balcony. He drained his raki
and refilled his glass.

* * *

'You know, when things fall apart, they can come together again too. But in
a different form, otherwise there'd be no movement. No progress' said
Satanaya.

It was much later that night. She and Mustafa were lying atop the bed
in the brief cool before dawn, gazing out at the stars through the open
window.

Satanaya wasn't sure why she said this. It was something she remembered from her father. 'Religion is like a tree, where all the branches point
in different directions. And the fruit of one branch imagines it is different
and separate from the fruit on the branch opposite. But all the branches
point upwards, and all the fruit falls to the earth. And when the tree dies,
the fruit still carries the whole tree in its seeds. The whole tree. Don't you
see, the point is in the fruit, what it carries inside it. The whole tree hidden
in the seed, the whole human potential in each person.'

Mustafa looked at Satanaya but he was seeing something way beyond
the little room where they lay, beyond these moments stolen from the
march, far beyond the stars of this dark night which held them now, close
as they had held each other.

'You once told me you wished all the religions to the bottom of the sea,'
she continued. 'But then what?' Satanaya sat up and looked him in the eye.

'When you have levelled all these old ways and there you are with your
great flock, where will you lead them? Are you just going to sit back as
Sultan in this new religion? Is that it? You exchange old for new, but the
people remain. Only the idols change their forms. Even the shepherd must

lay down his staff one day, and then what? You don't have sons and heirs; your friends, those few you have left, are now in your mould. What then?'

Mustafa drew on his cigarette and looked into the smoke above his head as he exhaled long and slow. Eventually he spoke:

'The children, the children's children, and their children. Let them dream new dreams when we have gone. But for now, in my lifetime and yours, my dream must hold fast. For as long as it takes for the old mould to be well and truly broken. Then there will be another thing, a different thing. Different from anything you and I could possibly dream of, but there will be no going back, that much I can see, that much I can promise. You called me a shepherd. Hah! For these sheep, yes, perhaps. But in my dream, each person must be a shepherd to his or her own flock, master and mistress of their actions, their hopes and fears. And each person will have their own dream to fulfill. But that is a long way off – my dream is only a beginning. You talk of a seed, of humanity's potential. It will take generations to plough and sow that land with this new seed. But if we are not paying attention, if we forget what we are really serving – that potential – weeds will spring up. Parasites from the old religion, they are so deeply rooted in the soil – they will return, and they will have to be rooted out again and again.'

'This dream, how do you know it's real and not illusion? Aren't we each just a mirror to an infinity of possibilities? What gives you the right to discriminate between, and choose. For everybody else?'

'It's got nothing to do with what I think.' said Mustafa. 'It's what I've been made to know. How can I explain it? If I say I see a mountain, you can say I've seen a mirage, but I *know* it is a mountain. Every atom of my being tells me this is so – that what I feel, what I have always felt for this country, is real. I cannot act in any other way. God help me but I would like to. To sit back and rest. But there is too much to do, and too little time. Rest will come for us all, when our job is done, even if the grave will be our bed. At least we can rest easy then.'

'And us?' said Satanaya. She was smiling now. 'What about us? Or is that too personal a question? Are we lovers? Or am I just some kind of quartermaster's store for you to provision those parts the army does not consider part of its remit?'

A feeling of nostalgia came over Mustafa as he looked at Satanaya. 'Lovers? I don't have time for love.' he said, 'There's too much to do, and too little time.'

'Ha, you say that, but you are the biggest lover I've ever known. The difference with you though is your mistress is a whole country. Don't say you're not a lover when I see how much you care for her, about all the little things; how you put her before yourself all the time; how patient you are with her when she falls, and how impatient with her caprices. No, you're a lover alright. A great lover.'

THIRTY-ONE

Long Life, Honey in the Heart

Constantinople, 1917

> *And the Hellenes scaled the hill and found quarters in numerous*
> *villages which contained supplies in abundance. Here, generally*
> *speaking, there was nothing to excite their wonderment, but the*
> *numbers of bee-hives were indeed astonishing, and so were*
> *certain properties of the honey'*
>
> **Xenophon, The Persian Expedition**

> *Modern travellers attest the existence, in these regions, of honey*
> *intoxicating and poisonous... They point out the Azalea Pontica*
> *as the flower from which the bees imbibe this peculiar quality.*
>
> **Grote, History of Greece**

HE WAR GROUND ON relentlessly. The Hotel Grand Antakya became an island refuge in Turkey's sea of troubles. There had never been any realistic hope of victory, but a simple sentiment persisted among the populace that an honourable defeat could not be worse than the prevailing oppression of the spirit and the physical starvation of war. Even the dogs, numerous in the streets of Constantinople in the best of times, were shadows of their former selves, creeping into houses if a door was left open, searching for food when once generous household left-overs would have been their daily fare. No longer the lazy princes of the boulevards, they had become scavengers snarling among themselves over thrice-boiled bones at the kitchen door.

That the party at the Hotel Grand Antakya would someday end, was always accepted. But no one had expected Zeki Bey's involvement to terminate in quite the way it did. Zeki Bey's escape route for dissidents had grown quietly over the years. The authorities had always suspected the hotelier's part in the hiding and dispersing of political fugitives, but neither Colonel Karagöz nor his minions had ever discovered how the system was operated. Early on in the war, the hotel had been searched regularly, but the secret passage had never been found. It was accepted eventually that perhaps one or two fugitives may have slipped in and out of the hotel before the authorities arrived, and it was left at that. The information that was fed to Colonel Karagöz, titbits of gossip concerning the indiscretions of Turkish businessmen, members of foreign legations and the expatriate European community when they were in their cups, was usually sufficient to satisfy the appetite of the Interior Minister's in-tray.

It couldn't last forever. Taalat Pasha, who became Grand Vizier – Prime Minister – in 1917, eventually lost patience. Enver Pasha's Special Organisation, the *Teşkilât-ı Mahsusa**, had gotten wind of an assassination plot: at least, that was how it was phrased when two members of the dreaded secret police turned up at the hotel with a warrant for Zeki Bey's arrest. According to their sources, two Greek men had been found carrying firearms in the vicinity of the Kuruçeşme Palace, the Bosphorus home of Enver Pasha and his Princess Naciye. They had then admitted under torture that they were waiting to assassinate Enver. With further painful inducements, the Greeks volunteered the information that Zeki Bey had

---

*   forerunner of today's National Intelligence Organisation – *Millî İstihbarat Teşkilatı.*

made arrangements for their escape. Of course, all of this was a fantasy concocted by Talaat, and no record of the arrests, of either the Greeks nor even of Zeki Bey himself, was ever published.

Zeki Bey went calmly to his fate. Initially he was taken to the General Prison, the Hapishane-i Umumi. This was an old building, originally the palace of İbrahim Pasha, the one time favourite and Grand Vizier of Suleyman the Magnificent. It was a bleak place, in the Old City of Stamboul, just across the Hippodrome from the Sultanahmet Mosque. It was never designed to be a prison and was constantly under repair. It held nearly a thousand prisoners, and had special cells called 'black holes' where the sun never reached. Many of the prisoners were without bedding or even clothing; they depended on charity, with support from their families and bribes to the wardens whose salaries were always well in arrears. Because Zeki Bey's crime was political, not criminal, once he had been formerly charged he was transferred the following day to the infamous Bekirağa Section, a building within the grounds of the Seraskeriat, The War Office, further up the hill from Sultanahmet at Beyazit. Here some of the worst crimes of the Committee and their Special Organisation took place. Zeki Bey was put in a solitary cell, to await his fate.

But Zeki Bey had prepared well for such eventualities. Immediately after his arrest, Satanaya was on the phone to Amina Khanoum, who spoke to the Colonel Efendi, who put wheels in motion among his contacts in the War Office. The duty officer in charge of the Bekirağa Section issued a permit for Zeki Bey's 'Moroccan wife' to visit and bring him his dinner that night, as it might well be the last time they would see each other. One may wonder how in such extreme times, this ease of access to a prisoner could be effected. It must be recalled that Zeki Bey held too many notes of incriminating information regarding the Committee's lackeys, that only a fool would risk his career by denying these not unreasonable last wishes.

* * *

After many trials and tribulations, Xenophon with his army of 10,000 Greek mercenaries, returning through Armenia from his failed attempt to unseat the Persian King Artaxerxes, reached the Black Sea in the region of Trebizond. With their cry of 'thalassa thalassa' *– the sea! the sea! – their souls drank in the visual ambrosia which the sea represents for this maritime people. They then sat down and feasted on the local ambrosia they found in* *hives all around, the honey from bees fed on the rhododendrons growing in the Pontic Range. Specifically, the two or three species of rhododendron the nectar of whose flowers contain the substance grayanotoxin. In Turkey, the honey from these flowers is known as 'deli bal' – mad honey – due to its effect when ingested in any quantity. For Xenophon and his troops, it caused vomiting and diarrhoea, loss of bodily control giving the appearance of mad behaviour, and paralysis. Of perhaps even more interest was the ability of the honey to lower blood pressure to the point where a body might appear, to all intents and purposes, to be a dead body.*

* * *

When Satanaya appeared at the Seraskeriat, veiled in full *chador*, with the Bastilla pie that she had spent all the previous day cooking, (a Moroccan celebratory dish served at weddings, of pigeon cooked with eggs, honey and almonds and baked in a semolina pastry, a dish so paradisiacal in taste that it would awake in the meanest soul the aspiration towards the light of the next world,) neither the sergeant-at-arms who signed her in, nor the guards in Bekirağa Section, suspected anything but the purest intentions of a grief stricken Moroccan woman bearing her last supper to the condemned man whose fate, by his mere presence in the building, was effectively sealed.

The next day the hotel's trusty concierge Fatih Bey arrived at the prison guardhouse, ostensibly to bid farewell to his friend and employer on his journey across the river of death.

'Too late, my friend,' said one of the guards, as Fatih Bey presented his identity card, 'Sadly Mr Zeki Bey did not make it through the night.'

'Yes,' said a second soldier, 'you might as well have brought a coffin and the Imam.'

Fatih Bey feigned shock. He crumpled to his knees onto the floor of the guardhouse and began to weep.

'There, there,' said the first guard, 'it could have been worse. At least he didn't have to undergo the interrogation. Why don't you come and sit down inside for a while.'

The soldiers comforted him, sat him down in the little guardhouse, brought him tea, gave him a cigarette, and explained how well Zeki Bey had seemed the night before.

'When his wife came with a meal, he seemed fine,' said guard number

two. 'Perhaps it was the thought of the interrogation which got the better
of his nerves.'

Late the previous night, they told him, after the woman had visited
and Zeki Bey had eaten his pie, the prisoner started to behave strangely,
stumbling about in his cell like a drunk and screaming obscenities in
Arabic.

'We went and checked on him.' said the first guard, 'He was vomiting
and he had messed himself. Then he collapsed on his bed and passed out.
We thought he was asleep and so left him.'

'This morning we tried to wake him but we couldn't even find a pulse.
The cell stank horribly,' said the second.

And that was how Fatih Bey found him. Permission was given to
remove the body of his friend. Fatih Bey generously tipped the guards who
were glad to rid themselves of a smelly corpse.

'For the mess to be cleaned' he said, as they feigned humble gratitude.
He knew full well that the guards would pocket the bribe and some poor
prisoner under threat of a beating would clean up the cell.

An *araba* was found, conveniently waiting in the square outside the
Seraskeriat, the very square where Satanaya and Amina Khanoum had
witnessed the assassination of General Mahmut Şevket Paşa years before.
The cart was driven by one of the waiters from the hotel. After washing
the 'corpse' and wrapping it in a green cloth, with many pious recitations,
the two men, their demeanours fittingly drowned in grief, carried their
erstwhile boss to the araba and set off in the direction of Galata.

Zeki Bey's 'corpse' was brought into the hotel through the rear kitchen
entrance so as not to alarm the clientele. There, in the cold storage larder,
he was carefully lifted from the coffin, wrapped further in a thick blanket,
and laid to rest on one of the long marble shelves that lined the walls. From
another stone shelf, another body, similarly swaddled in green cloth was
now placed in the coffin.

These arrangements had all been permitted due to the chain of inter-
ventions which began with Satanaya's plea to Amina Khanoum, eventually
reaching a cousin in the War Office, a certain former-Captain now Colonel
Anwar, late of Cyprus, Silifke and the road to Karaman, the duty officer
responsible for the Bekirağa Section

Colonel Anwar had watched Satanaya arrive from his desk in the
War Office. He came down in person to sign the entrance chit for the

'Moroccan Lady', and longed to peer through the gauze of her chador and behold those fondly remembered cornflower blue eyes. In the brief exchange in which no words were spoken, merely the passing of paper between the officer's gloved hand, and the henna-dyed fingers of a soon-to-be widow from the Magreb, had Satanaya recognised her lover of old? He had put on weight, and wore a beard, but he still had that boyish grin. Was she aware he was married now, and happily so, to a woman with a good sense of humour and a fond embrace, who had provided him with children who were the delight of his own brown eyes? Yet, nonetheless Anwar allowed himself a moment of sweet nostalgia in remembrance of that week riding through the Taurus Mountains and conversing under Anatolian skies, and the quiet passion of their nights of love under canvas by the sky blue waters of the Göksü River.

It had not been difficult to find the substitute corpse. These were times in Constantinople where life was both cheap and priceless. Any number of bodies would be removed each day, death by malnutrition in most cases, and in the winter from exposure, from the alleyways of the city and beneath the trees by the seashore. It took little inducement among the street community for a suitable candidate to be found. Such and such a size. Such and such a colour. It didn't matter too much if the features had suffered a little decomposure, for this would easily be passed off as the effect of the poison which it was assumed the prisoner had hidden on his person and taken with his meal.

A funeral would have to be held, of course. Under Fatih Bey's direction, two of the pastry cooks worked wonders with marzipan, food colouring and isinglass to make up the unfortunate street corpse to a faithful likeness of the deceased patron. Meanwhile, the real Zeki Bey was carried upstairs to his room in a laundry basket, where Satanaya and Madiha spirited him through the secret passage to the hidden apartment. Here, with the help of a good bath and many cups of Ethiopian coffee, he quickly recovered his wits sufficient for his onward journeying.

But like all great divas, Zeki Bey insisted on having his swansong. On the second day, with the help of expertly applied maquillage, he affected a passable resemblance to a Sarah Bernhardt of an earlier period. She draped herself in an exuberance of chiffon, lace and pearls, and presented this vision of old world coquetry at the bar, where she began to make eyes at Colonel Karagöz. Zeki couldn't help it. In a few hours he would be leaving

Hotel Grand Antakya, perhaps never to return. Karagöz, whose easily intoxicated imagination vanquished sober reason in matters where women were concerned, was completely taken in. But the Colonel was there on an official errand. He had come to verify the corpse before burial. Nevertheless, with oily charm, he introduced himself to this vision and added,

'Please let me invite you to a drink, but first I must go downstairs and identify a corpse. I won't be a moment.'

Zeki Bey couldn't resist the opportunity.

'Oh, how terribly exciting! Has there been a murder? May I accompany you?' and without waiting for an answer, firmly attached herself to his arm. Colonel Karagöz, in anticipation of future delights, allowed the 'lady' to accompany him. The smell in the larder was quite awful, and as they peered into the coffin, Zeki Bey let out a little squeal and collapsed onto the policeman.

'Oh no! how ghastly!' She whimpered, and pretended to faint.

Colonel Karagöz, with one hand holding up the lid of the coffin, had only a moment to take in the smiling, shiny glazed marzipan visage of the street deceased before catching the full weight of the indisposed female at his side and letting the coffin lid slam shut.

'Yes, it's him alright.' he said, as he helped the lady to her feet and signed the release for burial. As the two reached the top of the stairs and entered the bar, Madiha, who by now had been primed by Satanaya to come to the rescue, charged towards Colonel Karagöz like a fury. Zeki Bey *à la* Bernhardt grabbed the moment to let out another squeal, and a giggle, and disappeared to the far side of the bar while Madiha, in full sail, grabbed the Colonel, haranguing him for his faithlessness, and then seducing him with soft words and simpering looks from trembling lips and drooping cow eyes.

Meanwhile Satanaya was tearing her hair. Why couldn't Zeki Bey let it go? It was a serious situation and here he was behaving as if on stage. But she had to give him credit – Colonel Karagöz had countersigned the death certificate right under Zeki's powdered nose and the coffin was already on its way to the cemetery. Now it was just a matter of the real Zeki's safe departure.

Eventually, through certain contacts in the Embassy of the United States and a not inconsiderable cash donation to the charity Near East Relief, Zeki Bey acquired a genuine American passport and travelled to

New York as 'Mrs Smith'. Once there he made a new life for himself by opening a club in the early years of the burgeoning jazz scene. When prohibition made his club unprofitable, he turned his hand to organising 'booze cruises' beyond America's three-mile coastal limit, and smuggling whisky in from Canada. In time, after the new Turkish Republic was declared, Zeki returned to Constantinople, for a while running a small, exclusive jazz club in Pera's Çicek Pasajı. Eventually, finding the new political scene a little too earnest and dull, and hankering for the excitement of the old life, he made his way home to Egypt. There he enjoyed minor celebrity status as entrepreneur and general fixer during the Farouk years, even, it is said, persuading Josephine Baker to perform in Cairo during World War 2 on behalf of the Free French, on which evening it is said that in spite of Egypt's neutrality, even the King was present.

THIRTY-TWO

My Husbands To Aleppo Gone

Syria – Palestine, 1917

OVE IN TIMES OF WAR is time out of time. A raft to cling to in a tempest of fire. Satanaya and Mustafa's nights together had the quality of a true dream, a brief awakening in the chaos of a world of conjectures and miasmas. But the respite for Mustafa was all too brief. Within days he was off east again, by train to Aleppo. Here General von Falkenhayn, the overall commander of the proposed Baghdad campaign, had set up headquarters.

However, things now took a different turn. The Germans decided it would be unwise to make an immediate push across the desert to Baghdad without first securing their southern flank. Turkish and German forces under Djemal Pasha, Governor of Syria and the third in the Triumvirate, had barely been holding the line in Palestine against British forces in Northern Sinai since 1915.

June the following year had seen the beginning of the Arab Revolt against their Ottoman masters, with Mecca falling to the tribes shortly afterwards. A second attempt to capture the canal in July 1916 saw Turkish-German forces pushed back to the Mediterranean coastal town of Al Arish, on the edge of the desert of Northern Sinai. In December they were forced to retreat further north to Gaza. By January 1917 the British had taken the whole of the Sinai Peninsula and made two attempts on Gaza. It was only a matter of time. Soon Jerusalem would be within enemy sights.

✳ ✳ ✳

Mustafa paused from dictating, barely containing his rage. He had been ordered to bring the 7th Army to the Sinai front where General von Falkenhayn's plan was to push the British back to Suez, and then turn the army round and march on Baghdad.

'Salih, the man's impossible!' he said to his cousin and ADC. Salih looked up from the table where he was typing his commander's report.

'Look at the state of things. Three Turkish armies, and one front line – it'll be chaos! Who exactly is in charge, I wonder? We get orders from Constantinople from one failed General who still thinks he's going to lead a holy war to India, while here the army is barely equipped to defend itself, let alone pursue a major offensive. It's difficult enough supplying water for the troops, let alone the horses and camels – this is Palestine, damn it! Even Saladdin didn't take on the Christians without first making sure of his water supplies. We should just maintain a defensive position. And as for Baghdad, don't even go there! It's just another of Enver's schemes like the Caucasus. He really believes he is some kind of Mahdi* sent to unite the Islamic world. He's quite mad.'

Mustafa was on his feet, pacing round the tiny space before the open flaps of his field tent. Salih continued sitting at the table, silently waiting for his commander's outrage to blow over in order to complete the dictation.

'And, if you ask me,' Mustafa was getting into his stride, 'the Germans would be very happy for us to get bogged down here holding up the British, while they move into Iraq and the oil fields. It's got nothing to do with helping Turkey maintain its empire. Why else have they been pushing out

---

* 'The Rightly Guided One' (Islamic Tradition) who will appear with Jesus before the End of Days to kill the Anti-Christ. There have been a number of pretenders to this position.

that railway project to Baghdad for decades now? Not for our benefit. It's quite the opposite, really; they want us on our knees so they can take the oil for themselves. Well, Enver can either put me in overall charge, or they will have to manage with one less general. I'll resign!'

He paused and a calm came over him. The fine thread of patient acceptance, maintained so long since his last outburst after Gallipoli, had finally snapped. These thoughts, so frantically expressed in the heat of the Syrian afternoon, took form as a whole.

'Salih Bey, please take a letter: "To the Minister of War, Seraskeriat, Constantinople... It is with deepest regret..."'

Salih put a clean sheet of paper in the typewriter. When Mustafa finished dictating his letter of resignation he turned to his cousin. 'You know Salih, this isn't going to end at all well. We've lost the tribes, and we may yet lose Palestine if we carry on this way.'

✴ ✴ ✴

Mustafa's resignation left him without funds. Before leaving Aleppo he returned all the gold that had been allocated him by General von Falkenhayn on his appointment to the 7thArmy – what had been effectively an official bribe, although Mustafa had insisted then on giving a receipt, which he now insisted be returned. The one member of the Triumvirate still sympathetic to Mustafa was the Governor, Djemal Pasha who purchased Mustafa's stable of fine Arab horses at a good price. Only by this was he able to make the journey home. Djemal later re-sold the horses on his friend's behalf for a big profit, thus enabling Mustafa to fund the activities which would keep him occupied for the next two years.[*]

---

[*] The chaos that followed in Palestine was as Mustafa had predicted. A third battle for Gaza took place at the end of October 1917, with the British, now led by General Allenby, fooling the Turks into believing they were making another frontal attack on the town. In fact, Allenby understood well the necessity of maintaining a good water supply, and while half his forces were bombarding Gaza, the other half slipped off to the east, to the legendary Wells of Beersheba. And here, where the Prophet Abraham had at Sarah's request sent his concubine Hagar and his first child, Ishmael, into the wilderness, the cavalry of the Australian Light Horse overran the Turkish trenches and secured the wells before they could be poisoned. Continuing north, Allenby's forces then split the two Turkish armies. The Turkish 8th Army made a hasty retreat from Gaza shortly afterwards. Jaffa fell to the British, who then headed east through the Judaean hills, and a month later Jerusalem was surrendered.

* * *

The long journey from Aleppo ended finally at Haydarpaşa Station from where a ferry conveyed a travel – and war-weary Mustafa across to Karaköy. Standing on deck gazing across to Stamboul, he wondered what his return to Europe would bring. Each time he crossed these straits it felt a weight was being removed, only to find another awaiting him on the approaching shore. Yet these brief minutes all at sea were a relief from everything. Below, the wintry waters of the Bosphorus churned green and cloudy, the colour of village olive oil. Banners of cloud streamed above the distant minarets of the Old City. Astern the Princes Islands were obscure shapes on a fading horizon. Steamers drifting south, at one with the tide, made no greater impression in the water than a large bird swimming upon the surface of the sea. The air was cool but not cold, and the grey light, soft but glowing like mother of pearl, cushioned his tired eyes.

Ashore, it was the irksome weight of his resignation that had to be dealt with. Enver pleaded with him, but Mustafa was adamant that he could no longer work under German command. Which reading between the lines meant he was unwilling to work with the Committee in its present form. Enver even offered to reinstate him in his old command of the 2nd Army but he refused. Rather than make public display of this disagreement between the Minister of War and the hero general of Gallipoli, which would have been a disaster both for army and public morale, Mustafa was given a month's leave.

THIRTY-THREE

A New *Sharia*

Constantinople, 1917-1918

USTAFA TOOK rooms once more at the Pera Palas Hotel. A long soak in the magnificent six foot enamel bath went some way to restore his sense of well-being. A couple of bottles of raki in the late afternoon shared with friends in the bar, nibbling *leblebi* and white cheese went further in covering the accreted smut of war, before he headed over to the Hotel Grand Antakya. He knocked on her door.

'Yes, who is it?' called Satanaya, who was at that moment in the process of wrapping her wet hair in a large towel.

'Je reviens.'

'Oh, it's you again?' she said as she opened the door, trying to sound as disinterested as possible.

'What are you standing there for. Come on in.' She pulled him inside, shut the door and embraced him fondly.

'I'll just be a moment. It was a busy kitchen tonight. Let me finish getting cleaned up.' She disappeared into the bathroom and returned a few minutes later, dressed. She looked at Mustafa, who was sitting by the window.

'So, you're back. I thought you'd be out there defending the wells of Beersheba and the walls of Jericho and Jerusalem. You've heard the news I suppose?'

'Yes, we've been discussing it for hours down at the Pera Palas. The Christians are masters in Jerusalem once again, the new crusaders. Of course, if Enver and von Falkenhayn had taken my advice, we'd have withdrawn north to Damascus and Beirut. From there we could have defended the line easily. We were too weak, the front was far too long, the command wasn't coordinated and half the troops were ill or deserting. We needed time to get our strength back, and certainly we shouldn't go traipsing across Iraq just to please the Germans.'

'I can't say things are much happier here' said Satanaya. 'The Tokatlian Hotel has run out of vermouth and gin, and I understand the Pera Palas doesn't fare much better.'

Mustafa laughed. 'Is it that bad? They still have plenty of rakı.'

'True, as do we, and plenty of fine wine. But seriously, it hasn't been easy since Zeki Bey departed. All we hear are complaints against the government. Food is scarce, people are going hungry. And not just the poor, but the families of the troops, the officers too. And nothing happens without a bribe. Trying to keep the kitchens supplied has become almost impossible. Thank God we laid down good supplies of grains and pulses, but even these are running low. No one trusts anyone any more. Things are falling apart, just like you said.'

'Yes, but it didn't have to be like this. When a fish stinks, it starts with the head. Look at what they've done.' Mustafa paused. 'You know I've resigned my command.'

'What! Again? What are you going to do?'

'I'm not sure, really. But I have a little money. I sold my horses to Djemal, so there's plenty to be going on with.'

'I'm sorry to hear that – the horses, I mean.' Satanaya knew what fine horses he had, and what a personal sacrifice it would have been for Mustafa.

'Anyway, I'm talking to people. Maybe there's a chance we could settle a peace, separate from the Germans. We aren't going to win this war, that's been clear from the start. We've always been on the defensive – except when Enver gets one of his crazy schemes – and see what trouble that lands us in.'

'Come on, Mustafa, you're beginning to sound like the rest of them. What's happened to my man of destiny?' Satanaya could sense Mustafa's despond, and knew he needed cheering up. Why else would he have come to her?

'Hah, you're right of course. But what next, that is the question?' Then he brightened: 'Go and get a bottle of that delicious Domaine de Misericorde, I think we need a little help here. In fact, get two, let's make a night of it.'

It was already two in the morning, but Satanaya went downstairs, returning shortly with a tray containing a good ration of *kuru fasulye**, some steaming bulgur, and the wine.

Mustafa opened a bottle and poured two glasses. He sniffed.

'Hmm, the '95, it's almost peaking'

'No, it's got a way to go yet, you'll see. Another five or six years should see it right.' Satanaya was tilting her glass to the light and looking at the fine edge of burgundy tinged with autumn gold that shone around the rim.

They clinked glasses and took a long, easy swig. Mustafa's eyes were grave. He peered at Satanaya over the rim of his glass. It was a look both penetrating and distant.

'You know, they say that wine weakens the will, which is true, I know – I'm already looking at you with wanton eyes – but it also opens the soul and loosens the tongue. So, what's on your mind?'

She thought for a moment. 'Last time you were here you were saying the big problem was religion. I want to hear more.'

'Oh yes? Was I?.' Mustafa drank again, and was silent a while.

'Let's take this business of '*sharia*'' he began suddenly in earnest, 'Religious law – it's worked up to a point. The prophets came to people

---

* kuru fasuliye – dried white beans cooked with tomato. One of Mustafa's cooks in later years was Halit Atay, a Bolu man who died aged 95 in 2008. He said 'Mustafa Kemal Atatürk's favourite food was kuru fasuliye, and we would never know when he would want them, so we always had to have them ready. We would prepare them every morning, and if he didn't eat them, we would chuck them out and make them again the next morning. Even when we traveled by train, our first job was to make kuru fasuliye.' – www.gastroorganic.com

with different needs, at different times. Perhaps religion was necessary for our evolution. But I think we're missing something now.'

'But this evolution hasn't stopped.' said Satanaya. 'We change, we grow, and religion adapts to take on the colours of our surroundings.'

'Exactly.' said Mustafa. 'But that's my point. Something new has been happening. The time is finished for seeing a religious leader or an emperor or sultan as the ultimate authority, between a person and their idea of a god, their concept of reality. We need to rethink this idea of '*sharia*'; we need universal laws for all of humanity, based on common human values and the rights of the individual.'

'Like the laws of mathematics, or nature? Laws that are applicable everywhere?'

'Yes. Laws based in reason, that benefit all. Surely out of all these thousands of years of religion we must be able to extract the common denominators, the conditions that apply to everyone, rules of behaviour that respect the individual rights, while serving the greater whole of a society.'

'And what if their personal beliefs clash with these new laws? Must they then keep their beliefs to themselves?'

'If someone wants to sacrifice a goat to satisfy their sense of their relationship to a higher reality, or not eat meat at all, so be it. But let them do it privately.'

'So where does this new law come from if there are no new prophets?'

'We each have to discover and know what is best for ourselves, and then to take responsibility, jointly and individually, for ourselves and our communities.'

Satanaya laughed and took a swig of wine. 'That's a lot to ask, don't you think, when you consider the state of things. We've not all been educated according to this enlightened vision of yours. Try explaining that to the refugees out there.'

'You're right,' said Mustafa, 'it's hard enough discussing this with educated people. Still, we have to start somewhere, and putting religion in its proper place, and educating people to develop a sense of personal responsibility, to know themselves – these things should not be incompatible. Doesn't it say in the Koran that there should be no compulsion in religion?* Which mullahs conveniently forget when they wave their black flags of *shahada†*, and shout *Allahu akbar‡*. And didn't Mohammed say we should seek knowledge "even as far as China"?'

So much of what Mustafa said resonated with Satanaya's own feelings. It corresponded too with much of what those sheykhs and dervishes who came to the konak in Beylerbeyi had been saying.

'Go on,' she said, 'this is interesting. But here in Turkey this religion, this '*sharia*' is an organisation, and organises everything even in our daily lives, from the top down.'

'That's because we let it. Imagine if these mullahs and sheykhs no longer had the power to dictate. Imagine if we taught our children, the girls as well as the boys, to think for themselves, to make up their own minds.'

'But if you take away the power of the religious, they will become an opposition – it's only human nature.'

'Of course, but it's not Divine Nature. Look, if we consider the matter of '*sharia*' as a Divine Inspiration, and that there are no more prophets after Mohammed, does that have to mean that existence ceases to evolve? That wouldn't make sense, logically or metaphysically. Maybe it's still there – the revelation that is – out there for all of us. For heaven's sake, wasn't Mohammed meant to be the best example of man? So? Maybe we have to find this 'prophet' thing in ourselves, find that place where revelation happens in our own hearts and minds.'

Now Satanaya thought he was on to something, something she had been feeling for a long time, ever since she was young.

'You mean like love and beauty, or certainty about things, knowing something to be true without necessarily being able to explain how? Like knowing something in our heart?'

Mustafa paused. Something in Satanaya's words had struck deep, raising memories from long ago. He remained silent for a while.

'Yes, yes. This certainty,' he said finally, 'it's different from faith belief, from what we ask of our children. It must also be verified by reason and intuition. These questions concern first the individual. Then the state.

---

* Koran: 2:256

† shahada – the Muslim confession of faith: 'I bear witness that there is no god but God, and Mohammed is his messenger.'

‡ *Allahu akbar* – God is greater

The state must promote the best conditions to bring out each person's individual potential within this democratic context. Religion then becomes an inner quest. A personal concern. Then no man or woman can presume to lord it over any other human in the name of religion.'

'It's not going to be easy,' said Satanaya. 'After all, there is a Sultan and Caliph, who people still believe is God's Viceroy.'

'Well, maybe things are changing there already. When the Sultan signed the *fatwa** for this war which called the people to a *jihad*, you can bet Enver and Talaat were leaning over his shoulder dictating his words. Don't tell me that was an act of God. Their holy war has failed. Isn't that a sign? It's over, but they don't see it. No, we need a complete separation between the religious and the political order. And the political order has to stem from the real rights of the individual within the community.'

'Come on,' said Satanaya, 'Let's open that other bottle.'

'You go ahead. I need something stronger.'

He reached into his leather satchel and pulled out a bottle of raki and a bag of *leblebi*. He began to munch on the pale roasted chick peas while Satanaya got up and fetched two glasses and a carafe of water. She poured him a double and filled the second glass with water. He poured a little water in the raki and contemplated the slow transformation from clear to opaque white liquid. He was absent again, But this time his far away look was envisioning a future that he was determined to bring into the present.

'First we have to establish a free nation.' said Mustafa. 'Free and independent of interference. Free from our own history, certainly. And free of the control of foreign powers. Then we must work to be an example of what is possible for humanity to become. But that lot – the Committee members, Parliamentary deputies, the generals, the governors – they will then try and fix us in this 'nation' idea, because that is where their vision ends – they don't see that the nation state is also only a stage in time, like religion.'

'Isn't it just same for us?' Satanaya butted in. She was beginning to warm to Mustafa's drift. 'First we were just a mass of animals with a germ of sympathetic intelligence, a herd united by its strongest members. That's how the sultans ruled, and the way the prophets led their people, even if

---

* A decree was issued in November 2014 by the Sheykh al-Islam in the name of Sultan Mehmed V calling for a jihad (Holy War) against Britain, France and Russia.

their strength came from above. But when we discover our individuality, our private potential, then we too must have the freedom to be who we are, to discover our true selves, not just some model which our ancestors have arranged in their own image. Do you think nations will ever learn that they too are simply members of a single body? That we are one humanity? One world?'

Now it was Satanaya's turn to gaze into the crystal of her wineglass. She paused while Mustafa took a cigarette from his silver case, lit it, took in a deep lungful of smoke and breathed out slowly, savouring the tobacco's sweet, woody aroma and the nicotine's sharpening effect on his brain as it mingled with the alcohol in his blood.

'You mean with a world government? Yes, perhaps. But that will take a long time. And who knows? Maybe it will never happen. And if it does, then maybe this Constantinople will also be reborn to what it was intended. But for now, for this lot...' Mustafa waved his cigarette out into the night air, '... they're not ready. They've yet to discover the taste for this kind of unity. Let them sweat, let them long for this, let them learn. They must earn it – or at least believe they have to earn it. In the meantime, we shall give them Anatolia.'

He was quietly raving now: Satanaya recognised the look. It reminded her of Khalil. She hadn't thought of Khalil in years, but now she remembered his presence strongly, the beautiful young poet, sitting by the harbour in Beirut. She felt again the intensity and passion of his soul-searching, his pained struggle to bring his lofty ideas into poetry and art. But with Mustafa it was different. His vision was definitely rooted in this world, while Khalil's always seemed to be located in some transcendent universe that he could never quite bring to earth. Mustafa, she felt, was actually seeing the future in the present, not as some wistful dream, but in a carefully designed construction, like an architect's plan already drawn out in his mind and just waiting to be executed once the site had been cleared and conditions were auspicious. How strange is love, she thought, now for this one and and then that one, so different, but the same love.

Mustafa took a long draught of raki, leant back in his chair and closed his eyes, exhausted from the effort of concentrated vision. His cigarette continued to burn between his fingers, a spiralling mist of smoke rising and disappearing.

THIRTY-FOUR

A Rising Star

Constantinople, 1917-1918

HE ILL-OMENED moon of the Triumvirate was beginning to wane, while Mustafa's star, thus far occluded, began to shine in the Anatolian firmament, piercing the fog of war and dirty politics. Mustafa was more than an inconvenience to Enver Pasha. Here was an unemployed general with a popular following who was in complete disagreement with the government's handling of the war. And so it was that towards the end of 1917 in order to get him out of Constantinople, the Minister of War had arranged for General Mustafa to accompany the Ottoman Crown Prince Vahidettin, who had been personally invited by Kaiser Wilhelm on a courtesy tour of Germany. Enver had recommended Mustafa as his Honorary A.D.C. in the hope that this might also change this difficult General's views regarding Germany's chances in this conflict, now accepted as a World War.

From the steps of the Crown Prince's villa, high above Çengelköy, Mustafa looked down over the twilight city spread before him. He could see the distant silhouettes of domes and minarets, dark hills beneath paler skies and darker shores outlined above glittering waters. Constantinople glowed, infused with a soft violet light sparked with glints of yellow, as a purple cloth is edged and shot with gold.

'But,' he thought, 'no view of Istanbul is possible only in these imperial hues.'

He began to sense beneath the calm repose of evening a restive seething, disturbing the peace of his contemplation –flickering thoughts like cries from the underworld, the sighs of internal discontent heralding future eruptions.

Constantinople was a city frozen in self-hypnosis, catatonic from the creeping shock of prolonged war. But it would need to be awakened if it were not to sink irretrievably into coma and death. While there was much here to hate in what he saw, he knew there was so much more to love.

From far below came the sound of a foghorn as a ferry pushed out from the landing stage by the mosque in Beylerbeyi. The fleet of *sandals*, the little fishing boats that crowded the waters between Üskudar and Eminönü parted in its wake. It was the season of *lüfer*, the delectable blue-fish of the Bosphorus. The ferry surged into mid-stream, the lights from the crowded salon twinkling off the surface of the water, spreading a trail of stars upon the dark waves.

Later that night Mustafa met Satanaya. His kidney complaint had been giving him hell all day, and he lay down on the chaise longue in her room, with his feet up. It seemed to ease the gnawing pain of gravel passing through his left kidney. Satanaya brought him rakı, water and *leblebi*, and a glass of wine for herself.

'It was strange.' said Mustafa. 'All these chaps sitting in the audience room, dressed, you know, in *istanbulin moda* – frock coat, fez and trousers – a glum looking bunch, all of them, as if they'd had their tongues pulled. I'm sitting there waiting with Colonel Naci, and this other chap comes in, dressed the same. Just as silent. He sits down with us on the sofa and closes his eyes. So there we are, wondering when the Crown Prince will turn up, when this fellow leans over and greets Naci and me, quietly so, and very courteously. Then he tells me he believes we're going to travel together, and that was it. Audience over. It was rather pathetic, really. And this is the guy who's going to be our sultan when old Mehmet goes.'

'What's he like then?' asked Satanaya.

'He's small, a bit thin for a sultan. I hear he suffers a lot from hyper-acidity. Mid-fifties, a thick moustache, drooping shoulders. He's rather plain looking – seemed a bit sad really. He wears pince-nez. A bookish sort, I think. All those years hanging around, I guess, wondering what his purpose was in life. He even attended the University – studied history and *tasavvuf* – mysticism. He's got a couple of daughters, apparently, and he's giving them a modern education. He never thought he'd be in line for the throne, then his cousin Izzedin went and topped himself.'*

'He doesn't sound such a bad sort.' said Satanaya. 'So, when do you leave?'

'The day after tomorrow. I'm not looking forward to it.'

'Oh, come on Mustafa. You know you want to see Europe.'

'Germany in the middle of winter? In the middle of a war? Now, if it were Paris...'

'Well, you've Enver to blame for that.'

'Don't I know it. Still, I'm sure I'll learn something. And if what they say about the nightlife in Berlin is true...'

'You wish!'

✶ ✶ ✶

Regrettably for Enver, the trip did not have the desired effect of bringing Mustafa into line. The party set off on 20th December. It was a long journey by train through eastern and central Europe, to Berlin. It included trips to German positions on the Western Front, where Mustafa spoke with lower ranking officers who told him how they were short of infantry in the front line. He took the opportunity to criticise directly the judgements of the

---

*   Sultan Mehmet Vahidettin VI, like his predecessor, Sultan Mehmed V Resad, was a
     younger brother of Sultan Abdul Hamid II, all three being sons of Sultan Abdul
     Mejid I (reigned 1839-1861). He became heir to the Ottoman throne after the death
     by suicide in 1916 of Sehzade Yusuf Izzeddin, a cousin through Sultan Abdul
     Mecid's brother, Sultan Abdulaziz (reigned 1861-1876). Vahidettin became the last
     Sultan of the Ottoman dynasty in July 1918 until the Sultanate was abolished in
     November 1922.

German Chiefs of Staff, including Kaiser Wilhelm himself, for the lack of a concrete objective in their latest big push.

History proved Mustafa right in his view. The great 'Spring Offensive', the 'Kaiserschlagcht' – 'Kaiser's Battle' – did not make the decisive breakthrough the Germans had intended. For, as Mustafa had pointed out, no clear objectives had been established and although gains were made, it was only on strategically unimportant areas difficult to defend. Inadvertently this offensive helped the Ottoman position in Palestine, where the Allied advance north, already hampered by the winter weather, was further held up as Allenby's forces were reduced by 60,000 men in order to reinforce the defenses on the Western Front.

Although he did not make himself popular with the German High Command, Mustafa formed a bond with the Ottoman Crown Prince. Vahidettin was also worried about the way the war was going. He was concerned that in such a rich country as Turkey, the people in both town and country were going hungry, while the rail network, instead of transporting food stuffs was taken up with removing Turkish raw materials to Germany.

Mustafa arrived back in early January but by the spring, kidney trouble took him to Vienna for treatment, followed by more than a month recuperating in a clinic in Karlsbad. When he finally returned to Constantinople at the beginning of August, it was to a new Sultan. Mehmet V had died that month and Prince Vahidettin, now enthroned as Sultan Mehmet VI, became the last in the line of Osman.* Since 1299 the Ottoman dynasty had ruled an empire which at its peak had stretched from the outskirts of Vienna, to Baghdad and Arabia, through the Caucasus and Crimea, down into Syria, Palestine, Egypt and most of North Africa. But so many of its European estates were lost during the Balkan Wars, and its eastern Arab territories during the current conflict, that Vahidettin's inheritance was but a fruitless tree in a derelict orchard.

* * *

'So you're back at last!' Satanaya greeted Mustafa. Since Zeki Bey's departure, she was *de facto* boss of the Hotel Grand Antakya and had

---

* The deposed Sultan Abdul Hamid II, who since being rescued from his Salonica exile in 1912 had been fading away within the confines of Beylerbeyi Palace, finally gave up the ghost in February 1918.

moved into the penthouse suite. The escape route by way of the secret passage was now out of service; by this time most of those on the Three Pashas wanted list had either escaped or been arrested. She had initiated Mustafa into the mysteries of the building and provided him with a set of keys, so he was able to come and go as he wished via the apartment building next door. Nevertheless, he generally telephoned before he visited.

She sat him down, and he lit up a cigarette while she poured the raki.

'Tell me all about it then. How was Vienna? and Karlsbad?'

'Cold, mostly. And the hospital food was really dull.'

'But all those *Konditoreien*? Didn't you get to try the chocolate cake at Hotel Sacher?'

'Satanaya, you have no idea how many times I asked them to give me *kuru fasuliye* with rice, but they insisted that beans were not good for infected kidneys. They kept feeding me soups. Insipid broths. You know, no one makes soups like you.'

'Well, I'm preparing something special for you tonight, to strengthen your kidneys. And your liver, if that's still possible.'

When Mustafa had rung the day before she had put some lamb's kidneys and chicken livers to soak overnight in raki. Now, after she had drained them and removed all the membranes, she tossed them in a mixture of flour, seasoned with salt and pepper, a little paprika and ground cumin. She heated some butter in a frying pan and tossed in the meat, turning them quickly until the outside was crispy and cooked but still a little pink on the inside. She kept this warm while she prepared the *tirit*, a thick canapé of fried bread covered with red onions sliced and sautéed in butter with a little stock and pomegranate molasses. She poured the kidneys and livers over the *tirit* and brought it in to Mustafa.

Mustafa left his cigarette burning in the ashtray and began to eat.

'Mmm. This is good. They say one gets strength from eating one's enemy. I hope my liver is not going to become my enemy as well as my kidneys. I shall call the dish Mustafa's Liver, to ward off the Evil Eye.'

'Are you in danger of that?'

'In my position – always. I did a lot of thinking while in Karlsbad. I had little else to do – except read those novels you sent me, thanks for those. Especially about the government, those buffoons who call themselves pashas. I can't see how they can continue once this war is over, whichever way it goes. Djemal Pasha for instance. How does he afford to

live the way he does? It's obvious he helps himself to the gold the Germans
send. And Enver Pasha – well, we know he's in clover with a princess for a
wife. Though I can't figure out our relationship. He seems to like me while
at the same time he's insanely jealous of my success. He knows he blew it in
the East against the Russians, and that without our efforts in Gallipoli we
wouldn't be sitting here now. He could easily have made me Minister of
War, but instead he has insisted on calling himself Commander in Chief.
Only the Sultan has ever had that title. Except maybe İbrahim Pasha back
in the days of Suleyman the Magnificent, and he paid the ultimate price.'
Mustafa paused in thought.

'And Talaat Pasha?' said Satanaya.

'You know what they say, "once a postman, always a postman." The
man is no fool, but he is mechanical, and a brute. He's right about Russia,
we shouldn't trust their intentions since the Revolution, any more than
before. But he's a pure bureaucrat. Once an order is put in place, that's it. If
a letter is posted, it has to be delivered, rain or shine. Admirable qualities
for a postman, perhaps, but not for a politician or a diplomat. Or an army
officer for that matter.

'What's going to happen, Mustafa?' They exchanged glances, each
knowing that an end was coming, both hesitating to bring their intuitions
into thought, let alone speech.

She looked at him and noticed how the years of constant stress had
taken their toll. She remembered the dashing young officer she had seen
first in Syria; and then on the dance floor in Sofia, the military attaché with
his handsome face and sharp blue eyes that spoke of adventure and danger.
The man before her now had aged. The eyes were still blue, and the steel
was still in their gaze. They had certainly seen their fair share of danger, but
she no longer found him dangerous. And the face. It had softened, but it
was a man's face, and she found herself overcome with fondness for this
face, for the man who wore it, and for the fact that he dreamed dreams that
were worthy of a real man. This was a man worth loving. But how? What
was the manner of this love? Could she bring herself to love what he loved?
Could they share that passion? She found herself again in a quandary.
When they slept together, she would surrender herself to him, as he
surrendered himself... to what? She knew she had to be bigger than herself
to receive his passion. Bigger than her thoughts of personal relationship. It
was strange, this kind of love, the bond they shared was so close, like

members of a family. Like closest friends. Could it ever be one of marriage? Satanaya pushed the thought away, and it left with ease.

'I'm leaving again. That's one of the reasons I came tonight.' Mustafa's words brought her back. 'I've got a new posting. A good one, perhaps. I don't really know. We'll see. I've been made commander of the 7th Army in Syria and Palestine – it seems that Talaat and Enver are pulling the strings once more with our new man in the Palace. But it was Vahidettin Padişah himself who gave me my marching orders, so I couldn't exactly refuse. I'll be under Liman von Sanders again; no doubt sparks will fly.'

Satanaya was surprised to see, before they went to bed, that Mustafa had finished the plate of liver and kidneys. Although still not completely recovered he seemed to be in a good place in himself, not so much resigned to fate as accepting. Perhaps he had learnt a little patience in Karlsbad. At any rate, the fire was still there.

THIRTY-FIVE

The Last Battle

Palestine – Syria – Anatolia, September – October 1918*

> *"And he gathered them together into a place called in the Hebrew tongue Armageddon. And the seventh angel poured out his vial into the air; and there came a great voice out of the temple of heaven, from the throne, saying, It is done. And there were voices, and thunders, and lightnings; and there was a great earthquake, such as was not since men were upon the earth, so mighty an earthquake, and so great."*
>
> **Revelation XVI, 14-18.**

---

* The situation for the Ottoman Army in Syria and Palestine was now untenable. The Allies under General Allenby had consolidated their successes at Beersheba and Jerusalem with attacks into Jordan and north towards Nablus in March 1918; progress was hampered by the state of the roads during the winter rains, as well as the removal of troops to support operations against the German 'Spring Offensive' in Europe. The 8th, 7th and 4th Turkish armies –the so-called Lightning Group – together held a front stretching sixty miles from the East Mediterranean coast through the Judean Hills and into Jordan. General Mustafa was responsible for the middle twenty-five mile section.

PON A HILL in Palestine overlooking the Plain of Megiddo lies the ruined fortress of Armageddon. It is situated on the ancient trade route, the Via Maris, which connects Egypt to Damascus, Anatolia and Mesopotamia. It goes by way of the Plain of Sharon, which leads up from Gaza along the Mediterranean coast to Dor, where it cuts inland through the mountains to the Plain of Megiddo and the Plain of Esdraelon in the shadow of Mt Tabor, then meeting the Jordan Valley. The three passages of Sharon, Esdraelon and Jordan form a semi-circle enclosing the Judean Hills and the towns of Jenin and Nablus where Mustafa had his headquarters north of Jerusalem.

Ahab, King of Israel and husband of Jezebel built the fortress of Armageddon nearly 3,000 years ago. But Ahab wasn't the first to experience the strategic value of this location. In Constantinople, mid-way between the entrance to the Blue Mosque, and the Great Church of Hagia Sophia, rises the top third of the Obelisk of Thutmose III, one of the greatest of Pharoahs. Originally erected in Karnak, it reached its final destination upon a marble pedestal in the ancient Hippodrome, having been brought there by the Byzantine Emperor Theodosius in the 4th Century AD. For all the desert winds and storms of sand of three millennia, the hieroglyphs of eyes and owls, falcons and scarabs scribed in the smooth red Aswan granite are as sharp as if they were carved yesterday. Following the death of his stepmother, the female Pharoah Hatshepsut, Thutmose III began a long career of conquest when he took on the King of Kadesh, who along with the King of Megiddo was leading a rebellion against Egyptian suzerainty.

The first Battle of Megiddo would be the largest and most significant battle of Thutmose III's reign, and like his obelisk, his story survives, engraved in the walls of Karnak. A forced march up the coast through Gaza and the Plain of Sharon brought his army of more than 10,000 chariots to the ridge of Mount Carmel. Of the three ways to reach the enemy forces at Megiddo he avoided the easy routes to the north and south of the ridge, and chose what was considered the more dangerous and therefore least likely but direct route through the narrow ravine of Wadi Ara. His hunch paid off. The pass was lightly guarded and after a battle the rebels retreated to the fortress. A seven months siege brought about surrender of the rebel city, and further victories re-established Egyptian authority in the region.

* * *

With such prophetic, noble and bloody pedigree, was it any wonder that the inspired leader of the Allied forces, General Edmund Allenby, spurred on by his successes in Beersheba and Jerusalem, was drawn to follow in the footsteps of this legendary Egyptian warrior? But how to effect the necessary surprise? Deception would be the key to a favourable outcome. Then speed, superior forces and safe lines of supply and communication. Allenby sought to encircle the Turks by breaking through the Turkish 8th Army in the west with a surprise attack on Megiddo, and then outflank Mustafa's 7th Army forces from the north before they were able to retreat from Nablus.

From his headquarters in Jerusalem, Allenby spread disinformation to mislead the Turks into believing he would mount his attack in the east through the Jordan valley. By day Allied troops were marched openly east and trucked back under cover of darkness. Meanwhile by night he secretly strengthened his forces in the coastal area of the Plain of Sharon.

Tutmose III marched his armies along the Mediterranean coastal plain in springtime. The storks were flying north along the Jordan Valley, a good omen for the Egyptians. The weather was fair, the land was green and lush, and the rivers coming down the ravines of the Judaean Hills on their right hand were brisk with winter rains. Allenby's armies trod in the burnt dust of summer's traces, across dry riverbeds, with water scarce and daytime temperatures over 30 degrees centigrade. But among his troops were hardened Anzacs and men of the British Indian Army. They were well supplied, well equipped and armoured, and outnumbered their German and Turkish counterparts almost five to one. The Allies' air superiority imposed a virtual no-fly zone over the whole of northern Palestine and Syria, preventing Ottoman air reconnaissance from discovering the enemy's deceptions and revealing its actual troop displacements.

* * *

For Mustafa in Nablus, the situation did not appear promising. Even the *knafeh**, which had he taken the trouble to seek out, likely would not have improved either his mood or his liver. Less helpful even was the attitude of

---

* Middle Eastern dessert of pastry and sweet sheep's cheese. See: *Satanaya and the Houses of Mercy*, p. 139.

the Arab population, by now thoroughly infiltrated with Allied spies. The condition of the Turkish forces was pathetic, with regiments down to less than half strength, under-nourished and ill-equipped for the inevitable confrontation with Allenby's army.

The Turkish officers gathered in Mustafa's headquarters. Among them was Ali Fuat, his deputy and old friend from staff college and their days in Beirut and Damascus nearly twenty years earlier; also present was Colonel İsmet, his companion in the eastern Anatolian campaigns of 1916 and 1917.

'So what do we really know of this Allenby?' Mustafa leant over the table and studied the map.

'Ah, you wish to know your enemy.' replied Ali Fuat. 'Well, he's a very experienced soldier, in his late fifties. But he's not an old fossil. He's studied the art of war, and uses his knowledge intelligently.'

'But what's he like? What are his strengths... weaknesses...? I want to get inside his mind.'

'He's a big man, tall, good looking. But hard too, apparently he has a short temper. His men call him "the Bull"' said Colonel İsmet. İsmet knew English and read the reports of the war in the London Times when he could get hold of copies. 'He's tough on his subordinates, but he listens to them. He's a thinker, a strategist – as we found out to our cost in Gaza with all those false reports he put out over the radio.'

'He could have done even better if he'd known how weak our position was in Gaza. If he'd kept some of his cavalry back for that battle – there was never enough water to sustain his cavalry in the wells of Beersheba' said Mustafa.

'Maybe he's learnt from that. Maybe he will put his main force by the coast where he can maintain his supply lines.' countered Ali Fuat.

'You can bet he'll use his cavalry where he can. His mounts will need a lot of water in this season.' İsmet paused. 'You know he had a son in the army. Killed last year on the Western Front.'

Mustafa looked up from the map. 'Ah. So perhaps there is a flaw. But will it hinder or help him? He no longer has anything to lose; nor any reason to win. Which one will it be?' He thought a while. 'I think our time here may be over. Look at how he behaved in Jerusalem. Apparently he entered the city with his commanders on foot, and swore to protect the holy places, just like the Caliph Omar ibn al-Khattab. He let the Nuseibeh family, Muslims, remain as door keepers to the Holy Sepulchre, as they have been since Saladin appointed them seven hundred years ago. The Arabs see him as a liberator. A man with such integrity will be supported by Providence. We must take care now, as we forfeit the interest, not to lose the capital.'

'Will it come to that ?' said Ali Fuad.

'Think about it. He has more than twice our forces. They're well supplied. And he has been paying Prince Feisal £200,000 a month in gold to keep the Bedouin on his side, so you can bet his field intelligence is good.' said Mustafa.

'Then he is a worthy opponent.' concluded İsmet, and Mustafa smiled.

* * *

From 16th September, Allied diversionary attacks had begun in the east. Allied Arab irregulars, some under Colonel T.E. Lawrence (of Arabia), and some Howeitat warriors under the fierce and fearsome Auda Abu Tai had been harrying the Ottoman forces for more than a year, disrupting communications and troop movements by blowing up trains on the Hejaz Railway. Auda had ridden with Lawrence to capture Aqaba, so giving the Allies a port to supply their Egyptian Expeditionary Forces, and now they had their sights on Damascus.

Under Prince Feisal, a group including Arab army regulars, some Arab Ottoman army deserters, and French Algerian and Indian support, moved north along the Hejaz railway in the Jordan Valley in order to attack Deraa.

* * *

Ottoman Command Headquarters, Nazareth, 17th September.

Mustafa was bedridden again with kidney trouble, but he sat up from his cot when his adjutant entered, breathless.

'We've just captured an enemy deserter, sir.'

'And?'

'We've questioned him. He's an Indian N.C.O., sir. A Muslim. He says the main attack will come from the west, along the coast. Tomorrow, after midnight. He says the attacks here and in the Jordan Valley are just diversions, and the main body of troops has been moved secretly west.'

'Did he give this information freely? Or was he 'encouraged' to speak?'

'He seems genuine, sir. Shall we bring him in?'

'Yes, but let me get up first.'

Mustafa dressed, and the solder was brought in. He had obviously been encouraged a little – he had a black-eye and his boots had been taken. But he stood proudly at attention and his look didn't waver when the Turkish commander questioned him.

'Why are you telling us this? You know you will die if the British defeat us?'

'I want to fight for the true faith.' the Indian answered.

'Take him out.' Mustafa ordered.

He sighed. Mustafa abhorred disloyalty, even when it brought him advantage. He convened a meeting with his staff officers, Colonel İsmet and Ali Fuat, and Colonel Refet, another compatriot from Salonica days, now a corps commander from the 8th Army on the coast. Refet asked to withdraw his troops north to slow down the attack, which all now agreed was more likely to come from the west.

But General von Sanders thought otherwise. While he allowed for some contingent preparations, he wasn't convinced by the Indian's story. No withdrawal would be permitted.

Two days later a little after midnight, communications went down between the GHQ in Nazareth, headquarters in Nablus and the 8th Army in the west; telephone and telegraph lines were cut and a lone Handley Page aircraft bombed the railway junctions and exchanges in Afula and Messudieh.

Shortly after, in the early hours of 19th September, having amassed a huge artillery and mortar compliment of nearly 400 guns and with two destroyers offshore, the Allies began a heavy bombardment of the Ottoman defences on the coast below the ridge of Mount Carmel. There then followed a 'creeping barrage' upon the Ottoman entrenchments in which a line of artillery fire shifted forward at a rate of one hundred yards a minute, with the Allied infantry advancing behind it, across the now-destroyed barbed wire. In hours the Allies had broken through and their cavalry divisions were heading north along the coast at some speed. The Turkish forces were routed, and those Ottoman troops not outflanked and taken prisoner fled in retreat. Colonel Refet was cut off by the swiftness of the advance. He reached the safety of Tyre a week later, evading capture by travelling at night, riding his horse at walking pace and saluting but not speaking when he encountered the enemy.

At the same time Mustafa's headquarters in the Judaean Hills came under heavy bombardment. The Allies were hoping to effect an encirclement by coming around to the north of Mustafa's 7th Army.

Twenty-four hours after the engagement had begun, the Allies held the ridge of Carmel, allowing their troops to pass through to Afula and Beisan. Nazareth came under attack and General von Sanders and the Ottoman GHQ were evacuated.

Mustafa knew he had insufficient strength in the 7th Army to take on Allenby's forces. On the night of 20th September, to prevent being outflanked, Mustafa abandoned Nablus, withdrawing to just south of Damascus. But even here the line could not be maintained.

In Damascus the Turkish troops had to contend with Arab street fighters and as the retreat continued, Mustafa barely escaped with his life. The city fell on 1st October, and Beirut shortly after. There followed a staged withdrawal as far as Aleppo, but still the Allies pushed on relentlessly into Syria. Nazareth fell, followed by Haifa and Acre on the coast a few days later.

The Allies continued to advance. In mid-October Homs, which had been the headquarters of the 4th Army, was destroyed. After fighting broke out around and within Aleppo, Ottoman forces abandoned the city. Most of the troops retreated into Anatolia, encamping near Iskenderun in the Belen Pass above the plain of the Orontes, defending the southern gateway into Anatolia. Mustafa remained with a small force about thirty miles north of Aleppo, near the village of Qatmah. Here he made a token last stand, seeing off a British attack. For Turkey, it was the final battle of the war.

With defeat in Palestine and Syria, the penny finally dropped for the Ottoman High Command, for when they realised they could not come back from this defeat, everything began to fall apart again. On 4th October Sultan Vahideddin sacked Enver Pasha from his position as Minister of War, and the government controlled by the Triumvirate resigned ten days later. Turkey's erstwhile ally and buffer state, Bulgaria, had been defeated at Salonica, and the Austro-Hungarian army had been dissolved. It was time to seek a separate peace while they still possessed the integrity of Anatolia.

The Armistice between Turkey and the Allies was signed on 30th

October 1918. In common with German officers within the Ottoman territories, General von Sanders relinquished his command, leaving the sad remnants of the three armies of the Lightning Group to General Mustafa.

Mustafa himself left for Constantinople two weeks later and installed himself in the Pera Palas Hotel.

'At last,' he thought to himself as the slow train made its way across the Anatolian plains, 'Perhaps now the real work can begin.'

THIRTY-SIX

Occupied

Constantinople, November 1918

IGHT UPON THE WATER, grey sheen of mother of pearl, fluctuations dimpling the surface of time. The grey battleships cut a grim furrow, brooking no resistance as the waters of the Dardanelles opened a way. The minesweepers had gone ahead, removing the pickets that had prevented entry, and a transport vessel had docked at Çanakkale where troops of the victorious British army had disembarked in order to take over the forts guarding the Straits.

Ten days earlier on British battleship HMS Agamemnon, in the harbour at Mudros on the Aegean island of Lemnos, the Ottoman government and the Allies had signed the armistice bringing hostilities to an end.* In reality it was a humiliating surrender, giving the Allies the right to

---

* A week later in France, negotiations began between Germany and the Allies. Kaiser Wilhelm II abdicated on 9 November, and the armistice signed on 11th November 1918 signified the end of WW1.

occupy the Anatolian heartland wherever they felt their interests might be jeopardised.

The irony in that Homeric name, *Agamemnon*, commemorating the leader of the victorious Greek expedition against the Trojans, could not have escaped the classically educated officers of her complement. Perhaps the more prescient among them even glimpsed in this allusion the seeds of tragedy yet to unfold.

The combined Allied battle fleet of fifty-five warships cruised up the narrow waterway, passing on their port bows the small villages and towns from whose meagre fortifications and shore batteries three years earlier brave defenders had halted the onslaught of these same navies, and from where the Ottoman army had mounted the successful resistance to the Allied landings on the Gallipoli Peninsula. The convoy continued out into the Sea of Marmara, the line of ships extending a full sixteen miles, before reaching Constantinople.

That same day, Mustafa stepped out of Haydarpaşa Railway terminal onto the quayside. In the grey afternoon he observed one after another the gloomy warships drop anchor opposite the noble domes and walls of the great city. It was a violation. As if thugs had entered the private rooms of a great lady, intent on despoiling her, and he could only look on impotently. He felt sickened, as he took the ferry across the Bosphorus to its berth by the Galata Bridge at Karaköy; the very same old paddle steamer that had bravely seen off a British submarine three years earlier, though he had no idea of this now, as it bobbed and weaved with the humble dignity of the defeated within the congestion of dreadnoughts and destroyers lording it around Saray Point.

* * *

From the konak's terrace at Beylerbeyi, Satanaya and Amina Khanoum watched the grey ships arrive. British, French, Italian, even a few ships of the Greek navy. One by one their dark steel hulls filled the near horizon from below the old city of Stamboul, stretching up along the Bosphorus and obscuring with their bulk and billowing smokestacks the palaces of Dolmabahçe and the blackened ruins of Çırağan at Ortaköy.

Amina Khanoum sighed. 'We have lost so much territory, and now even here we are occupied. You know, I'm not even sure what my nationality is any more.' She looked glum. Inside she felt afraid, for in spite of the hope she had felt when the Colonel Efendi had brought the news that the fighting was over, she knew things would be changing. Their personal fortunes lay in the oilfields of Mosul, and God knows in whose hands these pots of gold would end up. Already the British had occupied the Ottoman possessions in Iraq.

'Life goes on, doesn't it?' said Satanaya. 'People still need to eat. I should get back to the hotel, for these İngiliz will need feeding just like all the rest. And besides, it will be good to be in the middle of things – these are historic times.'

'Yes, it's historic. Constantinople has fallen from the inside. But I'm worried. The Greeks, the Armenians, they will want revenge, surely. I prefer to watch from over here. You and Colonel Efendi will doubtless keep me well informed.'

Satanaya smiled reassuringly. 'Don't worry, Amina *canim*, things didn't go badly in Egypt or Cyprus. I'm sure these Europeans will behave in a civilised way.' She was looking forward to seeing new faces, and hopeful that food supplies would improve and the hotel could expand its menu again after the privations of the war years. And Mustafa would return soon. No doubt he would have much to tell her.

✶ ✶ ✶

As Mustafa made his way via the Tünel up to Pera, he was more than glum. His deep frustration had flared into all-out anger. The armistice specified demobilisation of the half a million strong Ottoman army, currently spread around Anatolia in various locations. It also allowed an occupying force of 50,000 Allied soldiers. He was glad he had resisted the orders to disband the remaining 24,000 troops of his own command, the Lightning Group, and had taken steps to spirit away large caches of arms and munitions to secret hiding places. He had also encouraged other confidants of rank to do the same. What made him really furious were the conditions allowing foreign troops to occupy Anatolia itself. He knew this had to be resisted, and was searching for a way to make it possible.

For now, he seethed in silence. In shops and businesses in this pre-dominantly European and Christian area of Pera, the mood was strangely buoyant. Some pale flags in blue and white were displayed in the windows of Greek-owned buildings. Even the Turks he had encountered at the waterfront were curious and quietly excited after the tension of the past four years. Mustafa had also noticed the sunken shoulders of the remaining German officers; these old familiar infidels no longer carried themselves with the aloof swagger of colonials among the natives; the armistice had bestowed on them an impotence more humiliating perhaps than that which Mustafa sensed among his own defeated comrades in arms. Most were desperately trying to depart by boat to the Black Sea ports and back to Austria and Germany. In their place was this impending presence upon the water, bearing a new infidel to the very threshold of the heart of the domain of Islam.

With Enver, Talaat and Djemal now out of the picture – for the 'Three Pashas' had fled Constantinople within days of the Armistice being signed – Mustafa began the groundwork for the future. In the bar of the Pera Palas Hotel, where he had taken rooms, he met up with a group of journalists, mostly Turkish, but including a Mr Price from the Daily Mail. They stood him drinks well into the evening, while Mustafa gave chapter and verse on his own early political and military background, his diplomatic interlude in Bulgaria and wartime activities, and what he felt was necessary now to ensure the territorial integrity of the nation following the armistice. His declarations were published in a number of articles, hailing him as the one unconquered hero to emerge clean from the inglorious debacle which the Three Pashas had inflicted upon the country. Over the next few days he began to establish contact with various comrades from his Salonica days, and from within the Committee and Army, discreetly sounding them out for the future.

* * *

'I thought you'd been avoiding me. I heard you've been back almost a week. A new girl, perhaps?' Satanaya produced a particularly alluring pout from her repertoire of '*la femme abandonnée*', as she welcomed him into her apartment at the Antakya.

Mustafa, whose thoughts were altogether elsewhere, took her jibe seriously just for a moment. 'No, no...' he stuttered, then seeing her smile at catching him out, he threw up his hands. 'Sorry. No. It's just my feet have barely touched ground since I arrived.'

'Where are you staying?'

'I was at the Pera until yesterday, but it's so expensive. Now I'm staying with a Syrian friend in Şişli until I can find a place of my own.'

'You could stay here, you know.'

'*Canim*, I know; and I would love to, truly. But at the moment I have to see and be seen among certain people. Everyone who matters, or will matter, is there: in Beyoğlu, in Harbiye, the parliamentarians, the diplomats, the officers. And the Sultan in the Palace down the road. The war is over, but the country is still in danger. The real struggle begins now. Besides, I'll be near my mother.' The tone in which he made this last comment, in a low voice as if expressing an intimacy, surprised Satanaya. Mustafa so rarely mentioned his mother, she had almost forgotten her existence.

'And me? You won't forget to call from time to time? We do get some very interesting people through here nowadays, you know. Fatih Bey and Madiha are both well informed as to what goes on in the street as well as behind closed embassy doors.'

'Don't worry, I'm relying on you to keep me well fed, and well informed. I need someone watching my back in more ways than one.'

'Are you in danger?'

'Not at present, I don't think. But you know, with the coal shortages, and no street lighting, even I think twice about venturing out alone on these dark nights.'

Satanaya brought in some mezes from her kitchen: a little '*fava*' bean paste made from pureed broad beans, olive oil and dill; some freshly made '*müjver*' courgette fritters; a bowl of *muhammara,* the hot red pepper and walnut paste, *dil peynir* (tongue cheese) and fat Gemlik olives. Rakı, ice and water came next, and they sat down for a long talk.

Mustafa gave her a rundown of the Palestine campaign, and then he began to expand on his hopes for the future. But he was restless. Being with Satanaya could calm him for a night, but a different fire was burning in him now that no amount of tenderness could assuage. When she awoke later in the chill early hours, the space next to her empty.

She saw his silhouette by the open window, and his face an intermittent pink glow as he drew on a cigarette.

Mustafa stood, staring out beyond the shrouded city into the dark sky shot with starlight. He sighed. 'How does it change so?' he said to himself.

He turned to see Satanaya looking over towards him.

'What are you talking about?'

'How does the beauty change from our love making to this?' He waved his arm into the night sky. 'To this nowhere I can put a finger upon, to this no body, no arms embrace; and yet it needs to be embraced by these small arms of mine? No eyes where my eyes can alight? And yet my heart, my poor heart's vision is straining to encompass all this and beyond; it spills out like a wave afraid of discovering it is an ocean.'

'You know,' he went on, 'this making love has so many forms, but it is all the same in the end. ' Then, like a wave that has expended all its energy upon some vast receiving shore, he turned back to her. 'Look at you, you have been a gift to me, like a key to love, for a beauty that goes beyond you and all my imaginings. Like the beauty of this night, so full of potential, you are no less a mystery.'

Mustafa had never spoken to Satanaya like this before. It was quite new, and she wasn't certain whether he was talking to her, or to his muse. Perhaps there was no difference.

'Close the window.' she said finally. 'And come back to bed, it's freezing.'

'Sorry, I've got to go. Some Laz chaps I need to see down at the docks. Don't worry, it's all arranged. I said I need someone to watch my back – they're for my protection. And they are helping us to smuggle arms out of the city by boat. I'll be back when I can. Promise.'

The Laz people to which Mustafa referred were members of the fiercely independent seafaring race from the eastern Black Sea regions of Trabzon and Rize and beyond into Georgia.

'*Kolay gelsin.*' Satanaya laughed. 'May it be easy. You know they say, behind every Laz man there's a Laz woman with a sword.'

'Hmmm. And what's behind a Cherkez woman, I wonder?'

'A whole nation, if I'm to believe what you say.'

✳ ✳ ✳

Mustafa visited Hotel Grand Antakya again later the following afternoon, with a bundle of newspapers under his arm. He took coffee with Satanaya in the office she had taken over after Zeki Bey's departure.

Satanaya put down the newspaper she was reading. 'They really have made you out to be quite the hero, haven't they? Or were you putting words into their mouths.'

'It's what they want to hear. A little positive regard helps everyone in these difficult times, don't you think?' Mustafa was getting used to defending himself against Satanaya's teasing.

'Okay. But what are you going on about here, where you say "the best

government is the one that is the most powerful, in every sense"? I thought
you said the government was impotent now. Then you go on to say this
force is not just a matter of military might, but must be strong spiritually
and scientifically, as well as being virtuous and knowledgeable. What's that
about?'

'It's what I've been saying all along. What the last lot never took on
board. We need well-educated people running this country, from the top
down. People with a sense of the spirit of the nation, people who understand and are trained in modern scientific techniques so we can compete
on equal terms with these Europeans. We need the independence that
comes from that. And we need to demonstrate real moral standards in
government.'

'And you think this is possible?'

'Certainly, once we shrug off the old ways, the ways of the mullahs and
the nay-sayers who want to go back to the past. We found a new way in the
war, in the army. We found a strength and a power even with our lack of
weapons. We were united in our belief in ourselves, in this land. We were
prepared for the ultimate sacrifice. This gave us the strength of will of
virtuous men. How else did we succeed in Gallipoli? Even if we are only
left with Anatolia, the heartland, it will be enough. As long as we don't let
them divide it. A nation is a very powerful spiritual force if the people's will
is undivided. And that will be more powerful than all those battleships
down there by the Golden Horn.'

'Oh Mustafa, I love it when you talk like a revolutionary. You glow.'
Mustafa gave Satanaya a quizzical look. She smiled. 'And Vahidettin? How
do you think that will work out? You say he insists on staying as Sultan and
Caliph, temporal and spiritual head?'

'We have an understanding. I believe he trusts me.'

'And you? Do you trust him?'

'He's not the difficulty. It's the system, the people around him. There I
can't see, but time will tell.'

* * *

At the house in Şişli, Mustafa met regularly with his friends. With the
collapse of the Three Pashas regime, and subsequent dissolution of the
Committee, Mustafa's old friend Ali Fethi had begun a new political party.
Its aim was to pressure Parliament to challenge the increasing encroach-

ments by the Occupying Forces on the State's sovereignty. But the Sultan, conscious of his need to preserve his position as both spiritual and political leader, dissolved Parliament at the end of 1918 and postponed elections indefinitely. Mustafa and his associates saw Vahidettin's withdrawal of power to himself as a retrenchment to the bad old days of Sultan Abdul Hamid II.

Meanwhile, the Allies grip on the Empire increased. While it had been agreed in the Armistice that only the forts of the Dardanelles were to be manned by Allied troops, within days of the fleet arriving, British soldiers were seen marching in the streets of Pera and Galata. The French, coming from the west after the fall of Bulgaria, had reached the Porte the day before the British, taking control of the old city of Stamboul. Early in February 1919 Italian troops and *carabinieri* took up policing duties, eventually making themselves at home on the Asian shores of the Bosphorus at Üskudar and Kadıköy. It was a wholesale military occupation, and the Greeks and other Christians who made up nearly fifty percent of the city's population, were jubilant, imagining that the days of the *Megáli Idéa** – the Great Idea – were nigh. The Turks of the old regime became increasingly nervous.

Almost simultaneously there began a stealthy encroachment in Anatolia itself. In February 1919 the French occupied Adana with four battalions, hoping to extend their Syrian mandate into Anatolia. Further incursions by British and French troops in the south-east region brought Maraş under Allied sway, as they began to repatriate Armenian refugees to the town. The French took over the coal mining port of Zonguldak on the Black Sea, and further along the coast British troops occupied the port of Samsun. Konya in Central Anatolia, and Urfa, the ancient city of Abraham just north of the present day border with Syria came under British control, while the Italians took the sleepy east Mediterranean coastal region including Antalya and Fethiye. It was a carve up.

---

* *Megáli Idéa* – The dream of Greeks since the time of Turkish rule of re-establishing a pan-Hellenic state based on the former Byzantine Empire which would include the areas of Thrace, Macedonia, the Aegean and Ionian islands, the western Anatolian coast, Crete and Cyprus, with its capital Constantinople.

THIRTY-SEVEN

Love, Food and Death

Constantinople, November 1918 – May1919

 HE FIGHTING ENDS. But war continues in thought and word and heart of the combatants. Exhausted, victor and vanquished lay down arms, while from their frozen passions bitter poisons rise.

On the streets of Occupied Constantinople strange atmospheres co-mingled: the wariness of the Muslim Turks, cautious to the point of surliness as they trod their familiar city; the openly boisterous expressions of expectation on the faces of the Greeks and Armenians; the strutting confidence of the Allied troops: all betrayed the illusion of peace.

Yet within this agitated climate of sadness, resentment and barely suppressed gloating and of overbearing arrogance, Satanaya and her team at the Hotel Grand Antakya strove to create a neutral enclave of harmony and respite.

Although few of the original kitchen staff now remained, an influx of dispossessed Russians since the 1917 Bolshevik Revolution had provided the city with a surfeit of competent chefs trained in the French manner. Satanaya had interviewed a small group of well-qualified candidates. From these she chose a couple of men of Circassian descent, the only ones who had declined her offer of a glass of vodka as they stood before her in the office, kalpaks in hand.

* * *

'We need to have some sort of celebration,' she said to Fatih Bey one morning. 'Something to mark the end of the war, and a new beginning. We need a new menu, one that will please all the various nationalities who imagine they have occupied our city. But a menu that will turn the tables, so that it will be Constantinople that occupies them, here in the Grand Antakya. Once we have conquered their stomachs, their hearts will be easy prey. We shall no longer have anything to fear by their so-called occupation. Then we can hunt them at our will.'

'My dear Satanaya, that is fighting talk. What's got into you?'

'Seduction, my dear Fatih Bey. A more intimate form of flattery than dull obedience. We shall entice them with food, and seduce them with beautiful ladies. And then strip them of their haughty will through mirth and pleasurable enjoyment. They are already weak. We shall tenderise them further for the cooking that must inevitably come.'

'Inevitably? So what do you propose?'

'Oh, nothing strange or startling. Let's start with a night of *La Cuisine d'Entente* – presenting the great dishes of the world. French and Italian dishes. British too if we can find someone to cook a decent Spotted Dick. And for the Greeks, well, we'll just call it 'Eastern Mediterranean', they won't tell the difference; we'll just not use pork in the moussaka.'

She sequestered herself in the office with Takla's Cookbook. After sitting quietly for a while she opened it, seemingly at random, at a tipped-in letter in the Cairene's familiar hand. It had been a long time since she had consulted the book that had accompanied her from her ignominious departure from the Convent of Seydnaya as a young teenager, and what she read now she would swear she had never read before.

"*Union, or the Way of Food and Love,*' it began. *"and the Transformative Power of Death."* Then a further sub-title: *"Why it is important to consider the meaning of the phrase 'absolutely you become what you eat'."*

"The importance of food:" wrote the Cairene, *"the material food as the representative and emissary of the Divine Nourishment and Taste. So, the preparation of the dish, and its ingredients must be in conformity with the highest knowledge and aspiration with which the cook is blessed, whence it may deliver benediction in accordance with the original intention, without interruption or deviation.*

"This is why we are enjoined to cook with love, for love is the movement of that origin – which we variously designate the Divine, the One, the Reality – *to be known. And the most essential and direct way of knowing is certainly knowing through taste. And the acquisition of this knowledge of the real is arrived at through the union of taster with that which is tasted – in the eating, whereby we may 'eat' of the essence, and so be nourished directly from our essence.*

"So, to cook with love, to appreciate through the cognitive action of taste, to be intimately penetrated by the union that is the reception by body, soul and mind of the essential nourishment, and to manifest praise of this union through the enjoyment, the taking of pleasure, that is the ultimate joy to be aspired to and God willing be attained through the cooking and eating of food.

But the prerequisite of this union is death. Not death of the body. That will come anyway and all too soon. But an extinction prior to that. A removal of all that separates us in our minds, our behaviour and our substance, from that origin. A relinquishing of our dependence on opinions and imaginations formed by our so small experiences of life, a willingness to let go of these preconceived notions of likes and dislikes. And learning to taste for the first time directly of the thing perceived, whether it be a dish of food, the face of the enemy or the embrace of the beloved. To know through taste we first must abandon perceptions based on information acquired through hearsay. We have to see for ourselves, and know for ourselves. And such a death can only be through love. Love is the only real service we can give to our essential being. And by love, this union that always is becomes known."

Satanaya closed the book and sat a while before taking up a pen and beginning to write:

Hotel Grand Antakya
welcomes the Allies
to
Constantinople, Great City of the World
with
An Evening
of
Great Dishes of the World

Then she went down to the kitchen and together with her new chef began to compose the menu.

For the hors d'oeuvres, they decided not to fuss about. It was simply a matter of transposing Turkish mezes into Greek mezedes, so that cheese and spinach börek became spanakópita, humus with tahini translated as choúmous me tachíni, cacık and dolmas were now dolmades and tzatziki, patlıcan salatası appeared as melitzanosaláta, and so on.

The fish course was a dish to honour the memory of the British Navy. A fillet of salmon (to represent the Scots) and a fillet of Dover sole (for the English), lightly brushed with lemon forming the two sides of a sandwich stuffed with lightly sauteed Dublin Bay prawns (for Ireland – although of necessity the langoustine had been fished in the Marmara Sea) and finely chopped leeks (for the Welsh), seasoned with fresh dill, the whole then coated in a thick bechamel sauce using fish stock and a little grated *kaşar* cheese, covered in breadcrumbs and gently fried, then served with potato chips. The accompanying pink sauce, to represent the global nature of Britannia's empire, was a light bisque made using prawn butter (boil the minced prawns heads and shells in butter, add a little brandy and paprika, then strain through muslin). She named the dish simply 'Fish and Chips Mary Rose', a further nod to the long lost flagship of the Royal Navy of King Henry VIII.

A French theme was chosen for the poultry course – a dish of roast pigeons on a canapé with truffles and foie gras, accompanied by pears braised with cinnamon and red onion. The pigeons were local. Very local in fact for since taking on her role as Kitchen Manager, Satanaya had promoted the feeding of pigeons on the roof of the hotel. Cages had been built and regular broods reared for the table. A simple dish of pigeon cooked with green olives and onions had become a staple of the menu during the war. Goose liver had been supplied by the Colonel Efendi from his poultry farm, and the truffles came courtesy of the cook of a French battleship – the same cook who had supplied the Pol Roger vintage 1900 champagne, now at its best, as well as a case of very fine cognac.

The meat course was whole lambs, slowly spit roasted with a stuffing of rice and pistachios – in ironic representation, perhaps, of the Turkish surrender and its pending carve up, though no one was so undiplomatic as to bring this thought to speech.

Since the arrival of the fleet off Constantinople, and the re-opening of the Dardanelles, the food situation in the city had begun to change. The ever-resourceful Fatih Bey, through the agency of his brother who ran a chandlery business down in the docks, had insinuated himself into the comestibles supply chain with the pursers and chefs of the various foreign vessels arriving in the port. A barter system prevailed whereby Fatih Bey arranged supply of fresh vegetables and dairy products, fish and meat, and in return was provided with hard to find items such as chocolate and alcohol, especially foreign spirits, claret and champagne, as well as truffles and pasta from Italy. In addition Fatih was able to introduce the sailors to some of the more lively aspects of night life in Pera and connect them with some of the better class female escorts. Cargo ships were now arriving from Egypt and the Levant bringing early season vegetables and fruit.

For dessert, icecream seemed most appropriate in paying homage to the gay Italian spirit. Individual little cakes comprising vertical stripes of pistachio, melon and pomegranate ices represented the colours of the Italian tricolore, encased in a palisade of miniature Savoiardi sponge fingers, and topped with a chocolate dome reminiscent of St Peters in Rome.

Once the menu for the opening week had been settled, Fatih Bey used his many contacts to broadcast the Hotel Grand Antakya's new menu by leafleting the various foreign gendarmeries and military billets throughout the city. A small stream of regulars on the first few nights, quickly grew into a flood as word spread of the unusual and unusually good cuisine at the Antakya, and soon advance booking became essential. A floor show was put on each evening, of traditional, mostly Balkan, music. And though Madiha would dance a tantalisingly teasing, though essentially modest,

version of the Seven Veils, to old timers the magnificent presence of Zeki
Bey was sadly missed. On occasion Spotted Dick did make it into the
menu.

The initial flood of custom settled down into a steady flow of dining
regulars. As warmer weather approached, Satanaya got it into her head
that a *bal masqué* would be a fun way to celebrate the coming of spring.
Notes were sent to the various diplomatic missions and military staff of the
occupying powers. Of course the top brass and ambassadors had their own
embassy parties and regimental dinners, but the Hotel Grand Antakya had
its loyal clientele, and tickets quickly sold out.

A masked ball might be likened to a sea cruise, in that where pelagic
vastness overwhelms the voyager, bestowing a certain timeless anonymity,
so too the mask and costume releases us from mundane conventions of
behaviour, freeing us to recreate ourselves in our own oceanic imaginations.
No longer inhibited by gender or race, colour or culture, where size no
longer matters and we are free for a brief moment to express that long
suppressed desire to be other than who we appear to be – the drab sparrow
may become a bird of paradise, the timid are now heroes, the conformers
plunge headlong into eccentricity, the reticent appear bold, and the meek
become magnificent.

The party got off to a jolly start. Trays of champagne did the rounds
without pause as the guests arrived, and the band played an assortment of
popular melodies from all the European countries represented. A grand
buffet had been prepared, leaving Satanaya free to meet and mingle with
the strange parade of characters as they presented their tickets. In a city so
used to costume, it has to be admitted the foreigners outdid themselves in
their originality. One French couple came as the Arc de Triomphe,
constructed in two parts joined across the middle of the arch. While this
ensemble worked quite well when dancing as one, the two halves looked
somewhat adrift as they parted into the arms of gorillas, South Sea maidens
à la Gaugin and Biblical prophets. Shakespearean characters were the stuff
of the British contingent, with Lady Macbeth partnering Hamlet, and a
bushy-bearded Othello arm in arm with a dainty Ariel in diaphanous
dress. An Italian couple presented themselves as a Cardinal and a nun,
which seemed a little incongruous until it was pointed out that they were
Borgias. Casanova arrived with two young girls in tow, all wearing Venetian
masks. When a troupe of Greeks entered in skirts, stockings and pompoms,

the uniform of the Presidential Guard of the Evzones, the Italian contingent
pointed out that they should have had more imagination than to wear their
ceremonial dress. The Greeks protested that they would have come in
togas as Socrates, Aristotle et al., but the weather was too cold.

Mustafa was one of the last to arrive. With characteristic aplomb he
appeared in the Janissary uniform he had worn years before in Sofia. With
a contingent of friends similarly dressed he marched into the hotel as
honour guard to a splendid Sultan Mehmet the Conqueror in flowing silk
robes complete with jewelled turban and ostrich plumes. A rumour spread
that it was Sultan Vahidettin himself, in disguise and out for a night on the
town in the manner of earlier sultans checking up on their subjects behaviour. But the man in question was in fact an old eunuch from the time of
Abdul Hamid who had been retained to look after the historical garments
and imperial robes in the Topkapi Palace; a corpulent man with a penchant
for pretty young boys, he had been lured into taking part in this charade by
a couple of eligible young captains on Mustafa's staff.

Mustafa greeted Satanaya, herself made up for the evening as a young
Circassian warrior, with fake moustache, bandoliers and a massive fur
kalpak.

'Tell me, is General von Sanders here?' Mustafa asked. 'I thought he
was in Germany, but I swear that's his Mercedes parked outside.'

'Yes, that's his car all right. But it now belongs to that tall fellow over
there.' Satanaya nodded towards a group of guests. 'He's a British Captain,
in charge of their intelligence service. He even speaks Turkish. Shall I
introduce you?'

'No, not just yet. I'd like to know more about him first.'

The character Satanaya indicated stood out even in that motley gathering, due in part to his height and the shock of blonde hair. Unmistakably
English, with the slim mask over his eyes, a little green hat with a parrot
feather in the band, long legs in green tights, short jacket, a quiver of
arrows over his shoulder and a longbow, it had to be Robin Hood. For a
spy, for that he was, it was a little too obvious a disguise. But there were few
there who knew the young English intelligence officer who spoke passable
Ottoman Turkish and was responsible for issuing travel permits to
members of the now-defeated Ottoman army. This was Captain John
Bennett. Tonight he was to be the object of Madiha's attentions, and if all
went to plan, of her affections too.

Dressed as the tragic Nubian princess Aida, heroine of Verdi's epony-
mous opera, Madiha approached the table where Captain John, alias Robin
Hood, sat with friends. The Englishman rose and greeted her with a bow:
'Good evening, Madam.' he said, 'Do we find a damsel in need of
assistance? Perhaps you are fleeing the wicked Sheriff of Nottingham? We
are at your service.' And he then introduced Little John, Will Scarlett and
Friar Tuck, all fellow officers dressed in a variety of coloured tights and
rough-cut cloth jackets and monkish habit. 'Are you by any remote chance
the Maid Marian?'

In the hubbub of the noisy ballroom Madiha misheard her own name
and for a moment thought her cover was blown. She had no idea at all what
this character was on about, so she gave him a simpering look and breathed
out slowly, flaring her nostrils, then turned sideways allowing him to
appreciate the fullness of her figure and announced:

'Aida. Aida of the Upper Nile.'

Captain John bowed again, and as the band had begun to play a waltz
he proffered his hand. She accepted and together they took to the dance
floor. It was evident to Madiha that Captain John was tipsy, and ready to
enjoy himself. His work in the intelligence department had meant he had
barely slept more than a few hours each night since arriving in Constantinople, and the few glasses of champagne he had drunk, now produced in
him a pleasant lightheadedness in which he was ready to go wherever the
evening led. That it ended in the early hours in Madiha's bed cannot be
confirmed. Or denied. Not that it mattered. The members of his merry
band assumed it to be.

Meanwhile the festivities were in full swing. Fatih Bey's kindly
ministrations among Pera's ladies of the night throughout the war now
bore sweet fruit. A party of more than a dozen of the most beautiful
maidens, ladies of the Balkans, Ukrainians, Russians, Circassians, Greeks,
Arabs, Turks, all arrayed as odalisques of the seraglio, decked out in finest
antique silks courtesy again of the retired eunuch of the Topkapi Palace,
had followed the Sultan and Mustafa's janissaries into the hotel and had
spread out among the assembled parade like celestial presences turning in
the night sky, stars attracting to themselves in their graceful curving
motion the singular unattached planets of young officers of the occupation.
And while few had insufficient weight to resist the pull of these heavenly
bodies, and many crashed and burned in one glorious night of champagne

supernova, some like returning comets maintained a steady orbit of their celestial partners over many months to come, surrendering much dark matter of information in exchange for the stardust of pleasure. And the fallout of these discreet conjunctions, whether quincunx or sextile, trine or opposition, in whatever mansion, was a most valued aspect of the evening as far as Mustafa and his colleagues were concerned.

THIRTY-EIGHT

Gun For Hire

Constantinople, Spring 1919

O, WHAT ARE WE going to do with you, Mustafa?' Sultan Vahidettin gave the General a langourous look from across the ornate marble-topped table upon which lay two coffee cups, both now empty.

They were sitting alone in a private audience chamber in the palace. The small room looked out through tall French windows over the Bosphorus Strait. The surface of the water was grey and choppy beneath a sullen *Lodos** wind which had been blowing up across the Marmara Sea since early morning. The warm air laden with the dust of Africa was causing headaches among the inhabitants of the city, and neither the Sultan nor his

---

* *Lodos*: a strong south-westerly wind in the Marmara Sea/Aegean region.

subject were immune from this irritation. Both men were weary but neither let their weariness show. Few boats had ventured forth that day, for this ill wind made the currents devious and unpredictable.

'Well, you could always appoint me to head the War Ministry' suggested Mustafa.

'Yes, yes, we all know you would like that. And no one could deny you have the qualifications. But would it really be the answer? You would be stuck here just as I am, surrounded by all this… a prison really.'

Vahidettin waved an arm, by this gesture indicating both the huge English battleship that lay barely a hundred yards offshore, and the encumbrance of the Occupying Forces. Or perhaps, thought Mustafa, his glance taking in the gilded furniture, the cascades of swagged curtain and ornamental pargeting of the room's painted ceiling, the Sultan was referring to the House of Osman itself, the Palace and its six hundred years of encrusted bureaucracy.

'You need room to move, Mustafa, and I need someone who can move for me. Someone able to bring together what's left of our poor estate.'

'Then let me go back into Anatolia. I will work to ensure that the Army doesn't disintegrate into factions. You know there are so many of us who haven't accepted this defeat. Some you might consider as 'loose cannons', who are looking for a cause. The country will be prey to all sorts of dangers if we don't bring them into a single body.'

The Sultan considered this and his face sank. He adjusted his pince-nez on the bridge of his nose and looked at Mustafa.

'Ah, yes. Yes.' he spoke slowly, pausing between his sentences. 'Everything becomes its opposite in the end. My dear late brother, Mehmed Reshad, God's mercy upon him, told me this. "As long as a quality isn't unified in its essence, it is in danger of becoming its opposite." He was a dervish, you know. A Mevlevi. A mystic in his own way. They – Enver's lot – they tried to turn him, but he was beyond all that, I believe. Are you beyond all that, Mustafa? Are you unified in your essence?'

Mustafa didn't know how to answer this. While in Anatolia in 1916 and 1917, during the long periods of bad weather and lulls between the fighting, Mustafa had had time to read. And he had read a lot: as well as military texts and history, he devoured the writings of the medieaval Islamic philosophers and theologists: Avicenna, Averroes, Al-Ghazzali, as well as the Sufis – in particular, Ahmad Hilmi, whose works were banned

by the Committee. Ahmad Hilmi* was Mustafa's near-contemporary
whose thought is steeped in the notion of '*al-wahdat al-wujud*' – 'the unity
of being'. Mustafa preferred to view the concept of antinomic affirmation,
with regard to the relative world, expressed in its correlative in modern
scientific thought, in the idea that every action has an equal and opposite
reaction.

'No, forgive me, that's unfair.' Vahidettin continued. 'None of us can
answer such questions. But we know you as we have seen you. The Dardanelles. Syria. You are trustworthy. Like the Prophet, upon whom be peace,
you are '*emin*'. Our caravans are safe in your care.'

'And you? Are you safe, as Sultan? As Caliph?'

'Oh, I don't think we need worry about our British shepherds, for now
at least. They have as many and more of the Faithful in India for whom I
am also their Caliph. They must keep them on their side.'

✳ ✳ ✳

For the time being, Mustafa enjoyed the confidence of the Sultan; and
within the intimate confines of the private audience room, they understood each other and trust persisted. Later, separated by geography and
unable to speak face to face, their communications came to be interfered
with by the go-betweens of the bureaucracy of state, and this so delicate
confidence was sundered.

This future breakdown of trust, and the subsequent rupture betweeen
Mustafa and the Sultan – for the young general currently enjoyed favoured-
courtier status – perhaps may be viewed as being 'in the grand scheme of
things', inherent in which is always the possibility of perdition or salvation.
Only time would tell who had been lost and who had been saved.

✳ ✳ ✳

Mustafa met with Sultan Vahidettin intermittently during the six months
following his return to the capital from Syria. Outwardly the Sultan con-
formed to the wishes and pressures of the Occupying Forces, cooperating

---

* Ahmet Hilmi (Şehbenderzade Filibeli Hilmi, born 1865) was a Turkish Sufi, writer
  and newspaper publisher. As a supporter of the Committee of Union and Progress
  he was exiled to Libya until the Young Turk revolution in 1908. Later he became
  critical of the government of the CUP. He died by poisoning in 1914.

under the terms of the armistice, while in the '*enderun*'* of his private relationship with Mustafa, a different picture for the future was being
discussed.

With the dissolution of parliament, the Occupying Forces rounded up
dozens of former members of the Committee and imprisoned them in the
notorious Bekirağa prison attached to the War Ministry. Many of those
arrested, politicians and military officers, were then sent into exile in Malta
by the British, who feared they would undermine Allied plans to dismember
the Ottoman Empire. At the instigation of the Occupying Forces, but
within the jurisdiction of the Ottoman Courts, trials were held for those
accused of ordering or taking part in the forced evacuations and massacres
of Armenians during the war, and some executions took place.

Mustafa, the national hero with strong influence in the Ottoman
military, was left alone. Nevertheless his movements were being watched
and noted with interest by foreign parties. In spite of his being under the
Sultan's protection, the Occupying Forces didn't hesitate to harass the
soldier through his family, raiding his mother's house on at least one
occasion.

Mustafa's situation was fast becoming critical. Two army officers
among his closest confidants had already received official postings into
Anatolia, and now encouraged him to join them. But Mustafa wasn't to be
rushed. He needed an official posting if he was to put his plan into action
with any degree of legitimacy. In Constantinople Mustafa gathered round
him a cabal of like-minded officers, supporters on whom he could rely, as
he worked on getting himself posted out of the city.

A new government was formed in early March 1919, now purged of
any former Committee members, most of whom had been rounded up
and arrested that month. Mustafa's old friend and wartime comrade Fethi,
who had served as Interior Minister in the brief period after the collapse of
the Triumvirate's cabinet following the armistice, was also in custody. But
the War Ministry had been stacked with sympathisers sharing Mustafa's
ambitions to free the country.

Now the Ministry proposed reorganising the remaining forces of the
Ottoman Army by appointing a number of inspectors to oversee the col-

---

* *enderun* (Persian), the interior, intrinsic, heart. Pertaining to the Palace, i.e. to the
Sultan's inner circle, private domain, domestic apartments etc.

lecting and secure quartering of ordinance, and the demobilising of the troops in Anatolia. They were also expected to put an end to the continuing violence between various partisan groups, Greek Christians and Kurds in particular. The Ministry nominated Mustafa for the post of Inspector of the 9th Army, covering eastern and central Anatolia – effectively all of Turkey east of Ankara. The details, which had been conceived mostly by Mustafa himself, also gave him authority in the areas to the west and south. It was a very broad mission, and only by a little bureaucratic sleight of hand on the part of his colleagues in the Ministry did he manage to get the order passed, signed and sealed.

In spite of the official brief, Mustafa's own plan was simple: to raise an army in the hinterland from those forces that as yet had not been demobilised, staffed by officers he knew to be loyal to the idea of the Turkish state; to maintain possession of all the military hardware that remained in Ottoman possession, and then with a provisional government, working in conjunction with the Sultan and parliament in Constantinople, to renegotiate the armistice to free the country of foreign forces and establish its independence. Essential would be the support of the civilian population in the countryside, for the will of the people was the key to success in any revolution. And for that the acquiescence of the Sultan would be paramount. That was the plan, in rough; inasmuch as any plan could be made when launching an entire country into the unknown. Mustafa's passion was alight again. But there was one final hurdle: he still needed the permit from the British to leave the city, which came with a risk of being rescinded before he got away.

* * *

When Satanaya returned to her room in the afternoon she found Mustafa standing by the table near the window, pouring intensely over a book he had opened. After some time he looked up.

'You see, it says it all here… "the cause of ignorance is either lack of aptitude…or else it is getting lost in the distractions of the world." Exactly! This work will only be achieved if we never for a moment lose sight of our aim.'

Satanaya knew he was reading from her copy of Ibn Arabi's Fusus al-Hikam, the Bulaq edition.

'Yes, but that's referring to God, to the Divine Knowledge.'

'But don't you see, Satanaya? Is it any different? Now *you* are separating. If our work is real, then it is the same thing. "As above, so below".'

But Satanaya had more things on her mind than to argue metaphysics.

'Did you get the permission?' she asked.

'Everything but the permit from the British. But it's in hand. I go to collect it from Captain John – or should I say Robin Hood – tomorrow from British Headquarters. I wonder if he'll recognise a fellow outlaw?'

THIRTY-NINE

A Romanov Holiday

Constantinople, April 1919

OLLOWING THE success of the New Year party, business remained brisk at the Hotel Grand Antakya. The Russian chefs had settled in well. With their knowledge of French cuisine, coupled with the excellent Turkish cooking of the local staff, they were well able to satisfy the tastes of their growing clientele, both among the Occupying Forces and the occupied. Madiha, Fatih Bey and their loyal troop of escorts continued to harvest useful information on current affairs, from overheard conversations at the tables and bar, or from what was let slip during more intimate moments in the bedrooms. Collated and supplemented by Fatih Bey from his own special sources, this was then passed on to Satanaya, who in turn gave Mustafa chapter and verse on what went down on the streets and behind closed doors of the embassies, ministries and military offices in Pera and Stamboul. More than once it had been possible to forewarn a colleague, a politician or Ottoman officer, of his imminent arrest and deportation to Malta by the British. The secret passage came back into use, and Mustafa's Laz irregulars could be relied upon to spirit away the fugitives into the relative safety of Anatolia.

But Satanaya still had enough time on her hands to make regular visits to her friends in Beylerbeyi, where she could relax and share gossip with Amina Khanoum and the Colonel Efendi. In April all the talk was of the continuing civil war in Russia. As unconfirmed details slowly leaked out of the murder of the Tsar and his family the previous summer, a trickle of surviving members of the Russian aristocracy started to appear in the city.

The Colonel Efendi always had the latest news. One cold morning early in April, he looked up from his breakfast coffee and peered out over the misty waters of the Bosphorus. Through the gloom he could make out the dark grey shape of a large warship making its way north towards the Black Sea. All the little fishing boats and ferries were laying back inshore, giving it a wide berth.

'I suppose that must be HMS Marlborough – the British battleship sent to collect the surviving Romanovs from Yalta' he said, and went back to his breakfast.

It was quite consciously a tease aimed at his wife, and she took the bait.

'What? How do you know? Who are they going to collect?'

'Oh, the Dowager Empress Maria Feyodorovna, I believe. You know, the mother of the Tsar.' he said, as if imparting common knowledge. 'And the Tsar's sister Xenia. And a whole pile of nieces, nephews and cousins. The walls really are closing in on the old regime and the English just aren't going to allow the sister of their Queen Alexandra to be taken by the Bolsheviks, not after what they did to the Tsar.'

'And to the children, poor things,' added Amina. 'But we must find a way to see them when they return. Can we arrange something?'

'Well, you know it's all meant to be hush hush, but…'

* * *

Amina Khanoum couldn't wait to tell Satanaya the news, and phoned her immediately after breakfast, inviting her for lunch.

'I've pestered the Colonel to arrange a launch for us. They are going to be here for Easter it seems. Apparently some of the passengers wanted to celebrate in the Church of the Hagia Sofia, but it was explained to them that it was now a mosque, and had been for rather a long time. Really, these poor things, most of them have never left Russia before. Apparently the captain of the battleship is having an awful time persuading the Dowager Empress to leave Russia. Everyone is terribly sad, it seems, having to leave it all behind, the palaces, the treasures, all that land.'

Satanaya, whose family had been forced to flee their homelands by the ancestors of these very same Romanovs had little comment to make when it came to the plight of the dispossessed aristocracy. She had also read a little Tolstoy in French translation, and her sympathies lay mostly with the peasants.

'Yes, I suppose it could happen to anyone.'

'You think so? You think it could happen here?' Amina looked suddenly quite alarmed.

'Not like that, no. Even when the Committee deposed Abdul Hamid, they let him keep his wives. His family have continued to rule.'

'After a fashion. But now, with this occupation, who knows?'

'Well, the British aren't going to depose the Sultan. He seems to be getting on well with them.'

'And your friend General Mustafa? What does he think? Is he really the revolutionary they all say he is?'

Satanaya laughed. 'No, not at all. He's very much a man who likes order. And he's not given to unnecessary violence. He's a strategist, and a humanist, the plight of the peasants affects him a great deal. He really believes that the wealth of the nation is the common man. Not like Enver or Talaat.'

'You know the British want to arrest him, don't you. The Colonel told me so.'

'Yes, but they won't do anything as long as he has the ear of the Sultan. Which he does. You know he's had half a dozen private meetings with Vahidettin. Heaven knows what they talk about.'

'Anyway, Satanaya, what I really want to discuss is our invitation to the Russian Royals when they pass through. I thought, perhaps you might be able to have your new chefs rustle up something suitable to make them feel at home. You know, some good Russian fare? What do you think they would like? If the Colonel manages to find a big enough boat, we could have a party on board. I think we still have some of that special champagne left. You remember, the Louis Roederer Cristal*. And I know you know how to get hold of the best caviar. So, blinis, sour cream, caviar, champagne…?'

'And the rest. I gather they've been rather starved of meat during their stay in the Crimea.'

✳ ✳ ✳

A week later the battleship Marlborough departed Yalta in the Crimea, carrying the remnants of the Imperial Russian Family. A day's sailing brought them into the Bosphorus on a grey and misty morning. The ship anchored off the islands of Prinkipo and Halki†, the largest of the Princes Islands, twelve miles south-east of Constantinople in the Sea of Marmara.

Some days later the Colonel Efendi arrived home with the news that a navy launch had been arranged, and permission to visit the refugees on the battleship had been granted. Already as the Bolsheviks advanced, thousands of Russian refugees had fled the Crimea on British ships and disembarked on the islands for processing. But the accommodation was inadequate, with insufficient water and food supplies. The refugees were now to be transferred, initially to Malta. At present they were quarantined on the islands for fear of spreading epidemics in the city. The Colonel had visited the camps, now under French administration, and was disturbed by what he saw.

'The state of these poor people, you wouldn't believe that some of them used to live in palaces' he told his wife and Satanaya. 'We have had to fumigate their clothes, of course, because of typhus, but they were only rags anyway. And as for their accommodation, I've seen sheep and goats housed better. Anyway, a boat is arranged for tomorrow to pick up some of the younger members from HMS Marlborough for a picnic. The Dowager Empress prefers to stay on board. I said we'd provide the food and drink – I think they're looking forward to this.'

The day proved glorious. Spring had finally come to Constantinople, the weather sunny and warm. The launch picked up Satanaya and her

---

* The favoured champagne of the Romanovs since the days of Tsar Alexander II.

† Now known as Büyük Ada and Heybeli Ada.

Circassian catering brigade from the Karaköy ferry station early in the morning and after collecting the Colonel Efendi and Amina Khanoum, motored out upon a calm sea towards the great grey mass of the British battleship lying at anchor off Halki Island. Accompanied by a few British naval officers, a motley bunch of rather overdressed Russian aristocrats with worried looks on their faces stepped nervously down a canvas-covered companionway.

'*Bienvenue en Turquie!*' The Colonel Efendi welcomed their guests aboard. French would be the *lingua franca* of the day as only Satanaya and the cooks could speak Russian with any fluency.

When introductions had been made – most of the guests, even the children, were titled Prince or Princess, with the odd Grand Duke or Duchess – Amina Khanoum announced a cruise along the shores of Constantinople before lunch. The Russians were thrilled to hear this, as they had seen little through the mist on the day they arrived and had been stuck twelve miles away ever since. For political reasons none of the party would be allowed to come ashore in the city itself, but on such a beautiful day much could be seen from the sea.

They motored first across to the western edge where the visitors sighed and marvelled at the great walls and towers at Yedi Kule. They followed the shore east past the Church of Saints Sergius and Bacchus*, and the Sinan masterpiece of the Sokollu Mehmet Pasha Mosque, then the grand imperial mosque of Sultan Ahmet with its six minarets. Below the Aya Sofia, the Church – now Mosque – of the Holy Wisdom itself, the boat paused awhile as the refugees gazed up with tears in their eyes and prayed for the delivery of Mother Russia from the scourge of the Bolsheviks, and perhaps, silently, also for the delivery of Constantinople from the infidel Turks.

It was a relief then, to pass beneath the harbour walls below the Topkapi Palace and wonder at the mysteries of the harem, now no longer inhabited by the Sultan's odalisques. Weaving through the massed ranks of the Allied battle fleet, they entered the Bosphorus Straits. Along the green slopes of the shores, between the gaily painted villas and grand palaces of pashas and Egyptian princes, the Judas trees poured down their magenta jewels. That such magnificence of architectural riches could exist outside

---

* Built by Byzantine Emperor Justinian I in mid-6th Century, converted to a mosque by the Ottomans, now known as Küçük Ayasofia Camii.

their own wonderland of St Petersburg, however, only saddened the poor wretches further, so Satanaya had a brief word with the Colonel Efendi, who nodded to the waiting staff, and soon the sound of champagne corks popping shook the morbid Russians from their disconsolation. As glass after glass of Louis Roederer Kristal were quaffed in the sunshine, the mood lifted and conversation brightened.

'You know, this is so kind of you' began one Princess to Satanaya, 'We had no idea what would happen to us once we left Russia. We still don't, but so far the British officers have been most gallant, looking after us on board, and playing with the children. And having to put up with poor old grandma Maria Feodorovna. She's been quite a handful. But then, she's lost so much.'

'But you all have.'

'No, I mean her son. She was devoted to him. They killed him, that's for sure. And almost certainly the Tsarina as well, and the children, our cousins. So her grief is great. And she feels responsible. She really didn't want to leave. The people, that is.'

'But the people had a revolution?'

'Yes, that's true. But it's not that simple. Changes would have come, I'm sure.'

'Perhaps, but not in time.'

'Not perhaps. But certainly not in time. That's the great pity. We had our chance. We had too much time. We didn't use it well. Now this...' the Princess paused, and looked at Satanaya. 'They are thugs, you know. Gangsters. The worst of the worst. Heaven help poor Russia.'

Satanaya felt sympathy for this individual, tied to the destiny of an empire that was now caught in the maelstrom of civil war. The largest country on earth perhaps, an empire that grew by swallowing smaller nations in a kind of global gluttony, now wracked with violent intestinal disruption.

'And you have the British and French? How is that?' the Princess asked Satanaya.

'It's not looking good. We too have had our own share of thugs. We wouldn't be in this mess otherwise. Now they're gone and we are being slowly dissected. The Sick Man of Europe, they called us. And we are impotent like the soldier whose limbs have all been amputated but lives on, unable to move.'

'Perhaps you can grow new limbs?' She gave Satanaya a strange look of hope, as though bestowing the energy of her own hopeless hopes and impotent desires as a gift.

Satanaya thought of Mustafa.

'Yes, perhaps there is hope yet. In the meantime we manage as best we can.'

By early afternoon the boat party arrived back at the Princes Islands. A picnic was arranged in a small sandy cove. By now everyone was hungry, and the cooks ferried pots of food ashore. Tables were set up and everyone set to. The Russians finally divested themselves of their fur coats and military overcoats to reveal figures which bore witness to their recent privations.

Sure enough, they ate as if they hadn't seen food in weeks. The caviar and blinis were consumed in seconds, washed down with more champagne. Two large kazans full of steaming borscht and trayloads of pirozhki had barely been placed on the table before they vanished into hungry mouths. The pace slowed a little when the Boeuf Stroganoff arrived, alongside platters of rice and cabbage, but all were cleaned up with ease.

'You have no idea what it is to eat real meat again.' whispered the Princess to Satanaya, between mouthfuls of Stroganoff.

'Is it true you had to eat donkey?'

'That's only the half of it.'

The Colonel Efendi hadn't bargained for the quantity of champagne needed, but one of the officers, seeing a crisis looming as the last bottles were opened, sent the launch back to HMS Marlborough for more wine and vodka.

Eventually the feeding frenzy passed and everyone relaxed. The afternoon became quite hot and the party rested in the shade of the pines which grew along the shore. Some of the officers swam in the bay.

'Why didn't the Grand Duchess join us?' asked Satanaya

'She's in no mood to socialise. Ever since arriving here she's been seeing refugees from the camps and listening to their tragic stories. She feels it's her job now to give them moral support in their hour of need, especially since her son is no longer able. She won't accept that he's been killed, and the communists won't admit responsibility. They just say the Tsar and his family have been taken away. It's all been quite upsetting for her. She has this lovely ornamental egg made by Fabergé that Nicholas gave her for Easter in 1916. It has his picture on it, and inside a miniature of him as a child. She keeps bringing it out and looking at it, and then she starts to cry. She is living with an impossible hope, but we can't say anything. Now with Easter coming upon us…'

In late afternoon the launch took the Imperial party back to the battleship, where the Romanovs received the news they were departing for Malta in the morning. Returning to Beylerbeyi, their erstwhile hosts were in a pensive mood.

'Poor things. You can't help but feel for them.' said Amina Khanoum. Inside she was thinking about her own situation.

'Oh Amina, you are a silly thing.' said Satanaya, intuiting her friend's unspoken worry. 'Whatever may happen here, you will be fine. You are rich, you have your connections, to the Sultan and to the Khedive. The British may take control, but they like to keep things in good order. You know they learnt about bureaucracy from the Moguls in India, who are Turks too, and that's how they rule. They need their Suez Canal, to keep open the route to the oilfields in Iraq, and to India. They won't want to upset the applecart.'

Amina wasn't convinced. The wars had been going on for too long, and nothing seemed resolved. Everything was still up in the air and no one seemed to be sure how things would land. Satanaya wasn't convinced either by her own words. She knew enough of Mustafa to know he wasn't going to put up with this occupation indefinitely. She was sure things would change sooner rather than later.

FORTY

Laissez-Passer

Constantinople – May 1919

 APTAIN JOHN seemed to be in a perpetual state of bewilderment. The spectrum of his state of unknowing had first
revealed itself to him following a shrapnel wound on the
Western Front a year earlier. The intervening period had
brought him by a strong and fateful current to his present destination.
From that brief but wounding exposure in the trenches, he had been
shunted through marriage, his father's death and his own, premature
fatherhood, to the War Office for an intensive course in Ottoman Turkish,
followed by a long and wine-fuelled train journey across a broken Europe
in the aftermath of war, to terminate at the G.H.Q. of the British Army of
the Black Sea, in Constantinople. Here this tall and tender, fair-haired boy

of twenty-two years took up his post as Assistant Liaison Officer, with an office in a room sequestered by the British in the Turkish Ministry of War. The same building outside of which misfortune had fallen upon the noble General Mahmut Şevket Paşa. And here, on account of his knowledge of Turkish, and the fact that his boss was otherwise engaged with a demanding Russian mistress, Captain John toiled day and night dealing directly with many of the high-ranking officers and ministers of the defeated Ottoman Empire.

Today his mood of bewilderment seemed more so than usual. Among the papers on his desk lay a pile of official documents bearing the Ministry seal; permits to leave the restricted area of Constantinople. He looked at them again, and then at the Turkish officer opposite.

Mustafa looked back across the desk at Captain John and at the vital *laissez-passers* he was holding. The British Intelligence Officer was hesitating, glancing from the documents, to Mustafa and back to the documents.

Normally the task of issuing such high ranking permits would have been undertaken by his superior, but as usual the Major was absent. Captain John had felt so unsure of the legitimate purpose of these documents, prepared by the Turkish War Ministry regarding Mustafa's appointment to Anatolia that he had first referred them to his own G.H.Q near Taksim Square.

'It looks more like a War Party than a Peace Mission, if you ask me' he had said to the Staff Officer on duty.

G.H.Q. had then consulted the British High Commission. The order came down from above that General Mustafa enjoyed the highest confidence of the Sultan. So that, apparently, was that. Still, the young Englishman had his own misgivings. He was fast becoming disillusioned by these people of rank who occupied positions of responsibility, and yet were governed so often by their own petty, personal preferences and prejudices.

With a sigh Captain John took up his pen and with the air of someone consciously entering that space between the devil and the deep blue sea, he signed the papers, and placed them in a brown manila envelope which he handed over in silence. It contained permits for Major General Mustafa, his fifteen staff officers and other Ottoman military of high rank, and a platoon of soldiers, to leave the capital and travel to the port of Samsun on the Black Sea, and further within Anatolia as the situation demanded.

Had Captain John known he was handing over a nation, would he have released Mustafa so easily? Would he have released him at all? Standing before him was the most successful Turkish general to come out of the war, a hero respected by the people, never actually defeated in battle, and he was sending him into the heart of the nation where he was expected to disarm and collect the weapons of his own troops. It seemed such an obvious recipe for a revolution. But even if his instincts told him one thing, he was unable to do otherwise. The pull of the current was too strong. On days like this, perplexity glowed strongly in the spectrum of his unknowing.

'The trouble with you English, Captain John,' said Mustafa, placing the envelope in his attaché case, 'Your silence says so much. Only, you never say what you really mean. You seem incapable of returning property you have borrowed without holding on to a set of keys.'

'I suppose you are referring to Suez, and Palestine?' said the Englishman.

'Perhaps...Yes, that too.'

Mustafa rose to leave. Captain John stood and both men saluted and shook hands as they parted at the door. Once outside, Mustafa, accompanied by his A.D.C. and his bodyguards, returned quickly to Pera.

* * *

After Mustafa had left, Captain John took a carriage down to the Bosphorus shore at Kabataş. He stood watching the small boats and ferries weaving between the warships. He noticed how they first headed up close along the shore where the current was weak, before turning to cross, and riding the downward flow to bring them by an easy way to the opposite side.

Life, he mused, came down to a choice of swimming with the stream or against it; to the source or to the sea – the trick was in knowing the tides. But the Bosphorus current goes in both directions, the saline water from the Sea of Marmara flowing upstream three metres beneath the sweeter downstream surface current from the Black Sea. The question in the English captain's mind was, did the Turkish general march with the tide or against the flow? Time would tell.

Mustafa had no doubts. He was to sail upstream, to the headwaters. And perhaps from this origin, in the high steppe and highlands of Anatolia, his vision of the country's greater destination would become clear.

With his *laissez-passers*, Mustafa was elated. But he knew the road ahead was long and full of danger, and that it was futile to depend on the sun for help in bringing his vision to light, when the sun – in this case the Sultan's support – was occluded by the tenebrous mists of the Occupying Forces. He needed a different lamp to light the darkness of defeat and bring daylight back to his benighted land.

* * *

Mustafa's departure plans were hastened to urgency by events beyond his control. Barely had he received his permits, and was considering his next step, when startling news arrived in the capital. At first it was a rumour, but quickly confirmed by reliable sources: the Greek army had landed in Smyrna (İzmir) and taken control of the city.

At the Paris Peace Talks in early May, Britain, France and America had agreed to allow the Greeks to occupy Smyrna on Turkey's Aegean coast. On 15th May Greek troops landed. The unrest between the Christian and Moslem communities in the city which had been brooding since the armistice now flared into open conflict. The touch paper had been lit that would eventually ignite the country into full scale civil and military resistance to the occupation.

For Mustafa the die was cast. It was imperative that he depart Constantinople without delay, before the British had time to rescind his permits. He knew that from now on he was in danger of arrest – more so now that his intentions in Anatolia would be under scrutiny – and he needed to disappear from his usual haunts until his departure could be arranged. He must see Satanaya immediately, but didn't want to be seen entering the Grand Antakya. Like all the best hotels in Constantinople, the Antakya's bar now sported spies of every denomination. He sent a message for her to meet him on the Galata Bridge. Here among the crowds which were always so thick and mixed, coming up from both sides, shuffling between each other, it was easy to pass unnoticed.

In the mid-point of the bridge they leant against the railings with their backs to the passing parade, gazing into the churning maelstrom of ferries at the entrance to the Golden Horn, looking out across to Üskudar. Flanking them on either side men in thick coats and dirty turbans fished for mackerel and anchovy, which they kept alive in buckets of seawater at their feet and sold to passersby, or to the *'balık ekmek'* boats – the fish sandwich vendors at Eminönü – or if the catch was plenty, to the fish market at Kasımpaşa. From time to time a tram rattled down the centre of the bridge, and the crowd would part like a rolling wave, pushing them against the railings.

Mustafa turned to Satanaya and looked from deep inside himself. But his look went far beyond her wind-chapped cheeks and watering eyes.

'I am leaving, and I don't know when I'll be back.' He hesitated. He didn't need to say 'or if'. Much passes between the hearts of lovers in the language of unsaying. 'There is so much to be done.'

Satanaya was silent, but her face was a question. Was this the end? Had she completed that work which had drawn her from Beirut, through Konya to Constantinople? It was such a hard thought for her. He had left her once, in Sofia, and that had built something in each of them. Not a wall. But, how to describe the expansion of soul that struggle brings? Where even in suffering there is a deeper glorification of the being? She felt the pain again, certainly, in these threshold moments. And the glory? Was this real – the intuition she now felt in spite of her breaking heart – the certainty that all was truly in the hands of providence, once the choices had been made? She prayed she had made good choices.

'You know, Satanaya, it will be like the Battle of Sarıkamış. When the snow falls in the mountains, all the known frontiers become hidden, as if returning to the unknown, and sight becomes blind. Armies are defeated without even meeting their foes upon the field, for the battlefield too has been lost in the snow. But the difference is, now we shall be the snow.'

Satanaya looked at him. She had never seen him like this. Though their faces were inches apart, he seemed so distant, like a prophet walking alone into a wilderness.

'What are you saying? Do you want me to come with you? Is that it?'

'No. It will be dangerous. Better you are here, and better for me that I know you are safe – and perhaps you can be of help from the inside. But...'

He hesitated again and looked over towards the Asian shore, before turning back to her.

'Why don't we get married? Now, before I go.'

Satanaya took some time to reply. She looked down into the water, through the dripping tangled skeins of the fishing lines. A light drizzle had begun. They huddled closer to each other within their coats.

'You remember that night on Mount Vitosha? And that night when you came to the hotel? Well, you know something happened then between us that was closer than any marriage could ever be. Since then, with every breath, every move, every thought for each other, we have been penetrating each other deeper than any marriage vow, building into something more lasting than any long night of love. It's love's way, before we even know it. Love loves love. Nothing can ever break that union if it is for love alone. Not even death.'

Satanaya's words were like a long line cast into the sea of Mustafa's soul, and with each word she drew him slowly from his well of vanishing.

'I know you're right.' he said. 'But afterwards. When this is all over...' The 'this' was a vague move of Mustafa's being, a throw of the dice of his own possibility into a future he yearned to grasp into presence. But he knew it was impossible. The future had yet to be built.

'Let's see.'

'But for now? Something for now?'

'We have this, don't we? We will always have this, whatever happens.'

He beheld her face, her voice, her blue eyes now almost black in the fading light of an overcast afternoon, her scent of rose and lily of the valley. He wanted to hold her, to join her, to disappear for an eternal instant from that fearful future he had just beheld. To vanish from himself in her. Then the moment passed, and he saw her clearly. She was a woman. And he... well he was who he was. It was suddenly very simple. He knew he had touched upon a perfection, but the perfection was not hers, nor anyone's, except the moment itself. It had shown itself to him in Satanaya, and once tasted, he knew he only needed to hold on to the certainty that such a thing existed, and persisted in him, whatever the circumstances. The same perfection and completion he held as an ideal for himself, for his country, for this reality he chased within himself each day. That beautiful perfection exists, if only beyond the thinnest of veils, in everything.

He took her hand, and turned around. The rain had passed. Beyond, above the hills of old Stamboul, the last embers of the sun were peeping through molten clouds between the minarets of the Suleymaniye Mosque, cascading off the wet surface of the tumbling domes and roofs in silver light.

Mustafa already had the keys for the secret apartment in the building next door to the Hotel Grand Antakyan. He could come and go in secret, should he so wish. Parting on the bridge, in the coal-smoke smitten mist of evening as the steamers blared their fog horns, cabin lights streaming, whirling fireworks upon dark waters and so many passengers, passengers, passengers. It seemed to these two that whole universes raced away around them, while they by clinging to the railing held on to themselves, embracing the wet metal as if by that they could remain.

Curtained within the collars of their coats, they stole a kiss and bravely pushed each other away. He went to meet his staff and arrange their departure. She returned to the hotel.

Satanaya's emotions were in turmoil. Up until now she had enjoyed the easy, if intense, nature of their relationship. Perhaps it was the war – with Mustafa she was the one who had always felt safe, in spite of the appalling situation of the country. Now all she had thought and imagined in theory, about Mustafa's aims for Turkey, was about to come out into the open and be tested for real. The war that had just ended would be a simple affair in comparison. Those battles had all taken place on the outside. What Mustafa was venturing now was unpredictable. It was revolution in the heartland. And it was frightening.

But then he hadn't changed. Not one bit. He was the same man fired with an unforgiving resolution that had both awed and amused her as they rode the mountains above Sofia. The same man who had returned war weary but drenched in love and compassion from the mud and dust of Gallipoli and Palestine. No, he hadn't changed; but he had become more certain, more full of the fire of his ideal. His talk of marriage now was his own illusion. She knew there could not be three in this marriage, even if one was a country. After all, he was not the Sultan. And anyway, it would never be just three. There were times Mustafa simply needed a woman as a sedative. Whoever he took after his nights of raki with his friends was his business. There was no blame here, but Satanaya knew she would never be that kind of wife.

And she? She still had family in Palestine. And Pelin in Beirut with whom she had kept in regular if sporadic communication. Perhaps it was time now to go back to the land she had once called home. If only for a full farewell. And then move on.

FORTY-ONE

The Parting

Constantinople, May 1919

FTER AN EVENING of meetings and briefings with his comrades and staff, Mustafa came before dawn, by the secret way, to Satanaya's room. He slept a few hours before leaving again to join his staff at the docks at Galata.

SS Bandırma was a venerable old lady of 300 gross tons, built in the Clydeside shipyards some four decades earlier. She had operated under various flags, British, Greek and Turkish, as passenger and cargo vessel before being being taken on by the Ottoman Shipping Administration in 1910 as a mail carrier. She was by any estimation a humble vessel for Mustafa to embark on a journey destined to mark a profound turning point in the country's history. Bandırma looked very small along the dockside, dwarfed by the backdrop of grey warships lying offshore in the foggy waters of the Strait.

As Mustafa arrived at the quayside, the British troops who had been searching the old vessel for illegal passengers, arms and contraband, were filing ashore.

Satanaya came down to the ship around midday, bringing extra food supplies from the hotel. Seeing them stowed safely in the galley, she joined Mustafa in his cabin.

'So, is this goodbye then?' Mustafa spoke as if to himself. As if he had already taken on the mantle of a destiny as hazy as the Bosphorus beneath the light drizzle of the afternoon. It was a question that Satanaya had been turning upon all night. They both knew the answer, but the question held more of the present, of the love and longing that anchored them safely against the storms of anxiety that any thoughts for the future might bring. The question – was it good-bye – allowed affirmation, and denial, in a single moment. Tears then came to Satanaya's eyes. Was this how completion felt? This tearing away from the past? Why was it that the past could not be dropped as easily as a gown, a shoe cast off, or a hat thrown in the air? But she knew it was a part of herself that was being shed. And that hurt. Her new skin felt too raw for these winds. Mustafa took Satanaya in his arms and pressed her into himself. They kissed, not furiously, not with lust, but lingering, tenderly, lips embracing lips, gently breathing together. And in that moment whatever of reality of love existed for these two lovers held them safely in their hearts.

Such fond kiss is ne'er forgotten but remains for ever as stellar light, returning from time to time to illumine the empyrean of our being in the dusk of fading memory. Such was the fareweel with heart-wrung tears shared between Satanaya staying, and Mustafa parting.

Satanaya did not remain to watch the little ship pull away from the dock. Did not see the good ship Bandırma set forth, picking its way between the Black Sea caiques, and the little skiffs of the local fishermen, pushing out past the scuttling ferries and the gloomy foreign warships. Satanaya walked within her own cloud of silence, by the Ottoman Bank, past the Genoese Tower, up the steep cobbles of Yüksek Kaldırım. She did not stop, not even waver, as she passed the green grill and marble mausoleum known as The Place of Silence which houses the tomb of the Mevlevi poet Sheykh Ghalib, though if she had, her thoughts might have dwelled upon his great poem, 'Husn-i-Ask' – 'Beauty and Love', and upon the trials that Love undergoes in his journey to discover essential identity with the beloved Beauty.

Instead she strode on up to the top, back to Hotel Grand Antakya, up to her room, and onto the roof from where through gaps in the buildings she could make out the dividing waters of the Bosphorus as the mist finally lifted. And just as once upon a hillside in Lebanon long ago she had watched her lover Khalil sail to America, and later cried over the departing spirit of her mentor Lady Gülbahar, she stood and gazed down upon a pathetic little ship cradling the hopes of the nation, and the longings of a girl now a woman, as it steamed north towards the Black Sea.

And although this time too she cried her heart out, it was not sadness that overflowed her heart but a profound nostalgia. Not hopeless tears for herself, but simply a deep longing for the beauty that had been there with Mustafa. She knew she would miss him terribly. Damn it, she missed him already, missed the precious moments of their time as in her presence he glowed, shone, as his words pouring forth on this and that, complaining of Enver, raging over von Sanders, describing the victories and praising his men, all the time looking at her with such love, and joyful in finding such appreciation in his listener, enjoying even her arguments and mocking laughter; and she loving the fact that somehow, his vision came to light in his looking on her and loving her.

Now she feared for him knowing the dangers he would face, imagining the mountain range of opposition he would have to circumvent in order to bring his vision to birth in the minds and flesh of the people, the earth and stones of his land, with blood and steel, as much as with words of love.

And she remembered his kiss. What was it about this exchange between the lips so intimate, more so even than all their making love? Is it that the simple physical exchange between bodies is in the end of far less consequence than the mingling and exchange of loving breath, which joins our souls together? And in joining that part of ourselves which leans and longs into eternity, that longing becomes united in the permanence of spirit? One day we may discover the intimate connections, the intelligent discourse that exists between the lips and the human heart. Then will we learn to know this heart not by the head but by the heart itself?

Then after the tears, and the memories, something else. The slowly growing sense of a journey completed. And with it, a feeling of relief. Not that she was in any way glad to be rid of this man. Quite the contrary. She knew he would never leave her heart. Something else. The words that came to her were the words of an old man she had once known, something about work to be done. And even though she knew this wasn't an end, that the work might never be over, she realised that for her something in the nature of this work, something she had not even been aware of during its process, had been finished. A stage completed. And as she watched the vessel round the point where the Mosque of Sultan Abdülmecid juts out into the water at Ortaköy, and disappear from view, something else. A new opening arrived in her being. A new step was asking to be taken, and she felt a thrill. For a moment, all the weight of the years of war and her fears for Mustafa fell away. All the history vanished, like a picture painted on glass and washed off in the rain leaving it clean, in the gentle rain of evening she sensed the light of a beckoning dawn.

* * *

Meanwhile, upon the deck of the Bandırma, Mustafa followed her going, hoping for a last backward glance which did not come. But she had told him she wouldn't. And Satanaya was true to her word in such things. Full of sentiment, but not sentimental. He watched her disappear among the carters and their carts, the bent-back porters, the baleful camels and donkeys, that were busy with unloading and loading sacks and bushels back and forth between the godowns and the multitude of sailing craft crowding the quay. He knew if he was to succeed in this venture, he too could not look back. He swallowed the inevitable rising of tears for the beauty he had left, and looked away.

As the vessel cleared the moored warships and gained midstream he glanced back briefly, down towards Saray Burnu and the domes of Topkapi Palace, the Aya Sofia and Sultan Ahmet Mosque, and all the other fabulous symbols of this City of Ottoman Empire prostrated now beneath the onslaught of a new era. Even the great Mosque of Süleyman on the high hill above them all seemed occluded somehow of its magnificence by the deluge of current events and impending storms. He was sorry, and also not. A curtain was falling on a past that he believed would never rise again, and although that included much he loved, he was convinced it had to be that way. A great cutting back, so a new tree could be planted.

The insistent throb of the little 50 horsepower steam engine echoed back across the water from the near bank as they passed beyond the Dolmabahçe Palace, and the darkly fenestrated façade of the Çirağan

Palace, standing still after the fire nearly ten years earlier. A gloomy mist
clung in the trees of Yıldız Palace. Rounding the point at Ortaköy, the
captain brought the vessel closer inshore to avoid the strong currents. On
the far shore beyond Beylerbeyi and Çengelköy the peaked towers and
long white walls of the Küleli Military School glimmered briefly. They
passed close by Bebek with its summer embassies; the twin forts of Rumeli
and Anadolu Hısar where Sultan Mehmed the Conqueror had first
threaded the noose that brought the great Byzantine city to submission;
the inlet of Istiniye with its naval dockyards, and then Beykoz with its
fountains of sweet water. On and on, past the little fishing village of Sarıyer,
the lighthouse of Rumeli Feneri and into the Black Sea.

Little maritime traffic was abroad, a severe weather front was coming
in from the north and few fishermen were venturing beyond the Bosphorus. As she tossed and rolled in the rising waves, the old ship creaked and
whined incessantly. The young officers sharing Bandırma's deck with
Mustafa eyed each other ruefully, wondering whether they would actually
make it safely to port in Samsun. There had been rumours that the British
Navy might simply sink the ship once it was out of sight of land, but it was
as likely the weather might do the job for them.

Mustafa was beyond worrying. Either they would make it to Samsun
or they wouldn't; what mattered now was that he was free. Free of the
Occupying Forces; and free too of the city, that great theatre of discontent.
He had given his hand to destiny, and he felt certain she would not abandon
him.

After two days sailing in rough seas, in a heavy storm, SS Bandırma
made the quayside in Samsun, and destiny hauled Mustafa ashore.

* * *

For Satanaya, the next few weeks were a frenzy of activity. She had made
the decision, standing that afternoon above the rooftops of Pera, as the last
wisps from Bandirma's funnel faded into the fog, that her time in Constantinople had also come to an end. She made arrangements with her bank to
give Fatih Bey power of attorney for all the hotel's accounts, endowing the
capable hotel manager with fifty percent of the profits until either she or
Zeki Bey returned. On her last evening she threw a small party. It wasn't a
very gay party as all the staff were in tears, except for Madiha, who was
planning her own departure, intending to continue her European tour

now that hostilities were ended. During her sojourn in the Hotel Grand Antakya, she had developed her singing voice with a good repertoire of European melodies to accompany her toned-down yet still risqué cabaret act, and she had tentatively agreed to a season's booking at a grand hotel in Berlin later that summer.

All the staff received a generous bonus; Satanaya gave the cook a raise in the hope he would stay on, and packed her things. Now the Ottoman Bank was paying out in gold and foreign currency again, she arranged her own finances, then made her way back to her friends in Beylerbeyi to plan her next move.

Departing from Amina Khanoum was a far more emotionally tearing affair than leaving the hotel. In spite of the war and the continental division between Pera and Beylerbeyi, the two ladies had remained as close as sisters can be, keeping up a constant communication throughout the past four years. But Satanaya had made up her mind: to return to Beirut, and to Kfar Kama; to revisit her past. Her dear old horse, Tarçin, she left in the care of the gardener. Tarçin was too old now to travel; or indeed for much more than nuzzling weeds and grass beneath the olives and fruit trees the Colonel had planted on the slope above the konak in the years before the war.

By the end of June, as the peaches from Bursa were reaching their peak of honeyed sweetness, and the black Napolyon cherries as big as golfballs were bursting with delicious lip-staining juice, Satanaya boarded a steamer for Beirut. It was a hot day and the water was calm all the way through the Sea of Marmara, as it had been on the day she captained the brave paddle steamer to fight off the ravening British submarine. It was calm too as she passed through the Dardanelles in the cool of evening, a full moon spreading its silvery balm upon the now silent slopes of Gallipoli. At times like this, she thought to herself, it was easy to believe in forgiveness, to believe that pain and struggle has an end, as if agonies past held no greater permanence in the mind than a bad dream, from which eventually one would find the strength to waken. The constant arrival of a present vanquishes the past as the tides of the sea drink in the wake of passing ships, leaving the surface as though it had never been disturbed. So life swallows death, she thought. And while history leaves its imprints upon hearts bound by time, a heart that loves knows no such bounds, but is constantly in motion, making all futures possible in the present; leaving no footprints, only the scent of morning.

FORTY-TWO

Breaking the Ties that Bind

Lebanon – Palestine – Anatolia, 1919-1920

ATANAYA FIRST NOTICED the palm trees, waving their dusty fronds above the rooftops in muted welcome. And then the mulberries – their absence. Her memory was of a city spread within green acres of mulberry trees which fed both the fruit stalls and the silk industry. Where glorious verdure once reigned, mangy patches of bare ground lay like withered wreaths between the hovels of refugees and the encroaching streets. Behind the city, the once-lush orchards which terraced the mountains tumbled in disarray.

Silk and mulberries were synonymous with the Beirut she had known. Half of the population of Mt Lebanon, that quasi-independent area of coastal Ottoman Syria supervised by France since the military intervention in 1860, had been economically dependent on the silk industry. It was a marriage between French money and technical know-how, with Lebanon's supply of land and labour, and accounted for more than half the value of the country's exports before the war. Ottoman alignment with Germany prevented France from continuing its participation, and production collapsed. In the subsequent poverty, many of the orchards were reduced to firewood for the needy.

But now the French were back, and the docks, once piled high with bales of raw silk, housed encampments of French soldiery and military equipment.

Satanaya found Pelin waiting for her in the little restaurant *La Veuve du Poisson Anonyme* in the lane behind the harbour. The old patronne had passed away, but not before handing over the secrets of her bouillabaisse to a suitable candidate: another young widow with aptitude and taste, thrown up by destiny on the shores of the Levant.

Pelin rose from the table at Satanaya's approach, beaming with joy. The two friends gently embraced, and then both burst into tears. They had frequently corresponded over the past fifteen years, and now, on meeting face to face, those tangible waves of love and sisterly affection, overflowed between them once again. They sat down, gazing at each other in silence for a long while, then bursting into quiet laughter and more tears.

'You haven't changed, Pelin. You look just the same, truly. How do you do it?' Satanaya said at last. It was true the little Ethiopian mistress still had the glow of innocent youth about her, but her eyes, always a well of experience, seemed deeper, darker, even more intense than she remembered.

Pelin laughed: 'And look at you, Satanaya, you really are a woman now. And even more beautiful. How you didn't marry that Turk, I really don't know. Although the bigger mystery is how he ever let you go.'

'Hah! you didn't know him as I did. He was impossible really. Impossible not to love, certainly. But also in so many other ways. Anyway, that's done. I doubt he'll ever marry, and if he does find someone willing for such a sacrifice, I pity her. She'll always be one among many. But now, tell me what's been happening here since the Turks left? How has it been, really? And Gérard and Clotilde, what news of them? And the Beyt?'

A shadow crossed Pelin's face. She lowered her voice.

'It hasn't been easy here.' She took a long breath before continuing. 'For a while, when we still had our autonomy, not a lot changed. But that finished when Djemal Pasha came with the Turkish army in 1915. He was a Committee man, like Talaat, brutal with the local nationalists. Conscription began, and we had to hide our sympathy for anything French.

There were hangings in the main square here. They didn't call him *al-Saffah* – the Shedder of Blood – for nothing. Gérard and Clotilde fled early on to Cairo. I believe they got work with French garrisons there. I haven't heard anything from them since.'

'And the Beyt?'

'A Turkish commander took it over. That's when I left; he brought his own staff. He was supposed to pay us rent, as you know, but he never did. Just left a pile of requisition slips for me to try and cash in, but I suppose they're worthless now. All the horses and animals went to the army. He drank up most of the wine, what I couldn't squirrel away first – I did manage to hide a few dozen cases of the good stuff, waiting for you. The crops were harvested, but nothing replanted. All the men had either fled or been conscripted. Within a year of Djemal Pasha's coming, the country was starving. Then there was a fire in the Beyt – I think it was set on purpose, when the Turks were retreating last year.'

'What's left?'

'The stone walls are still standing. Refugees have taken over the ruins, but there's precious little for them. They try and grow a few vegetables and keep chickens. I can't throw them out, they've nowhere else to go?'

'I noticed the mulberry trees have gone.'

'And the rest. So many trees cut down by the army for firewood or fuel for the trains. Well, you've seen the beggars. It was never like that before, and it was even worse before the American ladies came.'

'Yes, you wrote you were working in an orphanage.'

'You know I was orphaned myself once. And people helped me. So, when the American Committee for Relief in the Near East[*] needed an interpreter, I applied and they gave me a job. Actually, I don't get paid, but I love the work. We have taken over a disused silk factory a few miles south of the city. We have over five hundred orphaned girls, many who came out of Anatolia escaping the massacres. You know about the massacres?'

Satanaya nodded as she recalled her conversations with the American ambassador's wife, Josephine Morgenthau, regarding the Armenians, 'Yes, of course, in Harput...'

---

[*] Founded in 1915 in the wake of the Armenian massacres in Anatolia, later named Near East Relief, it has organised humanitarian aid and development projects in the Middle East and Africa for over a century.

'So, I am teaching the children sewing, dressmaking, even cooking. And also hygiene. And where possible, some manners too. They come to us like frightened little animals. They've been living rough in bands in the streets, scavenging what they can. They've seen things no child should see. They are damaged, not just in their bodies. Their minds have been hurt. And rape of course. But they won't speak of that. That is war. It leaves unspeakable traces. Then we cover it all up and we forget, don't we? Everyone forgets. I suppose it's the easiest way. I just think of our dear Lady Gülbahar, who knew that love was the best healer. Love and work. Keeping busy, but with a smile. And trying to keep their little tummies full.'

By now Satanaya was crying again. It was not that she hadn't seen terrible things herself, in Gallipoli, and the subsequent effects, the maimed soldiers, and then the refugees from Russia and Macedonia begging on the streets of Pera. What touched her now was the simple uncomplicated compassion with which Pelin was dealing with the situation. Pelin, the little Jewish orphan who had walked from Ethiopia in search of the promised land, herself left for dead at a desert way-station, now in natural submission to necessity, caring selflessly where others might throw up their hands in despair. Little Pelin had grown big in her heart.

The soup came, and in spite of her sombre mood, Satanaya was delighted to find that the taste was as she remembered. Here the passage of time had stolen nothing. The old widow's spirit had continued to flourish in the new incumbent. From discarded fishheads and bones, and a few bruised vegetables, the shop had survived the poverty of war by its anonymity. The sign in the shape of St Peter's fish had weathered well the storm.

* * *

For the next couple of months Satanaya made herself useful in the orphanage kitchen. There were so many mouths to feed, and no shortage of little hands to help wash vegetables and little fingers to pick out stones from the lentils. Some of the older girls showed an aptitude for cooking, soon managing simple recipes on their own. As the heat of the summer waned, though, Satanaya's thoughts turned to the south; to her intended, and strangely dreaded, return to her family in Kfar Kama. Then one of the American ladies who directed the Near East Relief organisation offered her a lift by car into Palestine, and she knew it was time to move on.

The now swift passage upon the French-built road and sudden arrival in Haifa after a few hours motoring was almost too much. She put up for the night in the German hotel, from where next morning she hired a driver and car to take her east. She hadn't planned it that way. In her imagination she had always returned on horseback, perhaps in a caravan, leisurely along the coast as she had done with her father more than two decades earlier, or riding down the Plain of Esdraelon with the two young Circassian gallants. Nazareth passed in a flash, along with Mount Tabor; and in the late afternoon she arrived in Kfar Kama. The motor vehicle could not negotiate the narrow streets, and she had to enlist a donkey and driver had to be enlisted to carry her luggage to her family's front door.

As she trod the cobbles between the stone-walled cottages of her childhood, she found herself entering a dream of her past. So familiar yet somehow unreal. But it was only a moment. There was her father standing at the front door, as if he had been expecting her. His appearance was much older, and he now leant on a stick. His beard had turned white and he seemed to have shrunk a little. But then he smiled, dropped his stick, and almost ran to greet her. Never it seemed had a father been more happy to welcome home a long lost daughter.

They had been in communication since the armistice. Satanaya had written also from Beirut and had received the news of her mother Gülay's passing in the last month of the war. Something in Gülay had given up. She had received precious little news from Satanaya over the years, and even less of her daughter's putative husband Timur. It had been hard times for the little Circassian settlement, with all the men off to war, and so few returning. Perhaps it was the unconfirmed report that the man she understood was her son-in-law, the handsome lad who had galloped off with her daughter through the streets of Kfar Kama so long ago, had been reported missing presumed killed in one of the final skirmishes of the war that she decided she had finally had enough. That and the fact that her daughter was still without children. Perhaps it was for the best.

Now, though, it was time for father and daughter to catch up, and to take stock.

FORTY-THREE

Father Daughter Talk

Kfar Kama, Palestine, 1920-21

 ANSUR *DEDE* HAD REACHED the stage in life where his title, *dede*, meaning ancestor or grandfather, was not merely an honorific applied in respect of his years, but a recognition of the wisdom he embodied within the context of *khabze*, the spiritual lore of the Circassian, or Adige, people. He was known also as *efendi* – master; sometimes simply as 'the *Baba*', meaning father, but also in the sense of spiritual father or patriarch. Such was the breadth of respect shown him that at times some of the Jewish settlers even addressed him as Rabbi. His home was an open house, and he regularly entertained groups of students for conversation and instruction in *khabze*. In the time since Satanaya's mother died, he had begun cultivating her little kitchen garden, keeping the herbs going, and that summer he had raised a good crop of peppers and tomatoes.

It was a few weeks after Satanaya's return to Kfar Kama, and she and her father had just finished a simple supper of bean stew and greens, flat bread, water – nothing extravagant, in spite of Satanaya's comfortable financial position. Diced carrot, onion and celery were sautéed in olive oil with a little spicy pepper and tomato paste, a couple of bay leaves and some parsley, then seasoned and cooked in stock; she added soaked and pre-cooked white beans, finally baking the pot slowly to marry the flavours. In the economic strictures of the post-war period, it would have been unseemly to serve anything too rich, and in any case, Mansur Dede had become accustomed to a spare diet since Gülay's death. Nevertheless, Satanaya was able to insinuate a few tasty comestibles into the otherwise humble fare. She had brought fat olives from the Marmara shore, and rich olive oil from Ayvalık. On the wooded slopes of Mount Tabor she collected mushrooms and dried them, and planted aubergines and okra in the kitchen garden.

Coffee was one luxury that Mansur did not deny himself, and as they sipped their little cups, the conversation turned to current affairs.

'In Constantinople,' said Satanaya, 'sometimes at the konak, I met people. People you would recognise, Papa. Wise people. They spoke about the meanings of things, about war, about suffering, about time.'

'Yes, we know them.' her father replied. 'They are also of us, of the *khabze*. They may not be Cherkez. They may or may not be Muslims. Perhaps they don't call themselves anything. They wear their knowledge beneath a cloak of anonymity, but they are there all the same. They are the anchors in this stormy world. Or maybe they are the captains. No one knows them but themselves. The fact that some have shown themselves to you, and you have recognised them, is a great blessing. It shows you are included within their cloak.'

'But how do they know what they know?' said Satanaya. 'I mean, you wouldn't look at them in the street, most of them, yet they speak with an authority that cannot be denied.'

'Not denied by you, certainly, Satanaya. But just look at the way the mass of people behave. Look at the populations, how they blindly follow their leaders who mostly rule by their own desires, even though they only hold their positions by chance or force. These people are distracted by the appearance of nature and identify only with their bodily functions and needs. These other people are living at a different level of being, their actions happen from the source of existence, not simply from the effects.'

Mansur Dede's words carried her back to her time with Yeşil Efendi, the strange dervish whom she had met in Konya years before.

'This world, as we see it, is simply a place of trial.' Her father continued in the same vein. 'A place where the human possibility is exposed. We are all evolving. Not simply in the way Mr Darwin has shown us; our forms certainly have developed from the depths of the sea, each new appearance taking its form from the previous. But that is just our animal nature, our vehicle for this world. But the being – our existence, our spirit – that also evolves from an ocean, one we do not see, yet we have never left it. Our hearts, our spiritual minds, that place of origin from which our conscious-ness emerges – that comes out of an ocean of being, and we are in evolution in the being of existence itself. And when there is a movement there, in the very depths of human existence, the place the religions call God, its devolvement can be witnessed here in this world. We call that evidence 'change'. Sometimes we consider it progress, sometimes catastrophe. It depends on the point of view. But it is simply a movement in the heart of our being. If we resist or deny this movement by divorcing ourselves from that interior existence, if we oppose that flow in our heart, then difficulties arise. We become disunited from our source. Then the integrity of our world, the harmony in our lives, becomes broken.'

'So we should try and follow the flow?' asked Satanaya.

'Yes. As long as we discriminate between the flow that simply follows an imagined route for the human journey, which might simply lead us into a desert of non-existence, and the flow that is from the origin, the original intention for humanity, to know itself according to that origin.

'At certain times a great movement of the spirit occurs, and a huge change is necessary in the human consciousness. It is the inability to accept the changes that bring the difficulties, such as war and social conflict; our inability and unwillingness to accept and process what this interior move-ment signals, when what is required is expansion of our vision. It is due to an ignorance of the inherent mercy, the goodwill that accompanies this process, which if we were to submit ourselves to, would transform us, and bring us to a knowledge of our true heritage. The movement in the heart of existence, that origin in being from which we are all formed, and to which we ultimately return, is a movement of love. Our task here is to know and express this reality of the human being, each in his or her uniqueness, knowing that all stems from a single, absolute, undivided identity.'

Mansur Dede paused, and in the silence Satanaya felt an expansion in her thought. Time, space, all changed. And even though she remained seated by the fireplace in the room, she felt herself inhabiting a different sphere of existence altogether; and her father's words were like a light, and their meaning clear in a way that thinking alone never reached.

'But this change?' she said, 'I only see its effects. Everything is broken. Everything has been torn apart. Empires are falling. Look at Russia, our Ottomans, the Austrians. What does it mean? Where is the movement of love in this, when we are left in chaos?'

'This is the flood of time. It continues to flow, like tides, back and forth. What we have seen is just a beginning. We, this human emergence, we have been brought to our knees because we need to dig deep for the treasure inside. But to dig is to admit that we don't know; and when we discover an existence so much bigger than we ever imagined, we resist, we are afraid to give up this pathetic attachment to our limits and enter a bigger place. It could be so easy, to accept our hearts as the place of true knowing, and admit that our heads, our relative minds are merely the sorting office of the information. We have become so important as postmasters and telegraph operators, receiving and sending messages with our brains. Like that Talaat Pasha, he was a very efficient telegraph operator. So much so that he became a monster who destroyed whoever didn't fit his timetable. But in a way we have created these monsters, as a mirror to bring us back to ourselves, through fear. But that is so wasteful, this way of fear. And sad. Better to hold to the rudder of love.'

As Mansur spoke these words, Satanaya thought of Mustafa, whose task now seemed so important. To change the minds of a nation. To go beyond the forms. To break down the conditions of the old systems of belief and relinquish outmoded traditions. She mentioned this to her father.

'Yes, it's the way now for the future. But it will still take time. First the nations. Then the world. We cannot experience union, whether in the world or in the spirit, without first becoming individuated, otherwise our union is only with our own idea, another reality not THE reality; our little world, not THE world.'

'But for how long? And for what? Where is this world going?' Satanaya was almost pleading. In spite of all she had uncovered of herself in her years of journeying – with the wise lady of Beirut, and the dervishes along the way, with her lovers, and her experiences in this changing world, her Mustafa – now, sitting at her father's feet, she was as a little child.

'How long? My dear, as long as it takes. Please God it doesn't take so long there are none of us left to enjoy it. But probably not in our lifetimes. Maybe, who knows, our children's children's children…? If the human being doesn't come to its senses in this era, and begin to recognise its potential, in this time, then more wars, and other disasters will undoubtedly follow.

'You see, we are of one existence. One human from a source we call divine, eternal – however you like to see it. And our planet, this earth – it is as a second skin in which we live. We are connected just as much in the exterior world, by the elements of our composition, by the breath we breathe, by the soil we tread, by the sun that grows the food we eat, and by the love we make and by which we reproduce. Our birth is our asking for fulfilment of our possibility. But it doesn't stop with birth. Our development depends on our continued asking. We are not like the minerals and the plants, or even the animals, which exist in a natural state of request. We can choose to ask, to wake up to our end, if we want to return in completion.

'The wheel has been set in motion since before time, before space, from the single heart of existence. Don't ever imagine this is unconscious or accidental. Everything necessary for this completion is there. Even the religions which guided us in the past. For humanity to evolve as a cohesive and cognitive whole, a new dispensation will be necessary. The signs are there. The whole world can now communicate with itself, at least on the surface. And yet all we seem to want to do is crawl back into the little caves of empires and nationalities, religions and old civilisation. And when we find cracks, we try to plaster over them. But the force of this tide, which is no other than the movement of existence itself, cannot be resisted forever. Knowledge, real knowledge, knowledge of the heart – this is contagious. It spreads willy-nilly because all the hearts are connected. Not by arteries, like roads that can be blocked, but because they are of the same substance. What happens in one of us, resounds in all. The pathways of the heart are holographic.'

Mansur stopped speaking and took the last sip of coffee. He poked the fire and tossed on another piece of wood. Winter was approaching, and although the weather was still pleasant, the days were shortening and the nights cool.

'It's late. Too late to talk of such things. Tell me more about the beauties of the Bosphorus, and your picnics by the shore. Tell me more of your journeys in Anatolia, so I shall sleep dreaming of the Sweet Waters of Asia and the terebinth trees of green Meram.'

In spite of her telling, Satanaya lay awake for ages, thinking on her father's words, spoken so calmly, yet with the quiet certainty she had heard him talk all her life. She remembered, too, things that Mustafa had said with such urgency and passion, enlivened by copious draughts of raki. Each seemed to inhabit and inform from a platform of certainty that so far evaded her own sense of her intellectual self. Not that she couldn't taste the truth of their words. But they were their words. She knew she had to find the words in her own language, and so far the only language she felt certainty in speaking was that of food. There she felt at home: truth in a plate of beans and rice, cooked to tender perfection that was her service to the potential of the beans. Truth in the simple earth of lentil soup. Reality in the sweet scent of thyme wafting off the chicken in the pot. These were her words. Words that could be eaten and digested, words that transformed in their nourishment of body and soul. For now, anyway, that would be her language.

The next morning at breakfast her father added a postscript to their conversation.

'You see,' he said, 'the devil is in the details – the divisions, the separations – because there is always that which loves to take things apart. And keep them apart. But everything has a limit in time. In the long run, worlds reconfigure. You'll see. But we are in for a long run of chaos, and disintegration before it is reformed. Changed. Reconfigured. New. Not what we could imagine from this point of breaking up. So we need something to hold on to in this flood. And there is only one thing to hold on to, when all else fails: the being, the existence, the one, God, love, beauty, whatever you want to call it, however it comes, by taste, by intellect, by a feeling or a movement in the heart, it is the human reality. You, Satanaya, be certain in that, it is your boat, your ark, in this flood of time. Only that will bring you to your destination.'

Not long after this, Mansur Dede mentioned the subject that she herself had been pondering, and wondering how to broach it with him.

'So, I expect you'll want to be setting off soon.'

Satanaya looked at her father. How could she leave him here alone? Who would look after him? Wasn't it a daughter's duty to look after her aged parents, just as they had looked after and protected her in her infant helplessness? And she loved him so much. At the same time the situation vexed her, for she knew she had to move on. She had sensed a door to be opened, and it wasn't here.

'Oh, don't worry,' he said, noticing her pained look. 'Your cousins are eager to look after me. Before you arrived, they were always feeding me, bringing me little dishes of food. They've been checking up on me ever since your mother left us. It's quite endearing, and I have no objection to being cared for. It makes life easier. They want me to move in with them, but I shan't. I would get no peace at all then. At least now the students all leave when it gets dark, and I have time to myself, time to contemplate the night. I think you know how it is. You've travelled alone so much. Time alone with oneself can be hard, but it can also be a pleasure, a luxury even.'

'And Mother? Don't you miss her?' asked Satanaya.

'You know,' began Mansur Dede, ' when your mother died, it came as a much greater shock than I could ever have imagined. I had become so accustomed to her always being here – in the home – for more than forty years… People think that when old couples have lived so long together that they take each other for granted – well, maybe it is like that for some – but with your mother it was different. She was a mirror to me. She reflected myself back to me in all my moods, and it was as if I saw the world described through her. Then she was no longer there, and it was suddenly as if that mirror had vanished, the mirror that showed me how I appeared in the world, and how the world appeared to me. And for a while I could no longer see myself, feel myself. Who could I talk to? Who could share my thoughts? So I retreated into my inner world and relied on that mirror we all have inside – the god we pray to in our hearts, the place we have recourse to when our outer world collapses, that part of ourselves which is so close even though we may not see it, even when we doubt it.

'And I spent a long time looking into that mirror, looking to see, to find some vision; gradually my heart became still, and showed me myself, whole again; then when I looked at the world, the mirror that she had been was there again, wherever I looked. In all the rooms of the house, in all the details, wherever my eye fell, I found myself; it was there in the earth, the plants, the sky, and in everyone I met – now the whole world has become a mirror and nothing is missing any longer.'

'And mother?' said Satanaya.

'She is here too, her presence, everywhere, whenever and wherever I want. So, as I said, nothing missing. Nothing missed.'

When eventually the time came for Satanaya to depart, they wept on each other's shoulders. True, they were sad. They knew that these would likely be the last moments they would share together on this earth. But also, each knew that distance did not exist in this heart they shared, that companionship followed wherever their destinations drew them, and that help was ever available from the same deep and magnificent source in all their journeying. And on each breath was a prayer from their being to the same origin in the unknown.

FORTY-FOUR

The Jew's Tale

Haifa – Beirut, 1921-1922

ATANAYA RETURNED to Haifa, to the German hotel on Mount Carmel.

Sitting in the bar one evening after supper, she was taking a coffee and reading one of the European papers when she came across a short article referring to events taking place in Turkey. According to the report, a Turkish general and former A.D.C. to the Sultan Vahidettin, one General Mustafa, had been sent to the interior of the country to disarm the defeated army. Once there he had, in contravention of his orders, set up a national movement to resist the occupation of the country by the Allies and to repel the Greek invasion. What struck her was the reference to Mustafa as 'the Jewish leader of the Angora government'.

Satanaya put the paper down and sat back. She gazed at the ceiling where a large fan turned slowly above her. Her action did not go unnoticed. A small, good-looking gentleman about her own age, dressed in the European style, got up from the bar and came over to her. Doffing his Homburg hat, he started to speak.

'Good evening Madam. I couldn't help seeing you sitting here on your own. You are evidently not a local – I thought perhaps you might enjoy some company, for the conversation. We get so few visitors these days, apart from the military.' He spoke in French, grammatically correct but slowly, with an accent.

'Please.' Satanaya gestured to the chair opposite her. 'I'm returning to Beirut after a family visit. And you?'

The man was a journalist for one of the Jewish papers, but had studied in Europe. He gave his name as Mr Ben-Avi.

'I'm here canvassing for support to start a new Hebrew-language newspaper. This hotel is a good place to meet well-heeled Jews visiting the homeland. But please forgive me, as a journalist I am so inquisitive. What was it in that paper that gave you such pause for thought just now?'

'It's the news from Turkey.'

'Ah yes, the dashing General Mustafa. He's definitely gone and thrown the cat among the Allied pigeons.'

'Oh, it wasn't just that. The paper here says he is Jewish.'

'That's interesting.' said Ben-Avi, 'Let me tell you a story. I met him once – twice actually – in the Kamenitz Hotel, in Jerusalem. Do you know it?'

'Yes, I've heard it's the place to stay. Very modern, elegant, good European cooking and French wines. Or so I'm told.'

'Yes, again, it's a good place to meet people. Well, one night, it was winter, just before the war – the Balkan War that is. At the end of 1911, as I recall. I was sitting there at the bar, just as I do here. Chatting with the owner. He pointed out to me a Turkish officer, a Captain, who was sitting at a table drinking arak. "One of the Committee men, an important chap in the new organisation. You should try and get to know him." And so I did. We got very drunk together on a couple of occasions. He could really knock it back, I tell you – and still remain coherent, if a little emotional.

'Anyway, we got to talking about religion, social change, that sort of thing. I am a Jew and interested in bringing back Hebrew as a living language, but using the Latin alphabet, as a way to revivify our people, our culture. And he tells me he would like to do the same with Turkish, to have it written in the Latin script, and use the Turkish language, the words which the people actually use in their day to day speech, not the language of the bureaucrats and religious which is full of fancy Arabic and Persian.'

'Yes, that's right. I heard him say much the same.' said Satanaya.

'You knew him?'

'Yes, in passing.'

Satanaya felt suddenly hollow inside and almost unable to breathe, as she remembered Sofia and their ride back from Mount Vitosha, when Mustafa had explained the peculiarities of the Ottoman language. She remembered Constantinople, and she could smell his cologne, his cigarettes and the raki on his breath. She knew that to talk of him now would somehow be a betrayal, a debasement of the intimacy they had shared. How could she speak of Mustafa to a complete stranger? And how would he understand their relationship anyway?

'It was before the war. He visited Beirut. The Beyt'ur-Rahim, Lady Gülbahar, perhaps you knew... I spent time there.'

'My goodness, yes. Of course. Never visited, mind. She had died while I was off studying in Europe. Some of my friends however, Arab writers, poets... there was a chap called Khalil, he went to America... Anyway, so you knew Lady Gülbahar and the Beyt... Gosh, that is fascinating.'

The mention of Khalil came as if a mention of the dead. A strange but familiar shade lingered briefly in her mind. This conversation was beginning to feel quite unreal.

'But go on. You were saying, about this Captain Mustafa?'

'Yes, he was quite passionate about this language thing, and other ideas he envisaged for Turkey. It was when the Italians had invaded Tunis and Libya, and he was on his way to join Enver and organise resistance among the local tribes.

'Another night – we were quite drunk again – he starts telling me that he is descended from a character called Sabbatai Zevi, a Sephardic Jew of Smyrna, and a Kabbalist, hundreds of years ago. This Sabbatai character believed he was the Messiah, and began a movement, but the Sultan put him in prison and threatened to execute him; so he put on a turban and converted to Islam, as did hundreds of his followers. But the story goes that

this conversion was a sham and secretly they carried on being Jews, after
their own somewhat heretical fashion. Captain Mustafa told me his father
taught him to say our Jewish profession of faith, the Shema: "Hear O Israel,
the Lord our God, the Lord is One.'"

'Yes, he was like that, Mustafa.' said Satanaya, 'He would often speak to
people in a way that would make them feel at home, to gain their trust. He
would say anything really in order to get his own point across. As I recall,
he didn't have any real problem with the essentials of religions. It was the
way they were practiced that he found objectionable, when people used
their beliefs to divide humanity. I imagine he found that prayer of yours no
different than the Muslim *shahada*. He was interested in unity. But he
wasn't a Jew, if that's what you're thinking.'

'Maybe, but I tell you he spoke that prayer from the heart.' said Ben-Avi.

Satanaya was trying to keep her comments vague, but this reference to
the Jewish prayer interested her.

'Of course he did. It was given him by his father, wasn't it? And his
father died soon after. Of course he would cherish such a memory. But his
father removed his son from the religious school so he could have a
modern education.'

'But he told me he admired this Sabbatai Zevi,' said Ben-Avi, 'and that
we Jews would do well to follow his path.'

'Yes, perhaps. Though that may have been the arak speaking. You
know, later, he studied the books of Sufis. And he was a lover. Perhaps he
had read the Arab poet who said '*My heart is capable of all forms, it is the
temple of idols, the Christian monastery, the Books of the Koran, and the
Bible, but I follow the religion of love, wherever it leads me.*'

'Now I would drink to that!' said Mr Ben-Avi. 'Wherever it leads! Will
you join me in a glass of champagne. It's still early, and I'd love to hear more
of your story, about Lady Gülbahar and her extraordinary villa in Beirut.'

Satanaya was not unaware of an ulterior motive in the journalist's
seemingly-innocent invitation. His eyes had taken on that well-known
gaze, the mild look that belied the inherent lusty desire. She understood
the male gaze, in which she was merely an object of his pleasure, and not
an equal partner in a relationship. And yet, she also found in him a certain
charm and open-heartedness that likely would have made him a good
lover. But just as she was no longer naïve, neither was she in search of
adventure. Mustafa, even the memory, would satisfy her needs for a long

while yet.

'No, I think not, thank you. I've an early departure. But it's been very interesting talking with you. So I shall say goodnight. And best wishes for your newspaper. What will it be called?'

'I'm thinking to call it "The Daily Mail" like the English paper, but in Hebrew of course.'

'Oh. Yes, well, why not? Will it deliver the truth, or simply facts. Or perhaps rumours and gossip? There are so many ways to tell a story, aren't there? I shall look out to see which way you take. Good night Mr Ben-Avi.'

'Good night, Madam…?'

Satanaya smiled as she rose, teasing him with a female gaze of her own, and left the bar.

✳ ✳ ✳

In Beirut, the winter sun flowed low over the sea in the late afternoon. Satanaya loved this light. Warm upon the face, golden in the water and upon the walls of the dusty city, gently touching the edges of her mind like the sweet wine they were sipping in a cafe by the water's edge.

Pelin was describing to Satanaya something she had seen as a child while crossing the Red Sea from Africa in the pilgrims' ship that took her to Yanbu on the Arabian coast.

'It was a beautiful morning. I was sitting out on deck just after sunrise. The sea was quite calm, and barely disturbed by our boat making its way slowly in the light breeze. The water was a shining blue mirror. Suddenly the surface was broken by a fish, which leapt up and flew ahead of us like a bird. It went for yards and yards, gliding with its fins, before dropping back with a little splash. Then another and another, until there were dozens, jumping and flying along – they might have been shiny pink angels or jinn gliding on their feathery fins. At that moment I knew I must find a way to fly too. To fly above the difficulties of this world. I knew it, I just knew there had to be a way. That's why I didn't talk much when I first came to Lady Gülbahar's. I still thought there was something I had to escape. But then she started teaching me things, and I discovered there was so much inside me waiting to come out. Now when I fly it's just for the pleasure of letting go. '

As Satanaya listened to Pelin's story, her own aspirations rose, leapt, like the great rays of the pink flying fish of the Red Sea which leap from the water in joyful expectation of taking flight. She knew that scientists would claim that the fish flew simply to escape a predator, or maybe to show their desire for union with their opposite sex. Perhaps, but was that so different from the innate desire of creation to animation, to fly beyond the predations of the earthbound state, that urgent cry of the spirit to grow, evolve and join again its origin? Even rocks will rise up from the depths of the earth when a field is ploughed.

But how to achieve this union? She knew that in essence there was nowhere it couldn't be found. But also each of us has tracks that demand to be followed. Like a treasure map, we hold inside ourselves. A map which reveals itself only in time. And it is up to us not to miss the moments of its epiphany.

Satanaya knew that the tracks in Syria and Palestine were now closed, had run their course, and the same for Anatolia. Anyhow, there was war there, and she'd had enough of war. Europe? It tempted her, but something in her soul told her this wasn't it's time either. America? Now here she felt warmer waters moving in her heart. But not North America. Something, perhaps it was the memory of Khalil, was not safe, felt hard, in this proposal. And in any case, she had heard that the United States had closed its borders to immigrants at present, fearful of importing the diseases rampant following the war.

And so it was that she found herself in the office of the agents of Lloyd Brasileiro Shipping Lines booking a modest stateroom for Rio de Janeiro.

But what was she going to do in South America? Pelin had asked.

'Horses.' Satanaya replied. 'I hear they love horses there. I shall breed Arab horses. I shall find the best bloodstock from here, and bring Arab horses to breed in America. There are so many going cheap since the war ended. The Australians are not taking theirs home with them. I shall purchase the best I can afford, and start a stud farm.'

It was a grand idea, and allowed Satanaya to occupy herself completely in the time before she sailed, rather than dwell on what she was leaving behind. She knew what was called for was an absolutely new start in life; a complete break with the past in order to allow her as-yet-unknown future, waiting patiently for her, to arise.

FORTY-FIVE

From Samsun To Smyrna

Anatolia, May 1919 – September 1922

USTAFA STOOD ON the rainy dockside of Samsun harbour and breathed the damp air laden with wood smoke. It was a relief to arrive safely after an uncomfortable three days sailing in S.S. Bandırma with a broken compass along the Black Sea coast. Yet the path before him remained as obscure as the hillsides surrounding the small town, now draped in misty cloud.

He took another deep breath and stepped forward, his entourage following. Into the unknown. It had always been thus; why should it be any different now? Nevertheless, Mustafa's goal was bright in his mind: nothing less than a completely free and independent Turkey, democratic and a republic.

The Greek invasion had cast the die which would determine this future. An effective army would have to be organised, from the broken remnants of years of war. Aside from the Occupation Forces in Constantinople, there was danger from the new Caucasian states of Armenia and Georgia now hoping to reclaim much of Eastern Anatolia and the Black Sea coast; in addition France and Italy continued to maintain troops in the south-east.

But Mustafa knew that victory depended on uniting the disparate forces, both military and civilian, at his disposal. An army is only as strong as the people it purports to protect, and he knew he must successfully carry his vision to the Turkish people. With a parliament in Constantinople still at the beck of a Sultan now hostage to the Allied naval guns trained on the city, Mustafa had to provide a viable alternative.

Over the coming months, with trusted comrades from his army years he welded a grass-roots political organisation from the villages and towns of Anatolia. Committees formed and congresses met with delegates from all over the country. He initiated alliances with the newly founded states of Azerbaijan and Dagestan, and negotiated arms deals with Bolshevik Russia.

By October 1919 the Nationalist movement had gathered sufficient political force in the country that the 'official' government in Constantinople was compelled to enter talks, effectively giving recognition to Mustafa's campaign. When the Sultan called elections for a new parliament, Nationalist candidates took part, and Mustafa won the seat for Ankara.

Meanwhile, at the Paris Peace Conference* the Allies were cooking up a new course for the Middle East. It wasn't a dish of herbs. But then, neither was the Turkish ox fat. The talks became effectively a division of the spoils.

For Mustafa, the pressing necessity was to protect the geographical integrity of the emergent state. Without an army sufficient for a major campaign, a guerrilla insurgency was undertaken. Many former soldiers and officers joined bands of resistance fighters under the leadership of local '*efes*' and '*zeybeks*' – rebel leaders and irregular soldiers – with the

---

* The Paris Peace Conference held in 1919 set the terms of peace. It involved 32 countries and was controlled principally by Britain, France, Italy and United States. Although various treaties, such as the Treaty of Versailles were prepared that year, the process was not fully concluded until July 1923 with the signing of the Treaty of Lausanne.

aim of interrupting the enemy's communications: attacking command posts and blowing up bridges, telegraph lines, railways etc. The French and British had little appetite for fighting after their great losses in the war, and the Italians preferred to come to terms without resorting to armed conflict. The Greek army, on the other hand, newly landed on the Aegean coast, was relatively fresh, and filled with zeal for realising the "Megáli Idéa"; the dream of the greater Hellas.

The new parliament in Constantinople contained a predominance of Mustafa's Nationalist deputies. Though short-lived, it brought about one significant change – in January 1920 a 'National Pact' was agreed, demanding independence and sovereignty for Turkey within the boundaries declared in the October 1918 Armistice. This was a step too far for the Allied leaders. The final Ottoman Parliament was closed down in March, and British troops occupied the streets of the capital once more, rounding up and imprisoning on Malta many prominent parliamentary members.

A new political will became established in Ankara, and consolidated among the population of Anatolia. Throughout 1920, under Mustafa's charismatic and forceful leadership, huge efforts were made to build the army's strength. Initial field engagements with the Greeks were not successful, however, and the newly formed National Army was in danger of defeat.

✳ ✳ ✳

The serious fightback to recover Turkish soil began in early 1921. A regime change in Greece had precipitated a new offensive. In January, and again in March that year, the National Army successfully defended against Greek attacks in what became known as the First and Second Battles of İnönü, greatly enhancing Mustafa's standing with both government and the population. Reverberations were felt at the Paris Peace Talks.

The Greeks renewed their offensive, in July 1921 advancing to within fifty miles of Ankara at the Sakarya River. But the Greeks' supply lines were over extended and ammunition was low. The Turks dug in and waited.

A month later the Greeks attacked again, capturing the strategic heights of Mangal Mountain. This loss only hardened Mustafa's resolve. Though the Greek army was superior in men and materiel, the Turks were fighting for the soil of their birth.

The battle of Sakarya River was unrelenting. It lasted for twenty-one days and at times Mustafa believed he would die with his soldiers, for there was no possibility of surrender. But, as he had declared, the successful outcome would be achieved, not by human effort and skill alone, but 'Tevfik Allah'tan' – 'Success through God's help.'

The Greeks had reached the end of their logistic tether. Turkish cavalry had interrupted their supply lines, food and ammunition stocks were low, and the Greek commander, General Papoulas, ordered a rest day. The Turkish army too stood down, exhausted after more than ten days of continuous combat.

Mustafa recognised that the Greeks were weakening. He wasted no time in mounting his counterattack, and soon they had retaken Mangal Mountain and pushed the invaders back across the Sakarya River. It was the turning of the tide in Turkey's War of Independence, at a cost of nearly 6,000 killed and 18,000 wounded, on both sides.

Throughout September 1921 the Turks pursued the retreating Greeks west, back to Eskişehir and Afyon, where defensive positions were re-established on both sides in early October. Here they would remain until late summer in the following year.

* * *

Around Mustafa's headquarters, a simple little camp nestled in the hills west of the Sakarya River, there were still a few trees and shrubs. The area had been relatively untouched by the daytime bombardments, and at nightfall when the firing stopped and the heat passed from the day, the birds returned and chirruped a song of consolation – small angels alighting with bigger hopes in anxious hearts. When times allowed, Mustafa would leave his bunker to wander among the troops, receiving salutes, checking passwords, and sometimes, if invited and the mood was right, he would stop to listen to the men at their campfires.

At one such encampment a dervish soldier was relating the story of a Sufi sheykh, Sünbül Efendi – 'Mr Hyacinth' – who lived in Constantinople at the time of Süleyman the Magnificent.

'Towards the end of his life,' said the soldier, 'Sünbül Efendi was conversing with his students, asking each what changes they would make if they were to become sheykh. One by one they gave their bright ideas for

---

* The Young Atatürk, George W Gawrych, (I.B.Tauris, 2015). P.153

the future, how they would change this or that, each according to their personal taste or vision.

"'And what about you, hiding back there?" Sünbül Efendi asked of a man, an insignificant looking fellow, who never spoke, but always attended the dervish meetings, sitting quietly behind a pillar at the back of the *tekke*.

"'Who? Me?"

"'Yes. What would you change?"

'The voice from behind the pillar sounded surprised.

"'Why, I would not change anything." he said. 'Everything is in its centre*.'"

'In time this lowly dervish, at Sünbül Efendi's bidding, took over as Sheykh in charge of the *tekke*, and ever afterwards was known as Merkez Efendi – Mr Centre.'

The conversation among the men then turned to the question: to change or not to change.

'How could he say this "not change anything"?' said one soldier. "Surely we need to change if we are to progress? Didn't the Prophet, upon whom be peace, say we must seek knowledge even to China? Why would he say this if things were not meant to change?"

"'And didn't our Sultans change things for the better for hundreds of years?" offered another.

"'And made a mess of it often enough." complained a third.

Noticing their commander Mustafa listening in the shadows, the soldiers fell silent and shuffled to their feet, saluting.

'At ease, *sayın efendiler* – gentlemen, may I join you?' said Mustafa.

'Welcome, *paşamız*, please.'

'Tea?'

'Thank you. But carry on with your conversation.'

'Tell us what do you think, pasha? Is change a good thing? Or is everything as it should be? Is everything already in its centre?' said the dervish soldier.

Mustafa sat and stirred the sugar in his glass of hot tea and pondered the question. The light from the small fire glinted in his eyes as he gazed above the heads of the assembly of noble warriors. The fire flickered and hissed, the birds had fallen silent hours ago.

---

*   Turkish: 'Her şey merkezinde'.

'Perhaps,' began the General, 'most of the time, when everything appears to change, really things stay the same. One moment we are here in this great room beneath the stars, speaking. The next we have travelled far, to our homes perhaps, and are silent. The scene has changed. The action has changed. But have I? If I were fearful here in the heart of battle, but relaxed when in the arms of my woman, have I changed? Am I no longer fearful? The same is true of this country. We have always been ruled by our circumstances. Sometimes easy, sometimes difficult, but always we are either fearful or happy. But do you think Mr Hyacinth, or Mr Centre were between fear of pain and death, and hope of love and happiness? I like to imagine they had reached a place beyond these opposites, these contrary positions. That they had found the still centre in themselves, to see what the winds of necessity brought into view. If they were really sheykhs, then they were in control of their personal feelings. Free of the effect of circumstances, they could move and change with whatever circumstances brought, without leaving their centre.'

'Take our battle here, for instance. We plan a big push against the enemy. How do we know it is the right thing to do? How do we know the right time to attack? How do we plan all this? Is it one man's idea, one point of view? That would be very limiting, don't you think. No, it is necessary to look at the situation from every conceivable point of view, calculate on the information at hand, if necessary send out spies to gather further informa-tion, discover our enemies' strengths and weaknesses and if possible their intentions. Isn't this your 'seeking knowledge even unto China'? Before we act, we need to be informed. Then it is a matter of bending to the dictates of climate. We sow in the spring if we want an autumn harvest. But we sow early or late depending on the inclination of the year, the time of the moon etc. Or perhaps we leave fallow. We retreat from a valley here, we bypass a difficult hilltop if necessary, perhaps we break new ground, unexpectedly, and wait until the time of attack is more auspicious for our long term aims.'

'I believe that change itself dictates its own terms. It gives us signs to follow, and to follow the signs is our only chance of remaining free of blame. If we try to change things from our own opinion, our personal preference of how things should be, we are on a narrow road to nowhere. This battle has a conclusion. There will be victory, and defeat. What will be our portion is our choice. But our commitment must be total. Either way change will occur. Our best protection is to find our centre, and hold fast to that.'

* * *

The Western Front of Turkey's War of Independence now stretched for around 400 miles from Izmit, south-east of Istanbul, south in an arc around Eskişehir, Kütahya, down to Afyon and west to below Smyrna, encircling most of Aegean Turkey. A large area covered in rugged hills, it gives natural advantage to the defending army. Summers are hot and dry, with temperatures nudging 40°C at times, while in winter the land becomes covered in snow, and temperatures are known to fall below minus 25°C.

The Greek forces were displaced over two main areas – before Eskişehir and Kütahya, and around Afyon further south.

Mustafa believed his army's best hope was to concentrate an attack with the bulk of his forces in a single place – Afyon – to break the Greek line with artillery bombardment followed by a frontal infantry attack. At the same time his cavalry were to overrun the Greeks' right flank and penetrate deep behind the front line, thus opening up the possibility of an encirclement. Troops were gradually brought up to the line under cover of darkness, avoiding detection by the Greek spotter planes. Meanwhile Mustafa established himself in a forward observation post upon the hill of Kocatepe, at an altitude of 6,000 feet, just south west of Afyon. The Greek Commander in Chief, General Hatzianestis, gave his orders from hundreds of miles away on a warship in Smyrna harbour.

The Turkish offensive began before dawn on 26th August 1922. The initial artillery bombardment caused heavy casualties among the Greek front lines, the Turkish cavalry forcing a passage through and cutting off communication and supply lines to the west.

Within days the Greek army was in disarray along the whole front and fleeing towards the coast, the Turks following in hot pursuit. Chaos, due in large part to the breakdown in communications within the Greek High Command and collapse of morale among the ranks, took over. There was no serious rear-guard action, and within two weeks, on 9 September, the Turkish army entered Smyrna*.

---

* In the north, the situation was similar. The Greek army abandoned Eskişehir. Bursa fell shortly afterwards and by 18th September the remnants of the occupying army fled by ship from ports on the Aegean and the Marmara Sea.

FORTY-SIX

The Great Fire of Smyrna

Smyrna, September 1922

APTAIN FOGARTY peered through the morning mist which blew across the white limestone cliffs of the Karaburun Peninsula, the western promontory which guards the entrance to the Gulf of Smyrna. He had steamed north by night through the straits which separate the island of Chios from the mainland of Anatolia. Chios is known to the Turks as Sakız Adası after the abundance of mastic trees which produce '*sakız*', the aromatic gum used in scenting rice dishes and lokum, and chewed to sweeten the breath. But as the ship rounded the point and turned east into the gulf, it was not the sweet smell of *sakız* which was carried on the breeze, but bitter herbs and gall, the pungent fumes of holocaust. From Manisa, some 40 miles inland from their destination, the winds of perdition reached the bridge, for the

Greeks as they fled to the coast had put to the torch this ancient city of Ottoman princes.

In peacetime, Smyrna was a regular call on Captain Fogarty's route, which took in most of the major ports in the Eastern Mediterranean. The service had been interrupted during the War, and only recently reinstated to carry migrants to Marseilles prior to on-passage to the Americas. Due to the on-going conflict in Anatolia, Smyrna had been taken off the route. But a request by a supporter of the American charity Near East Relief, negotiated by Pelin and Satanaya, had persuaded Captain Fogarty to divert his vessel to help in the impending emergency evacuation of Smyrna. By the time the ship reached the area, the Turkish army had taken the city.

The retreating Greek army, in fleeing the land it had occupied but briefly, had instituted a policy of slash and burn, that is: slash the Muslim civilians and burn their fields and houses. The response of the pursuing Turkish army on arrival in Smyrna, had unsurprisingly been one of victorious celebration mixed with anger and revenge.

Rounding Karaburun Point the ship headed south-east down into the gulf. It was a perfect morning, the sea glowing limpid blue in the soft Mediterranean light. They steamed past Uzun Adası, the long island which the Greeks called Makronisi, and the smattering of smaller islands to star-board, before turning to port, east between Pelican Point, and beneath the Sanjak Fort opposite, the guns of which guarded the entrance to Smyrna Harbour. It was immediately obvious to Fogarty that it would be impossi-ble to berth here. The harbour was packed with vessels anchored a couple of hundred yards out from the long quay that fronts the city. These included a score of battleships flying the White Ensign of the Royal Navy, and Tricolores – variously starred according to the rank of Admiral on board – of a French fleet, some U.S. Navy and Italian warships and various mer-chant vessels. Cutters, caiques and rowing boats, crowded to the gunnels with refugees, plied the water to and fro between ship and shore.

As Fogarty brought his vessel to a stop, a navy cutter came along side and through a loud hailer a young officer informed him that the harbour was off limits and no landing was allowed. Fogarty was an old hand and not put off. He brought the ship about and pulled back out of the harbour and into the lee of the small islands south of Uzun Island.

'Don't worry, ' he said to Satanaya, who had been his companion on the bridge since they entered the gulf, 'we can put you ashore at Voulah landing near the quarantine island, and lay up there in Gülbahçe Bay. It's a *barınak*, a sheltered haven to sit out storms. The harbour master and I are old drinking buddies, he'll see us right. We can unload a cart and horses at the jetty there, and you can be in Smyrna in a couple of hours – it's less than twenty miles away and the road is good.'

Satanaya left Voulah early that evening, in the company of a middle-aged American couple, Christians from Wisconsin, Sam and Debbie, who worked with the Near East Relief organisation. The road was filled with refugees, men leading thin bullocks pulling carts loaded with worldly goods, children and women wrapped in cloaks and blankets, going this way and that but mostly in flight from Smyrna. But no soldiers, and no one bothered them as they made their way through the sad groups in the dusty afternoon haze. They had the sea to their left, and to their right the famous orchards of Smyrna figs, fields of tobacco and olive groves. Beyond rose low hills and chalky slopes of the ancient vineyards of Voulah.

They reached Smyrna after dark, entering through the southern part of the city mainly occupied by the Turks and Jews. They avoided the main thoroughfares near the waterfront where the human traffic was thickest and wound their way through the narrow back streets near the railway line where poorer people lived, and to the European quarter known as Paradise. It was an area within the Greek and Armenian quarters, towards the apex of that deep triangle of the city formed by the convergence of the railway line from the south and the two-mile-long harbour waterfront, the Quay, which the Greeks call Prokymaea. Here in a school compound they found the Americans who were helping organise the orphan evacuations.

The city was in turmoil. Although the Greek army had already escaped by sea, the arrival of the Turkish forces hot on their heels brought an atmosphere of doom to the remaining Europeans, Ottoman Greeks and Armenians. For hundreds of years this Christian population had lived in relative peace within the Ottoman state, and Smyrna had flourished as a centre of modern culture in what was perhaps the most advanced of the Europeanised cities of the Eastern Mediterranean. The Greek Army's invasion three years earlier had not been welcomed unequivocally by many of the established Ottoman Greek families, who had for the most part enjoyed good relations with their Turkish suzerains. Now they could only watch in dread as the jubilant Turkish army flooded into the city.

For the next couple of days Satanaya and her companions busied themselves with collecting orphaned children and finding them suitable temporary guardians among the refugees. Each morning and evening they accompanied their wretched cargo back to Voulah, where Captain Fogarty accommodated them aboard awaiting final departure.

News came one day that General Mustafa had arrived in Smyrna. Satanaya's curiosity eventually won out, and she decided to make a brief sortie out of the American compound. Why, she didn't really know. She knew there was no place for her in this new world of his. It was a wish simply for confirmation: to look, to see, to help her own understanding of what was happening, much as had been her intention on that earlier trip to Gallipoli. As she approached the guardhouse at the entrance of Command HQ she was surprised by a cavalry officer coming to greet her.

'Satanaya *khanoum*, what on earth are you doing here?'

It was Colonel Anwar, her lover of the moonlit passes of the Taurus Mountains, her boon companion of the sky blue waters of the Göksu River. They had not seen each other since the time Satanaya had collected the 'corpse' of Zeki Bey from the Bekirağa prison during the War.

'Anwar!' Satanaya sighed, lost for words, but feeling relief and joy in finding her dear old friend amidst the nightmare of this plundered city. Anwar's delight at seeing her again showed in his huge brimming smile.

They embraced warmly and went into the guardhouse. Chairs were brought, and coffee, and each excitedly brought their stories up to date. During the past three years Colonel Anwar, with his Palace connections, had been one of the 'go-betweens' relaying vital information between Constantinople and Mustafa's deputies in Anatolia. He had arrived in Smyrna via a British warship to facilitate the negotiations that would inevitably follow the Greek defeat.

'And General Mustafa? How is he?' Satanaya asked.

Colonel Anwar gave Satanaya an understanding look. 'He's deep in talks, day and night, with his own officers. Even I haven't yet managed to speak to him directly. He moves about constantly, and never spends the night in the same place twice for fear of assassination. A meeting would be difficult just now.'

'No, no, I just want to know how he is. Is he well?'

'They say he's lost weight, with the stress of the campaign. You know, he's been ill, though he tries to hide it. And the struggle isn't over yet. There are still the British to see off. He won't stop until Constantinople is free, of that you can be sure. But why are you here? This is the last place I would have expected to see you. Though I should know better. Still on your adventures, I suppose.'

Satanaya explained her situation, how they hoped to gather the abandoned Greek children and evacuate them to safety.

'Our ship is along the coast, we couldn't get into the harbour.'

'Yes, the Allies don't want to interfere, so they're doing the next worst thing which is nothing at all. I think they're fearful of upsetting Mustafa, now his star is in the ascendant. If you ask me, they're afraid of losing influence, especially with the Mosul oilfields at stake. They won't risk another war.'

A commotion from beyond the building brought them both to their feet.

'Wait here.' he told Satanaya, as he stepped out into the entrance yard.

A bevy of officers descended from a wide staircase in the big building opposite and spilled out into a line of waiting automobiles. Small but prominent among the dozen or so uniformed men in navy caps and army kalpaks was a figure in an army greatcoat that seemed too big for its wearer. Compact, contained, concentrated, and yet with a look deep in his eyes that went beyond exhaustion. It was Mustafa. As quickly as the group appeared, the motorcade swept out of the enclosure, horns blaring, as it headed away up the street in the direction of the castle behind the city. As they passed by, Mustafa turned his head and looked towards the gatehouse where Satanaya stood in the doorway, taking her in as he might take in the sight of a beautiful woman in the street, a vicarious capturing by the mind's eye. She never knew whether the recognition in his eyes was of her, or something in him, a desire that she would never fill.

She called to Anwar: 'I'm sorry, I can't stay. I must get back to the orphans, before it gets dark. If you get a chance, send Mustafa my love and good wishes.'

'Satanaya, please, don't go back out there. It's too dangerous!' he pleaded with her.

She shook her head: 'There are children waiting for me.'

She turned away and Anwar watched her go with a heavy heart.

Satanaya headed back towards the European quarter. Evening was approaching and the narrow streets were hard to navigate in the gloom. The atmosphere had changed since earlier in the day. Where before the

refugees who filled the streets with their possessions and children were a
sad, muted crowd, now they seemed motivated by a sense of panic border-
ing on hysteria; angry and confused cries came from the Armenian quarter,
distant explosions sounded from afar, and with this came the smell of
smoke. Turkish soldiers were roaming around in groups, but with little
coordination or order to their movements. Many were drunk, on victory
or alcohol she couldn't tell, as they pushed among the crowds, singling out
men of military age for internment. Dressed in European clothes, Satanaya
had imagined that she would have been safe in Smyrna, and so far she had.
But now she realised that many of the Greek and Armenian residents, in
contrast to the peasant refugees from the hinterland, were similarly attired,
and so no less subject to assaults from the soldiers.

'Hey, *fahişe, gâvur*!, infidel bitch, come here and make a soldier happy!'
The lewd call came from a group heading towards her. She attempted to
walk past them, but they were blocking the street. She turned back the way
she had come, thinking perhaps she could find Anwar.

A hand grabbed her shoulder and spun her round. A soldier, a sergeant, pulled her towards him, his filthy unshaven face with its garlic
breath and unwashed stink pressed close as he tried to kiss her. She shook
her head wildly as she tried to push him away.

She was taller than her assailant, and as he stretched his face up, she
closed her eyes and bit hard on the end of his nose, that tender antenna
designed to warn of danger through great sensitivity, especially to pain.
Satanaya felt a distinctive crunch, as of biting through gristle on a chicken
bone, and she spat.

She shouted out in Arabic, '*Bism'allah, audhu billah* – In the name of
God, I take refuge in God!' then looking the soldier in the eyes she
screamed, 'Would you assault a Muslim woman, who could be your sister
or your mother?'

In extreme pain the soldier released his grip. He turned his bloody
face round towards his friends. Seeing their boss thus scotched, they burst
out laughing. He turned back to Satanaya, who now had her pistol out and
was pointing it at the soldier. For a split second, a moment which seemed
to expand beyond time, the two faced each other. Holding the gun now
with both hands she fired a shot into the air above his head. The soldiers
stepped back, unsure of how to deal with this unexpected opposition.
Satanaya backed off slowly, getting a little distance and some bystanders

between her and the soldiers. She then turned on her heels and ran.

But it was a case of out of the frying pan into the fire. The smoke she had seen earlier was now manifesting everywhere and she soon lost her sense of direction. She entered a street to her left, only to be confronted by a wave of people fleeing towards her screaming, clutching parcels, pushing carts, dragging children and animals while beyond through the smoke she could see leaping flames as old wooden buildings in the Armenian quarter caught fire. She turned again, running before the crowd, and at the intersection where moments before she had faced off the soldiers, a further stream of humanity came pouring down the road in full panic. The smoke was becoming intense, and the sounds of old wood crackling and the crash of breaking glass as buildings buckled in the flames and began to collapse, filled her ears. Her eyes were stinging and she was in danger of being trampled as the crowd hurtled towards her. She knew she had to keep ahead of them, to keep running. She sensed the direction she must go and lifting up her skirts she bolted down the cobbles, jumping over the scattered belongings jettisoned by those fleeing ahead.

When she tripped over a loose stone and found her feet no longer giving purchase as she flew forward, everything went into slow motion. She flailed with her legs, but was unable to prevent herself falling. And just as she would have crashed to the ground, something took hold of her from above and lifted her up. She remembered wondering, in that split second which seemed to last an eternity, whether an angel had taken her soul. But then by some intrinsic sense she recognised the rough hand that wrenched her up and planted her across the saddle, and now held her in its tight embrace. It all seemed so familiar, the dust of the street, the sound of hooves, the smell of leather and the strong arm holding her safe upon the shoulder of the horse. The rider drove his mount through the stampeding mass, jumping over discarded baggage, not stopping until they had escaped the burning streets and reached the safety of the Army HQ.

Both Satanaya and Colonel Timur were too breathless, and stunned by the preceding actions, that when they dismounted it was some time before either could speak. Satanaya just stood there shaking her head in shocked but happy disbelief.

'It was the pistol shot.' said Timur.

'But how did you know'

'Anwar Bey told me'

'But why?'

'You're still crazy, Satanaya. No one would have gone in there once this fire had started.'

'But don't you see, I had to get the children.'

'Yes, I saw the Americans. They got out just in time with the cart, loaded like the ark. I realised then you must be in there somewhere.'

They were both still too wound up to fully appreciate what had happened. Tea was brought and they sat in the guardhouse drinking in silence. Satanaya gradually put her thoughts in order.

'But Timur! You're alive! Oh thank God! I had no idea. We hadn't heard from you so long, we feared for you. And Murat...?'

Colonel Timur looked up at her, and down again. 'It was in the retreat from Eskişehir. He'd ridden back to pick up one of our wounded... then a sniper... he managed to get back to our lines but...'

The irony of this, given their recent escape, hung in the air like a kind of karmic judgement, the providential taking and giving of life. Outside the sky was lit up now, almost like day, as not a mile away a city burned with the noise of a furnace. They were silent again.

'I'm so sorry. And you, how are you?' She looked at Timur.

'Me?' He seemed surprised at the question. He hadn't thought of himself for so long. 'Oh, I'm fine, really. You know, in war. So many dead. You learn to deal with it. You bury your feelings with the dead. Hopefully, if there is a day of resurrection, those feelings will return.'

Then he looked again at Satanaya, and something recognisable of himself seemed to emerge.

'But you, you're not here for Mustafa, are you?' Timur asked her. They had met briefly once in Constantinople during the war and she had confided her affair to him.

'Well, not really. Just passing. My ship is moored at Voulah. I'm moving to South America. Horses, you know... a stud farm, maybe...'

'Ah, a good thing, horses...' Timur paused. 'You know about Mustafa? And Latife?'

'No? What "Latife"?' Satanaya frowned.

'I don't really know, but apparently there's this young Turkish lady, educated, a lawyer, speaks French, from a wealthy family. Coming to Izmir specially to meet him. One of these modern types. Knows her own mind. And speaks it. An independent woman, just like you. Even rides like a man, none of this side-saddle stuff.'

'It'll never last.' Satanaya snorted.

'Don't tell me Satanaya is jealous?' Timur dipped his head and smiled as he looked at her from under his brow.

'Not at all. No. Not of her, at any rate. But she'll discover. No one can compete with destiny's child, especially when its mother is a country.'

Since seeing Mustafa earlier that day, Satanaya knew that the destiny which had always ruled in him, had now overtaken her personal Mustafa; and that she no longer had a part in it. Her work, whatever it had been, if only as a mirror to his own thoughts and passions, was finished.

Her mourning was for what had been. It was really more nostalgia than grief, for she knew that even as the bad times never last forever, so too the good is constantly in process – demolition and reconfiguration, and the good too must be let go. How else could there be growth and move-ment, which is the soul of life itself, if she remained with the past?

Satanaya was well aware one cannot freeze love in time or place. Without the passion – without even the simple warmth of affection – the fire that is love inevitably dies. Still, she felt for the human person in Mustafa, the warm soul hidden now somewhere deep behind that steely-eyed visage, that thin hard face of the military commander portrayed in newspaper photographs, and again in that face this morning, distant in almost transcendental detachment.

A lieutenant appeared at the door, with an update on the situation and requiring instructions from Colonel Timur. A couch was arranged for Satanaya in a corner of the guardhouse where she could lie down and rest, if not sleep, through the hellish storm.

'Try and sleep, we'll talk more tomorrow.' said Timur, heading for the door.

✳ ✳ ✳

Outside, under cover of the night apocalypse descended, a furnace reflected down through clouds of smoke, giving the city an otherworldly glow. A cacophony of cries and crackling fires lit up the city, and exploding timbers filled the air with ash and sparks. Attempts by firefighters to stem the spread south into the Jewish and Turkish quarters would have been in vain had not the wind turned and pushed the flames back. Hemmed in between the sea and the railway, the conflagration had taken on the diabolical nature of a cornered beast, roaring and screaming, devouring and destroying itself and everything within its infernal maw.

Morning saw the fires still raging, but the flames appeared dimmed in the daylight. A thick smoke cloud hovered above Smyrna and beyond, obliterating the sun. The Quay had become the last refuge for many of the inhabitants, desperate to escape, and although the stone buildings along the waterfront provided a little protection from the heat it was poor solace to the crowds of refugees, caught literally between the devil and the deep blue sea. Feeble attempts at evacuation resulted in many capsizings and drownings in the roiling water.

Timur re-appeared a little after dawn with a pot of coffee. He looked haggard, his face smeared with soot and his uniform blackened from the fallout of ash and smut.

'Look, Satanaya, there's no chance of getting back to the American school. If it still exists. You best return to your ship. I've arranged a horse and an escort for you, and I will come to Voulah later. I'd like to talk to you before you go, but here's not the place.'

FORTY-SEVEN

The Proposal

Aegean Sea, September 1922

VERYTHING HAS AN END, unless it is an aim. An aim that is a non-existent point in the imagination which directs the arrow of our intent. A point which when it seems we reach, it disappears, and another distant goal is shown. For our wanderers on the silken road of the spirit, those nomads voyaging within the ark of love, the aim is always to seek the higher things, even when they appear in lowliness. And the aim of love, the essential elevation to which the contraries have no reach, is endless.

But war and peace are two parts irreconcilable, the breathing in and breathing out, and the pause between. Each demands the continuation of the appearance of things, one by death, one by life, joined by the moment, by the pause.

It was a week since the fire began and smoke still blackened the western horizon eighteen miles distant where the city continued to smoulder. Captain Fogarty's ship was getting up steam; they would embark within the hour. Satanaya looked at the documents that Timur spread out in her cabin. She was puzzled. One was a marriage certificate, signed by her father, Mansur Dede, and Timur's father, Kılıçzade, the hero blacksmith of Plevna. Here the names of the two betrothed parties, Timur and Satanaya, were clearly inscribed in Arabic letters. The other paper was a *laissez-faire*, signed by the Governor of Jerusalem, giving permission for the married couple to travel within the Ottoman Empire.

'But... I don't understand?'

'It was just in case. The only time I used the marriage certificate was when I was registered in the army, so I could get a married man's pay. It also makes it easier to get a discharge. That's what I want to talk to you about.'

'What do you mean?'

'Well, I've been thinking. Since Murat died, and especially now the fighting is probably finished... and seeing you again... Mustafa will win independence for Turkey, there's no doubt now about that, it's only a matter of time. But I can't go back. Not to Palestine. I'm not sure I even want to stay in Turkey any more.'

'So what were you thinking?'

'You said you are going to America. Is there anyone? You know, someone?'

'No. Not at all. Just... well, I too feel like you... there are too many memories here of what no longer is.'

'That's it. I want a new life. This one seems to be over. And I'm not sure there's a place for me in what's coming under General Mustafa.'

'So?'

'So, as I said, I've been thinking – why can't we be married? At the very least on paper, and as partners, so to speak, while we figure things out.'

'You mean...'

'I mean, what if I was to come with you to America. Right now I will have to go on with Mustafa to Constantinople. It may take a little time, but I should be able to leave within six months.'

Satanaya didn't know what to think.

'This is very sudden.' she said, 'Don't you want to stay and help build this new *vatan*? Isn't that what you've been fighting for?'

'Yes, but now I ask myself: what is my homeland? Where we used to live will no longer be part of any new Turkish republic. The British have promised Palestine to the Jews of Europe as their homeland: but will the Soviets invite us back to our home in the mountains of the Caucasus? A home we only know from songs and stories, a home our parents were driven from by starvation and massacre, a home where neither of us have ever lived? Do we have to go to war again for this, like the Armenians or the Georgians?

'None of us can stop the era, but I've had enough of these old fights. I want a new life too, Satanaya, just as you do. There's nothing left here but memories. The good ones will stay with me, the bad ones I'll leave behind.'

'But what would you do? You're a soldier.'

'I was once a blacksmith. Not a very good blacksmith, I admit. But I do know horses. And I can handle men. Would it be out of the question for me to come and help you set up this stud farm in America, as a manager or something? Now that would be something...'

Satanaya saw something grow in Timur's eyes, a light that she had not seen since their days in Palestine. Only this time it was not a hidden, immature glint, but a confident glow, a look of certainty, and she found it pleasantly reassuring.

'I hear the land stretches for thousands of miles.' he added. 'Surely between us we could afford a little piece...'

Satanaya was amused by this proposal. And yet the idea didn't seem so far fetched. They had journeyed together in the past, after all. And there were obvious practical advantages.

'Yes, perhaps it would be good to have a partner. A friend.'

Satanaya's mind was racing. It was a curious thing to discover after all this time that she had been married all along. And an adulteress to boot! This new situation was going to take a little getting used to. Yet in her heart she felt no resistance.

'Look, I have a boat to catch. And you have a war to finish. Let's give ourselves time to consider the best arrangement.'

'So it's not a 'no' then?'

Satanaya laughed.

'Of course not, we are married after all. We just have to work out exactly what a 'yes' entails. That may take a little time.'

She parted from Timur as they had always done, one turning back to the land and one to the sea. Would their relationship always be defined by an incompatibility of elements? Or, she wondered, could what appeared as incompatible on one level be complimentary on another?

* * *

In the late afternoon, when the refugees had all been stowed safely on the stern decks and in spare cabins, each huddled in their private caves of sadness: as the chug chug of the engine beat its soothing rhythm over the calm of the sea, and the vessel penetrated the flat expanse of water under a lowering sky, Satanaya emerged from her cabin and went up to the foredeck. She sought respite from the clinging smell of smoke and the anxieties of the day which buzzed in her head as a noisy fog.

Gradually the fresh breeze and the open sea worked to bring her ease and she rested in her centre again. And her heart, that strange organ of true perception, now expanded to wherever she placed her attention. Her body welcomed the wind's caress, her ears greedily drank in the splash of the waves upon the bow, and her mind's eye surrendered to the infinite depths of the sky. All her senses rejoiced in a freedom where her identity was released of limits, except the limits of her heart, which she knew were none at all.

And something more. From the natural love of an untied heart came now a sense of affection from knowing that all perception was of no other. And that this love too was unconditional. In the end it came down to this: what was love? She had known so many movements of the heart, movements that translated themselves to thoughts, to feelings, to bodily impulses and desires.

She remembered* the warm embrace of the earth as she lay on the hillsides of Kfar Kama as a child, when the spring sun warmed her legs and arms, the back of her neck, and the earth held her close like a mother, with the same heartbeat, the same breath, the same body.

She remembered too the quickening delight of her first kiss with Yusuf, the young goatherd at Seydnaya, and again it was a memory of

---

* The events, characters and relationships related here refer to Satanaya's earlier life, set forth in *Satanaya and the Houses of Mercy*.

annihilation, the disappearance of time and space in the joy of closeness to this beautiful boy, the desire to know this strange opposite.

And Khalil – such complete physical, mental and emotional abandonment there had left in its wake a soul on the edge of destruction, so penetrated by the force of his making himself known in her that her own being felt shredded, her identity blown away.

Then Lady Gülbahar, the real mother of tough love: when completely stripped of all her conceit and self-indulgence, came as restoring balm the pure kindness of Lady Gülbahar's gaze. And Pelin, dear, gentle, all-forgiving companion and confidante, as strong and reliable as tempered steel.

And Captain Anwar. Charming, romantic, Anwar, simply for their mutual pleasure, in a journey out of time. A physical love, certainly, but no less complete in that, for it was a joyous love, without complications. No regrets.

She thought again of Mustafa – an altogether different love. Something that continually expanded beyond their simple relationship. The deep affection he showed for humanity itself – even while orchestrating a battle which might see thousands slain in sacrifice for an ideal. And then the holy detachment of their lovemaking – lovemaking which came as a remedy for the conscience of the great man, drawing down the light of his vision, for just a moment, bringing him back to himself as a creature: hungry, needy, warm, with human blood flowing in his veins, so vulnerable; and then vanishing again as a wind that falls, leaving her each time as comrades in arms part before battle, never looking back

And now Timur. Three times he had come to her rescue. Three times he had saved her life. It had to mean something. Even in their so brief adventures they had already grown old together, grown accustomed, wholly accepting each other, never depending but wholly dependable.

'Timur? Well, why not?' she thought. 'What's to lose?' She continued to muse. No illusions, that's for sure. But love? Passion? Now there's a thing. The flame. The fire. Didn't passion take so many forms, ever more and more subtle? In the end it came down to the object of love. Love needs an object, just as any movement needs a destination.

Satanaya looked out upon the sea. The sun extinguishing itself in the distant line of the horizon. Fire into light. It came as fire and ended as light. But there can be no end to light, as there can be no end to existence. The pale glow intensified in the dusk. Not brightening, but garnering a differ-

ent, deeper luminescence, drawing her in as the sea's depth draws the imaginative vision, pulling her into an unseen as palpable as the sea itself, no more an empty void than infinity is a limit. Only from the side of birth, the cloak of ignorance and longing, is this unknown a darkness. Its reality is pure light.

But how could she cultivate an affection for this state? How was it possible to love such purity in the absence of things, for this absolute, the 'what it is' which tied all things in a whole?

'Shall I call you beauty,' she wondered out loud, 'for you are what makes the things beautiful? Those things where you breathe your strength and scents of sweetness, that find reception in my heart?'

She knew it wasn't the things themselves, they were simply signs pointing beyond. But perhaps the sign itself shared in a portion its destination, something, a glimpse, a flash of beauty revealed to her open heart. Like a shadow revealing the presence of its origin.

But sheer, unconditioned beauty, for that to appear? She knew it was impossible, in this changing, time-corrupting world. For beauty, the real beauty, must be incorruptible. She had no name for this 'what it is' other than beauty. Her only description came in absolutes, and she knew that absolutes deny description. No matter, 'it' remained 'what it is', however inadequate her thoughts were. And yet 'it' did appear to her. If not in what her eyes saw, but in the heart's mirror that beheld the vision of the beautiful. For as long as beauty looked upon her.

It bestowed a kind of paradise. Not the paradise that the good books told her lay in wait beyond the grave, beyond the Day of Judgement, with thrones and gods to sit on the right hand of, by rivers of gold with black-eyed houris and beautiful young men, banquets and fabulous birds – but something right here and now. Not as a reward for good works, but purely for love. Something that could come and show itself at any moment, in a glance, the light on the meadow, the sound in the breeze and the cool spray it carried from the sea, anything in which the 'it' chose to reveal itself, to say to her 'here I am, always, and if you remember me, I shall remember you'. It came as a covenant, both as promise of what was to come and confirmation of what already was for her, a taste of paradise on earth. Beauty was now her true companion. Perhaps it had always been so, there behind the things, like the actor in the mask, the beauty that made Yusuf so lovely, made him lovely for her in her heart, and made her want and desire, and cry at the loss. The same which made her ache for Khalil, and it wasn't Khalil that was ever attained, and therefore never lost, but this same mysterious beauty that tricked her awhile, enlivening him so she could taste a little and yearn for more – so that even when Anwar came, she could be free to let her body enjoy, her soul to yearn and her heart to stay safe, for only beauty itself ever penetrated that sacred space, the *temenos* of her being. With Mustafa, they had journeyed to the mountain and for a time they had climbed together. Now he was in sight of his promised land, he had no need of her.

But what of Timur? Was such a thing possible? As she let herself consider his proposal she felt a huge sense of relief. As if an enormous weight had been lifted. But what kind of love was this? There was affection, and trust between them, and she had complete confidence in his goodness. With him she was certain she could be herself. What did they have in common? Well, horses for a start. It had to be worth a try.

In the morning, as the ship with its cargo of salvation approached Mytilene, Sappho's island which the Greeks call Lesbos, Satanaya finally understood something. She had sat up all night, trying to figure out how to pray, how to address her soul, but unable to see the way. And now, as the dawn broke behind over distant Anatolia, and the blue calm of the Aegean Sea surrounding her reflected the sun as a luminescent mirror, she knew that the fire that had burned so long in her was gone, leaving in its place a delicious, beautiful light. At last she knew how she should pray. For all these years since burning the aubergines in the convent kitchen of Seydnaya, she had been building the landscape for her prayer. It was the landscape of tears and joys and surrender, a landscape of her own heart, within which a vast and overarching sky encompassed the totality of her aspirations, where clouds of generous rain hovered, awaiting the supplication of her thirst. And within the purview of her longing, mountains rose whose heights of possibility demanded prostration while inspiring dignity. Lush meadows of contemplation, green and rich unfolding; lakes of purest water spread before her as a forgiving balm to her beseeching eyes, and earth beneath cradled her in its embrace. Tall trees stood by to protect and companion her, streams flowed with ease to guide and urge her on with gurgling song. And along the hidden path revealed with each trusting step, an invisible hand led her, a hand of confidence that said 'don't worry, keep on going', extended by a providence that reached out from deep inside her and now showed itself, the source that she knew sustained her from beyond her birth.

She knew that this source, this 'It', was her, and also not her; that when she left her self she was no 'other', nor had she ever been 'other'. She knew that this It was always there, with her, in her, as her, and would never leave her, nor she It.

This covenant with herself, she would forget awhile, become distracted, fall, fail, pray again, and return to find herself once more in the landscape of her soul. And It would be there, ever present, hidden in the steps of time, like the scent of the beloved, bringing her to safety, to herself, always.

For the first time she truly felt the inheritance of her namesake, Satanaya, the heroine of the Circassians. And she knew that the sacred land, the homeland that beckoned her to kiss its sweet earth, was no longer confined within the mountains and valleys of the Caucasus, nor the hills of Lebanon, nor the shores of Gallilee, but was present wherever she chose to walk in the pastures of her own heart.

FORTY-EIGHT

Jacob's Afterword

Southern Turkey, 1980s

PUT DOWN my dog-eared copy of *Ataturk: The Rebirth of a Nation* by Lord Kinross, and looked over to Prince Mehmet.

'So what happened afterwards?' I asked him. 'Did Satanaya and Mustafa ever see each other again? And Timur? Did he follow her to South America?'

It was the mid-1980s, and we were sitting under a grape trellis in a quiet pension by the sea in Southern Turkey. Beyond the terrace, framed by vine leaves drooping in the late summer heat, the sea heaved like a resting belly quietly breathing under a languid sky. The scene reflected my mood. I had once again come to an impasse in my researches over Satanaya, and Prince Mehmet had long become bored with my persistent questioning. He looked up from his own paperback which rested open on his lap, yawned and lit a cigarette.

'My dear Jacob, I wasn't even ten years old at the time. How could I know what was going on? Mustafa had gone to the country – it's all there in the history books, how he went against the Sultan and set up a provisional government in Ankara; at least that's how they put it – as if all along he had planned to go his own way. But it wasn't like that at the beginning. They were in regular contact by telegraph. It was all the doing of those sycophants in the Palace, and the ministers in Constantinople. Who knows whose pockets they were in? I am told they held back his telegrams, kept the Sultan out of the picture, concealing things so he only heard from third parties what was happening in Anatolia, without Mustafa being able to explain. In the end Mustafa thought the Sultan had abandoned him. So, naturally he had to go it alone.'

'They say he rebelled.' I said, 'That he wanted to finish with the Sultan altogether, and abolish the Caliphate.'

'No, it wasn't like that. Not to start with, anyway. But the Sultan also thought Mustafa had abandoned him, and the trust between them broke down. It was very sad, but perhaps that was in the destiny of things. You never know. The Sultan had his hands tied, not just by his courtiers and the Constantinople government, but by the fact of the British occupation. So someone had to deal with the Greeks.'

'And Satanaya? What happened to her?' I asked him. 'Did she and Timur get together?'

'Ah well, there I'm not sure. Well, I believe they settled down in South America and started breeding horses.'

'And children?' I persisted. 'Did she ever have children?'

'They say she adopted some Armenian orphans and took them to South America, but who can say. She was only forty years old. Anyway, they all lived happily ever after. Is that what you want to hear? And there were many descendants, many great nieces and nephews, and she was a splendid grandmother to them all, though they were often a trouble to themselves.' I was sure he was mocking me now, but I wasn't put off.

'And then?'

'Then? Well, I suppose it all became rather domestic. And then came the war, the second one. But that is another story. Understand, Jacob, the die had been cast long before. Some say our lives end at forty. Some say they only begin then. It all depends on your point of view.'

He was humouring me; I tried to get more out of him, but he didn't

AN ARK IN THE FLOOD OF TIME

seem to be interested. Yet there were still questions, so many questions. I asked his opinion about what I'd written.

Finally Mehmet became exasperated.

'Look, Jacob, the stories do not belong to us.' he continued, 'We are not their creators; they exist in the universe of infinite possibilities. All we can do is try to make ourselves suitable for their reception. To bring them to expression "without let or hindrance" as the passports say. Saying what demands to be said, and not revealing what asks to be kept hidden; and in their own time.'

'And what of the truth?' I asked. 'Surely we must say it like it is?'

'Never say it like it is, for that presumes you know all the ramifications, that your point of view is the real one. Only God knows all the ramifications!' Prince Mehmet shouted this last, for emphasis. It was his way of making sure I had heard. 'You can say "Maybe it is like this." or "Perhaps it could have happened in this way." Always we are involved in similitudes. That way we don't let the facts get in the way of the story. Similitudes may lead us to meanings. Facts merely have surface value.

'The truth of the matter is not in our hands, for truth will out. If and when and to whom it wishes.' He shrugged, then added quietly, 'It is discreet, a matter of the heart.'

Mehmet was always at his clearest when at his most abstruse. Often he said things which made sense at the time but eluded me when I tried to recall our conversations later. As if in his presence I was hearing with different ears. And though rarely could I remember what he had said exactly, a strong sense remained that something real had passed between us.

'The facts do not impinge, and neither do the falsehoods. So much is unknown when it comes to be written down, and so the heart makes bridges with the imagination as it sees fit. So for this, the heart must be prepared. It must constantly be kept clear of our own conjectures.'

I thought he was no longer talking about writing, and tried again to get him back to the story of Satanaya.

Mehmet sighed impatiently. 'Those letters I gave you in Istanbul. That day, after we cast Lady Satanaya's ashes into the Bosphorus. Have you been through them yet? I'm sure there were some from Constantinople and Beirut, from after 1919.'

'Yes, but they were mostly in Amharic. I assumed they were from Pelin.'

'Oh, so you haven't read them?'

'Well...no. Just some bits in French or Turkish. Actually it's been difficult enough with the Turkish letters – at least, the ones when she was still
writing in the old script. I haven't been brave enough to try Amharic.'

'Come on. What is it Mr Holmes says? "once you have eliminated the
impossible, whatever remains, no matter how improbable, must be the
truth." So, maybe you have to dig a little deeper.'

'Yes, elementary my dear Mehmet.' I muttered to myself.

Prince Mehmet stretched back in his chair and took up the Agatha
Christie paperback he had been reading; conversation closed. At times he
could be infuriating. But he was right; I hadn't had the nerve to start on
another language with its own script, certainly nothing so remote as
Ethiopian.

∗ ∗ ∗

Some time passed before I finally braved the strange script of the Abys-
sinians. It occurred to me that these mystifying runes might conceal
things which Satanaya and Pelin wished to keep private to themselves.
Interspersed between long paragraphs in Amharic were passages written
in French; innocuous chit-chat, mundane descriptions of daily life in the
Constantinople hotel and Beirut during the war, nothing salacious, certainly nothing incriminating. There were also a few letters written later,
to and from South American addresses, and later even, letters from all
over Europe. But why the Amharic?

So, I began with the alphabet, writing over and over each consonant
and its variant forms with vowels, then syllables and simple words until I
had a rough proficiency in reading. I looked at the letters again, searching
out any word that seemed familiar through repetition. I poured over the
Reverend Isenberg's 'Dictionary of the Amharic Language' of 1841.
However much I looked, I drew a blank. None of the words written either
by Satanaya or Pelin seemed to correspond to known Amharic vocabulary.
Perhaps I had finally eliminated the 'impossible' – that is, my learning
Amharic. So, did truth, the 'however improbable', remain? I slept on it. I
woke up with the question. I stared at it in the foam on my face in the
mirror as I shaved. I stirred it in my breakfast tea and tried to read it in the
turning leaves which floated on the surface. Nothing.

One morning in desperation I transliterated as best I could a whole paragraph in a letter picked at random, from her early years in the Beyler-beyi konak. Painstakingly I copied the text letter by letter. In the end the solution came like the picture which emerges when developing a photograph, the dawning out of darkness of a recognised landscape. It was a code, with a very simple key, meant simply to ensure privacy from the casual observer. The casual observer who couldn't read Amharic, to be sure. Once the key had been seen to fit the lock, the doors of the letter opened and the text became clear. They had used the Amharic alphabet to spell their messages phonetically in French. After that it was an easy task to unravel the content.

The letter revealed a lighter side to Satanaya; gossip about the officials attending the soirées, frivolous innuendos concerning the ladies she met on their Bosphorus jaunts, not necessarily complimentary and so best kept from prying eyes; nothing that seemed important to me at this distance in time. But my pen was weary, and it seemed that for now the story was done. For now I knew not what secrets those other letters held, and whether the story of her further journeys would ever come to light.

FORTY-NINE

Appendix

Operation Nemesis

HEN WE PRISE OPEN the coffin of history's corpse, among the dust-encrusted relics of our past crimes what evidences will we find to soothe hearts which ache for closure and eternal rest? Will the shaking up of dry bones return the flesh and breath to speak the truth? Life, eternity's thread stitched in time, once unravelled, knits not again on pathways already travelled. Still, for the restless mind that delves for proofs of existence even into stagnant pools, we poke about this crypt and pray not upset the sleep of ghosts.

∗ ∗ ∗

In September 1918, while Mustafa led his army in a desperate but measured retreat from Palestine and Syria, defeat for Turkey was imminent, and the 'Three Pashas', Enver, Talaat and Djemal resigned the government.

And at the very time the armistice was being signed, these thugs who had brought the Empire to this sorry pass, escaped Constantinople in the dead of night of 2nd/3rd November on a German ship, north to the Crimea and thence to Berlin and Switzerland.

The following day, the Ottoman newspaper İkdam reported that they had fled, saying that Talaat, Enver and Djemal's response to eliminate the Armenian problem was to attempt the elimination of the Armenians themselves. In the subsequent military trials held in Constantinople in 1919 and 1920, these three, among others, were sentenced to death *in absentia* for organising the massacres of the Armenians and Greeks.

None of the Pashas would be permitted a quiet retirement after their crimes; for each was a marked man. Over the coming years, in their own appointed time, they would meet their nemesis.

* * *

Berlin, 1921

Frau Stellbaum had been pleased with the new tenant for the room in the house in Augsburgerstrasse where she was employed as the concierge. Solomon was a foreign student. The tenant who introduced him was also a foreigner and spoke little German. But Solomon had paid his rent up front without fuss, and he was polite and caused no problems. A modest, kind young man, she thought. At her age – she was 63 – she didn't need tenants who couldn't pay or were noisy or drunkards. But she was also concerned for the young man who seemed a troubled soul. So often he would come in with a sad look on his face, go to his room, and sit in the dark playing sad songs on his mandolin. She had seen his type often in the years after the war, young men wandering from city to city, rootless and unhappy. He had moved in just before Christmas, and had been ill on and off with fainting fits. At night she would hear him talking in his sleep, or sitting with his friend smoking and making music.

Just occasionally she would hear him whistle, and she would think to herself, 'After all, a man cannot be sad all the time.'

Solomon told Frau Stellbaum that he would stay until the end of May. One day in early March, he returned to his room in an agitated state. Then a few days later, he found new accommodation, a ground floor room well lit by the sun, in nearby Hardenbergstrasse. The weather was still quite cold when he moved out.

Frau Dittmann was the landlady at 37 Hardenbergstrasse in the Charlottenburg district of Berlin. About a week after her new tenant had moved in she was sitting by the window of the drawing room in her upper floor apartment sewing, when her maid appeared at the door, looking a little flustered.

'Sorry to disturb, Frau Dittmann, but it's the new tenant. There's something wrong. I think I can hear him crying in his room; he's making a strange sound. I thought you should know.'

'Thank you Mathilde.'

Frau Dittmann put down the pillowcase she was repairing and went downstairs. She was concerned as the new tenant had seemed such a nice, polite boy, and so tidy. She had noticed how pale he looked, and thin too. But then, they all were, these young men after the war. She knocked on the door.

'Yes' came a voice from inside the room.

She found Solomon sitting with his mandolin in his hands. On the table in front of him was a glass and a bottle of cognac, a third of which had been drunk. This didn't bode well.

'Is everything all right? My maid heard something and thought...'

'Yes, everything is good.'

Frau Dittmann looked from Solomon to the glass and the cognac, and then back to Solomon, with a questioning look.

Solomon gave her a weak smile.

'I am not strong. I faint sometimes. The cognac, just a little in my tea, it helps.'

'Yes, of course. But my maid. She said you were crying.'

'No, just singing. My country's songs. Very sad.'

'Yes of course. Sorry. Can I get you anything?'

'No. Thank you. All is good.'

Frau Dittmann looked at the young man, and her heart felt full of pity. She didn't want to interfere but she felt all was not so good for Mr Solomon.

'Good morning, then.'

'Yes. It is a good morning.' said Solomon, looking out of the window towards the house opposite.

After Frau Dittmann had left, he moved his chair closer to the window from where he had a better view.

* * *

Solomon Tehlirian was an Armenian, from a village in the eastern Ottoman province of Erzerum. He was twenty-four years old when he reached Berlin. His parents, and many members of his family had been murdered in the massacres ordered against Ottoman Armenian citizens by Talaat Pasha in 1915 on the specious argument that the Armenian population, as Christians supposedly sympathetic to the Russian enemy, posed a threat to national security. In what amounted to a process of intentional genocide, as many as a million or more civilian Ottoman Armenians were driven from their homes, robbed and murdered.

Solomon had been briefed by Shahan Natali, assassin master of the Armenian Revolutionary Committee in Tiflis. He had armed himself with a 9 mm automatic pistol, German Army issue, with a magazine of eight rounds, and after various ramblings had traced Talaat Pasha to Berlin. The former Grand Vizier was living with his wife under the alias of Ali Salih Bey in a comfortable apartment in the fashionable suburb of Charlottenburg, their identities known only to an intimate circle of expatriate Turks. Here Solomon had waited. In February he had spotted in the street a man with Talaat's appearance. Surveillance of the area confirmed Talaat's address, and Solomon took up residence in an apartment on the other side of the avenue.

* * *

Solomon continued to sit by the window, in the sunlight, watching the house opposite. From time to time he looked at his German grammar book and tried to focus on the words. At eleven o'clock a movement on the balcony opposite caught his eye. A man came out. It was Talaat Pasha; he knew him from the photographs. Talaat Pasha looked relaxed, content even, standing on the balcony in the sunshine. Solomon got up and opened the window. He began to pace about his room, still holding his textbook while continuing to observe the Turk, who shortly afterwards went back inside his apartment. Solomon relaxed.

A little later Talaat Pasha came out of the front door in the building opposite and turned to his right. A heavy-set man in his late forties, swarthy complexion, a thick moustache, wearing a long dark overcoat and Homburg hat, he began to walk along the wide pavement of Hardenberg-strasse, swinging his cane slowly as he went.

Solomon reached into his trunk for his pistol. He threw on his dark Ulster, grabbed his hat, and stuffing the pistol into an inside pocket he ran

outside. Talaat was still visible on the opposite pavement further down the
street, walking in the direction of the Tiergarten. The Armenian followed
briskly until he was level with his quarry and then crossed over. Hardenbergstrasse is a broad avenue, and by the time he reached the other side, his
target was already thirty or forty yards further on, almost opposite the
elegant facade of the University Art School. He increased his step until he
caught up and passed the man. He turned back and as Talaat passed him,
Solomon drew his pistol from his pocket and fired from behind at close
range, aiming between the collar of Talaat's coat and his hat.

The victim pitched forward. Solomon had seen something like this
before. In a Paris restaurant – a long narrow dining room with tables either
side, and from the kitchen, a step down a couple of yards into the room.
The waiter dashing with the cresting souffle tripped, and flew forward
headlong, still holding the dish. But it wasn't a souffle that smeared the
pavement of the avenue in Berlin. And where in the Paris restaurant the
maître d'hôtel had led a round of applause for the crestfallen garçon, here
gasps and cries of shock from the passersby now followed the echo of the
gunshot in the cold air.

The whole affair passed in barely three minutes. The assassin made no
serious attempt at escape, dropping his gun and only running off to save
himself from the blows of the crowd that gathered. He was quickly appre-
hended on Fazanenstrasse by a local butcher and a keen young servant
from a nearby dwelling, and taken to the police station.

✳ ✳ ✳

The trial took place over two days, a few weeks after the murder. It was a
curious affair, a *cause célèbre* even, which occupied many column inches in
international press for a brief season. The pathetic picture of the defendant,
pale and sad, his head bandaged from the beating by the mob; the motley
crew of witnesses: prim Hausfrauen from his lodgings, the Royal Gun-
smith, two locksmiths, a roofer, a painter, a pharmacist and a brick
manufacturer; no less than seven 'expert witnesses' in the form of psychia-
trists and physicians who deliberated upon Solomon's likely mental state.
The court even managed to bring in that leading German military advisor
in wartime Turkey, General Otto Liman von Sanders, to comment on the
Armenian question.

The case became something of a platform for the exposure of the

Armenian massacres orchestrated by Turkey's wartime government, a subject which seemed to have become obfuscated by the everchanging requirments of the various peace talks, Sèvres and Lausanne, during which the lines of the new Middle East were drawn and redrawn following the ending of hostilities.

No one, neither the defendant himself nor the witnesses, denied that Solomon had committed the murder in question. His guilt, however, hung upon a subtle legal point: whether or not he had been in control of his mental faculties at the time. In the event, it was decided by jury that, due to his illness, Solomon's mental capacity was temporarily impaired, depriving him of free will, and therefore not responsible for his act. He walked free.

There was likely a number of political elements at play here, not only with regard to the assassination itself, but to the necessary outcome of the trial in favour of the defendant. It has been suggested that the Armenian did not act alone, that he was funded by Armenian parties under the direction of Shahan Natali, and also that British Secret Service aided Solomon in the location of his victim. The verdict of not guilty not only freed Solomon, but allowed Germany to appear even-handed in their treatment of Talaat, former leader of their wartime ally Turkey which in 1919 had passed the death sentence on Talaat.

For, as Defence Attorney Niemeyer argued, 'If a German court were to find Soghomon (Solomon) Tehlirian not guilty, this would put an end to the misconception that the world has of us. The world would welcome such a decision as one serving the highest principles of justice.' Much later it is revealed that prior to the Berlin execution, Solomon Tehlirian had earlier assassinated an Armenian quisling in Istanbul.

Notwithstanding the outcome of the trial, in 1943 during World War Two, the remains of Talaat Pasha were returned to Istanbul for reburial with full military honours, paraded upon a gun carriage escorted by hundreds of troops with military and civilian dignitaries, both Turks and Nazis, in attendance. Turkey's position during World War Two, while ostensibly neutral, at times appeared ambiguous.

＊ ＊ ＊

Tbilisi, Soviet Republic of Georgia, July 1922
The intermission which occurred between World Wars I and II, which for the major belligerents began in 1918 as 'armistice' and signified an almost-

believable ceasefire – expressed in one of the early modern examples of 'post-truth' as 'peace' – barely took hold elsewhere. Geopolitical surgery and demographic transplants were the cause of chronic post-operation trauma in the Middle East and Africa; the ink had barely dried on the paper of Turkey's own armistice with the Allied powers when it rolled out its great War of Independence across Anatolia. And in the bridge of peaks and passes of the southern Caucasus, a short-lived state of Transcaucasia governed from Tbilisi the area which now constitutes the Republics of Georgia, Armenia and Azerbaijan, before a brief Ottoman military recovery reclaimed Erzerum and Kars in eastern Anatolia, and Soviet Russian expansionism swallowed up for the next seventy years the hopes of these small states becoming independent democratic nations.

By July 1922, Tbilisi was firmly in Bolshevik hands.

Djemal Pasha had not been idle in retirement following his escape from Occupied Turkey. Infamous for his brutal Governorship of Syria during the war, where he was know by local Arabs as '*as-Saffah*, 'the Blood Shedder', as well as being implicated in the Armenian atrocities, lately he had been cosying up to the Bolsheviks and developing contacts among German arms manufacturers. Following the Anglo-Afghan war of 1919, Great Britain withdrew the privilege allowing Afghanistan to import arms and ammunition from India. Where previously Afghanistan had been forbidden relations with other foreign governments, under a new treaty the Amir Amanullah opened diplomatic relations with the Bolshevik government. With a keen eye for opportunities in military adventuring, Djemal Pasha travelled to Kabul where in 1920 he secured a position as Chief of Staff responsible for modernising the Afghan military.

Stepan Dzaghigian was an Armenian from a village in the mountains above Trabzon on the Turkish eastern Black Sea coast. Dzaghigian was an experienced assassin, part of Shahan Natali's secret execution squad tasked with eliminating the major perpetrators of the Armenian massacres. He was also a long-time member of the Armenian Revolutionary Federation known as the Dashnaks*.

In the summer of 1922 Djemal Pasha was travelling to Berlin via

---

* Dashnak (*Hay Heghapokhakanneri Dashnaktsutyun*) – a socialist revolutionary organisation founded in 1890 in Tbilisi to unite Armenian groups advocating political reform in Armenian areas in the Ottoman Empire. It remains a minor political party in Lebanon and Nagorno-Karabakh Republic.

Tbilisi in the role of military liaison officer to negotiate an arms deal with
the Soviet Government. Around 4 pm, when the heat of the day had
passed, he was walking with two bodyguards in the sunlit boulevards of
the Georgian capital. As he passed near to the building which housed the
Cheka, the Soviet state security organization, he and his companions
found themselves surrounded by a group of young men. Gunfire broke out

Dzaghigian, the chief of the assailants, had earlier received the coded
telegram from his superiors: 'Send the package', which communiqué confirmed that Djemal Pasha was travelling via Tbilisi. From then on events
took their course.

Tbilisi was a city favoured by the Russian literary elite and the
Romanovs alike. In the wide boulevards of the busy metropolis, modern-
ised in the 19th century in European style, with splendid buildings and
electric trams, it was not difficult to arrange an ambush. Escaping was a
different matter. Following the shooting, Dzaghigian was arrested, along
with around a hundred other Dashnak suspects, by the Cheka secret
police. After the intercession of the legendary Dashnak, General Dro, an
Armenian warrior who held some influence in Bolshevik circles, all
detainees except Dzaghigian were released. Stepan Dzaghigian himself
remained in custody, eventually disappearing into the Soviet gulag system
whence he was never heard of again.

As for Djemal Pasha, following the brief firefight on the streets of
Tbilisi, the former Minister in the Ottoman Government and Governor of
Syria, the 'Butcher of Beirut', lay dead.

✴ ✴ ✴

Dushanbe, Russian Turkestan, August 1922
Was it the assumed proximity to the heavenly spheres which mountain
peaks possess that drew Enver to this land of heights and vastness? Had
some premonition of his imminent translation from the earthly realm
drawn him to this lofty valley, in the shadow of the Pamir Mountains
where Peak Garmo, now Peak Ismail Samani, rises just short of 7,500
metres? Or perhaps it was the apricots, glabrous and glistening, nurtured
at high altitudes in remote glens, which golden fruit, the juiciest and sweetest in the world, are watered surely by a paradisiacal dew, which led him
into these uncompromising uplands?

Dushanbe in present day Tajikistan takes its name from the Persian, meaning 'the second day', after the weekly market that took place at a crossroads village every Monday. Unlike Tbilisi, which had time to develop over 1500 years and become a respectable metropolis with European-style buildings and railway connections, Dushanbe in 1922 had little to distinguish it from its first appearance in the 17th century as a dusty Asian bazaar.

At the time of the Bolshevik Revolution, Dushanbe was a fortress town in the Tsarist vassal state ruled by the Emir of Bukhara in Russian Turkestan. Here the last Emir of Bukhara took refuge fleeing the Bolsheviks, before continuing his escape south into Afghanistan.

Enver Pasha, who was now under one death sentence in the Turkish capital, and under another from the Armenian Revolutionary Federation, still hadn't got the message. His request to Mustafa's revolutionary government in Ankara to join the army of resistance was denied him. Now like some narcissistic politician toppled from a great height, the former Minister of War dusted himself down and went in search of a new pedestal upon which to re-erect his vainglorious image. He still harboured his messianic desire to lead a Pan-Turkic revolt across Central Asia, and Turkestan beckoned. The developing rapprochement between Turkey and Russia following the 1917 Revolution gave him hope that currying favour with the Bolsheviks might provide a stepping stone to this end.

Late in 1921 Enver Pasha was in Moscow, where he managed to convince Lenin to send him to Soviet Turkestan to help put down a rebellion by Islamic revolutionaries, the Basmachi. The Basmachi had been a thorn in the side of the Tsarist regime since its policy of conscription had latterly included Muslims; now the rebel faction continued their armed insurgency against the Bolshevik policy of forced secularisation.

Once in Bukhara, Enver secretly made contact with the leaders of the various Basmachi groups, and having united them under his own command, led them against the Bolshevik forces in a number of successful engagements. Not content with the simple glory of victories against the Bolsheviks, this self-bedizened little Napoleon now styled himself 'Commander-in-Chief of all the Armies of Islam, Son-in-Law of the Caliph and Representative of the Prophet.' Now he conferred upon himself the title 'Emir of Turkestan', a contumely to the exiled Emir of Bukhara, who, along with Amanullah, the Emir of Afghanistan ceased to provide him with military support.

Such hubris would not go unpunished for long. It was 4th August 1922, during the *Eid al-Adha*, the Feast which commemorates Abraham's sacrifice of the ram in place of Isaac. Enver had given his troops leave to celebrate, and himself had remained in a village near Dushanbe with a platoon as bodyguard.

There are at least two versions of what happened next. The account given by his own ADC, Suphi Bey, might have been written by Enver himself. A dramatic and heroic final scene in a life of high drama, it sees him on horseback, Koran in one hand, pistol in the other, leading a mounted charge against a surprise attack by Red Army cavalry, and dying in a hail of bullets.

The leader of the Red Army cavalry, however, tells a different story. Hakob Melkumian was an Armenian from Karabagh in the Caucasus. His memoir tells how Enver fled the field of battle on horseback and hid out in another village for four days until Melkumian's forces discovered his whereabouts. A battle ensued and Melkumian claims to have shot the Pasha himself. One way or another, the last of the Triumvirate of Pashas had met his final nemesis, far from home cornered like a hunted animal in an insignificant little conflict on the arid steppe of Central Asia.

FIFTY

A Postscript from Gezi Park

Istanbul, May-June 2013

OPPY SEEDS lie dormant in the earth a hundred years. When the earth is turned they germinate and come to light upon the face of the land.

Within the human clay sleep seeds which when the heart is harrowed push out towards the light, even if it takes the fires of a hundred years.

And as a flower contains a multitude of seeds, so too the aspirations of one who speaks the truth may plant that kernel in a hundred thirsty hearts, which when disturbed, that truth will out, demanding to be heard.

A flight of birds appears above the trees, whirling home to roost, their chirrups ringing clear as water, as bells upon a dancer's ankle, her swirling skirts entwining her limbs to rest. *I close my eyes. I am hearing Istanbul.*[*]

---

[*] 'İstanbul'u Dinliyorum' by Orhan Veli Kanık (1914-1950)

✶ ✶ ✶

(When I first embarked on the story of Satanaya and her journeys, as related by Jacob Merdiven de la Scala, it was in the spring of 2013. I was staying in Istanbul on the Asian shore in a flat borrowed from my friend Meral, over-looking the Bosphorus between Beylerbeyi and Çengelköy.)

In Kadiköy, the evening of music and food in the gallery by Yoğurtcu Park is winding down when the smartphones begin to beep. The protest – the '*direniş*' – has begun.

Only days before I had gone with my friends, young Turks, students, artists, writers, and tech people, to the European side of Istanbul. We had walked through Gezi Park crossing the concrete wasteland that was now Taksim Square, on our way home from an exhibition of felt work: 'They're going to build a shopping centre here, and apartments, and a huge mosque also.' said Merve.

'And they want to cut down the trees in the Gezi Park.' said her sister, Bahar. 'But we won't let them. There will be '*direniş*'.

'?'

I wanted to know more.

'Protests, demonstrations.'

That was then. Now, in Kadiköy, the twitter-feed begins to trickle, then pours down into the gallery on all the smartphones.

'It's kicking off at Beşiktaş and at Gezi Park.'

'They've stopped the ferries.'

'People are marching over the Bosphorus Bridge.'

'Come on, we must join them.'

A warm night in May. We are on the street. I look at my friends, all young. The '*genç*' of Atatürk's new Turkey, now a nascent global economic power. The light that shines in their eyes is enough to make me weep. I have been there, in '68 and '69. Protesting Vietnam. Aboriginal landrights. I know this vision. I know this solidarity that comes, and goes beyond our individual selves to a place of purity. The passion for truth which once glimpsed, remains.

I leave my young friends at Dörtyol where they all pile into taxis. It's another party for them; more dramatic than any love affair. Or the same. I am unable to join them. My poor heart. I gave up on late nights, the excitement. I am filled with the sweetest envy. I go with them in all but body.

Back in Üskudar, I pass a crowd by the ferry station. A bonfire is burning and people are gathered round, young men and women singing, arms upon each others' shoulders, dancing Kurdish-style. I wonder, 'Am I seeing the beginning of a revolution? Will it go further than dancing and singing?'

In the next days I read the news on the internet. Bad things by the police happening in Beşiktaş. Tear gas and water cannon. I am unable to meet friends who are here for a shipping industry conference as their hotel in Beşiktaş is cut off from our meeting place.

Still, the protest at the Gezi Park continues. In the coming days things calm down. There is an official apology for police behaviour. Gezi Park is left alone. I decide to visit.

Emerging from the underground station at Taksim, it is impossible not to notice the large building overlooking the square, the Atatürk Cultural Centre – the Opera House. Hanging down from its roof-line, almost covering the whole of its horizontal facade, a collage of giant posters in every shade of political colour and expression, each a cry for its particular freedom. On the square leading to the park hawkers sell 'Anonymous' masks, goggles and water against teargas, cans of spray paint, whistles, tee-shirts with Atatürk's portrait, Turkish flags – all the necessaries of a velvet revolution. A group of dark-haired girls and boys laugh and sing and dance arms linked around a man carrying a Kurdish flag, a red star in yellow sun upon a green field, and a banner with the fierce-browed face of the imprisoned leader Apo. The atmosphere is as much of celebration as of protest.

In the park itself, beneath the canopy of new-leaf plane trees spreads a campsite of little dome-tents of every colour, crowded together between foodstalls, political stalls, LGBT stalls, message walls and meeting points; here is a vegan kitchen, there a man selling huge slices of freshly-cut watermelon. Next door to a first aid post, köfte kebabs sizzle and smoke in rows upon an open charcoal grill, and trade is brisk.

A band plays upon a stage under a banner declaring 'Taksim Solidarity', the music interspersed with earnest speeches by politicos, ecowarriors and student leaders.

Like the floating pennants of some medieval fayre, banners surround the site: '*no to the plunder of nature and life*' declares one, '*a world without borders, a world without class*', says another. All echo one way or another the aphorisms of Mustafa Kemal Atatürk, the heroic saviour and founder of the nation, of whose threatened legacy they now stand in fierce defence.

Stretched between the trees, a banner picturing the leftist poet Nazım Hikmet, is inscribed with lines from his famous poem, echoing the same sentiments now abroad in Gezi Park:

> 'I am a walnut tree in Gülhane Park
> an old walnut, all knots and hacked about
> Neither you nor the police notice it ...
> ...with a hundred thousand eyes
> I watch you, and Istanbul.'

Nearby a fierce and fearless lady holds forth passionately doing her piece to camera for local TV.

Graffiti artists are having a field day. Clingfilm stretched between two trees provides a wide canvas for a cartoon of a 'çapulcu' (protester, rebel, one who fights for his/her rights) knocking away cannisters of teargas with a baseball bat inscribed with the word 'halk' (the people). A grim stencil of the prime minister is titled 'Tayyıp, without honour.' Adorning a banner being erected over the main walkway in the park is the by now iconic image of the 'lady in red' depicting the female teacher being pepper sprayed in the eyes by a miniature policeman in helmet and gasmask. There is no evidence of police at all within the park, although plain clothes men are in plain sight, in their jeans and pressed blue shirts, close cropped hair, hardened, unsmiling faces, Raybanned eyes. It is the time of the phoney war.

I return to Beylerbeyi and continue with my writing project.

Two weeks later I am going home to Scotland. On my last night in Istanbul I check into my favourite Büyük Londra Hotel in Meşrutiyet Caddesi. From here, an easy taxi ride to the airport. Out of the way of Gezi Park, but still in walking distance. In the afternoon, with my goddaughter Anna, her husband Ben and two year old son Reuben, we stroll down İstiklal – the old Grande Rue de Pera. It is 'çok kalabalık' – choc-a-bloc – with Saturday crowds heading down to Taksim Square and Gezi Park. The city has caught the mood of the *direniş*, and the local population are making a '*gezi*' (tour/stroll) to Gezi Park. The crowd is enjoying the festive atmosphere, and the pavement hawkers of teeshirts, facemasks and goggles have multiplied tenfold since my previous visit.

Yet Taksim looks different. And then I notice. Parked at almost every approach to the square, rows of 'TOMA'; huge tank-like vehicles, armoured water cannons, which are now reported to have a chemical irritant added to their mix. Hundreds of riot police stand around in groups nearby. They chat and smoke, apparently unconcerned, like youths loitering aimlessly on street corners on a Saturday afternoon. I sense an air of unseen menace, and yet the crowd seems oblivious. It is a Titanic moment. We are sailing in the unsinkable ship of democracy and material security. Sun is shining, everyone is out for a stroll to see the famous Gezi Park protest camp, enjoying vicariously a little sense of people power.

I feel uncomfortable, and head back to the hotel. That evening I dine in Haci Abdullah's – slow roasted knuckle of lamb wrapped in aubergine, followed by quince compote with clotted buffalo cream. İstiklal is busy, but I have an early flight and return to the Büyük Londra. My room overlooks the lane opposite the corner with the Thai restaurant. I am on the first floor and can see both ways, down into Meşrutiyet Caddesi, and up in the direction of İstiklal.

It's ten thirty p.m. or so, and I'm preparing for bed. Then the explosions start – big bangs, repeating at regular intervals. Followed by the shouting. It all sounds like a football crowd returning from a match. I look out of my windows. Nothing at first, then young people begin to appear, first a trickle, then a flood, coming down the lane below my window, and passing into Meşrutiyet Caddesi in the direction away from İstiklal, Taksim and Gezi Park. Kids in summer clothes, handkerchiefs tied across nose and mouth, like bandits in a matinée western, the 'çapulcu', some equipped with facemasks and goggles. Suddenly I am transported to the present. This is Gaza, this is Tahrir, Tienanmen… Some stop and sit on the ground while others pour water on their faces. Then a mist comes drifting down, as if a following wake. Looking out I see a teargas canister land in the lane outside, emitting a steam of gas. A youth picks it up and hurls it back up the lane. Another canister follows. I open the window for a better look. Foolish. A strange dry smell invades my room. A waft of teargas hits me, in the throat and in the eyes. I am momentarily blinded. I slam the window down and rush to the sink, drink water and rinse my eyes furiously. The blindness eases. The acrid dry smell hangs in the air.

Although the rush of fleeing protesters subsides, the bangs and shouting continue throughout the night and I sleep little before my early morning call. At 5.30 there are still a few stragglers wandering down

Meşrutiyet Caddesi like all-night drunks wondering where the next party is. I am worried that I won't find a taxi. The night manager is so apologetic, on behalf of Turkey it seems, for the problems of the night, and finds me a ride within minutes. I am sped on my way through deserted streets, Sunday morning coming down over the Golden Horn calm as a mirror and onto Kennedy Caddesi, the coast road below Topkapi Palace.

The highway to the airport is lined with hanging banners advertising a political rally that day for the incumbent AK Party. On billowing drapes between the lamposts the prime minister's face, neatly suited and tie-ed looks down on us mile after mile all the way to Atatürk Airport. I cannot help but picture the rallies in Nüremberg in the Germany of 1937.

✷ ✷ ✷

That was in June 2013. Since then, Turkish democracy, the fragile but deeply rooted legacy of the Republic's first President, Mustafa Kemal Atatürk, saviour of Turkey in World War I and hero of the subsequent War of Independence, has been subject to continued attack from reactionary forces aided by internal corruption and imported religious propaganda. The precarious peace between the Turkish State and Kurdish PKK insurgents broke down. The war in Syria overflowed its northern border, resulting in a refugee crisis and ISIS bomb attacks on civilian areas in Turkish cities.

What might have been a Turkish Spring has become more like a slow-fuse Kristallnacht as personal freedom of expression has steadily been eroded and removed, with medieval Islamic rules and extreme religious attitudes being promoted by the State. In addition women who have been adopting modern western dress, the norm in educated middle-class Turkey for over ninety years, are now being exhorted to wear the headscarf, stay at home and produce children.

After the so-called 'failed coup' of 2016, which the public has been cowed into accepting further government crackdowns on what it sees as opposition – the most obvious and most insidious of which have been curbs on free speech and the press. The Turkish government imprisons more journalists and writers, *per capita,* than any country in the world.

As we see the walls closing in elsewhere, with return to gangster-fascism in near neighbours in Eastern Europe and ex-Soviet Russia, the recent four year Idiocracy of the USA, the smug 'no room at the inn' of so-called Christian Europe, and England's uncontrolled desire to emulate an ostrich, while global pandemic holds the world in its maw, one is driven to ask: how long will we cling to our caterpillar skins while searching, learning, dissolving and evolving in this imaginal soup before emerging winged into a new light?

Glossary

açma (T) – a kind of soft breakfast bread ring covered in nigella seeds,
   (see:https://www.youtube.com/watch?v=tV_hzV3OLzM)
anne, annem (T) – mother, my mother
araba (T) – carriage, wagon, cart; car
ayran (T) – a cool drink of yoghurt mixed with water

baqa' (A) – remaining, enduring; eternal
barınak (T) – a harbour, shelter
bey (T) – a notable person, gentleman; ruler, chief, prince
binbaşı (T) – Major (*military*)
börek (T) – cooked pastries with savoury fillings, most often soft cheese
Büyükler (T) – the 'Great Ones' i.e. the saints

canım (T) – my dear, my soul, my life – (a term of friendship)
çapulcu (T) – raider, pillager, rebel
cezve (T) – a small copper or brass pot with spout and long handle for
   making coffee
çınar – plane tree (*bot., Platanus orientalis*)
cumba (T) – bay window

damad (T) – son-in-law; a man married into the Ottoman Royal Family
darbuka (A) – a skin-covered metal or earthenware hand drum
dede (T) – grandfather, old man, sheykh
destur (P) – permission; by your leave, hence: make way!
dümbelek – a kind of hand drum

efe (T) – leader of Turkish irregular soldiers and guerillas; swashbuckling
   nomad, leader
efendi – sir, gentleman; term of respect
emin (A) – safe, secure; free from doubt; trustworthy; a steward or trustee
erguvan (T) – Judas Tree (*bot., Cercis Siliquastrum*)
ezan (A) – the call to prayer, i.e. *hiya ala salat...* etc.

fahişe (A) – prostitute, harlot
fana (A) – passing away; transitory

fatwa (A) – a ruling in Islamic law
fava (Gr) – broad bean purée
firik, freekah – young green wheat toasted then cooked as a pilaf in Eastern Turkey and Middle East.

gâvur (P) – infidel; non-muslim

hakîm – (A) medical doctor, physician; a sage; a Divine Name
Hajji (T: haci) – one who has performed the pilgrimage to Mecca (or Jerusalem)
halifa (A) – caliph
Halifetallah (A) – God's representative on earth, caliph.
hamal (T) – porter, carrier, stevedore, day labourer
hamsi (Gr.) – anchovy
hanım (T) – lady; woman; Mrs/Miss (after name);
haremlık (T) – private apartments in an Ottoman house
haydi gidelim (T) – 'let's go!'

inşallah (A) – God willing, hopefully
ıstağfurallah! (A) – God forgive me!
iskele (Gr.) – landing place, wharf, quay.
İslam (A) – a resigning or surrender to God and His Will; the Muslim religion
istanbulin (T) – a kind of frock coat

jihad (Turkish: cihad) – war against the infidels. literally: endeavour, struggle

kadın budu (T) – a type of köfte, (*lit: women's thighs*)
kafes (A) – wooden laticework over windows; a cage
kahraman (T) – hero
kalamatianos (Gr.) – a vigorous Greek folkdance, danced in a chain, holding hands, with jumps and squats
kanun (A) – a plucked stringed instrument, like a zither.
kardeş (T) – brother, sibling;
kardeşim – my brother
kavun – melon

kayık (Gr.) – rowing boat, caique

kazan (T) – cooking pot, kettle, cauldron

khanoum/khanum (T) – Lady; feminine equivalent of Khan, originally an
    aristocratic title. (modern Turkish: *hanım* – see above)

kız (T) – girl, daughter

kızım – my girl/daughter, my child (f)

koç yumurtası (T) – ram's testicles

kolay gelsin (T) – May it be easy. (greeting said to people working)

konak (T) – a mansion, residence; halting place, inn

leblebi (T) – roasted chick peas

lodos (Gr.) – a persistent, strong south-west wind in the Aegean and
    Marmara Sea

Mahdi (A) – (T: mehdi): the rightly guided one, who will come to cleanse
    the Muslim religion, prior to the Second Coming of Christ.

mangal (T) – indoor brazier for heating a room; barbecue

maşallah (A) – God has willed it (with the inferred wish that it continue
    so)

Mekteb-i Harbiye – the Military Academy

meltem – a light, gentle summer wind, a zephyr, an offshore breeze

Melâmi (A) – a dervish sect

menemen – a fried breakfast dish of chopped tomatoes, green peppers
    and spices mixed with egg

mercimek çorbası – lentil soup

meydan (A) – open space; public square

meyhane (P) – wine shop, tavern.

meze (P) – hors d'oeuvres; snacks accompanying drinks

moda (It.) – fashion

muezzin (A) – the one who performs the call to prayer from the minaret

ney – a reed flute

Padişah (P) – sovereign, king; Ottoman Sultan.

papaz – priest, monk

paşa/pasha – lord; *paşamız* – my lord

rebab (A) – a three-stringed instrument played with a bow.
rembetika (Gr.) – traditional popular Greek music and songs

sancak (T) – flag, banner, standard
sandal – a rowing boat
saz (P) – a plucked, stringed instrument
selamlık – main public reception area in an Ottoman house
sharia (A) – Islamic religious law
simit – a bread-ring coated in sesame seeds, Turkish cousin to the bagel
sohbet – conversation, chat; converse of a spiritual nature, with a sheykh
    in a *tekke*
şalvar – shalwar, baggy trousers

tasavvuf (A) – Islamic mysticism, Sufism
tarika (A) – a religious order, order of dervishes; (*tarik* – way, path, road)
tayyib (A) – clean, good, pleasant, pure
türkü (T) – folk song
tekke (T) – dervish lodge or convent where dervishes gather for group
    practices, meals, and often accomodation
tuğra – ornamental seal of the sultan

vatan (A) – fatherland, one's native country
vapur (F) – ferry

yalı (T) – waterside residence; shore,

zeybek (T) – irregular militia fighter; a dance where the dancers stretch
    out their arms simulating birds of prey
zikr (A) – vocalised affirmation of the Divine Presence; remembrance;
    mentioning

Select Bibliography

Mustapha Kemal, Between Europe and Asia. Dagobert von Mikusch, London, 1931

Atatürk, The Rebirth of a Nation. Lord Kinross, London, 1964

Atatürk: The Biography of the Founder of Modern Turkey. Andrew Mango, 1999

The Young Atatürk: From Ottoman Soldier to Statesman. George W. Gawrych, I.B. Tauris, London, 2013

Gallipoli. Alan Moorhead, London,1956

The Last Sultans, Bulent Rauf, Cheltenham,1995

Witness: The Story of a Search, J.G. Bennett, London,1974

Fusus Al-Hikam: Ismail Hakki Bursevi's Translation and Commentary, Bulent Rauf, Oxford, 1986.

Maps

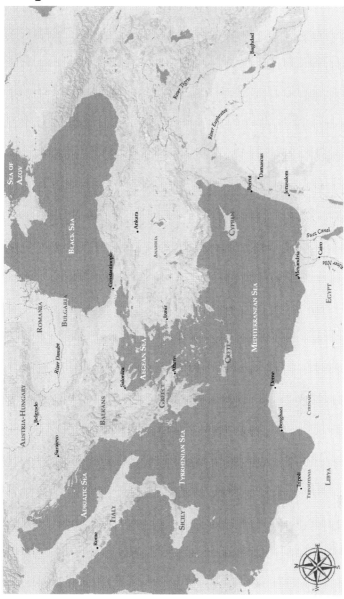

Mediterranean Sea

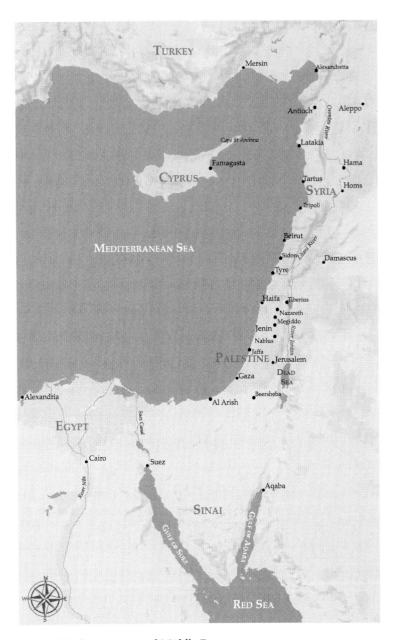

Eastern Mediterranean and Middle East

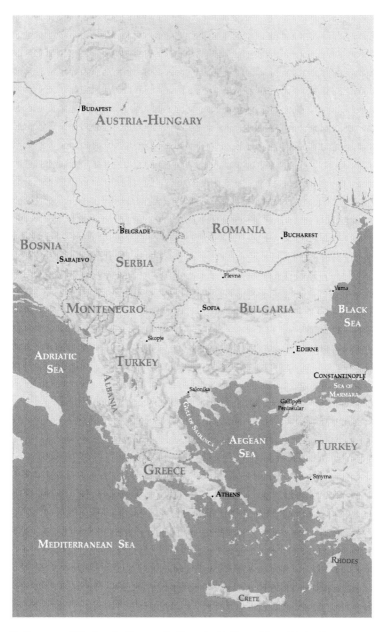

Balkans and Turkey in Europe before the Balkan Wars 1912-13

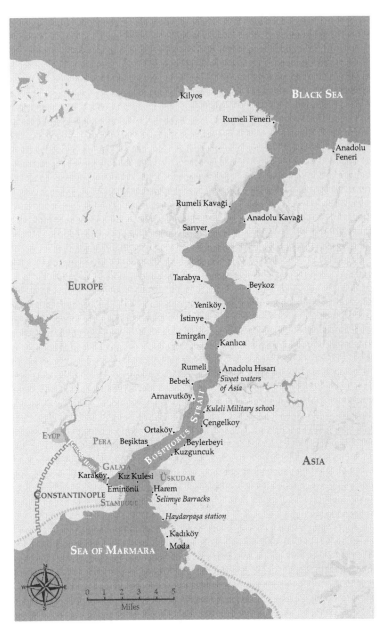

Bosphorus Strait

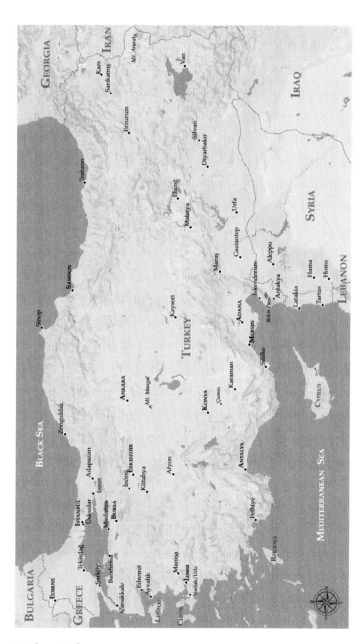

Modern Turkey

Also by Christopher Ryan:

FICTION:

The Story of the Damascus Drum

Daud, a successful trader, Takla a young cook, and Shams, an old billy goat from the hills above Damascus take us on a journey of love and self-discovery in time, space, and beyond through the Syrian landscape of the 19th century. An adventure replete with entertaining storytellers recounting tales of mystery and love, villainous villains and hospitable goatherds, clerics both wicked and wise, memorable feasts and a lot of goats....

'A fabulous adventure story, scented with magical realism, resonating with a talking goatskin drum... set among the monuments of Syria, and the old khans and mountainous hinterland of Damascus in a timeless Levant... valued spiritual teachings within a fast-paced plot.'
Barnaby Rogerson, Eland Books.

'a portrait of the Syria which I recognize as my own country and really miss... takes me to times I have never witnessed, but which my imagination has already visited and lived in."
Ruba Khadamaljamei – translator at Syria TV تلفزيون سوريا

'A journey of self-discovery and rebirth...sympathetic characters who reach out to the living even after their death - a work of Sufi Realism and a beguiling tale...I highly recommend.'
David Paquiot, SUFI Journal.

'delightful and quirky, it catapults us directly into the old world of Damascus... a magical piece of escapism with a lesson to teach the weary 21st century soul.'
Marion James, Sunday Zaman, Istanbul.

'profoundly human, funny, wise and it's a good tale.'
Sebastian Ritscher, Mohrbooks AG, Zürich

(Available in German translation as 'Die Damaszener Trommel')

Satanaya and the Houses of Mercy

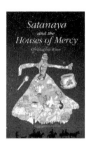

Satanaya, the young daughter of Circassian refugees in Ottoman Palestine, is trainee cook in the kitchens of the famous Convent of Seydnaya near Damascus. An innocent affair with a local boy hastens her exit from the convent. Her departure comes with a strange inheritance: an old cooking pot, a wooden spoon and a cookbook, left many years earlier by the legendery cook Takla. The book contains Takla's recipes and the correspondence of an Egyptian Bey, in all a treatise on good taste in food and love.

When Satanaya fetches up at the villa of the Lady Gülbahar, whose parties and soirées are renowned throughout the Eastern Mediterranean for their good food, fine wines and illustrious company, she enters the wider world of fin-de-siècle Beirut, then administered by France. Under Lady Gülbahar's tutelage, and with Takla's Cookbook as her *vade mecum*, she plunges wholeheartedly into the new life of an emerging modern world.

Satanaya is an explorer of mysteries: of food, of love, and most of all of her own self. A true nomad of the spirit, she experiences the dangers and delights, the heartbreaks and homecomings, while travelling through the Levant and Turkey in the twilight years of the Ottoman Empire.

"Part travelogue, part romance and part celebration of all things culinary, evoking the ravishing loveliness of the Middle East before the ravages of contemporary conflict -the mood is joyful, playful, sensual, while in the mysterious figure of Captain Mustafa, there are hints of darker shades to come."
Katherine Tiernan, author of the St Cuthbert trilogy.

"Ryan brilliantly recreates the Middle East in the late 19th and early 20th century... interweaving history, geography, food, and a deep sense of spirituality - contemporary and highly relevant."
Martin Gulbis, Steiner Academy

"A book to be savoured, in every sense of the word, for lovers of food and late nineteenth century Middle Eastern history and most importantly the human spirit."
Norman Latimer, Cornucopia Magazine online

NON-FICTION:

A Child Prisoner of War
Changi and Sime Road Camps, Singapore 1942-45
91 pages Hakawati Press, Hawick, TD9 0AN, U.K.
(publication due 2021)

*The author's account of his father, Thomas Ryan's experiences as a young
teenage seaman with Canadian Pacific ships during WW2; his being sunk
in the Atlantic by a German bomber; rescued by the Royal Navy's HMS
Tatar; then sunk again off Singapore by the Japanese on troopship RMS
Empress of Asia and his subsequent time as a POW in Changi and Sime
Road camps until the war ended. He relates how his father returned to
education in the secret prison camp school, his working in the camp
hospital, and the awakening of a desire to study medicine. His post-war
enrolment in Liverpool University and subsequent qualification as a
medical practitioner.*

The Author

 Christopher Ryan has travelled through-out Turkey and the Middle East for more than fifty years. He is the author of three novels set in the Middle East and Turkey during the latter days of the Ottoman Empire, up to the founding of the Republic of Turkey.

Professionally he has always been involved in food and writing. He has owned and run a number of restaurants in Cambridge and Scotland over the years.

He studied Persian and Ottoman Turkish at the University of Oxford, and has been a perennial student of Beshara since 1971. He was a director of the Scottish educational charity, the Chisholme Institute, from 1979 until 2016, and remains closely involved in its activities. He is also a co-founder of the international shipping and commodities information company, Infospectrum Ltd. His articles on shipping, food, travel and mysticism have been published in Lloyds List, the Financial Times and Cornucopia Magazine, and he has contributed to academic symposia and journals in UK, USA, Germany and Turkey.

He lives in Hawick in the Scottish Borders where together with his wife he now runs the Damascus Drum Café, Books and Tribal Rugs.

Printed in Great Britain
by Amazon